The
Keeper

By
C.A. Fiebiger

Cover art work by Gary Markley

Website by Gary Markley

www.cafiebiger.com

DEDICATED TO ALL THOSE WHO BELIEVED IN ME.

CONTENTS

PREFACE

Tom Palmer was a keeper of bees and much more. This gentile, kind and loving man, lived a life dedicated to serving God and others. He died a bachelor, but had grown to love his nephew as if he were his own son.

Larkin Palmer, seventh generation Keeper of a different kind, grew up in the farming country of New York, Madison County, to be exact. He lived a bikes' ride from the town of Brookfield, on the acreage his ancestors settled on in 1792. Returning from Washington, D.C. to attend the death bed of his Uncle Tom, he was apprehensive as to how his life was going to change and how his family would react to his new life since he had begun college at UMD.

His greatest fear was "them" however, for they had told him to go away for good, or his family would suffer the consequences. That was only six months ago. But he didn't care at this very moment; his uncle was dying. And of course he was, "The Keeper" of *The Eraser*…

Chapter One

The Preparation

Harry's phone rang and rang. Finally, on the eighth ring, Sally said, "Larkin Palmer are you going to get that?"

He looked at her and jumping up from his seat as if under her command, Larkin raced over to pick it up. "Hello?"

"Larkin, this is your Dad."Larkin could tell from the tone of his voice that something was wrong, "You need to come home Larkin. It's your Uncle. He's not expected to make it much longer."

"What is it, Dad?"

"It's his heart."

"I'll be there as soon as I can."

"I'll tell your Mom. Bye."

"Bye."

Sally could see there was a problem. "What is it?"

"It's my Uncle Tom. He's dying. We have to go right away."

"I'll call Mr. Shipley and your counselor at UMD. They will understand I'm sure."

"I'll call the airline and get packed. Then we'll take you over to your place and get some clothes. You are coming with me, aren't you?"

"Why yes, Honey! Why do you ask?"

"I just couldn't tell from your statement about Shipley and Dr. Perkins."

"Oh. Well I was going to include myself, too." Changing the subject she added, "But you know this does pose a small problem, don't you?"

"What's that?"

"We will have to tell them about- *us*." She motioned with a sweep of her hand, finger pointing at the both of them, back and forth like a metronome.

"Oh. Yeah. Well, God has His reasons. We just go along for the ride." He didn't know if his words made any difference to her, but without responding, she looked at him with confidence and trusted him steadfastly.

They managed to get everything arranged quickly. This all happened as Harry, his landlord, slept upstairs. Larkin packed, especially his sports coat. 'Too bad I won't have my new suit,' he thought. Then he remembered that he'd forgotten to pick up his suit the day before. Picking up the phone one more time, he dialed Stephen, the tailor. He didn't know if he'd be in, but he could try. Stephen picked up and Larkin said, "Hey Stephen, this is Larkin. I forgot to come and pick up my suit yesterday. Can I come to get it now?"

"Sure. I'll be here for another hour."

"Thanks."

Harry woke to all the commotion and came out of his room to see what was going on. "What's up, Larkin?" he yelled down the stairs.

"My Uncle Tom has taken ill and isn't expected to make it. We will be gone for a few days, Harry", he said walking up the stairs to the back door of the downstairs apartment he rented from him.

"I'm sorry. You will be in my prayers."

Sally came up the stairs, too, and asked, "Are you ready to go, Honey?"

"Yeah, but before we go to your house for your stuff, we have to stop and pick up my new suit."

"Okay." She came up to Harry and gave him a peck on the cheek. "Bye, Harry. Pray for us."

Seriously, the graying man replied, "I haven't prayed this much in a long time, Sally."

Larkin looked up into the overcast skies as they walked out towards the truck and got in. Harry opened the gate to let them out and Larkin looked to see if there was anyone watching them- no one to be seen and no one to see them. After the two stops, they made it to the airport just after dark and in time for the Tuesday night red eye to New York. From there, they could get a flight to Albany and rent a car to drive to Larkin's home.

When they took their seats on the flight, Larkin could sense Sally getting a bit nervous. He asked, "What's wrong?"

"I didn't expect it to be this way. I thought I'd have time to prepare before I met your family. I really don't know anything about them yet. Can you tell me more before we get there?"

"Don't worry. They will love you. But, I'll tell you more."

Larkin told her as much as he could about his Dad, Mom, and especially his Uncle Tom, and what he meant to him. By the time they arrived in New York City, Sally was becoming a little more at ease and he hoped she would be okay when they finally arrived in Brookfield. He hoped *he* would be okay, especially with the Masons there.

As they drove from Albany to Brookfield in the dark, watching for deer along the way, Larkin told her about *his* concerns. "I never told my parents that they had threatened me. That's why I went away to D.C., but it wasn't the fact that I might be in trouble. No. It was that they had threatened *them* that I was worried about. They just can't leave anyone I love alone."

"They'll leave you alone for this, won't they? I mean, especially if he dies?"

"You would think so. But, we had better not stay too long. We need to get back as soon as possible. Don't let them talk us into staying for Christmas. We can't do that!" he said emphatically.

"I understand, Honey."

"Good. I'm so sorry."

"What did I just say? *I understand.*"

They drove the rest of the way in silence. Sally was thinking about if she would be accepted and Larkin was thinking about telling them about her. But in the forefront of their minds, was Tom. Through it all, Larkin had kept him in his prayers. Sally had done the same. Just before they arrived, Sally smelled something. "Do you smell something, Larkin?"

"The chili just got to me."

She slapped his arm and said as she rolled down her window, "Thank goodness that didn't happen to the poor people on the plane!"

Larkin drove into the driveway and looked around before he got out. He didn't see the Lincoln, so he figured his parents were gone to be with Tom. They got out and went into the house carrying their things with them, except for the suitcase with the Palmer "things" in it, which they felt they must keep with them at all times now. There was a note on the table for him. It said:

"Larkin, we are over at The Homestead. He will not make it the night. He wanted to be there. Come as soon as you get here. Love,

Mom"

He sat his suitcase down and said, "Let's go, Sally."

They jumped into the rental car and drove as fast as he could to The Homestead. There were two other cars in the driveway when they arrived. The Lincoln, and from what he remembered, Dr. Flynn's car. Tom's car was in the barn. They walked in as quickly as their feet could carry them. When the door opened, Shirley came out of Tom's room to greet him. She was more than surprised to see Sally. His Mom kissed Larkin on the cheek and said, "I'm glad you're here, Honey. Who's this?"

Sally looked at him not knowing how Shirley meant the question quite yet and Larkin just said softly as to introduce her saying, "Mom, this is Sally. Sally, this is Shirley, my Mom."

Without speaking, Sally boldly went up to Shirley and gave her a hug. Smiling, Shirley said, "I'm very glad to meet you, Sally."

Matter-of-factly, Sally replied, "You, too. How's Tom doing?"

Larkin started toward the bedroom before she could answer. "Not too good. He wants to see Larkin, almost like he was waiting for him. Go in with him, too."

They sat their coats down and headed into Tom's room. Lawtin moved aside as they came in and nodded at his son, wondering who the woman was with him. The doctor stood on the other side of the bed. Tom looked up in the dim light of the room and saw Larkin come in, with Sally right behind. He smiled and motioned for him to come closer. They both walked over. Shirley came in and stood by Lawtin. Larkin went closer still, taking his uncle by the hand as Tom said, "Hello, Larkin. Who's your friend?"

"This is Sally, Uncle. I love her."

"I'm glad. Be good to her."

"I will, Uncle. I will."

"Everything is where we left it. I've willed the place to you Larkin; always "bee" a good Keeper." He smiled and winked, knowing his nephew understood the pun.

"I will, Uncle." He smiled back at him.

With that, Tom closed his eyes and gave up the fight. They cried for a bit, prayed for a bit, and after a bit, Lawtin motioned for them to go out into the living room. Lawtin closed the door to his brother's bedroom. Dr. Flynn shook Lawtin's hand and left, and then they were by themselves. Lawtin came over to Sally and said, "Hello. My name is Lawtin. I'm very glad to meet you." Reaching out, he gave her a hug. Now Sally knew Larkin was right. They did love her, because they loved their son.

They sat at the kitchen table and talked into the morning light about Tom, getting to know each other, sharing their past, voicing their concerns and expressing their faith. Most of all, Lawtin wanted to know if and what she knew when he asked his son, "Larkin, does she *know*?"

Larkin looked at Sally. She got up and with what seemed like resolve to his parents, went over to Larkin's' suitcase, and all the while the family watched her intently. She opened it and took out The Eraser Box. Walking over to the table, she sat it down firmly in front of them and said, "Yes. I know. And from now on, I will be the Palmer God wants me to be."

Shirley took her hand and Lawtin stood and said, "Praise be to God." They were relieved to hear it. Not only that, but that Larkin had become a well-established, mature son, and the kind of Keeper that would make the family proud, especially his Uncle Tom.

They called the funeral home in the morning to arrange the pickup of Tom's body. They just sat and talked while they waited; about what had happened in D.C. since Larkin had gotten there, including their meeting, their short courtship, and everything else. Larkin didn't tell them anything that may concern them or about the threats to the family. Finally, Shirley got up and asked, "Does anyone want breakfast?"

Sally said, "Yes, I'm starving."

Shirley said, "Larkin, go to the basement and get a ham would you?"

"Does he still have some down there, Mom?"

"I think so. You better bring up all of them so we can take them home, I guess. I don't think there will be that many."

"Okay. Sally, come with me." He smiled and motioned for her to come along.

Sally got up and the two went toward the trap door on the porch. Larkin flipped the light switch, pulled up the heavy door and they went down the steps. It looked like Tom had stored up a bunch of food stuffs. There were only three hams though. He unhooked them from the metal hooks hanging from the ceiling. Sally asked, "What's the trunk over there Larkin?"

"Oh. That's the Masonic treasure."

"Can I see it?"

"May as well. Its part yours now."

Larkin walked over and sat the hams down on the dusty stairs. Then seemingly methodically, he turned and faced the chest. It, too, was dusty and he figured that the last time anyone was in it was when Tom checked for the die. He never did get the picture Tom had promised he'd send. Turning on the lamp above it, he swept a cob-web aside, and grabbed the handle. Swinging the lid up, the dust flew around the room. "There it is."

"Wow! I've never seen so much gold and silver in one place in my life!"

"What's this?" Larkin picked up a note attached to a felt bag on top of the bars. It was from Tom.

"Dear Larkin,
I never sent you the picture of the die, because I thought you'd be here soon enough to see it for yourself. I've not been well for a long while and I've hidden it from your parents, my health and the die. So, I've kept the die out for you to see. Love to you,
Uncle Tom"

Larkin started to cry. Sally held him and waited for him to gain his composure before opening the bag. He finally did, brushing the tears from his face, and then he opened the bag that contained the die. Holding the round die up to the light, he exclaimed, "Wow!" It was just as he envisioned it. Surely Franklin and Gallaudet had, indeed, designed it. "By any chance did you bring a camera?"Larkin asked the enthralled Sally.

"Yes! I have my Brownie up in my purse."

"Go get it."

Scurrying along, she picked up two of the hams on the stairs and made her way up. She sat them on the counter by Shirley and said, "Smells good. Sorry it's taking so long, but Larkin wants a picture of something. Be right back to help you."

"Oh take your time, Dear. I'm doing fine."

Sally retrieved the camera out of her bag and went right back down to Larkin. She said, "What or um, how do you want this, Honey?"

"Let me hold this in the light for you so the picture turns out."

Larkin held the die up next to the light and Sally moved closer trying to keep it in focus; whatever that was, for a Brownie camera. The flash cube went off when she took it and Larkin said, "One more- just in case."

She took another picture and said, "I have to go up and help your mother. Close up the chest and come on up, okay, Honey?"

"Okay, Dear." Larkin put the bag back in the trunk and stuffed the letter into his pocket.

Sally picked up the last ham and went back up. When she got there, she sat it down, tried to wipe the dust off her hands and said, "What do you want me to do, Shirley?"

Before she answered, Shirley said to her without looking up from her work, "You know, I've called him "Honey" for years and he always hushed me. He must really love you, because he just called you "Dear", instead."

"I think he really does."

"So do I. Oh, set the table would you? The dishes are over there." Shirley pointed to the cabinet on the far wall.

Larkin came up the stairs and after closing the trap door said, "Mom, there's a lot of canned goods down there you'll have to try to use up."

"I thought there would be. We had a good year this year. I'm glad we sold all the apples off."

Larkin noticed his dad was not there. "Where's Dad?"

"Out in the barn; feeding."

He looked at Sally and said, "I'll be right back." Sally gave him a quick kiss and he threw on his coat, and hurriedly proceeded out to the barn.

Shirley, looking up from the stove said, "You can take the boy out of the country, but you can't take the country out of the boy." She didn't comment on the kiss, discerning that, indeed, the two had become a couple.

Larkin got out to the barn and found his dad with the mules. It had been a while since he had seen them. He didn't realize how much he missed his former way of life. He walked up to Lawtin and patted one of the mules on its head. Lawtin said, "You get around on that cast pretty good, Son."

"Yeah, well, you get used to it. But it sure itches. Especially way down by your toes. I have to get a pencil to scratch it sometimes."

Lawtin laughed, and then he got serious. "I'm going to have to hire someone to run the orchard for you now that Tom is gone. If you were here, you could do it, but you're not."

"I know. I trust you will do the best you can with it, Dad. If you have any questions you can call me anytime. We can see how it goes and evaluate it later. I appreciate your efforts so much, because I know it's not your problem, especially since Uncle left it to me."

"We are family, Son. Oh, and by the way, I'm glad God sent you someone. I worried you'd never get over Ginny."

"I have to admit, I still haven't, Dad. But Sally is different and God did send her to me. I truly love her like no other."

"I can tell. Let's go back in. Your Mom is going to yell for us soon." Just then they heard from the house, "Soups on!"

They all sat down to eat and Lawtin led the prayer. Taking each other's outstretched hands, Lawtin included them all and thanked God for His special blessings. After they finished eating, Sally and Shirley started to clean up and just then, the funeral director drove into the driveway with the hearse. Lawtin and Larkin got up to greet them as two men came to the door. Showing them where Tom's body lay, the reality of it all hit Lawtin again and he had to sit down. Shirley put down her wash rag and dried her hands on her apron. Coming over to him, she held his hands and comforted him. The men began to leave and reminded them to call Pastor Johnson. Larkin followed them out. He wanted to watch his uncle leave. Finally, they closed up the place. It felt-surreal. Empty. Larkin wondered if he'd ever be able to return to his new, old home. He was devastated.

The funeral was scheduled for Saturday afternoon. The weather had been good and the snow was gone. They planned to dig the grave and place Tom beside the rest of the Palmers there at The Homestead. Pastor Johnson arranged to have the service at the church and the ladies, like always, would do a dinner afterwards. Visitation at the funeral home would be Friday night. That would give them Wednesday and Thursday to get to know each other even better. Larkin thought it was God's way of bringing them together so that Sally would be accepted by them more easily. Ginny was a hard act to follow. However, Sally and Ginny were completely different, so it made it easier to love Sally just as much. But, Lawtin and Shirley could see one similarity in the two women-they both loved Larkin with their total being. And that was good enough for them.

When it was time to go to bed that first night, Shirley came to them and said, "I don't know how to ask this, but where, um, I mean, how?"

Sally understood and said, "Larkin will be in his room and I assume you may have another room for me?"

With sigh of relief Shirley replied, "Yes. There is spare bedroom next to his. You can share the bathroom. I have fresh towels in the closet up there, okay?"

"Yes. Thanks. Say Shirley," Sally paused, "can I call you "Mom"?"

Shirley came over to her and smiled giving her a hug saying, "Please do, Honey. I can't think of why not!"

Sally smiled, and said softly, "Thanks, Mom."

Larkin and Lawtin observed all of this and hunching over, Larkin picked up his suitcases saying like someone out of a horror movie, "Follow the bellhop with the club foot to your room, Miss."

"Why thank you, Igor." Sally knew which movie he was referring to.

Sally picked up her suitcase and followed him upstairs. Pointing toward the end of the hall he said, "That's yours down there, Miss. Mine is right here. The bath is in the middle."

"Thanks, Bellhop," she said.

She kissed him and went toward her room to change. He said, "Goodnight, Miss."

She replied, "I'm beat. Goodnight, Honey."

In the morning, Sally was sitting on his bed when he woke. Sitting up he asked, "How long have you been here?"

"Oh, not long. I slept like a baby last night. I was really tired. I hope you did, too. Considering, that is."

"Yeah, I did. As much as I'll miss my uncle, because we were so close, I know I'll see him and my uncle Harry again someday. It gives me peace to know that I'll be with them in heaven. I've never asked you about that and your family. Do you all have that assurance?"

"Yes, I believe we do. I sometimes worry about my brother, but for the most part, we all believe and trust in His promises."

"That's good. Now, who'll get the bathroom first?"

"I already went; your turn."

"I'm gonna take a shower. Will you go get me a plastic bag for the cast?"

"You bet. Be right back!"

Sally hustled off to the kitchen and he headed to the bathroom. He waited for her to return, feeling like she might try to pull something. He was right, because when she returned, she was giggling the whole time standing there and he asked sharply, "Are you going to leave now?"

"Oh, I thought I'd see if it worked out first."

"Oh no, you're not! Get out of here so I can take a shower!"

"Oh; alright." She said faking disappointment, giggling again, turning and walking toward the door. He started to pull off his pants and suddenly she turned back almost catching him. She laughed and said as he covered himself, "Gotcha!"

"Sally! Get out of here!"

Sally shut the door behind her and went down to the kitchen in her PJ's. Larkin's PJ's. She never thought about that and when she got there, Shirley was there starting breakfast. She noticed the apparel right away. "I see you have a new set of PJ's?"

Blushing, Sally said, "Oh no, Mom. Don't get the wrong idea. We have made a pledge; none of that until we are married. I tease him a lot, but it's not going to happen until its legal."

"I heard you tease him. I think it's funny."

"You do?"

"Yes. He's so innocent. He needs to grow up, I know. But at least you two are doing it right. I'm glad. Not many kids think about that anymore."

"Don't worry. We'll keep our promise. I just happened to need a pair of PJ's after I got all wet in the snow. These are so nice I use them every time I'm over."

"Every time you're over?"

"Oh; yeah. Let's talk about that. Sit down, Mom, and I'll tell you."

They sat at the table while Larkin was in the shower and Sally told her everything. How she had stayed some nights, teased him, and now how she was going to move in with him. Finally, she told her about the reservation at The Hay-Adams. She was totally honest. Shirley appreciated it and said, "I trust my son. And after our conversation, I trust you, too, Sally. But just between you and me, keep on teasing him, you'll drive him crazy!"

Larkin came in on that part of their conversation and said, "Are you two calling me crazy?"

At the same time they both said, "No, Honey, we're not."

They all burst out laughing.

Shortly thereafter, Lawtin came in from the barn and they sat down to eat. He asked Sally, Larkin thought as a test, to say the grace. She didn't flinch and began, "Dear Lord, we thank you that in the midst of adversity and hard times that you provide for us; our food, our faith, and the hope of life with you. Thank you Lord for this my new family and for your Son, Jesus. Amen."

They all said a resounding, "Amen!"

Lawtin picked up his fork, looked at Sally and said, "Thanks, Daughter."

"You're welcome, Dad."

Turning to Larkin he said, "Arville and Percy are out there, Larkin, and they'd like to see you before the funeral."

"Oh, that'd be good. I'll go out after breakfast. Okay?"

"You just want to get out of drying the dishes," remarked Sally.

"So you know he dries?" asked Shirley.

"Yup; he told me all about it. I'll dry today."

"I'll take any help I can get!"

The phone rang again. It had not stopped since the town found out that Tom had passed. Lawtin got it this time and spoke with Ginny's dad. Larkin got up, put his plate in the sink and motioned he was going out to the barn. Sally and Shirley started to do the cleanup. They talked as they worked and Sally began to understand what Larkin had said; true feelings and emotions come out when you share a common project, even as simple as doing the dishes. It was "dishwashing philosophy" at its best. Sally was glad to be a part of it and Shirley got to hear her new daughter's perspectives on much; including life and death. Consequently, the task took a while.

Larkin opened the barn door and upon doing so, smelled the familiar smells. Not as strong as many diary barns, because, it would seem, the guys were keeping it extremely clean. Larkin was impressed, especially by the new tractor that helped them do their job. For a country boy, this- was home. The radio was on playing a tune for the cows. He saw Percy and Arville and waived. "Hi Guys!" he yelled above the milking machines. He went over to Heidi and said hello, too. "Hello, girl. How have you been?" She remembered him, shaking her head and ringing her bell.

Percy came up to him and grabbed him in a bear hug, raising him up off the floor. "Hello Larkin! It's so nice to see you. I wish it was under different circumstances though. I'm sure gonna miss Mr. Tom."

"Me, too, Percy."

Arville came up and in his normal, overly shy way of just smiling with only the corner of his mouth said, "Hi, Larkin."

He moved on to his next task and Larkin said as he passed by, "Hi, Arville."

"I heard from your dad you brought home a girl with you. What's she like, Larkin?" asked Percy.

"Do you mean; 'Is she like Ginny?'. No, she's different, and she loves me. And I love her. God has truly blessed me again."

"I'm glad to hear it."

"So what's been going on here at the dairy?"

They talked about the dairy, and the improvements, and how many cows, and so many other "farmer" things. Larkin was happy to hear how well it was going and was impressed as to the condition of the grounds. They kept them immaculate. However, he had to ask, "Do you know anyone that could take over the orchard, Percy?"

"I have an idea. But, I think Lawtin needs to put out ads to fill it. It's going to be a demanding job. Tom was good."

"I know. That's the problem- too good. Kinda like you two. Sure looks good around here. Do you think Dad would be able to handle it if he can't find someone?"

"I don't think so. He needs to start searching right away."

"Thanks, Percy. I appreciate you."

"See you on Friday, Larkin."

"Bye."Larkin looked around the barn once more and headed toward the door.

Walking slowly back up to the house, Larkin found Sally sitting at the table talking to his dad. Shirley was on the phone talking to one of the ladies from church. He waved at Sally like "come on", pointed at her to his father as if to say, "I need her" and they made their way upstairs. When they got up there, she gave him a quizzical look, wanting to know what was going on. He motioned for her to keep quiet and they went into his room.

He shut the door and grabbed her. Taking her to himself he kissed her deeply. She drew back and said to him, "Whoa, boy! What got into you?"

"You can take the boy out of the country," he started to say, but she interrupted and finished it for him saying, "But you can't take the country out of the boy." They laughed and he released her. He patted her on the rear as she went to sit on his bed. Then he said, "I think Dad will have a hard time finding someone to fill my uncle's shoes. We need to make it a priority to pray the Lord sends him someone."

"I know. Otherwise the place will become run down."

"Yes. And it also needs to be protected from "them." They may get curious and try to find the chest. If they do, it will be bad."

"I know. But who can you trust to be there? They would have to *know* it's there."

"I know. It's a *big* problem. It's almost like I need to be here instead of D.C.. But I need to finish at UMD."

"What are we going to do, Honey?"

"God will let us know when it's time. It will become totally obvious."

"Yes, I suppose."

"Come here." He motioned for her to come over by the window. She bounded off the bed and stood next to him. "Take a look out there. This place is all I've ever really known. I would love to come back to it. Could you be happy here?"

"You know I would."

"Well, let's see what the Lord does and what doors He opens. We'll go along for the ride."

"Okay, Honey." She gave him a long kiss.

When he came up for air, he said, "Whew. Thanks."

"Let's go down and see your parents. I want to visit with them some more."

"Okay. But you're weird. Oh, just a second, I'll be down in a minute. I want to look for something. Go ahead."

"Okay."

Larkin went to his dresser junk drawer and looked around. There he found a transistor radio he used to use. He wanted to take it back to D.C. so he had something to listen to, because Harry's radio was definitely shot. This would work for the time being. He put it in the suitcase next to The Eraser Box. He wondered if he should leave the Journal and the other stuff here when he went back to D.C. He knew he would have to take The Eraser, but he didn't know if taking the rest was necessary. He'd have to think on that.

He went downstairs and joined the conversation at the table. Lawtin said, "Mr. Berry is looking forward to seeing you Larkin, and of course, meeting Sally. In fact, to be honest with you, I've told most of the people who've called that Sally is here. I didn't want to spring her on people."

"Oh I understand, Dad. I hope they give Sally a fair shake. They just need to get to know her."

"Oh, don't worry. If they see what we see, they will love her, too."

Sally blushed and said, "Thanks, Dad."

When Larkin saw this he said, "Boy, I didn't think you could blush, Dear. That's refreshing."

She reached across the table and swatted at him. Shirley said, "I've seen her blush too, Larkin. She's not as brazen as you think she is."

"Oh? Really? Well, I guess I'll have to try to get her to blush someday, too."

Sally said, "That'll be the day. You're a prude."

"Well, I never!" He said defensively. Then he laughed. Sally came over to him and gave him a kiss. It was the first time Lawtin had seen that. Looking at Shirley, she just smiled.

Larkin changed the subject and asked, "Is there anything we have to do to prepare for tomorrow evening or for Saturday, Dad?"

"Yes. We need to write the obituary and get it to the paper today. Want to help?"

"Sure. Let's go into the study."

When they had the new house built, they had changed one of the two first floor bedrooms into a study, and made the master bedroom bigger. That way, Lawtin had a room to do his bookwork in the house without making a mess. They sat down and wrote the obituary together following an example from the paper of the week before. It took longer than they had anticipated and by the time they were done and asked the girls to edit it, it was almost five. Lawtin called the paper to make sure they were still there to accept it for the next edition. The person who answered said, "Yes, we'll be here for another half-hour."

Lawtin replied, "We'll be there in ten minutes." Hanging up the phone, he said to Larkin, "Let's go. Grab your coat."

The two men grabbed their coats, kissed the girls goodbye, ran out the door and jumped into his dad's Lincoln. As they drove into town, for some reason his dad turned on Stanbro and headed towards the Homestead, (Larkin didn't understand why considering they were in a hurry), but Larkin noticed the changes since he had been gone; the new fence and road work at Five Corners, the Brown's had painted their house green, and the trees had gotten taller going up Dugway Road. But then something dawned on him and he asked, "Dad, where's Sam?"

"I didn't want to worry you, Son, but when Tom got sick, he just up and disappeared. We don't know where he is."

"Oh," he said disappointed.

"I'm sure he'll turn up, Larkin. Sometimes dogs sense this. Just wait and see."

They pulled up at the newspaper office and got out. Larkin looked around to see who might be on the Turnpike. A truck was coming in from Highway 99 and slowed as it went past them getting out of the car. He didn't notice who it was, but the men inside recognized him. They were Masons and they would soon tell the rest of the lodge who was in town for his uncle's funeral. The two Palmer men went in and dropped off the obit. Coming out, they decided to go straight home and skip any interaction in town. They were just not in the mood.

They got in the car and as they headed back home, Larkin thought about what had occurred; Tom's death and all, and God's timing in it. It made him think about what was really important to him. Did he really need a college degree? Did he really need to hide any longer? Couldn't he, like generations of Palmer men before him, just live his life there in Brookfield and pass The Eraser on to his son? He asked his dad, "Dad, could I take Sally out to The Homestead tomorrow?"

"Well sure, Son. Any reason?"

"I don't know. I guess I want to show her what Palmer life is like." His dad chuckled. "Palmer life?" he asked.

"Yeah. I have a lot of decisions to make. I want her to be part of them."

"I understand."

They drove up to the house and got out. There on the porch was Sam, and as soon as Larkin got out the dog ran to him and jumped up to greet him. "Sam!" he yelled when he saw him. "Good dog. I wondered where you were. Glad to see you back, Boy!" He rubbed his head and Sam ran ahead of him to the door. Larkin looked at his Dad and asked, "Does he come inside now, Dad?"

"Yeah, you're mom has him spoiled. Besides, he has his own little place by the stove."

Larkin let him in and the two men went to see where the girls were. They were in the kitchen drinking coffee and had made arrangements for flowers and the headstone for Tom on the phone. Shirley said to Lawtin, "I'm glad that Tom had picked out his headstone and made all of the other arrangements. He was a very thoughtful man.

I'm surprised he never got married. He would have made a wonderful husband for someone."

"Well, sometimes God never sends the right one," replied Lawtin, "sometimes He sends two." He winked at Sally.

Larkin came over and gave Sally a kiss and saw that Sam was sitting on the floor next to the stove, just like his dad had said. He asked, "What's for supper?"

"Fried chicken," said his mom.

"Oh man, thanks, Mom."

Turning to Sally he said, "My mom makes the best fried chicken on the planet."

"Not to be disrespectful, Mom," she said to Shirley, "but Larkin, *my* mom makes the best fried chicken on the planet."

"We'll just see about that! Mom, do you think you can win her over?"

"I'll do my best!"

"You always do."

As Shirley cooked, the three of them just stayed in the kitchen keeping her company and helping out as they could. It was like a bee hive, all participants flitting about doing their part to put it all together. They sat down to eat and said grace. Larkin offered the first piece of chicken to Sally. "What do you like Dear, white or dark?"

"Dark. Give me a thigh if you would."

Larkin picked out the piece he would have taken for himself. Sally looked it over, placed it up to her lips, and slowly took a bite. They all waited with bated breath for her to say something. Finally, she smiled and said mid-chew, "Don't tell my mother, but this *is* better."

"Yeah!" Larkin and Lawtin shook their heads in agreement as Larkin said, "I told you so."

He took a bite of his and said, "Um-um. This is good. I missed your cooking, Mom."

"Thanks, Honey."

Larkin didn't say another word and just kept on eating. Shirley winked at Sally and sat down.

After dinner they went into the living room to sit by the fireplace. Lawtin had put a log on the fire and it was cozy-warm in the room. The kids sat by each other on the sofa with Lawtin and Shirley in their chairs. Shirley knitted a set of booties for a new baby at church and Lawtin read the paper. The kids just watched the fire dance and crackle occasionally as it burned down slowly into glowing red-hot embers. They got sleepy in this self- imposed trance and Larkin began to fade off to slumber. Sally kissed him on his forehead and he woke up enough to smile at her and kiss her on the lips. His mother watched as she worked and smiled at the thought that Larkin was once again so happy and in love. It was more than she had hoped for him.

Larkin woke when his mom started to get up to go to bed. Lawtin had nodded off himself and as he got up to join his wife, he said goodnight to them all. Sally was still awake thinking about her situation. Larkin started to get up, but Sally pulled him back down and said, "Wait a minute, Honey, can we talk?" Shirley took the hint, and said goodnight and left the room.

"What is it, Dear? Is there something wrong?"

"Oh, no; just the opposite. Everything is *right*. What you have here is so wonderful; family, work, and a future. Why would you ever want to leave this?"

"I don't. If it were not for the Palmer curse, it would all be so *perfect*. And I'm glad you brought this up. I want to take you to The Homestead in the morning and talk about it some more. Would that be okay?"

"I'd like that."

"It's a date. Let's go to bed." Larkin rose and pulled her up off the sofa. They held hands and walked upstairs. When they got to the hall he kissed her. He didn't want to leave her to go to his own room, and his feelings were all over the place at this moment, but he knew he must. She smiled when she saw the disappointment in his eyes. She didn't want to tease him tonight. They both needed to part ways or break their commitment to one another. Larkin said as he walked away, "Goodnight, Sally."

"Goodnight, Honey."

Sally went to her room and closed the door. While preparing for rest, she thought about what she may be getting into. To other girls, this kind of family, this kind of life in the country would be boring. All they did was work hard, eat, sleep and just- sit there! What kind of life was that? Especially since they had little to do with people outside of the family and church because of- The Eraser. She said a prayer asking God for help and guidance, and went to sleep.

Chapter Two

The Burial Proposal

Early in the morning, Larkin was up and out to the barn to help with the milking. By the time Sally was up and dressed, he had come back in and was sitting at the table drinking coffee and talking to his mom. "Well hello, Sleepyhead. How are you today?"

"I'm good, Honey. Did you help with the chores?"

"Yes. It was good to be back out in the barn. I miss it."

Lawtin came into the room and said, "That's good to hear. You can go over to The Homestead and see how the animals are doing over there." He didn't want to let on he knew what Larkin had planned.

"I'm taking Sally over there with me, Dad. I can show her around."

"Sounds good to me."He smiled at his son, who returned the gesture.

After they ate, Larkin went out to get the old pickup from the side of the barn. Like it always had, it started up right away. The old Ford was rusty, had a cracked windshield and the body had scratches and dents all over it, but the best thing about it was it had a good heater. He pulled it up to the door and Sally ran out and jumped in with him. She waved at Shirley as they drove away and she settled in for the short drive. Sitting next to him in the seat as the cab got warm, he told her this and that about the places they passed. He explained that he always knew he would own the orchard someday, but never expected it to be so soon. Arriving at the Homestead drive on Chase road, he stopped by the mail box. He conveyed his story about how he and Percy had rebuilt it so many years before and how he was led to find the "Mail Box". He then drove up to where Tom used to park his Ford. Getting out right on top of it, he showed her where the old house used to stand and the footings now beneath them. Tilting his head toward the house, Larkin said "I'm not ready to go back in there quite yet. Can we just walk and I'll tell you everything I know?"

She nodded "yes".

"Let's start over there at the cemetery," he said pointing, "and I'll introduce all of the people that I've been reading about and even some that I haven't."

They walked past many things he would later come back to, for he had much to tell. Rather than go over to the headstone of Lawtin Sr., he stopped at Ben first. "This, Sally, is Ben. He is the first one who helped bring out Grandma Mary's gift in me. He left his own little treasure map in the Glory Box that I haven't told you about yet. Ginny and I," he paused and sighed, "Ginny and I found it over there under the big tree. I'll show you later." They walked around the family graveyard, Larkin introducing her to them all on this side of heaven and telling her all the stories he knew.

Finally finishing his stories, he took her to where the grave diggers had already dug Tom's grave. "This, as you probably have figured out, is where Uncle Tom will be, right next to Harry." He didn't linger there, which Sally thought was good, but rather, they went toward the apple barn. "The apple barn is new and the first one we built after the tornado.

Sally replied, "Tornado?"

"Oh. I never mentioned it? We had a tornado come through a few years back and tear down the old barn, which the Amish rebuilt last year." He pointed to the barn by the car. "They did a really good job and the other day was the first time I saw it. You wouldn't know it was new, well, unless you knew. It took out my parent's house too, and the one they have is a new modified reproduction."

Along the way, he told her about the new business where Tom sold apples both commercially and at the apple barn, and as they walked to the new barn, he told her about the day of the tornado and how black the sky had become. He opened the heavy barn door for her and said, "This is where I sat, right here in the door on that chair," he pointed, "and when the rain let up, I ran into the house with my uncles. If I wouldn't have, I would have flown up with the barn, like the witch in the "Wizard of Oz", I guess!" Sally laughed. He went on, pointing to the corner, "That is where I found the silver chest that's in the basement and how I got the idea to dig for Seward's chest at the Smithsonian." He walked over a couple more feet and said, "And this, (he stomped his foot on the ground for effect) is where I found Percifer Carr's treasure- right here." He told her about the mules and the loss of Tom's ox and how they used to have the water drum for showers on the roof until he paid to have the bathroom put into the house for his uncles. After they checked on the animals, they walked out of the barn and he said to her, "I've saved one place for last. Come with me."

He walked over to the big tree and said, "This is where I found Ben's treasure with Ginny. It was a beginning for me. We are also standing under what my family calls, "The Wedding Tree". Many of the people you just met were married right where we stand. It is where I want to do this." He got down on one knee and when Sally figured out what he was about to do she began to cry, but held it back but for a couple of tears, "Sally Britt, will do me the honor of being my wife?"

"Oh, Larkin, you are so romantic. Yes. Yes, I will be your wife!"

Standing up, he kissed her and asked, "Are you sure? Even after getting the whole picture about me and my family, and all we've had to go through? Are you sure?"

"Yes. I'm sure."

"Then we have a wedding to plan! Yahoo!" He took off the baseball cap on his head and flung it into the air.

Waiting a moment as she watched him retrieve it, she smiled and said, "Haven't you forgotten something else?" She paused, hand outstretched. "A ring?"

"Oh. Yeah. A ring. We'll get that first!"

He grabbed her hand and they walked back to the truck, no longer feeling the cold. On the ride back to the farm, Sally thought about her prayer just the night before. She smiled and mouthed, 'Thank you Lord.'

When they got back to the house, Shirley noticed how happy they were and asked them as they sat down, "What's going on with you two?"

Sally replied, "Larkin just proposed to me."

Looking at Larkin, his mom asked, "What did she say?"

"She said yes, Mom," her son said smiling.

Sally got up and Shirley came to her and gave her a big hug. "Welcome to the family, Sally."

Sally said, "He did it under, "The Wedding Tree." He's so romantic."

"Aren't I though?"

Lawtin came in and sat down. "What's going on? Why's everyone looking like- that?"

Shirley replied, "Because your son proposed to Sally."

"What'd she say?"

"Yes!" Shirley slapped him on the shoulder.

"Well then, it looks like we have a wedding to plan!"

"I didn't want to take away from Uncles' funeral, Dad, but I had the opportunity to ask her, so I took it. Let's wait until afterwards to announce anything. Okay?"

"Okay, Son, we understand."

They ate lunch and the focus of their day returned to Tom's funeral. It also became somber, as Lawtin became nervous and somewhat depressed at the thought of it all. Shirley tried to help, but thought it best to just let him work through it himself. Larkin was now quiet, too, and taking Shirley's example, Sally did the same. They cleaned up the lunch plates and Larkin went up to take a nap before the viewing. Lawtin did the same.

Sally followed Larkin up to his room and lay on the bed with him as he tried to get to sleep. He didn't say anything when she joined him and she draped her arm and leg over him, placing her head on his chest. Finally, they drifted off to sleep.

They woke to someone arriving out front. Getting up, Larkin looked out his window to see a family from church knock on the door and deliver some food from the ladies group to his mom. He went to the bathroom and when he came back Sally sat up on the bed. "What are you going to do now?" she asked rubbing her eyes.

"I'm going down to talk to Mom. I guess we had better eat before we go, but I'm not very hungry."

Sally didn't say anything, but went into the bathroom. Coming out, she found Larkin picking out clothes for the evening. He really had no choice- it was the new suit or nothing. He sure would be glad to get rid of the cast! Sally said, "I'm going to take a shower now and put my makeup on. I don't want to wait until the last minute, okay?"

Larkin looked up from his task and said, "Sure, Dear. Go ahead. I'll take my turn later."

Sally went to her room and got a couple of things. Larkin heard her in the shower and looked up after she came out of the bathroom. She was wrapped in a towel and was drying her hair with another as she walked toward him. She asked, "Do you think I should get my hair cut? It's been long like this for years."

She turned around with her back towards him, shook out her hair, and "accidentally" her towel dropped to the floor. She stood there, her long red hair reaching to the back of her legs, covering her nakedness. Still, he gazed upon her and couldn't help but see her beauty, her freckles, and the sacral dimples peeking out below her waist. Coming up to her, he picked up the towel, wrapped it around her and replied, "No, Dear. You are beautiful the way you are." He kissed her, slapped her on the behind and said, "Go get dressed!" She giggled and went to her room to get dressed.

Just then, Shirley came up the stairs and said softly to him, "I heard all of that you know."

Blushing Larkin said, "I'm sorry, Mom. She just drives me crazy."

"I know. I told her to."

She handed him a box. Pausing, not knowing how to react to her statement, he instead asked her, "What is this?"

"Open it."

He opened the box to find a wedding ring. "It was your Grandma Mary's."

"It's beautiful. Can I?"

"That's what I brought it up here for!"

They smiled at each other and Larkin kissed his Mom on the forehead and said, "Thanks, Mom."

Larkin left his mother and went towards Sally's room. Shirley went back downstairs. When he got there, he just opened the door without knocking and went in. She was standing there still half naked. She turned, covered herself and said teasingly, "Why, Larkin Palmer! What are you doing walking in on me like that?"

He went over to her and put his finger on her lips, telling her to be silent. He pulled the box from behind his back with his other hand and opened it. Sally's eyes got as big as saucers and she looked at him for permission to remove it from the box. He nodded and she took it and placed it on her finger. It fit just right. He took her in his arms, kissed her, and they fell onto the bed. She said, "Larkin, thank you."

"I hope you don't mind, but it was Grandma Mary's. Do you like it?"

"It means a lot to me. Yes, I do. I love it." She asked him softly, "Larkin, are you sure we have to wait?"

He was tempted in the moment. He was more than ready. However, realizing their commitment once again, he got up and said, "Ah, we can wait, Dear. You know I want to, but let's wait until we are married and live up to our word. Okay?"

Disappointed and yet relieved, she sat up and said, "Okay. Hand me my shirt."

He picked it up from the dresser next to him and handed it to her. She pulled it over her head and smiled at him. Larkin's mom called up the stairs, "Larkin and Sally, come to the kitchen and have something to eat."

"Okay, Mom," Larkin called out just like he had so many times before. Sally smiled hearing how it used to be at the Palmer house when he was growing up. They got up and went downstairs, hand in hand, now with a ring between them.

When they got to the kitchen, Sally went straight up to Shirley and gave her a hug. Showing her the ring on her finger she said, "Thank you, Mom."

"I thought you might like it. I've had it for a long time. It needed a new home."

"I'll keep track of it. I'm a Keeper, too!"

"You bet you are!" said Larkin as he gave her a hug.

Lawtin asked them to join him at the table and he said the grace, "Lord, where you take away, you give. In life and death we give you thanks. For this food and for all your blessings, thank you. Amen."

They ate while talking about the ring and Larkin's, Grandma Mary. The conversation came around to her "gift" and the apparent transfer of it to Larkin. "He has another thing to find," said Sally without thinking. She looked at Larkin and said, "Oops. I'm sorry, Honey."

He excused her saying, "Oh. It's okay." He looked at his folks and said, "I have to find a key to something for my research. It will solve lots of things, for my work and for us as a family. As you know, it all ties together."Larkin didn't tell them the whole story.

"Yeah, by The Eraser and the Masons," said Lawtin, continuing with his meal.

They finished up the meal provided by the ladies group and they all went to change to go to the viewing. Sally touched up her makeup and put on a dress and Larkin his new suit, which he put on for the first time. He didn't know how Stephen always did such a good job without him even being there. Sally came in and asked, "How does this look?" Larkin worried about how to answer *that* question. Sensing this she said, "Oh don't worry. I'm not like the other girls. Just answer the question."

He thought that if he were honest she would get a big head, because as she stood there in the light, hair hanging to her sides, with the white print dress with blue flowers under it, she looked as an angel in all her glory. Instead of that description he said, "You look great. How do I look?" He turned back and forth in the new suit for her.

"He did a good job. Even the pants fit the cast right. We better get downstairs. I think your parents are ready to leave."

As they started down the stairs, Larkin said to her, "Pray that everything goes okay. You never know what "they" will do."

She knew what he meant and she would pray.

Being the family, they arrived first to the funeral home. Lawtin parked the Lincoln next to the door like the director had told him to do. They got out and went in, feeling like they were being watched. At least the two kids felt it and they looked from side to side without being too obvious. They saw nothing and didn't comment on it as the two couples went in the chapel door and toward the viewing room. Neither the room itself, nor the funeral home, was anything special. It was just a local, small town affair. Lawtin was the first to go see his brother's body. Larkin came up next to him and said, "He looks at peace, Dad."

"Yes. He does." Lawtin put his hand on Larkin's shoulder.

Sally came up, stood by Larkin and said, "Your uncle had good taste. Everything is beautiful."

Indeed, the impressive casket of solid wood was of local hardwoods. He had designed it himself and had one of his Amish friends complete it. Even the flower arrangements were "handpicked" by Tom. He wanted his funeral to be peaceful and a reflection of himself. To his family, it looked as if he had succeeded. They went over by the door, signed the guest book and took a memorial card and pamphlet. It told all about him, but it didn't say much. It was brief and to the point, just like the obituary they had composed the day before. It didn't matter; Tom's life had been full, fuller than most men, but in a different way. He was private, compassionate, and kind. He loved the outdoors, the trees and fields, and especially his Creator, who provided it all. For that he was thankful. Enough said...

The people began to arrive for the viewing and they all came up to express their condolences to Lawtin, Shirley, and Larkin. Sally, for the most part, stood at Larkin's side, nodding her head from time to time and saying hello as she was introduced to more people than she would ever remember. Larkin was surprised when one of the local Masons, who never really was a problem to him or his family, walked into the room with his wife, who was a member of the church. They came up as the others had and said what they had to say. When the Mason walked away, without anyone else noticing, he palmed Larkin a note and kept on going. Larkin glanced at the folded note and put it in his pocket. He thought to himself, 'What now?' As the line had tapered off, Larkin excused himself to go to the restroom. When he got into a stall, he pulled the note out of his pocket. It said, "We had a meeting. They will leave you alone here. Congratulations on your engagement."

"Hum," he said out loud, "maybe they do have a heart?" But, he knew it was a rhetorical question and he wondered how they knew...

He came out of the restroom and the crowd was almost all gone. The director was starting to tidy up to close. Pastor Johnson came up to them before they left and told them what to expect at the church the next day. They said "goodnight" to him and he left. Picking up their coats, they headed toward the door. It had gotten colder, with a predicted zero that night, but there was to be no snow. They waited until everyone had their gloves on and out they went to brave the cold trip home.

They rode home in silence. Somehow, the ride in the cold and its similarity to death seemed more than obvious to them. It had been a long, eventful day.

The family said their goodnights and Sally walked upstairs with Larkin. She came into his room with him because she knew he was saddened by the thought of the loss of his uncle. He took off his suit and she her dress. He put on his PJ's and got under the covers.

She just climbed in with him and turned off the lamp on the night table. She cuddled up to him and they just fell asleep.

The next morning, Shirley called up to them and said, "Soups on!"

Sally got up and went toward her room, picking up her dress from the edge of the bed and hurrying down the hall in her underwear, somewhat worried that Shirley would to come up and find her there with Larkin. However, Shirley knew what had happened that night and trusted them both. Larkin stretched and got up to go to the bathroom. Sally came in with a pair of blue jeans on and her NY Yankee sweatshirt. Larkin had just finished, flushed and said, "I wish you'd let me finish before you come in. I clinch up even in front of guys at the urinal."

"Well, I don't."

She went over, pulled down her jeans and sat on the toilet. Larkin just turned around, threw his hands up into the air and got his toothbrush out of the drawer. He started to brush and she came over to wash her hands.

He started to talk with the brush in his mouth, "And, you should have gotten up and gone to your own room last night."

"Don't worry. We didn't do anything and your mom knew anyway."

"How do you know she knew?"

"I just know. It's a woman thing. Let's go see what's for breakfast!"

When they got down there to eat, Sally went over to get some plates and set the table. Lawtin, as most mornings, was sitting reading the paper. Larkin went over to his mom and said under his breath, "You're not helping, Mom."

Whispering back she said, "Not helping what, Honey?"

"With keeping her away from me. I'm gonna fail one of these times. She drives me crazy, if you know what I mean."

"Oh don't worry. She'll back off when she sees you have gotten used to the teasing. I trust you. You'll do fine. Besides, I'll give her the "Mom test"."

Not totally believing her, he just said, "The test, huh? Well, I hope you're right."

Not hearing their conversation, Sally asked Lawtin, "What time are we going to start over to the church, Dad?"

Without looking up he replied, "Oh, I think about ten or so. It begins at eleven. That should give them all time to tell us what to do."

They both chuckled and Larkin sat down by his dad. Shirley brought over a plate of pancakes with ham and her homemade maple syrup. Lawtin sat his paper down grabbed his son's hand and began the prayer. "Lord for this day we thank you and celebrate the fact that my brother is with you. Let us remember that today and look to the day we Palmers shall be together again. For this food we thank you. Amen."

Sally took a seat. Larkin said, "Mom made this syrup from our old family recipe this year. We planted a new grove of maple trees after the tornado. It takes a while to have enough trees to make it work, but this year she got some from the older trees out back. Hopefully, someday we can get enough to sell as we add trees."

"Sounds like you have more plans for the orchard, Son," said Lawtin.

Sally looked at him trying to figure out her fiancé. They actually all wondered what he would do now that the orchard and Homestead were his. He'd have to think on that. "Yes. Before I make any recommendations, I want to see who is available to take over managing the place. I don't want him to have to do something he cannot handle."

"That makes sense. We'll see who and what God provides. It's all in His hands."

Shirley sat down and said, "As it should be."

They finished up and did a repeat of the day before, getting ready to greet people and talk about Tom.

This day, Sally wore a black suit she usually wore to work. She was just as lovely in it as the dress the night before. She came into Larkin's room as he walked toward the hall and he stuck his hand in his pocket finding the note. He said to her, "Oh, look at this. I got it from someone at the funeral home last night. It's the only good news I ever received from a Mason." He handed it to her.

Sally took the note and opened it. "Huh. Maybe they do have a heart?"

He looked at her and asked, "Is that a rhetorical question?" They laughed, held hands and went down to his folks.

Shirley drove to the church. It was the first time Sally had seen it. The old country-style church reminded her of a Norman Rockwell painting. Parking behind the hearse, they went inside, and stayed in the back by the casket that the funeral director had already placed there.

25

Pastor Johnson had the service bulletin beside the door and Larkin picked one up for each of them. When the pastor saw them, he came over to greet them saying, "I thought I'd tell you, I had attended a funeral of a friend of your brothers' with him some time back at the Lutheran church over in Delanson. It inspired us both. He asked that I obtain the service and message from the pastor there and use it here today for his. I have taken the liberty to change the things that needed to be and what you shall hear is the best funeral you ever shall. They are not my words, but purely from the Lord."

"Thank you, Pastor," said Lawtin shaking his hand.

As Johnson walked past Larkin he asked him, "June wedding?"

Larkin whispered back, "Don't know."

Sally heard him and just smiled.

They waited for the mourners to all come in and the place was mostly filled. The family came to the front and Tom's body was brought in. Everyone took a seat and the service began. The pastor was right. The service was unlike any they had heard before, offering hope to all that heard. Afterwards, the family went out with the body and everyone else followed them to The Homestead for the internment. The long line of cars in the procession stalled traffic on the main road, (where four cars had to wait), and finally they arrived at The Homestead Cemetery.

They walked up to the grave and the pall bearers brought Tom to his final resting place. Sally looked around and thought that something was out of place. It didn't look the same to her as the day before when Larkin showed her the graveyard. Her mind was not on what was happening as she stepped back to look here and there, and moved from Larkin's' side to peer toward the pile of dirt. She knew it looked different. After a few minutes, the service was ended and they lowered Tom into the grave. Lawtin picked up a handful of dirt and threw it in. The rest of the people followed suit and walked silently away toward their cars. As Larkin and Sally got closer to the car he said under his breath, "Hold on. I'll tell you in a minute."

"Tell me what?"

"Why it looked different."

They all got in the car and started to drive away. Seeming irritated Sally finally asked loudly, "What did you do Larkin Palmer?"

Shocked, his parents looked at her and waited for their sons' reply. He spoke up so his parents could hear what he had to say as well, "Last night after you were all asleep, I came over here and got the tractor out. I dug the grave hole deeper, went to the basement and brought out the silver chest, put it in the bottom of the grave and covered it up. Uncle Tom is now buried on top of it."

They all were in shock and said in unison, "What!?"

Before the girls could chew him out Lawtin said, "Wait a minute. That's genius. In order to dig Tom or the treasure up, they'd have to get a court order. How did you think of that, Son?"

"Well, it just came to me. I thought that if you hired anyone to run the place we'd have to do something with the box. And we certainly couldn't explain it. So, I hope Uncle Tom doesn't mind. But he actually took his wealth with him. And the Masons don't even know it!"

"Wow. That was good thinking, Honey," said Sally.

"Thank you, Dear."

"But how did you sneak out? I mean, I was right beside you."

Larkin looked at her and she said softly, "Oops."

Shirley turned in her seat and said, "You can't fool an old fool, I always say. We know, and Sally, you knew I knew. We were kids once. We know you don't do anything yet. We trust you."

Lawtin looked in the rear view mirror at his son and said, "We do, but is it wise to tempt yourselves?"

Larkin looked out the window and thought about that, shook his head and chuckled. What was he going to do with her? He said, "Oh and I almost forgot, I took this with me." Larkin held up the felt bag with the die. "I wanted proof. No need for pictures this way."

When they got home, Sally and Larkin changed into blue jeans and they all sat at the table and had a cup of coffee. Lawtin asked his son, "So when will you go home?"

"As much as I'd like to stay, Sally has to get back to work. I don't want to jeopardize her job. Mine is somewhat different and I can do whatever I want now, but she can't. I think we'll fly back on Monday."

"I don't want you to go, but its good you'll be here for church on Sunday. Sally, I want you to meet all the ladies and their daughters. They will love you," said Shirley.

Sally turned to Larkin and commented, "What happened to Ginny's dad? He never came. I didn't meet him."

"That is strange, Dad. Have any idea?"

"Well, I suspect that having to see another woman at your side would only remind him of Ginny. It was probably more than he could take, especially at a funeral. Besides, he just lost a good friend today, too." Lawtin turned and faced Sally, "Don't take it personally, Sally. He has had a hard time with the loss of his wife and daughter this past year. When he finally does meet you, he'll be fine."

"I just hope everyone likes me."

"They already do, Sally," said Shirley reassuringly.

"I'm going to take a nap by the fire. Anyone else interested?" asked Lawtin.

"I'm going up to my room Dad, but thanks anyhow."

"Me too," said Sally. The kids got up from the table and made their way up the stairs. Shirley called up after them, "I'll call you for dinner!"

"Thanks, Mom!"

They went into Sally's room because she wanted to gather her things. She had hung most of her stuff in the closet, but the dresses of the last two days she had just took off and were laying on a chair by the door where she had placed them. She put some dirty things in a pile to wash and tucked others away in her suitcase. All the while, Larkin watched her from her bed. She finished and looked over at him. He lay on his side with his head propped up by his hand, but he had dosed off and was about to drop his head on the bed. Realizing this, she went over to him and crawled up beside him. She placed his head on her shoulder and they fell asleep as the winter afternoon sun made its way to the window, placing its warmth on the bed and the couple.

They had rested for about two hours when Shirley called up to them, "Soups' on!" Sally shook Larkin a bit to wake him and said, "Your Mom's calling."

"Okay. I got to pee."

"Okay. I'm going down with this little pile of wash. See you down there."

"Hey wait a minute. I have wash, too!"

"Okay. I'll go to your room and see. I'll meet you there instead."

Larkin finished in the bathroom and met Sally by his dresser. Since they had been there, he had taken his clothes off and threw them in a misshapen pile-except his suit, of course. Consequently, he had lots to wash. Sally said, "Man, you're a pig. Here, you take yours and I'll take mine." She picked up his clothes and handed them to him. She then picked up hers, turned him around, pointed him out the door and said, "Time for you to show me what you learned the other day."

They headed for the laundry room, which was off the kitchen. Lawtin saw the pile of clothes in his son's arms and said, "They only come home when they have laundry to do."

Sally laughed, held up the few things in her hands and said, "I only have this much."

Shirley said to Larkin, "Just put them down by the washer, Honey. I'll do them later."

Sally pushed Larkin into the laundry room, yelling back out to Shirley, "Oh no, you won't, Mom. He had a lesson the other day. No more pink underwear for him!"

Larkin rolled his eyes, looked at Sally and said, "Thanks." She giggled and helped him put a load of colors in. She added hers to the mix.

They went into the kitchen, which Sally had come to realize was the focal point of the Palmer home. They did everything there; read, talk, plan, pray, as well as eat. The first time she saw the house she had wondered why they built that room- so large and inviting. After being there with them this short while, she now knew why and how so many other families were missing out. Instead, other families did things they thought were important, but really weren't. Few families ever did this much together, much less still *ate* together. She went over to the cabinet and pulled out the dishes. It had become her job in just those few short days. Sally felt welcome, loved, and needed. She felt like part of the family, a daughter, a– wife.

When Sally saw that Shirley had made stew, she was excited. It was one of her favorite things, and the homemade popovers made it complete. No one in Tennessee made popovers. There, they made biscuits, so this was a special treat. And she was so grateful to be a part of it and hoped by watching she could learn some of Shirley's tricks in the kitchen. They sat down to eat and Sally asked as she stuck her hands out, "Dad, may I do the blessing?"
"Why, I'd be grateful if you did."
She began. "Dear wonderful and gracious Lord. Until these past few days I have only known you as a stranger, a God so removed from me, only for me to worship from afar. Until I saw your love through the love of my new family, I never knew what you were all about. How kind and caring You were. How You provide the right thing at the right time, and how You have shown us Your mercy. I thank you, Lord, for what You have done for me and us. As I become more a part of these people, I ask for Your care and watchful eye upon us all. May we never disappoint You. Thank You for Your providence in this meal and for the loving hands that have prepared it. Amen."
Shirley got up and started to cry. Lawtin said, "Thank you, Daughter."
Larkin smiled at her and said, "I love you, Sally."

Shirley came back to the table, grabbed Sally's head, and gave her a kiss on the forehead. Then, they began their meal. After her prayer, there really wasn't anything to talk about, but they just basked in the thought of it and how they had become a family in one short week at one sad time. This is what happens in kitchens like the Palmers'.

Dessert was raspberry cobbler from berries they had grown themselves. Shirley always made a few when she put them together and froze them to bake at a later date. She did that with apple pies too, which, by the way, were the best around. She always made her own whipped cream, of course, and when Sally tasted it, she could not believe how good it was- fresh on the farm. And the milk! She said, "The stuff in the store tastes like water compared to this."

Lawtin replied, "That's because it is. They water it down so much after it leaves here, you'd think it wasn't milk!"

Sally said when they were done, "Mom that was by far the best meal I have ever had. If I lived with you, I'd weigh five hundred pounds!"

"Come on back and let me try," said Shirley.

Lawtin said, "She does, too! Try, I mean."

Larkin said, "I only was thin because I worked my butt off."

Lawtin laughed and teased him saying, "What? I did all the work, you only watched."

"Aw, Dad!"

Sally said, "That's not what Larkin told me."

They laughed and Shirley asked, "Anyone want coffee?"

The all said, "No! We're too full."

They went in by the fireplace again. Larkin started the fire going and they talked until it was late. Even after the sadness of the funeral, they had grown into a loving family with Sally now, it seemed, replacing Tom. They sat in the places they had the night before and Sally rubbed Larkin's' back as they watched the fire and felt the heat on their sweaters and stocking feet. The kids had to keep moving in order that their pants didn't feel like they'd start on fire. It was a lazy comfortable night, one in which to think about life and wonder where it would go from there. And yet, Larkin was saddened that he was held in a life away from this place, even if it were for what he thought would be a short time. Maybe he could come back home if he found the "key". Maybe that was why "they" had been so confident all of these years in their persecutions and shenanigans; that "they'd" find it first, because the Palmers didn't know about it. So, he wondered, "How do I plan? What can I do?" He'd have to think on that for a while.

When the final embers faded, it was almost midnight and time for bed. They all said their goodnights like the night before. Only this time Shirley said to Sally as they started up the stairs, "Could I speak with you a minute, Sally?"

Larkin looked at Sally, shrugged his shoulders and made a face like, "I don't know what she wants", kind of face.

Sally said to Larkin, "Go on up, Honey. I'll be right there." She came back down the stairs and said to Shirley, "What is it, Mom? Is there something wrong?"

"No. Not at all. Here, take this." She put something in Sally's hand. "I say go for it, girl. You're as good as married. He loves you and you love him. Don't wait. Life is too short."

Sally looked into her hand- it was a Trojan. Her eyes flew open wide and she said, "Mom! I can't do that! It would hurt him too much. As much as I'd like to, and believe me I'd like to, I couldn't do that to him. He is the leader and I am his wife. I'll do whatever he wishes, no matter what."

"I'm glad you said that, Dear. You are all I could ever hope for in a daughter. Goodnight."

"Was this a test?"

"You did great, Sally. I love you. Goodnight." Shirley turned and headed toward her room.

Sally smiled and headed upstairs. She had passed the "Mom" test.

Larkin turned as Sally walked into his room. Smiling, she came up to him and took his hand. Placing the condom in it she said, "Your mother gave me this." Larkin looked down into his palm and read the label. His jaw dropped all the way to the floor.

Playing along as if he had not known, he said, "My *mom* gave you this?"

She was having fun with *him* now. "Yes. She said, "Go for it.""

"She did, huh?"

"Yes, she did."

Larkin was getting more suspicious with every word. "And I suppose she said we are as good as married and there's no reason to wait?"

"Why, how did you know that?"

"Because, I've been through it before. It's the "Mom" test. She did it with Ginny, too." He came up to Sally and got real serious, "And from what I figure, you passed with flying colors, too."

Sally looked downstairs and said, "She can be pretty sneaky, huh?"

"When she wants to be, but she does it all for my, or I should say, for *our*, good."

"But, she forgot something."

"What's that?"

She giggled, pointed at his hand and said, "That one condom."

Larkin chased her out of the room and said laughing, "Go to bed. We have to get up early." He placed it, the one condom, in his suitcase.

They got up and went to early service that last Sunday at home. It was cold and frost covered the windows of the Lincoln. Larkin had scraped the windows, but the fog inside the car made it hard to see on the way. By the time they arrived at the church it was finally dissipated.

As they got out Lawtin said, "Isn't that always the way?" Sally smiled at Lawtin's remark and took Larkin's hand as they walked into the church. She wanted everyone to know that they were a couple. They went to the usual pew, but today, Sally sat where Tom had sat for 80 years. She seemed, at least to the congregation, to be the one out of place- not Tom. But that was normal. He had been there longer than many of them had been alive. Sometimes change happens slowly. And so it is for churches...

They stood for the first hymn, and Lawtin saw Mike Berry standing next to his son, Andy, in the third row. Lawtin was glad to see them, and as Lawtin looked around, he saw that everyone was also looking at *them*. They all wanted to get a look at Sally. And from what he could see their reaction was, well, it was good. They finished the hymn and all sat down. Sally hoped the sermon was as good as at Tom's funeral. She was disappointed however, because it wasn't. There was something missing. She couldn't quite place what it was, so she decided to ask Larkin what he thought at home. She was surprised with herself that she was actually judging, or evaluating, what was going on. The Lutheran church she felt, was much more to her liking, even compared to her own Methodist church. She hoped Larkin would think the same now that he had a chance to compare them all as well. She hoped he would be objective about it. It was important to her that they have a common place to worship and not fall strictly on tradition. To her, doctrine and beliefs were more important than anything. 'I guess I'm more old-fashioned than I thought,' she surmised. Both of these young adults were evaluating their relationships with God, which under the circumstances was probably a very good thing, no matter where they decided to worship.

When they got up to leave, the people all stood up en masse and walked out together. It was strange how all churches do things differently. Many of them came and talked to Larkin and Sally, wishing them congratulations when they saw the ring. As Mr. Berry had sat in front of them, it took a while for him and Andy to make it out past them. He looked nervous, but he smiled as he approached them. Before Larkin had a chance to introduce her, Mike came up to Sally and said, "I didn't think there would ever be anyone that could take Ginny's place in Larkin's life. From what I've heard and seen of you Sally, I know I was wrong. I pray you have a long and happy life together. Congratulations."

Sally began to cry right there in front of him and replied, "Thank you, Mr. Berry. I know how much your daughter meant to him and the family. I know I can never take her place, but what I do know, is that God has sent me to love Larkin, and that is what I'll do."

Mike smiled, nodded and guided Andy, hands on the back of his shoulders toward the front door. Larkin wondered where Andy's little sister was and he whispered to him as they passed by him, "Hey Andy, where's Shelly?"

"She's been living with Grandma for a while."

Larkin understood and just nodded, as Andy walked out with his dad. After Mike left, the congregation greeted them all warmly, especially Sally. It was a difficult transition for them all and threw out all the gears of life; Tom's death, an engagement, and healing for a father. And now as the Palmers were about to go home, the realization that Larkin would be packing and leaving again. It made for a quiet ride.

Finally, being almost home, Larkin broke the silence and said, "Dad I have to make one last trip over to The Homestead. I want to bring all of the boxes over here where they are safe; all except the Eraser. While I'm there, I'll check the animals, too."

"Sounds good, Son."

They knew, though, that he also wanted to see Tom one last time.

After they had changed clothes, Larkin walked down the hall into Sally's room and asked, "How are you doing on your packing?"

"Actually, Honey, I'm almost done.'

"Do you want to go over to The Homestead with me?"

"Sure."

"Let's go then." He grabbed her by the waist and picked her up in the air like a ballerina. Holding her there for a moment, he kissed her as she hung above him and then sat her back down. Sally said, "Wow, Larkin. I didn't know you were that strong."

"Just don't gain any weight." She laughed. He wondered.

They took the truck and headed over to The Homestead telling Shirley before they left that they'd be back in time for supper. They drove into the yard and Larkin stepped out of the truck. He started to walk in, but paused, and waited for Sally to catch up to him as they walked towards the door together. He really didn't want to go in alone. He knew he'd miss his uncles. Taking out his key, he opened the door slowly. He went in first and Sally came in behind him and said, "Did they always keep it this cold in here?"

"Yeah. They burned firewood most of the time. And before they had a bathroom, they *really* kept it cool."

"I guess your dad should send Percy over to winterize the place."

"Good idea."

Larkin looked over by the desk for the cardboard box. It was still there. He picked it up and saw that it was as he had left it the previous summer. It seemed like so much had happened since then. It seemed like an eternity ago. "There's a lot of stuff in here I'd like to show you when we get back to the house. It's the family filing box."

Sally laughed. "Maybe you should get something a little sturdier," she recommended.

"I was thinking about putting it all in my suitcase and leaving it under my bed. All I really need with me now is the Eraser anyhow."

"That's true. You know, I've been thinking that some of the documents you've been using at work should be in there too. But that would be illegal wouldn't it?"

"Maybe not illegal, but certainly unethical. That's why I brought a copy of all of it in my suitcase- just in case!"

Sally laughed at him and he said, "Let's put this in the truck and go out to the barn."

They placed the box in the truck and went out to the barn. It seemed so empty to Larkin. He called the names of the mules and they recognized his voice. Placing some oats in a bucket, he went over to their stalls, and pouring some in each trough, he once more called them by name, Oliver and Hardy. It looked like Percy had been there to take care of them already, but he just had to say goodbye to his friends in the barn. They left the barn, Larkin closing the door ever so slowly as if he didn't want to leave, and then started to walk toward the cemetery. Sally had gone toward the truck and when she noticed he wasn't walking with her, she turned and ran to his side. She didn't say anything and they walked over to the grave. The headstone was already there. Tom had made sure it was exactly like Harry's and just a bit smaller than Lawtin Sr. Larkin went up to it, placed his hand on the cold granite, and let his fingers slide slowly across his uncles' name. He said to Sally, "I'm going to miss him very, very much." Sally had come up to him and put her arm around him.

She said, "I know, but we'll see him again."

He looked into her eyes and knew she was right. "Come on," he said. Taking her by the hand, they walked back to the truck and headed for his parent's house.

Larkin parked the truck by the barn and got out. Sally had the box on her lap, so he walked around and took it from her as she slid down to the ground. They walked up to the house and she stopped him at the front porch. Turning and pointing back to the barn she asked, "You really miss it don't you?"

"Miss what?"

"This." She pointed. "All of this; the farm, the orchard, the animals, church, your mom and dad- all of it."

"Yes, I do."

"When we get home we'll talk about it."

"We have lots to talk about and plan. We have our whole life ahead of us to plan."

"I know."

Sally opened the door for Larkin and his mom said, "I put your clothes up on your bed, Honey."

Sally said to her, "I told you not to spoil him!"

"Who else do I have to spoil?" Shirley smiled at her future daughter-in-law.

Lawtin said laughing, "I take issue with that statement."

Larkin chucked and said, "I'm going to take care of this box and I'll be right down, Mom."

"Okay," she replied as they started up the stairs.

Sally and Larkin took the cardboard box upstairs to his room. He took out his suitcase and placed all of the boxes into it one at a time. He picked up the medallion with the "PC" on it, which he had not seen for a long time, and put it in there, too. It all fit rather nicely and Larkin had placed the entire Seward file in the back of the Journal. He also placed Barton's letter with it and now the felt bag with the die. He placed the last threat letter from the Masons in Brookfield on top. When he finally got to the bottom of the cardboard box, he found his checkbook that Tom had used to keep his trust fund and cash. He opened it. Reading the balance he thought there must be a mistake. It read twenty million dollars! He thumbed through and found a note tucked inside the cover page. It was from his Uncle Tom. He read it out loud for Sally to hear, too:

"Dear Larkin,

If you are reading this, I have gone to my heavenly home. You must have noticed by now, that the balance is much more than you had earned. When I drew up my will, I did not want to place money in it for you to pay tax on, because you, nephew, are my only heir. I also took the liberty to sell all of Harry's and my personal portion of all our assets and place them in the account as well. The account draws interest, so if you use it wisely, you should never have need. Remember me with my bees, Larkin? They trusted me; as you should always trust the Lord. Proverbs 3:5-6. Until we see each other again in glory, Uncle."

Larkin sat on the corner of his bed and began to cry. Sally took his head in her hand and held it against her side. He had to get it out, this pent up sorrow, and this was the time.

When he had composed himself, he took his suitcase, closed it up and slid it under his bed. He stood up and picked The Eraser Box up off the bed, too. Sliding it into his pocket he said, "This is the safest place for it now and for the suitcase. Let's go downstairs and show this note to Mom and Dad." He picked up his checkbook and took it with him.

His folks were already at the table and when Larkin came in he said, "Look what I found in the box, Dad."He gave the note from Tom to his dad and he read it so Shirley could hear.

When he finished reading, he asked, "May I know how much he left you, Son?"

"Twenty million dollars."

Lawtin was floored! He said, "He squirreled away that much, huh?"

"He never went anywhere, Honey, and you know he was frugal.

He's been a good businessman all his life and the past few years, well, due to Larkin, have been very good. I'm happy for you, Son," said Shirley.

"Dad, you know that if you ever need any, all you have to do is say so. We are- Family Palmer."

"Larkin, you know we don't and won't ever need any. The farm is doing great and everything is paid for. God has been good to us and now to you."

"I can't believe it. I told The Secretary the other day I was a man of means, but I never dreamed I really was!"

Sally said, "Well I know one thing."

"What's that, Dear?" asked Shirley.

"I'm going to have a big wedding!"

They all laughed uproariously. Shirley said to her future daughter-in-law, "Come on, Sally. Help me with supper."

As they had done since they arrived, they talked about the little things that last night at the supper table. Larkin really wanted his cast off. Sally couldn't wait to move in with Larkin. Shirley and Lawtin wanted grandchildren. "What?" protested Larkin, "I just got- *engaged*."

"Well, you can always be hopeful," said his mom.

Sally just giggled a lot through all of that conversation, not really saying that she hoped for a family as well. She and Larkin had never talked about it and it was fun to see his reaction. Sally asked, "How many children would you want, Honey?"

Larkin blushed. "I've never thought about it. I don't know. One of each, maybe?"

"Is that all? Now that you are a rich man, you can afford to have a dozen of each."

"You really want that many? I'll wear you out."

Now it was Sally's turn to blush. "Well, I didn't mean that literally. I meant that we can do what we want as long as God provides."

"Good attitude. Is there more cobbler?" asked Lawtin as he licked the last bit of whipped cream off his fork.

Sally rose and started to pick up the dirty dishes. Shirley helped and Larkin said, "I need to finish packing. We need to leave by six to make the airport in time. I'm going upstairs, Dear."
"Okay, Honey. I'll be up soon and finish packing myself."
"Goodnight, Dad and Mom. See you in the morning."
"Goodnight, Son."

Larkin went up and switched some things around in his suitcase. He didn't have to worry about taking a second suitcase this time, though.

That would be easier, but he did want to take the old suit bag in the closet with him, so that his new suit didn't get crumpled-up like on the way there. He got it out of the closet and looked inside. No cobwebs anyway. Placing the new suit and the one sports coat he brought along into the bag, he zipped it up.

As he worked, Larkin thought about how this new money would affect him and his relationship with Sally. She had never seemed the type to need it, or for that matter, be spoiled by it. He hoped that things wouldn't change. It bothered him so much that when she came upstairs he just asked her up front, "Sally, I just have to know what you think about all of this money. Will it change anything between you and me?"
She smiled at him and came slowly over to him. She didn't crack a joke or make light of the situation. In fact, she replied very thoughtfully and seriously. Taking his hands into hers she said, "Larkin, I'm not your wife yet. It is your money. What you do with it is your business. Even when we marry, I know that you will treat me the same way you treat me now. I trust you to use it for the benefit of us both, now and in the future." She gave him a hug.
He gave her a kiss and said, "Thank you for trusting me. I won't let you down."

She smiled, let go of his hands and went into her room to finish packing. He went into the bathroom to take one last shower before the trip. He put the plastic bag over his cast and turned on the water waiting for it to get hot. Sally came to the door, looked in and said, "Can I help?"
"No. But you can have your turn after me." He flung the door shut, hoping she didn't see anything.
"Okay." She giggled.

She went back into her room and lay down on the bed. She had a long day and just fell asleep.

Larkin came out of the bathroom and when he didn't see or hear her, he went looking for Sally. He found her there on her bed asleep. He went back to his room and got ready for bed. When he finished, he went back to check on her. She still lay there in her clothes. He sat down beside her and asked her softly, "Are you going to sleep in your clothes all night?"

"Oh no," she said rousing, "I guess not. Will you help me?"

When she asked this, he didn't flinch like she wanted him to. This disturbed her somewhat. He took her shirt and lifted it over her head. Unsnapping her bra, she gave it to him and as he faced the other direction, he handed her his PJ top that was lying there on the bed. Then grabbing the cuffs of her pants, he pulled them off. He jogged across the room and threw the PJ bottoms to her as he put her pants and shirt by her suitcase. To her, he seemed to be getting too comfortable with this. 'Maybe I should back off,' she thought, 'if I don't, it may not be as special to him.' She'd think on that. 'Besides, am I being fair to him? What's' the point? Does God want me doing this?'

Larkin came back over to her and asked, "Comfy now?"

"Yup. Goodnight, Honey." She kissed him.

"Goodnight, Dear."

Larkin got up, closed her door and smiled as he left. He could tell by her reaction that she thought she may be doing something *wrong*. Her plan to embarrass him into action was backfiring, or was that what she was actually doing? He now knew his mom was right. Larkin slept well that last night at home. He began to drift off remembering the good times of his childhood with Uncle Harry, Uncle Tom, and Ginny, but then before he finally slept- thoughts of Sally.

In the morning things were very somber. No one wanted anyone to go anywhere. Larkin got Sally up and she went in to take a shower. She didn't ask him to go with, or participate in any manner with her showering or dressing. Maybe she was over her teasing. Hopefully, his mom was right. Shirley was a wise woman, using reverse psychology on Sally and being totally honest with her son.

He took his bags down with him and sat them by the door. He'd go get Sally's when she was done getting ready. He sat by the table and had a cup of coffee with his dad. Shirley was in the laundry room doing some of Lawtin's clothes. Larkin said, "I want to thank you for all you have done and how you have accepted Sally. A week ago you didn't know her at all. Now she is going to be my wife and you have accepted her as a daughter. Thank you, Dad."

"God works in His ways, Son. Tom's death brought us together. Life, takes us apart. I hope that one day you and Sally will be back with us again- for good."

"Amen," said his mom as she carried a basket of clothes into the kitchen to fold. That was unusual and Larkin looked at her like she had three heads. She said, "I'm not going to miss talking with you so he can have clean clothes." She began to fold the clothes.

Sally came in with suitcase in tow. "I'd have gotten that for you, Dear," said Larkin.

"No need to for you go all the way up there for me. I'm a big girl."

She sat the heavy suitcase down next to his with a thud and asked, "When do we need to leave?"

"In about ten minutes. You have time for a cup of coffee if you want."

"I do."

Sally went over to the cupboard, reached down a cup, and poured herself some steaming hot coffee. She sat waiting for it to cool and picked up Larkin's spoon to stir it. Sally was just as sad about leaving as Larkin and sat with her head down. No one really wanted to look at each other, for fear that they would cry. She finally sipped it down and Larkin didn't fill his cup again. Suddenly, they did want to leave, because they couldn't bear another minute of the pain they were going through. Larkin stood up abruptly and said, "Well, I guess it's time to go." He took his dad's hand and shook it, and then gave him a hug. He switched with Sally who had just hugged his mother. She said to him, "Come back soon, Honey."

"We'll try, Mom."

Lawtin asked, "Maybe Christmas?"

Larkin said, "We'll see, Dad."

"Okay."

Larkin and Sally picked up their bags and headed over to the rental car still sitting in the driveway where they had parked it upon their arrival. Sally called out saying, "Thank you so much. I love you!"

They waved and yelled back, "Goodbye!"

Larkin started the car and they headed toward Albany and the airport. Sally cried almost the whole way.

Chapter Three

The New and Old Stuff

The trip home that Monday was *exhausting*. Sally spent more time crying than not. Larkin sat next to a baby that did the very same thing the entire way. When they finally walked in the door to his apartment, Sally was so tired she collapsed. Rather than make her sleep alone on the couch he invited her into the bedroom. They put on their PJs and crawled into bed. She fell asleep as soon as she got in. Wisely, Larkin set the alarm clock for Sally, as she would have to go to work on Tuesday. Besides, he needed to go do some banking and transfer some funds around. Then, he needed to make some executive decisions about what to do with some of his money. When he finally put his head to the pillow, he wondered if he'd even get any sleep! But sleep he did. The next morning, he barely heard the alarm go off. He didn't turn it off- Sally did. Before she left, she came and gave him a kiss good bye. He immediately went back to sleep.

When he finally woke up, Sally had been long gone to work. He figured Harry was at work as well. Larkin got dressed and went to the kitchen to get a cup of coffee. The pot on the stove was still slightly warm from Sally's morning brew. Sitting down at the table, he saw the stack of Seward documents he had left sit there before they went to Brookfield. He could tell she had been looking at them that morning. She was a good helper. Larkin sat there assessing the situation and he felt guilty, at least now considering the circumstances, that she should go to work and he stay home. They didn't need the money now. What was more important? Getting to spend time with her or the money? He didn't have it planned this way when he first arrived in D.C.; he was going to hide under the radar. Work without "them" knowing he was there doing anything. And now look what had transpired! It was far from what he thought it would be. He wasn't in control. God was, but he had no idea what his purpose was. He finished his coffee and put on his coat and gloves. Today he was going to make some changes. There would be- new stuff!

When Larkin got on the bus, he didn't know what to do or where to go first, but he figured if he was going to use his money at all, he should get that in order. He got off at the first bank he came to.

Going in, no one paid any attention to him. He sat in the chair under a sign that said "New Accounts" by a woman that was so busy answering the phone, he didn't know if he'd ever get to talk to her. She saw him, but ignored him, and his patience started to grow thin. Finally, an officer behind the wall saw this and came out to help him. "May I help you?"

"Yes," Larkin replied, "I'd like to open a few new accounts."

Looking at his attire, cast, and simple country boy appearance, the man chuckled and asked, "Oh. Want to open a savings and checking accounts? Have a few hundred to sock away? Maybe open a Christmas club account?"

Larkin didn't like his attitude. He came back with, "Actually, I thought I'd deposit a few million, but if you don't think you could handle the deposit, I can go elsewhere?"

The officer snapped to attention. "Did you say, *million*? Please come and have a seat by my desk. Miss Summers, go get Mr. um?"

"Palmer."

"Go get Mr. Palmer a cup of coffee. Come here and have a seat, Mr. Palmer. Now, what can I do for you, Sir?"

Larkin took a seat on a comfortable leather chair and placed his cast out in front of him. "I'd like to open three accounts by transfer from my bank in New York and go home with some pocket money."

"How much cash would you require, Sir?"

"I'd like twenty-five thousand today."

"Good. And the accounts, Mr. Palmer?"

"As I said, I need three. However, what rate are you willing to offer on savings accounts?"

"We have regular accounts that now draw 8% and long term CD's that are paying 12% at this time."

"Fine. I'd like a checking account in my name with one million, a CD in my name with five million and a checking account in the name of Sally Britt with my name as co-signer for five million."

Miss Summers came with the coffee and handed it to Larkin. The officer gulped, not Larkin, and said, "And what funds will you be drawing from, Sir?"

He took out his check book and handed it to him saying, "Here's my information. You can call them."

He took it, looked at the balance and said smiling, "I'll call them right away. Please sit back and enjoy your coffee."

Larkin looked around the place and didn't notice anything out of the ordinary. It didn't take long for the officer to come back. He had a stack of new hundred dollar bills in the bands in his hands. He said, "I don't mean to pry, Sir, but I was wondering what you will be doing with the remainder of the balance in your current account?"

"I don't mind your asking. It already receives a good rate of interest, so I'll be retaining the account."

The man handed him back the checkbook and said, "That's fine, Sir. I already made the proper entries in your current checkbook for today's' withdrawals for you. Here are your new account books, and here's all of the paperwork for today's transactions. If I could have you sign here please."

Larkin signed all of the papers and the officer handed him the stack of bills asking, "Do you mind if I don't count out the cash, Sir?"

"As they are sealed new bills, no I don't. But before I leave I would like two things. First, may I have a bank deposit bag for the cash? Secondly, I saw that you offer premiums for new accounts. There's an AM/FM radio there I'd like. May I have one?"

The officer smiled and said, "No problem, Sir."

As Miss Summers had come to assist him, he asked her to get Larkin the items. While she was away, the officer said to Larkin, "I'm sorry if I offended you at the beginning, Sir. But your appearance made me think..."

Larkin cut him off and said, "Apology accepted, but it is a lesson for you today, isn't it? Don't always believe what you see on the outside. Know what is inside. That's what counts." He stood to take the radio and bag from Miss Summers and finished his comment, "It's kind of like a bank."

Appreciating what he said the man replied, "Thank you, Sir. I'm glad to have met you. If you ever need anything from me, here is my card. I'll be glad to help you." He stood and shook his hand, placing his card in Larkin's palm.

Looking at the man's card he replied, "Thank you, Robert. I'm sure that will happen."

Larkin started to walk away, but turned around and asked him, "Say Robert, would you be able to recommend a good car dealership?"

"Yes, Sir. I can!"

Somehow, Larkin knew he would.

Larkin had Miss Summers call a cab for him and he proceeded to the Ford dealer Robert recommended. When he got in the cab he said, "Take me to Hill and Sanders Ford in Wheaton."

"Wheaton?" asked the cabbie with dismay.

"Yes. I'm going to get my new car."

"You got it!"

When he got there the ride was fifty dollars, so Larkin peeled off a hundred, handed it to the cabbie and said, "Merry Christmas."

Excited, the cabbie said loudly, "Thank you, Sir! Same to you."

He shut the door of the cab and carried his radio box and bank bag up the stairs to the dealership. The sales people were just as busy as at the bank, except for one very young man that looked rather new to the job, sitting in his cubical. As he saw no one else helping Larkin, he came up and asked hesitantly, "Can I help you?"

Larkin asked him, "By any chance are you new here?"

"Yes, I am. Why?"

"No matter; you're the guy for me. I'd like to see the new Lincoln Continental. Where do you keep them?"

"Really?"

"Yes. What's your name?"

"Billy, Billy Smith."

"Have you ever sold a car, Billy?"

"Ah, no, Sir."

"Well, Billy Smith, today you'll make your first sale."

Billy led him out to the lot and they took a look at the cars. Billy tried to act the part of salesman, so he said, "This, Sir, is the new 1978 Lincoln Continental." He placed his hand on it and patted it a couple of times and followed up saying, "What color would you like?"

Without hesitating Larkin said, "I'll take the brown one. And Billy, how much do they pay you?"

"Um, three bucks an hour plus commission. Why?"

"Just make sure they give you the commission on this would you?"

"Don't worry. I need the money too bad for that not to happen!"

Larkin went back inside with him and Billy told his manager Larkin wanted the car. Larkin said to the manager, "I'll give you twelve thousand- cash."

"Where you gonna get that kinda cash, Kid?" he asked, chuckling.

Smiling, Larkin took out his bank bag and said, "Right here."

He showed the guy the stack of hundreds and the manager said, "Sold!"

The manager showed Billy how to write it up and they made the transaction. Then Billy handed Larkin the keys saying, "Thanks for the sale, Larkin. I really needed it. My wife will be real happy here before Christmas."

As they walked out to the car Larkin stopped and handed him two-hundred dollars saying, "Blessings on your Christmas, Billy."

"Gee, thanks Larkin. Thanks, so much." Billy almost started to cry, but smiled appreciatively.

"You're welcome."

As Larkin got in the car, Billy said to himself, "You don't meet people like him much anymore."

Larkin got in the car, sliding across the leather seat, started it up and took a deep breath of that "new car smell". He checked and was grateful that he could even get his cast on the pedal! He drove out of the lot with his first car, wondering why he had never gotten around to buying one before. Not what he ever thought he'd have one either, but it fit him now- for the time being anyway. He headed home reveling in the trip, the smoothness of the ride and all of the amenities, proudly parking in front of Harry's house. He wondered what Harry and Sally would say. He wondered what Harry would say when he told him he wanted to get his own place! That was the twenty-million dollar question! Going in the front door, he looked at his watch and saw it was almost time for the other two to be home. He went down to his apartment with his bank bag and radio, and quickly put the bag in the freezer and set up the radio on top of Harry's old, fried piece of antique furniture once called a "radio". He chuckled.

Larkin was tired. The cast still made him weary when he walked. Besides, he was still exhausted from the trip the day before. He could only imagine how Sally was feeling. He sat down in Harry's wife's chair. It didn't take him long to fall asleep. Sally woke him when she opened the back door and clomped down the stairs in her work shoes. "Larkin, are you here?"

"Yes, Sally. Come here. I want to talk to you."

She came over to him in the chair and plopped into his lap saying, "I want to talk to you, too. Everyone was so excited when I showed them the ring. They all want to know the date, but I told them we don't know yet. Even the Secretary was thrilled for us."

"That's great, Sally."

"What have you been doing today, Honey?"

"Get up off of my lap and I'll show you."

First, she gave him a kiss and then she got up. Larkin took her by the hand and started to drag her up the steps and into Harry's living room. Pulling her high heels off her feet and dropping each of them with a thud as she went she asked, "Where are we going, Larkin?"

He didn't answer but stopped at the front window and finally pointed out at the Lincoln saying, "Anywhere you want in my new car!"

"Nice car. You can drive it? I mean, you can get the cast in past the pedals?"

"Sure can."

"But are you going to park a brand new car like that on the street in front of Harry's house?"

"Well no, and that's what I want to talk to you about. But I wanted to see what you thought about all my ideas before I made decisions that will affect your life, too. Come on, let's go back downstairs and talk."

Larkin walked into his kitchen and sat down. He asked Sally, "Would you make a pot of coffee?"

"Sure, Honey." She got out the pot, Folgers coffee, filled it with water, and put it on the burner. The bank books were on the table and as she sat down she asked, "What's this, Larkin?"

"I opened a couple of new accounts that you should know about." Picking them up one at a time as he spoke he said, "This one is my new checking account for major purchases. It has a million dollars in it. This one here is a CD account with five million in it. This last one is yours, I can sign on it, but it is in your name. It has five million dollars in it. I really don't think you should use it right now and it's not intended to be used unless, well, you know, unless I die or something like that. I wanted to make sure you were taken care of."

Sally started to cry. "Don't say that, but I understand why. You sure have made me cry a lot lately, Larkin. Thank you so much. You are the greatest and I'll do whatever you want me too."

She stood up and gave him a kiss just as the coffee pot boiled over on the stove. She got up to catch it. As she did, Larkin continued, "I also would like you to quit your job and stay home and work with me on the Palmer family business. I can't think of a better person suited to do what God has appointed me, *no-us*, to do. Now, I know you love your job, but I want you to be by my side all of the time. We both know life is too short to be apart."

She started to cry again and said, "Quit that will you. You made me cry again!"

He asked, "Will you?"

"Will I what?"

"Quit your job?"

"What did I just say a minute ago? I'll do anything you want me to."

Composing herself, she sat down with a cup for each of them and asked, "You said you put a million dollars in your checking account. Why'd you do that?"

"I figured if we were going to get our own place we should have enough to do it."

"A house?" Sally began to cry again. This time she got up, came over to him and kissed him softly saying, "I love you, Honey."

"My question to you is: where do you want to look?"

"Well, I don't know. But Larkin, what is Harry going to say? He will be so disappointed. We just asked if I could move in. Now, we are going to abandon him."

"I've thought about that. I know he'll be happy for us. He'll come to realize we need our own place. Especially when he sees we are engaged. He'll understand, Dear. He will."

Just then the back door opened and Harry asked, "Anybody home?"

"Yes, Harry. We're here. Can we come up? We have something to show you."

"Sure, come on up."

The two started up and Larkin said, "Let me show him the car first; then you show him the ring. Okay?" She nodded and took his hand.

When they got up there, Larkin took Harry to the front window. He pointed out towards the Lincoln and said, "Someone got a new car and parked it out in front of your place, Harry."

"Yes, I saw that. I wonder who has that kind of money?"

"Me. I bought it today." Harry looked at it and Larkin in disbelief.

"Really? You bought a Lincoln? Isn't that your first car?"

"It is. And I never expected to buy a Lincoln for my first car. I always thought it would be like a '68 Chevy SS 396 or Mustang, or something like that. But I wanted to ride in style. It's kind of like my parents' car. Only, I think it's a bit longer."

"Wow. I'm glad for you."

"Thanks, Harry, but that's not all. Sally." He called her over to him.

Sally came over and stuck her hand out in front of Harry. His eyes got wider than they had ever seen them and he exclaimed, "You're engaged! My goodness when did this happen? How didn't I hear about this at work? News like this usually flies through the place!"

Sally said, "I told everyone not to tell you. We wanted to surprise you."

"Well you certainly did that. You almost gave me a heart attack."

"Sit down, Harry, and we'll tell you all about it," replied Larkin.

They all took a seat in the living room and they told him the whole story of the trip back home. When they got to the part about Larkin's inheritance, they could tell that this news saddened him. He asked, "Will you move back up to The Homestead, Larkin?"

"I suspect that someday we will, Harry, but for now, we've talked about finding our own place here in the city."

Looking down, he replied softly, "Oh."

"I know this changes everything Harry, but I want to be with Sally every minute. I know how short life may come to be, especially in our circumstances. I asked her to quit her job, too, so we can start our new life. I hope you will be happy for us, Harry?"

"Oh, I am Larkin. Come here you two and give me a hug!"

They both went over to Harry and had a group hug. He asked, "When's the wedding?"

Sally answered, "Don't know yet."

He said, "That's okay. Let's celebrate! I'll get the rum. You get the Coke!" Harry started to walk to his liquor cabinet, Sally toward the refrigerator.

"Sounds good," said Sally.

Larkin asked the other two, "What do they taste like?"

They laughed at him and Sally said, "I'll show you, Honey. You can taste mine first. You're so sweet." She went up to him and gave him a kiss.

They had a couple of drinks, talking and watching TV, and finally, the two excused themselves to their basement room. Harry was about to fall asleep in his chair anyway. Larkin led the way down the stairs and when they stopped at the bottom he asked Sally, "How did you think that went, Sally? I mean, telling him we would be leaving?"

"I think he took it pretty well. He loves us and doesn't want to see us go. But, he also wants us to be happy. He's a lot like your parents were this weekend, I'd say."

"Yeah, you're right. I'd say so, too. But that leaves us back with the same question I asked you before he came home: where do you want to look?"

"I just don't know. I have some names at the office I can call. When Mr. Shipley moved, he used a friend of his. He seemed pretty nice on the phone. Maybe I'll call him for some help."

"Which leaves me with a second question: when will you tell Mr. Shipley?"

"I'll give him notice in the morning, so that I'm done by Christmas. He won't like it and we may be uninvited for Christmas Day, but I hope he understands."

"I think he will. He knows the situation we are in- kind of."

"I'm getting ready for bed, Honey." She turned and went into the bedroom.

"Okay." Larkin went and turned on the TV. He wanted to watch the news.

Sally went in and got into a night gown from her suitcase; not Larkin's PJ's. It was more what Sally was all about. She was dainty and demure, soft and delicate, yet cozy to be with. She was all that Larkin had ever wanted or needed in a woman, and yet more than he had ever hoped for. She came out of the bedroom to tell him goodnight. As she came toward him, she seemed to glide as she walked, even more beautiful than when he had seen her in his room at home, in and out of her clothes. She came to him and said, "I'm real tired, Honey. I'm going to take the bed tonight, okay?"

When he looked at her, it was if he was in one of his day dreams, putting off an answer to the person who asked a question for just one more minute. He came out of it and said, "Yes, Dear, but just a second."He got up out of his seat and took her gently in his arms. He kissed her from the bottom of his soul, softly and deeply. When he released her, she didn't want to leave, as much mesmerized by his kiss as he was by her beauty. They stood and looked at each other for a moment. He picked petite Sally up and walked to the bedroom, not stopping to turn off the TV. He lay her down on the bed, on what had become "her side". He said to her, "If I don't leave right now, I know I'll be in trouble. I love you so."

He stroked her hair and kissed her head and said, "Goodnight."

She smiled trustingly at him and said, "Goodnight, Honey. Say a prayer for me."

"Do the same for me."

"I will."

He went back to the news and fell asleep after thanking God for her, his parents, and all that He had done for them.

The next day he took all of the Seward file, Barton's letter, and the pardons, to make another set of copies. He didn't want to risk losing all of it to the hands of thieves again. Sally had given him the roll of film off of her brownie camera, so he dropped it off to be developed while he was out, too. He loved driving his new car around town, but wondered if he'd be able to find a place with a garage big enough to park it. He guessed he'd have to find a big garage- with a house!

When he got back to the house the second locksmith was knocking on the front door. Harry had told him that Larkin would be there and Larkin was running late. Just as the guy from "Reliable Locksmith" was about to leave, Larkin rolled the window of the Lincoln down and yelled up from his car saying, "Hey! Sorry I'm running just a minute late. I'll be right up."

He parked, locked it up and ran up the stairs in his cast. The locksmith pointed at Larkin's cast and said in a Brooklyn accent, "You get around in that thing pretty good!"

"Aw, you get used to it after a while. Kinda like a three-legged dog!"

The locksmith laughed hard at that one and repeated it a couple of times saying, "That's funny! Kinda like a three-legged dog!"

Larkin took him to the door, had him change the lockset and give him three new keys. They talked about the Yankees and if the team was going to be any good that coming year. When he finished, he gave him the bill, and Larkin paid. Larkin gave him a tip and told him, "Merry Christmas". The guy said, "Hey, Merry Christmas to you, too! Thanks! Nice talkin' to ya." As he walked down the front stairs to his truck he said to himself, "Kinda like a three-legged dog. Ha!"

He laughed as he closed the door and Larkin went down to his room to work on the documents. It had been a while since he was actually able to work, much less possibly concentrate on it. He peered over them, over and over, especially document number thirty-seven. He still had no further thoughts or ideas as to the clue to the key. He still had no idea where it could be. Maybe he never would and if he couldn't, maybe "they" couldn't either! He hoped his "gift" would kick in. As he sat at the table his leg became increasingly uncomfortable. The Eraser Box was poking him. He took it out of his pocket and sat it on the table. He really didn't think he needed to carry it for protection, but so that it wouldn't be *stolen*. He remembered how he was amazed at how it was in such good condition after two-hundred eight years in the family when he first received it from his grandpa. He was still amazed. It seemed like it possessed longevity as well as the curse. *Maybe it did*. Even if he did want to, would he be *able* to destroy it? Damnable thing!

Larkin got up to take a break and turned on the TV. They had ad after ad for Christmas gifts already. One ad was so convincing, Larkin thought he might even want the "Hungry, Hungry Hippos"! It was only Wednesday, December sixth and Larkin had not even thought about what he might want to get Sally for Christmas. When he thought he was going to take her to stay at the Hay-Adams, he thought that would be enough, but now that he had a little more money, no, a lot more money, he wondered what he could get that would be special. Not a necessity. Not practical. Not something pricy, so as to make her think he was squandering his money. Not extravagant, nor elegant. What in the world was he going to get her? He'd have to think on that- not that he didn't have enough to think about already!

The news came on and he looked at his watch. It was five o'clock already. The time had really flown. The two would be home from the Smithsonian soon. Larkin went to the bedroom, grabbed Sally's suitcase and put it in front of his dresser. He rearranged what was in his only dresser and came up with two empty drawers for her things. He hung up the dresses in the closet and put the other stuff in the drawers.

He noticed her bras and looked at the tag on one to see what size it was. Even though he had seen "them" he didn't have any idea what she "had". He muttered out loud, "Hmm, 36C". Someone knocked at the back door and he quickly shoved it into the drawer. He ran out of the bedroom and yelled up the stairs, "Coming!"

When he got to the top, he saw Sally standing there with the old key in her hand. He opened the door for her and said, "The new locksmith came today and changed the lock. I have your new key downstairs. Give me a kiss."

She came over to him and gave him a kiss. When she finished the brief lip lock she said trying to move him to the side so she could pass by, "Come on, I gotta pee." She went down the stairs quickly and into the bathroom. He stood outside the door as she sat there and she asked him, "What have you been doing today?"

"I went and dropped off the film, got all of the documents copied, got the keys made, put your clothes in the drawers and the closet, did more studying of the documents and watched the news." When he finished saying all of that, she was still sitting there. He said, "Man, you must have really had to go!"

"I told you I had to pee!" She giggled and took some TP off the roll. Larkin turned to leave and she stopped him to say, "You put my clothes away?"

He replied, "Yeah. I figured the clothes you had were only the beginning of what you may bring over before the first. Maybe we can go get more this weekend and tell Mrs. Heidelmann all the news."

She walked over to wash her hands and said, "Sounds like a plan."

"Tell me what happened today at work."

"I had a real nice long talk with Mr. Shipley. He totally understood our situation and was glad that we will be getting married. My last day is the twenty-first. He is such a nice man."

"How about a realtor?"

She came out of the bathroom and said, "Oh, yeah. He said he would start showing us places as soon as I tell him when, where, what, and how much."

"How about going after church on Sunday?"

"That sounds like a good plan, too."

She took him by the arm and they went into the kitchen. She saw The Eraser sitting on the table and asked, "Need that today?"

"Nope, it was just poking me in the groin. I had to take it out of my pocket."

She giggled and said, "Go put it away then."

"Okay. I want to get some money to put in my wallet anyway. Make us a couple hot dogs would you?"

"Okay. That sounds good, too. Man you have a lot of good ideas today, Honey."

As he walked away he said, "Don't I always?" The fact was that he really always did.

He went into his room, put The Eraser in the top drawer and went back out to the freezer to get the bank bag. He wondered if that was a good place for it, so he thought about it while taking a few hundred out and put them in his wallet. He then took the bag back into his room and placed it in her underwear drawer. He smiled. He again went back out to the kitchen and said, "I put The Eraser in my top drawer. If you need any money, I put the bank bag in your underwear drawer."

"In my what?"

"You heard me."

"How much is in there?"

"Oh, I don't know. I think there's probably about eight-thousand left."

"Really? Is that safe?"

"Is anything safe?"

She thought about that for a second and said, "No, probably not."

She brought the hot dogs and a couple of cokes to the table and they sat down to eat. Larkin said the prayer as they held hands. "Lord for this food we give you great thanks. For no matter in what you provide we are thankful. Amen." They began to eat and Larkin said, "I was thinking I'd like to take you out for dinner on Saturday if you'd join me, Dear."

"Why that would be very nice. Where did you plan to go?"

"I'd thought we'd go for Chinese again. What do you say?"

"Again ? You called that a date?" She chuckled. "I think that'd be lovely. Say, Honey?"

Larkin looked up as if to say, "What?"

She asked, "Can we walk down to the liquor store and get some beer after dinner?"

"Yes, I think it'd be nice to get out for a walk. Even if it is cold, it's only a couple of blocks. And yes, it was a date- arranged by God."

She smiled and took his empty plate to the sink.

They finished up, bundled up, and went down the street toward the store. They went out the back and didn't disturb Harry. He had not called down to them when he got home. That always signified he had a bad day at work or he really didn't want any company. They had gotten to know him pretty well. As they walked, he held her arm as if to try to keep warmer, but it really did no good. Their breath showed with each exhale, and the street lights almost made the water in their breath glimmer as they watched it evaporate away. They walked into the store and the clerk looked at Larkin with an evil eye and asked, "Are you of legal age?"

Larkin answered, "No, Sir."

"Well then," he said pointing to the door, "you'll have to go outside." He then addressed Sally and he asked, "How about you?"

"Yes. I'm twenty-four."

"I'll have to see some ID." The overweight owner motioned to her with the palm of his hand for it and took the cigar out of his mouth with the other hand.

Sally said to Larkin softly, "Wait outside. I'll be right out."

"Okay." He left to go out into the cold to wait.

She went over to the counter and took out her ID. When he went out, Larkin felt kind of dumb, because they had not even thought about the fact he was underage. Sally bought her beer and came right out like she said. She was laughing when she came out. Larkin said, "What's so funny?"

"The guy told me I was robbing the cradle."

"Oh."

"That's not funny?"

Larkin didn't answer and they started home. They walked in silence after that. It wasn't that he felt insecure about it; her being older that is, but that he thought they all thought he was a kid. He'd not thought of himself as a kid for a long time. The Eraser had *made* him grow up. Maybe it was because he was so mature, or possibly innocent, that he felt the way he did. But Sally was sure trying her best to change all of that. She was the "Evil Woman" in that song on the radio by ELO. Realizing these thoughts were just a lot of nothing, he finally laughed out loud and said, "I love you, Sally."

"I love you too, Honey."

The next couple of days flew by, each doing their own appointed tasks. Saturday morning they went over to Sally's apartment. They took a list of things that Larkin didn't have for housekeeping and packed up as many clothes as they could in her two suitcases and the one of his they had brought along. Then they went up to tell Mrs. Heidelmann all the news. She reacted much the same way as Harry had; telling them how much she would miss Sally and how she hoped they would continue to go to church with her. Larkin said, "Don't worry about that Mrs. Heidelmann, we are finding your church to be very good for us. We will return tomorrow, if you let us sit with you again."

"Of course, I'd like that very much."

"Then we'll meet you like last time. Okay?"

They got up, said goodbye to her, took the suitcases out first, and then going back in, they each picked up loads of things in their arms and finally put it all in the trunk of the Lincoln. Sally said, "I can't believe that all fit in the trunk."

"Yeah. Big trunk," said Larkin proudly.

"Get the car started, Honey. It's cold!"

They drove back to Larkin's place and in multiple trips to the car, carried it all in. Sally wanted control of where it all went, so Larkin just put it all in the rooms she wanted them in and let her have at it. In a couple of hours it was all away, but Larkin had lost another drawer and his closet was now full. She asked, "What time is it?"

Without looking at his watch he said, "About time to get ready for our date."

"Yeah, I feel grubby after all that. I'm getting in the shower."

She went toward the bedroom to get her robe, which Larkin was glad to see as an addition to her apparel, and she came back out with her robe in her hand, in the buff as usual, sprinting in the cold to the bathroom. He just shook his head, laughed and said to himself, "Good start, but now she has to actually put it *on*." He also wondered why she had relapsed into doing that again. He thought she might have been cured of it that last day back home. 'Oh well,' he thought, smiling as he watched her close the door.

She got out of the shower and opened the door to the bathroom, billows of steam wafting from the room. She announced to Larkin, "Your turn."

"Did you leave me any hot water?" he asked as she stopped in the hall rubbing up next to him with her robe on.

"It doesn't matter, you need a cold one anyway," she said looking down at him. He didn't think it was that obvious, but he didn't care and was glad she was looking.

He took his turn and had plenty of hot water. When he had finished, she was ready to go, except for drying her hair and he got ready while she went back into the bathroom to finish. He put on the pair of blues jeans he had been wearing and a sweater, but looking at them he thought he might go buy another pair of jeans next week. He still had over a month to have the cast on and the cut pair of jeans was getting a little ragged. She came into the bedroom and said, "Ready. Are you?"

"Yup. Let's go."

When they shut the door and locked it they started off the deck past the truck. She said, "Hey! Let's take the truck like our "first date.""

"You are *so* romantic, Dear."

They hopped in the truck and even though it was cold, it started as it always did. She didn't have much kitty litter left in the back, in fact, just a frozen lump up next to the cab. However, the roads were pretty much cleared from the once-in-a-lifetime snow storm that they'd never forget. As they drove, it did remind them of that first time they spent time together; their "chance" meeting at the restaurant.

They had to park a couple of blocks away and as they walked they talked and laughed. They went in and the same waiter came to take them to a table. He recognized them and he took them to the same table they had shared before. This time, she sat next to him instead of across from him. They ordered a small family meal so they could share more than one type of dish, and if they were lucky, take home some leftovers, too. As they ate, they talked, and Larkin asked, "You know, Dear, we haven't really talked about a date for the wedding. I always thought I'd be married sometime in June when everything was in bloom. When I moved here after everything that happened this past year, I didn't even consider getting married until after college. I sort of thought that may still apply. But, I wanted to see what you thought about it."

The food arrived, giving her a chance to think about his question before she answered. As she picked up her fork she said, "Let's pray."

Larkin began, but she took over before he even had a chance to utter more than a syllable. He raised his head and letting her proceed, bowed it again and smiled.

"Dear Lord, you have blessed me so much in my life. I thank you for taking me to this place the first time I met Larkin. Lead us now as we make decisions in our lives. I thank you for your hand in what has come to pass and now we both thank you for your blessings. In Jesus name, Amen."

"Why thank you, Dear. Did you have a chance to think about my question?"

She put a bite of eggroll in her mouth and said, "Yes, but I always thought I'd be a winter bride. I like it this time of year, with the lights and cold, and all of the decorations, and parties. Maybe like after Christmas or before New Years? I don't know. And as far as the question of when: I'll marry you-as soon as you let me!"

"You know, we haven't told your parents yet."

"I know and I think we should let them know right away."

"Me, too."

They finished their meal and the waiter left the tab, and two fortune cookies. Larkin got up without taking his cookie and put on his coat to leave. Sally asked, "Aren't you going to open your fortune?"

"You saw what happened last time I did."

"How can you say it had any connection? If I remember right it said, "Beware of Strangers.""

"How many strangers have we met that were really rotten since then?"

"Oh. You have a point. Let's go."

Larkin left the money and a tip. They also left the fortune cookies.

When they arrived home it was only 8:30 p.m. and Larkin said, "Let's call your folks. It's an hour earlier there. It's not too late."

"Okay."

Sally went to the phone and picking up the receiver, dialed. "Hello, Mom? This is Sally. How are you? Is Dad there? Could you put him on the phone, too? I have something to tell you. Hi, Dad! I know I haven't been good about calling lately, but I've met a man and he's proposed. Yes, I know it's sudden, but I've already met his family and he has given me a ring. What? Yes, he does- lots. His name is Larkin Palmer. Yes, he's good looking. When is the wedding? We don't know yet, but we're talking about it. Have to go? Okay, I can call back later. An hour? Sure. Love you. Bye." She hung up.

Larkin said, "Well, I could hear your side of the conversation, but what did they *really* say?"

"I think they want to meet you."

"What was the part about "lots"?"

She giggled and said, "They wanted to know if you had any money!"

He laughed and said, "At least they have your welfare in mind. Why did they hang up?"

"They were just leaving the house. They want me to call back later."

"Okay. In the mean while, let's cuddle and watch TV. I gotta get something for my money!"

"You don't have to convince me. We have an hour."

Instead of just cuddling, she sat next to him and started to kiss him, which turned into an hour long make out session. He was starting to think he needed to go and *really* take a cold shower. He had to stop and he said trying to break the momentum, "Let's see if your parents have come home yet, okay?"

"Okay. But this time I want you to get on or put your ear by the phone, too."

"Oh. There should be a few ground rules I thought I should mention and I hope you'll agree with me, Dear."

"By any chance it wouldn't be any of the Palmer family business? Do you think I'm dumb or something?"

She was serious, so Larkin said, "Well, no Dear, but I don't want them to be in danger as well. The less they know about any of it the better. Ah, secondly?"

"Yes?"

"Please don't tell them I gave you five million dollars? I think that is between us and a private affair. You can tell them if I die. Okay?"

"Got it. Now see, I didn't need to hear any of those stupid rules did I?"

"No, you didn't. I guess you're not as dumb as you look."

"You better watch it, or I'll be able to tell them all about the money in just a minute!" She wacked him on the head with sofa pillow, got up giggling and went to the phone to call.

This call, they both were able to spend some time talking to her folks about the trip to New York. Her folks said they were sorry about Larkin's Uncle and hoped they'd get to meet his parents soon. The conversation came to Christmas and Sally just said she'd be staying in D.C. with Larkin and going to her bosses' house for the day. They didn't tell them she was moving in with him, quitting her job or going looking for a house the next day. They just had to follow a double standard with parental protocol. They could tell *his* parents anything because they would understand because- he was a boy. But, to tell the girl's parents everything about it all, well, they just *wouldn't* understand. They hung up feeling like they had made progress and that they thought he was acceptable for the first time they had ever heard of him, spoken with him, or got to know their future son-in-law.

"Whew, that was tiring," said Larkin.

"Yeah, that's almost as bad as "Eraser stress"."

"Eraser stress?"

"Yeah, whenever I have to deal with it, I get tired. Don't you?"

"I do." He smiled and was glad to see she was getting used to the fact of it though. There'd be more where that came from- sooner or later.

"Let's go to bed," he said.

"You mean?"

"Yeah. There's no need to sleep on the cold, old sofa. We did okay the other night. Besides, I trust ya. But, on the side of caution, don't get any funny ideas. The first time you try to go past first base, you're outta there."

She slapped him on the tush and headed into the bedroom. They got ready and went to bed saying a prayer. Larkin kissed her goodnight and yawned right afterward realizing that he really was tired. He thought about the situation he was in with Sally and knew he just couldn't continue to live without the benefit of marriage any longer, no matter how unsafe it was with the Masons threatening them. He knew he was "dancing with the devil" in how they were living as it all was so tempting, however he didn't care what other people thought, except Harry, and he knew what was going on, and that was- nothing. He prayed God would give him the answer.

They got up the next day and got ready for church. They had no trouble meeting Mrs. Heidelmann at the right time and they went to sit down in the customary pew. She was all smiles this Sunday and they supposed that she was this happy because she'd be able to tell her friends they'd be getting married. Larkin looked at the bulletin. It was the Second Sunday of Advent, December 10, 1978. He liked the rigidity of having what the Lutherans called a liturgy and following it all in the hymnal. He did have some questions about it, but he thought he'd talk to Pastor Olsen when they told him they wanted to become Lutherans and take classes. They began the service and they all stood for the first hymn. It was an advent hymn called, "Ye Sons of Men, Oh Hearken". He liked it and the good news it brought out from the Luke text it was based on. The message was long this time, but very good. Pastor Olsen had a way with explaining the plan of salvation in them and Larkin liked that.

As they left, walking to the back of the church to shake Pastor Olsen's hand, Sally was very happy and said, "Larkin, I want to come here and join this church. I'm so happy that I have found a place that isn't afraid to call me a sinner and then tell me I'm forgiven. This is what I've been looking for."
"Me too, Sally."

They finally got to the door and shook Pastor Olsen's hand, but before Larkin had a chance to tell him anything, someone else grabbed him and they had to go past and out the door into the narthex. They thought they could talk to him next week or they could call him soon. Before they could leave though, their escort, Mrs. Heidelmann, had to have them show all of her friends the ring and talk a few minutes. She was just too nice to be rude to and besides, she had no children to brag on. So, they stuck around for her for a bit and left her chatting with Mrs. Rolefson.

Burgers sounded good to them, and on the way home they stopped at Burger King, so they could have something to eat before meeting the realtor. Changing into something more comfortable when they got home, the realtor called to say he'd pick them up in about 15 minutes. It was all good timing and they were looking forward to going out and looking. Sally was really excited! In her mind she was already planning the furniture! Larkin didn't know how she could do that considering they had no idea what they would buy. Women!

The realtor was right on time and when he rang the bell in front, Harry let him in. "I'm here to pick up Sally and Larkin. Are they here?"

Harry said, "Oh, you must be the realtor. Come in and have a seat and I'll tell them you're here."

Harry thought the guy looked strange, big glasses that made his eyes bulge and hair all slicked down with BrylCreem, and he did a double take when he left the room. He went to the stairs and yelled, "Hey, Larkin. There's a guy here to pick you two up."

"Thanks, Harry. We'll be right up."

They went up and he introduced himself. "I'm Bob Robards. I was glad to speak with you the other day Sally. Mr. Shipley says so many nice things about you."

Sally shook his hand and said, "Why thank you, Bob. This is Larkin, my fiancé."

"Nice to meet you, Bob." Larkin stuck out his hand and the two shook them firmly.

"Well, so we don't waste any time, let's hit the road. I have about ten places to show you."

"Great," said Larkin, as they walked out the door. Harry waived a happy goodbye to them, but deep down, he was saddened by this and the fact he would soon be alone again.

They went to a few places in the downtown area, but none of them fit the bill completely. If they had the right amount of bedrooms, they didn't have enough baths. Some needed too much work and some were just plain ugly. And IF they did have a parking garage, it was too small for the Lincoln. Finally Larkin said, "Bob, is there any place you have to show us that has a great big garage?"

"Yes, there is one, but I was hesitant to show it to you because of the price. It's the most expensive listing I have."

"How much?"

"It's just shy of half a million."

Sally said, "That's a little steep, Honey. That's a lot more than some of the others. We can always look out of the city farther."

"I agree." He turned to Bob and said, "This is what I want you to do, Bob. You've seen what we liked today, but the problem was the garage. Keep track of all the new listings in the area with a big garage that are more in the three to four hundred thousand range. Then, if you find anything out a little farther that fits the bill, let us look at those, too."

"Okay Larkin, but don't you want to see this one anyway?"

"Where is it?"

"On Ridge."

"Okay. That's not too far."

After the short drive, they pulled into a space out front and the listing realtor was there holding an open house. They walked through and just loved it. Everything fit. Sally loved the kitchen the most as it reminded her of the Palmers'. The Victorian had just been remodeled and even had air conditioning. They took the listing information and the card of the realtor with them after Larkin saw the garage. It was perfect! They went back out to Bob's car. Bob asked, "So what did you think?"

"We loved it, Bob!" exclaimed Sally.

Larkin smiled and said to her, "You're a shopping wimp, Sally."

She laughed and said, "We're even, Honey, but I have to say, I could see us in this one."

"Me, too. But Bob, what will they take?"

"I don't know. Seeing as the market is a bit slow due to interest rates, we might be able to make a lower cash offer. You do have the cash don't you?"

Larkin pulled out his checkbook and said, "Yup. There's one million in this account. What do you recommend we try, Bob?"

"Let's shoot them a four hundred thousand dollar offer and see what happens."

"Okay. Let's go to your office and write it up. If they don't take it, we can still keep looking."

They went to the office and Bob drew up the papers and they signed them leaving a deposit as required. Bob said, "It's all in their ballpark now. I guess just pray they take it."

"We will, Bob," Sally and Larkin replied in unison, "We will!"

Bob dropped them off at home and they asked him to keep them posted. Harry welcomed them at the front door and asked, "Well, Kids, how did it go?"

"We made an offer on one, but we have no idea if they will accept it. I guess we'll see."

"Is it nice?"

"For four hundred thousand it had better be!"

"Whew! It had better," said Harry. "You guys hungry?"

"I'm starving," said Sally.

"I made a pot of beans and some corn bread. Want to join me?"

"We'll be up in a minute! I got to pee."

Larkin chuckled and said, "Me, too."

They ate with Harry because they felt like they hadn't been around him much lately. In fact, they hadn't. They had been busy, gone, or in their private world in the basement. Harry knew things would change if they got together, so he gave them their space. Tonight, they had the time to stay upstairs and talk with him, so they did. It was nice to just sit there with him and tell him about their plans and hopes as they dreamed about their future. And then he said something profound to them, "Always be there for the other and place the others' needs before your own. If you do, you can't fail."

"We will, Harry, and thanks," said Larkin.

Sally paused for a second before she asked Larkin if he wanted to leave, because what Harry had said meant something to her and she appreciated his thoughts. "Are you ready to go downstairs, Larkin?"

"Yup, I want to give Harry a break by not passing gas upstairs."

"That's right," said Sally with remorse, "you should have been there after your chili, Harry!"

"Or maybe not?" replied Harry.

They all laughed and said their goodnights as the kids went downstairs.

Sally went into the bathroom and Larkin to the bedroom to get into his PJ's. After what seemed like an eternity to Larkin, she came into the bedroom and got into hers, too. He thought, 'What takes girls so long in the bathroom?' She started out to the living room to sleep and he said, "We've broken the rules so much already, but we can't bend them any farther if you sleep here with me, okay?"

"Okay," she replied.

"You know Sally, what Harry said up there to us was the true definition of Agape love."

"I know, Honey. I thought the same thing."

She smiled, ran around to her side of the bed and jumped in. He got in and they said a prayer. Afterwards, he was glad that they were establishing a routine of praying together as a couple. Many older married-folks didn't even do that! He snapped off the light and kissed her goodnight. She snuggled tight in his arm and they fell asleep. He woke after a bit, turned over and faced the other direction from her, because he liked to sleep on his left side, and then it hit him as to what he would give her for Christmas- a wedding!

Even if he was tired, now he hardly slept all night, details rushing through his mind. Larkin finally drifted off just as Sally was getting ready to go to work. She came over to his side of the bed, bent over and looked closely at him. She smiled and gave him a kiss and left for work. As soon as she went out the door, he got up and sprang into action. The first thing to do was to call Mrs. Shipley!

He got her maid on the line and after explaining it to her; she went to get Mrs. Shipley. She was already up and in the kitchen going over the meals of the day with the cook. She picked up the phone there. "Good morning, Larkin! How are you today?"

"Just fine, Mrs. Shipley. Thank you for taking my call."

"How may I help you, Larkin?"

"By now Mr. Shipley has certainly told you the news that I'm stealing his secretary, am I not correct?"

"Oh yes, he's sad to lose her, but very happy for you both. Is that what this is about?"

"Yes and I have a great favor to ask of you."

He went on to tell her his plan and as many particulars as he had accomplished. When he was done she said, "That is so wonderful Larkin, I would be glad to allow you to use my home for the wedding. I even know a wedding planner that can help you put it all together. I'm so excited!"

"That is very nice of you, Mrs. Shipley. Are you sure you don't mind us taking your Christmas from your family?"

"Not at all. The girls will just love the goings-on. I'll have the planner call you today while Sally is at work. Oh, I just can't wait. You are such a romantic man. I wish my husband was still like that."

"Thank you so much, Mrs. Shipley. I will make sure that you are kept in the "know" the entire way. If there is anything that I need to do that you see or have any suggestions, please, feel free to make them."

"I shall, Larkin. Goodbye."

"Goodbye and thanks again."

He said to himself, "Alright! All I have to do is wait for the planner to call."

It didn't take long for Larkin's phone to ring. The wedding planner wanted him to come in right away, as there was no time to spare to prepare for a wedding in just 14 days! Consequently, he told her he would be in right after lunch. He was starving, so he ate the Chinese leftovers. There in the box was a fortune cookie. He threw it away.

He went in to see the planner and he was pleased to see that she knew her stuff. She asked about flowers and food, guests and gifts, attendants and bridesmaids, and the dress, which Larkin described in detail as to what he wanted: size, type, length, etc. They covered all the bases and she gave him a list of things to do, which wasn't much. She said, "This is not going to be a big wedding for sure, but we need to do many of the same things. What you will save in costs on quantity, you will spend on expedience."

"That's no problem, and cost is of no concern. I want it to be perfect."

"Then you will get what you want, Larkin. I'll be in touch!"

What he didn't know was how he was going to accomplish getting the license. He needed another favor or two.

He called Pastor Olsen at Mount Olivet Lutheran. "Pastor, this is Larkin Palmer. I've attended your church a couple of times with Mrs. Heidelmann and my fiancé', Sally. Do you remember me?"

"Yes, Larkin, I do. Is this about our conversation after church? Do you have questions?"

"Actually, I have many and two favors to ask of you. I know it is short notice, but may I come in to see you this afternoon?"

"Well isn't that odd, but I just had someone cancel a meeting with me. Sure, come in right away."

"I will. I'm only about a mile away. See you soon and thanks."

Larkin got there in less than five minutes and parked in the church lot. He went into the offices and found Olsen's secretary putting together something for Advent services. He said to her, "Hi! I'm Larkin Palmer. Pastor Olsen is expecting me."

"Yes, go right on in."

He walked in his office and said, "Hello again Pastor, how are you?" He stuck out his hand and the pastor stood up and shook it with verve.

"It's so nice to have you call me, Larkin. I assume you have something important you want to talk about?"

"Yes, we want to get married."

"I see. Maybe a June wedding?"

"As a matter of fact, in 14 days- Christmas Day."

Pastor Olsen panicked. "I can't do that Larkin. That is truly unorthodox. We haven't even sat down to speak and you aren't members. There are so many things."

"Don't panic, Pastor, please just listen to me." Larkin told him the reason that Sally and he were not in church the week before. He told him of their commitment to each other, their faith, and the desire to become members of his congregation. He told him of his plans and he also told him of his new found wealth, and that he would donate ten thousand to the church if he would officiate at Mr. Shipleys home that day in the afternoon. All he needed was that and a way to get a license and- keep the whole thing secret.

"You mean she doesn't even know she's getting married?"

"Well, not in so many words, but trust me Pastor, she will marry me that day. She has told me she will marry me at anytime. She won't be able to resist this."

Olsen said, "It is truly the most cockamamie thing I've ever heard of. Mr. Dan Shipley you say? Of the Smithsonian? "

"Yes, he's my boss."

"Larkin, from what I have seen and heard, I trust you. I usually don't do this, but I have a friend that may be able to get you the license. But, you'll both have to be there."

Larkin smiled sensing Pastor Olsen lightening up and said, "I know a way. Set it up Pastor and we'll be there. Just call me at this number." He wrote it on a piece of paper and said, "Thank you so much."

"I look forward to it. God bless you both." The pastor shook his head and smiled as Larkin left. Olsen said to himself, "Kids like this are the ones that will make this country great!"

Larkin got up and headed out the door an elated young man. Now he had to call all the parents! Consequently, he drove straight home. It was almost four o'clock when he called his mom. When she first heard of the idea she was hesitant, but conceded that it was romantic. Finally, after talking briefly with Lawtin, she agreed they would come. Larkin asked, "Do you think you could get Percy to take care of everything so you could stay a week or two?"

"What about your honeymoon, Larkin?"

"Oh shoot, Mom, I didn't even think of that! It's another thing to plan. I guess you better go home then."

She laughed and said, "I guess we had better if we ever want any grandkids."

"Aw, Mom."

"I'll be in touch, Honey. Let me know of all the final plans when you can. Okay?"

"Okay. Now I have to call Sally parents, too."

"Good luck. Bye."

"Bye, Mom."

He pushed the button down to get a dial tone again. He was glad Sally had written the number for her parents on the pad by the phone. He didn't know why she had done that. He dialed and it began to ring. He was really nervous when her mom picked up. "Hello, Mrs. Britt?"

"Yes?"

"This is Larkin Palmer, Sally's fiancé."

"Oh yes, Larkin, how are you?"

"Just fine. I've called to invite you to D.C. for Christmas. Before you say you can't, let me tell you why."

Larkin explained the plans and that he would pay for everything. "Larkin, that is the sweetest thing! Of course we will be there! Just let us know everything when you get it all firmed up."

"Will do and I'll sure be glad to finally meet you. Goodbye."

"Bye, Bye."

Another step was complete. It looked like he might be able to pull it off. No sooner than he had sat the phone down and went into the kitchen, it rang. "Hello?"

"This is Pastor Olsen, is that you, Larkin?"

"Yes, it is Pastor."

"I spoke with Judge Patterson and he will see you on December twenty-second at 11:30 in the morning. Can you make that, Larkin?"

"That is perfect, Pastor! We can."

"That's good. He's at 515- 5th Avenue, room 420. Got it?"

"Got it."

"Oh, by the way, it'll cost you. He didn't say how much, but bring your wallet."

Larkin laughed and said, "Right now that's the easiest part of my life, Pastor. Thanks so much. I'll be in touch."

"You're welcome. Goodbye, Larkin."

He hung up and said, "Thank you, Lord!"

After this, he really wanted to be able to talk to Sally to set up going to the judge to get the license and to feel her out as to where she might want to go for a honeymoon. When Sally got home, he asked her if she'd like to go have pizza. "Sure Honey, that sounds good."

"Want to try to go to Luigi's again?"

She came out of the bedroom after changing and said, "Again? Yes, I've been craving their pizza ever since the accident. Let's take the car this time though!"

They laughed and started over to Luigi's.

After they arrived, they couldn't believe they were actually sitting there and looking at the menu. Sally said, "I already know what I want." They both sang out, "Pepperoni!"

"How about having a salad, or something, too?"

"Can we split a salad?"

"Sure. What kind of dressing?"

"They have a new kind here called "ranch" and it's good. Want to try it?"

"I'm game. Want a beer, Dear?"

"I'd like one. Do you mind?"

"Okay, but just one and a glass of water."

They placed their order and finally started to talk. Larkin said, "I think we ought to go ahead and get a marriage license, so that when we do finally decide to get married, we won't have to wait. What do you think, Dear?"

"I think that's a great idea, Honey."

"And you know we have never talked about where we'd like to go for our honeymoon. I really don't have any place in mind. Do you?"

"Yes!" She didn't say where, but just sat there for a minute.

"Don't be funny. Just tell me."

"I want to go to- Costa Rica."

"Really? Costa Rica? Why there?"

"Because, it's the "unfound" vacation place. No one goes there. I've heard there are some places there that are totally beautiful."

"Do you have a passport?"

"Yes. Do you?"

"Well, no. How long does it take to get a passport?"

"Oh, it's not a long wait. I think it's about two months." Suddenly, Larkin's plan was going into a tailspin.

"Okay. How about having a second choice?"

"I always thought Hawaii would be nice, too."

"Me, too. I've never been anywhere."

"Well, we have time to think about it. But, it sounds like you had better get a passport. Here comes the pizza."

They ate, laughed, talked, and watched some Italian guy with slicked-back hair come in and throw a fit, because the cook had put anchovies on his pizza. The cook got so upset, that he started to yell obscenities at him in Italian. The tirade of the customer became an all out Italian verbal assault and the cook picked up a pizza and threatened the guy with it, telling him to get out and never come back. It was better than a floor show if they had paid for it. They ate the rest of the pizza and sat there for more than an hour watching people come in and out and just talking. They were really getting comfortable with each other. Although it was ever present, the sexual tension between them was subsiding and love was truly in bloom. God's peace was within them.

Larkin drove home and Sally sat next to him on the leather bench seat of the Lincoln. The radio played a song called, "My Girl" and Larkin sang along with the parts he knew. He didn't know a lot of the songs on the radio as he kind of skipped past some of the things other kids did. He was just always too busy and living in a farming community where the world seemed to just pass on by. When the song got over, Sally said, "You don't have too bad a voice, Honey. Why don't you try out for the church choir?"

Larkin had never thought about it before. He replied, "I'll have to think on it, Dear." What he at the least did know was: he didn't want to go to Costa Rica for a honeymoon.

He pulled in front of the house and they saw Harry look out the window at them. They got out, went in and Sally excused herself to the bathroom. Larkin took it as his opportunity to tell Harry about his gift and his plan. All Harry could say as he described it was, "Really. Uh huh. Really? Really?" When Larkin finished he said to him, "And make sure you keep this a total secret. Got it?"

"Got it. I think it's sweet."

Larkin started to go downstairs because he heard her making noise outside of the bathroom and he said, "That's great. He thinks it's sweet."

Sally was already in bed when he got downstairs. He went to the bathroom and brushed his teeth. When he got to *their* bedroom, because that's what it had become, she was already asleep. He changed and climbed into bed. He said a prayer and turned off the light.

When he woke, he got up right away, went to the bathroom and then to the kitchen to make them breakfast. He didn't think it was fair for her to go to work and he just sit there. Besides, she didn't know what he was doing the past couple days and he wanted to make it look like he was, in fact, doing something besides planning a wedding! He made some hot cereal and coffee, and cut a grapefruit for them to share. When he finished, he called to her in the bathroom, "Soups' on."

"Why, thanks, Honey. That's sweet."

"Oh great," he said to himself, "she thinks it's sweet." To her he said, "You're welcome, Dear."

She sat down and said to him, "I have to admit, Honey, I think it will be nice to be able to work with you on your project from home. I know people get up and go to work year after year after year, but I don't know if I could do that. Besides, I want to have a baby someday." She took a bite of her grapefruit, but when she took the next section from the bowl, it fell from her spoon and onto the table with a juicy squish. She giggled and wiped it up.

Larkin chuckled at what she did and kept to the point of their conversation saying, "I know. Being on the farm is so freeing. It is a way of life, not a job. And it's a great place to raise kids. I look forward to that. Also, I hope we can do what we need to do here and not have to punch the time clock. Besides, Mr. Shipley said he'd pay me. Not that I need it now."

Sally finished her food and she commented on his last statement, "I really think you should consider his offer. You may come up with another way to use his money and use it for good. Maybe give it to his children for college or something. Give it a thought." She got up, gave him a kiss and said, "I gotta go. See you later, Honey." She gave him a peck on the cheek.

"Bye, Dear."

She went up the stairs and he called the wedding planner.

The wedding planner already had things to tell him, but what he wanted to do is give her the job of getting the reservations for the family to fly to D.C. and back home, and for them to go to Hawaii for their honey moon after their stay at the Hay-Adams. He'd have done it himself, but he didn't know anybody. It would take too long and he didn't have the time. The big thing he asked her was to get a passport for him just in case Sally didn't like the idea of Hawaii and just had to go to Costa Rica. He wanted her to be happy. He knew the planner could handle it. He was right about her being so competent and he was glad Mrs. Shipley was, too. He also told her to keep Mrs. Shipley up to speed on everything that was happening and to let her offer suggestions at any time. The planner agreed and got to work.

When he finished talking to her, he prepared to go out himself. He wanted to look at something at the Temple. He felt they had, for the time being, decided to leave them alone, so he figured, "What the heck, I may as well go into the lion's den again." Before he left the phone rang. It was Bob, the realtor. He said, "I never would have believed it Larkin, but they accepted the offer. The place can be yours for the offered price."

"Really? Well, Bob, Sally is at work and I'll call her and let you know in a little while. Okay?"

"I'm at the office. I'll wait for your call."

Larkin hung up and called Sally. She answered and he said, "They accepted it."

"REALLY? The offer? When can we sign?"

"You don't want to talk about it?"

"NO! Larkin, I know you are playing with me. Quit it!"

He smiled and said, "Okay. I'll set up a time for us to go and sign, and give him the check."

"Like- today?"

"Yes. See if you can get off a little early."

"Okay."

"I'll call you back when I know the time."

"Bye, Honey. I'm so excited!"

"Goodbye, Sally."

He paused and grinned widely, hanging up the phone and thanking the Lord.

Larkin made his calls and set it all up with Bob and Sally for 4:30 p.m. at Bob's office. However, he still wanted to get to the Temple, so he got in the Lincoln and headed over there. He parked in a garage a block away and walked over in the cold, and by the time he arrived, his lungs hurt. He stepped inside the Temple and took a breath of the warm air. When he did, Dean saw him and looked truly surprised. As Larkin started to go upstairs Dean met him at the bottom and said," Hello Larkin, I'm surprised to see you here."

"Why would that be, Dean? I'm as safe here as anywhere in D.C."

"I suppose that's correct. Is there something in particular you'd like to see?"

"No, Dean. I would just like to look at the Pike collection of artifacts again; nothing big."

"Okay, Larkin, but you sure got balls. Go ahead."

"Thanks, Dean." He smiled on his way up the stairs.

He walked up the thirteen stairs and took a look at the Pike statue before he went in the museum. He walked around and around it, trying to see if there were any clues, even in a statue. He came up empty and decided to go into the artifact room. He looked at each and every piece reading the descriptions and comparing items of similar use and kind. It took him three hours, but he was just not making any progress. He pulled out his watch and took a look at the time. It reflected in the glass of the case he was standing in front of and as he snapped the lid shut, he looked up to find Dean standing beside him. He said, "I don't know where you got a watch like that, Larkin, but don't you find that to be an inconsistency in your life?"

"It's one of the *mysteries* in my life, Dean. It was passed down to me from the Button side of the family. A soldier named R. Button was, as far as I have determined, to be the only family member who was ever a Mason. I don't know why. Oh, and I use it to my advantage every time I can."

"I see. Have you found what you are looking for, Larkin?"

"Do you mean- the Key?"

"No, I didn't, but as long as you're asking, *have* you found it?"

"No and I know you haven't either. It'll take time, but I'll find it."

"Actually, Larkin, I hope you do."

"Thanks, Dean."

Larkin turned and walked away, surprised at Dean's statement. He had a 4:30 p.m. appointment to keep.

Larkin drove to Bob's office thinking about the Pike collection and what had just happened, not the fact he was about to give someone all that money for a house.

He was disturbed that he had not figured out this mystery about the Key yet. Maybe that was the problem- he was trying to rely on his intellect more than his gift. He'd give it time. He pulled the car into the parking lot at Bob's office and saw that Sally's truck was there already. He figured she would be, because she was really excited, and he didn't blame her one bit. Although he was concentrating more on the Key, he was a bit excited, too!

He went into the storefront office, which looked more like a used car lot rather than a realtor's place of business. Sally was sitting at Bob's desk talking about how she was going to furnish the house. When Larkin walked up to the desk Bob had just said, "If you care for the current furnishings the owners are moving to Saudi Arabia and have said they would sell it complete for twenty thousand dollars more. That's a bargain! Did you see all the antiques?"

Sally said to Larkin as he sat down next to her, "Did you hear that, Honey? What do you think?"

"We'd be foolish not to do it. We'll take it."

"Okay! I'll put that into the papers, too."

Sally said, "You're a "shopping wimp", Honey."

"I'd say we're both guilty of that." He bent toward her and gave her a kiss.

She said, "I guess it's time to get out your checkbook, Honey."

He pulled it out of his pocket and took pen in hand, and prepared to write the biggest check in his life.

After they signed the papers, Bob said they could move in on Sunday, only because the people needed time to get their personal effects out before they left for Saud on Saturday. He'd have the keys for them then, after Larkin's check cleared. They left, and Larkin walked Sally to her truck. She was actually dumbstruck and in shock, unable to believe she was part owner of a house, especially such a *nice* house. When they got to the truck, Sally began to cry profusely. She said she didn't deserve a man like him and that God was just so good to her. He held her in her total thanksgiving to God and said, "Our God is good. Thanks be to God."

He opened the door to her pickup for her and she got in. She said before she closed it, "I'll see you at home. No, I mean, at Harry's. I just need to take it easy tonight."

"Okay. Be careful."

Bob got on the phone. He said, "All set Dean. They're in."

"Thanks, Bob." Dean smiled as he hung up.

They arrived at Harry's and just went down the back stairs not really wanting to be disturbed that night. Sally went to the kitchen, pulled off her coat, gloves and hat, and threw them on the floor. She went to the refrigerator and took out a beer. Larkin watched all of this and stared in disbelief, because it was just so out of character for her to be messy. He picked them up for her and after she took a sip of the liquid gold, she said, "Would you like one, Honey?"

He sat her things on the chair and said, "Don't mind if I do, Dear."

They took their beers and went in to watch TV. They sat and stared and didn't talk much. Suddenly, Sally said, "What's that on top of the TV?"

"Oh, I got that for opening our accounts. It's an AM/FM radio."

Sally just started to laugh her socks off. She laughed so hard, she actually peed her pants. Larkin said, "Why is that so funny?"

She finally contained herself and said, "You put eleven million dollars in three accounts and all they gave you was an AM/FM radio!"

Larkin started to laugh too, and said, "I guess that is funny."

She got up, went to the bedroom and she changed her clothes putting on her nightgown and robe. It was softer than her, actually his, PJ's. She came back and sat next to Larkin and finished her beer. Neither of them was hungry, so they just sat there watching the tube. He remembered something and said, "Did I tell you I went back over to the Temple to look at the Pike collection before I met you at Bob's office?"

She looked at him like he had three heads and said, "You did what?"

"I know you heard me, but I wanted to look at all of the collection again to see if I missed something. I came up with zilch, even though I spent about three hours there."

"I can imagine what they thought about that!"

"Dean came up to me and told me I had balls."

Sally said brazenly, "Well I certainly hope so!"

She snuggled up next to him and they fell asleep watching the TV. The TV station signed off and the static woke Larkin. He rose from the sofa, picked Sally up and carried her to bed. He went back out to the living room, picked up the beer bottles and put them away. Then using the TV's light to guide him, he walked back to the living room and shut it off. Fumbling along the way, he went to the bedroom and being too lazy to do anything else, he took off his clothes and got in bed.

When Sally woke up in the morning, she found Larkin lying beside her in his underwear. She was startled at what she saw, but she didn't want to embarrass him, so she didn't say anything or wake him. She got up and got ready for work taking a long hot shower first. Larkin never did wake up, even when she dressed in the room, kissed him goodbye and left.

The next few days crawled by. Larkin and Sally were excited to get to move into their place and just wanted the wait to be over. They arranged for a moving company to take Sally's things over to the house the following Monday. She didn't even have to pack them. All of the furniture was Mrs. Heidelmann's, so all she had was clothes and personal effects, just like Larkin at Harry's house. They figured they could get Larkin's things themselves, as there were far less. Bob called and told Larkin he could pick up the keys and as far as they knew, they were all set to go.

When Sunday finally did roll around, it was hard for them to go to church as they were so excited. But, understanding where it all came from, (their possessions), and acknowledging whose it really was, they knew they needed to go to worship Him. They dressed and went to meet Mrs. Heidelmann at the usual place and time. They didn't speak with Harry before they left, because he was in the shower getting ready for church himself. They left him a note, "We'll call you later Harry."

The bulletin said, 'Third Sunday of Advent, December, 17, 1978'. Larkin sat next to Mrs. Heidelmann this time, as he wanted to ask a question or two as they went along in the liturgy. This was beneficial to him and he understood the underlying meanings of the liturgy better when she explained them. He knew he was sitting next to a woman who knew her theological stuff.

When the service was over, they got up and told Mrs. Heidelmann they wouldn't be able to stay and why. She was excited for them as well and when they got to the door to shake Olsen's hand she was busy telling her friends about it. It took the focus off of Olsen and their greetings which was good for Larkin, because as he walked out, Pastor winked at him. Sally didn't see it and it didn't matter anyway. They rushed and got in the car and headed to the new place with suitcases full of clothes Sally had packed the days before. They were ready!

They drove up and parked on the street. The two got out and looked up the stairs at their new home. Larkin didn't know if he liked some of the pink paint on the trim, but he'd not say anything to Sally yet before he tried to come up with a different color. They went up hand in hand and Larkin opened the door. Before she could step in he picked her up, Sally smiled at him and he carried her across the threshold. Indeed, he *was* romantic. She didn't comment on it, but she kissed him, which was more than words could say. He turned around and said, "I'll get the suitcases. You look around. Be right back."

He went down to the Lincoln and pulled the two heavy, full suitcases out of the trunk. He made his way up with only one, because he just couldn't manage the heavy things with his cast on the stairs. He sat the first at the top and went back down for the second. On the way back up he asked himself, "Did she pack rocks in here?"

He carried the bags into the front door and shut it. Before going any further with them, he looked for Sally and found her in the kitchen. It was the first and only place she had been. "Larkin," she said, "They left all of their stuff; the pots and pans, utensils, towels -everything."

Larkin went over by the phone which hung by the refrigerator. By it was a message board on which Larkin found a note saying:

"Larkin and Sally, We heard you'd be getting married and don't have a lot of things. We left many of our things which we thought you could use as you begin your new life together. It is our wedding gift to you both. Congratulations!
Signed,
Ed & Betty"

He took it off the board and handing it to Sally said, "Read this and find out why."

When she finished, she cried as usual and sat the note down. She came to Larkin and hugged him saying, "That's so sweet. Let's look around!" She took him by the hand and led him around; first the downstairs and then up to the second floor as fast as Larkin's cast would allow.

When they had traversed the stairs and had looked around, he asked, "Which bedroom do you want?" She had not thought about that. She was getting pretty used to sleeping in the same bed. Larkin waited for her answer hoping she would not ask to continue to do so. He was relieved and his chest fell visibly as he released the air he was holding in while he waited for her to respond.

She said, "I think I'll take the master until we get married because it has the bathroom. You take the one next to me."

He sighed with relief and said, "I don't know. I like the..."

She cut him off and said, "No. I get the master!" She ran into the master and jumped onto the bed giggling the whole way.

He followed after her and said, "Okay. You win. You are Queen of the castle."

And it was a role that they'd find would suit her.

He went to get each suitcase and brought hers up first so she could start unpacking. She just laid on the bed until he got there, hands behind her head gazing at the ceiling and all around the room, taking it all in with amazement and wonder. She wondered why God had blessed her so, even under the veil of the curse of The Eraser. 'Maybe,' she thought, 'He is making up for the curse with material blessings for us to live?' She didn't know.

Larkin arrived with the bag and shoved it next to a dresser saying, "Your bag, Madam." He bowed.

She jumped off the bed and came over to him saying, "Here's your tip, Bellman." She gave him a deep French kiss.

Larkin was surprised and said when she let go, "Do you always tip this way?"

"Only if it's you," she said as she started to open her suitcase.

He shook his head, leaving to go get his suitcase and said, "What am I going to do with you? But don't change, Dear."

As she opened her suitcase to begin unpacking she replied, "Don't worry."

They finished unpacking this first load and Larkin said, "I guess we better go over and get the rest of my things. Harry probably wouldn't want a stack of boxes sitting in the living room. Besides, we need to pick up your truck, so you can go to work in the morning."

She said, "Oh yeah, work. I'll be glad when I'm done on Thursday."

"Oh, by the way, I arranged for us to get a marriage license from a judge on Friday. Then we'll be ready to go."

"Oh, okay. That's good timing."

"That's what I thought. We can go before we check in at the Hay-Adams."

"That reminds me, Honey, I have to pack for that, too. We are going to be busy this week."

Larkin thought to himself, 'You don't know the half of it.'

The rest of the day was spent packing and unpacking. They maneuvered her truck into the garage and set boxes to the side, which left room for the things the movers would bring the next day from Sally's. But for Larkin, the best part was when he drove the Lincoln through the door of the garage. Smiling from ear to ear, he closed the garage door and turned up the heat. Yes, the garage even had its own heat! He was ecstatic when all the snow started to melt off the undercarriage and wheel wells. Now all he had to figure out was how to wash it in the winter time.

By the time they decided to quit working on the unpacking, they were spent. Trying to figure out what really needed to be unpacked because of what Ed & Betty had left made the chore of unpacking a little more complicated. Some of Larkin's' things just stayed in the boxes, but Sally made sure all the clothes made it up to the closets and bedrooms. Larkin's room seemed empty. Sally's, well, he knew Sally's would be full after tomorrow and maybe hers might run over into his! She had a lot of clothes. At least, that's what *he* thought.

73

They went down to the kitchen and sat on the bar stools by the counter. Taking a look in the refrigerator, Sally found a pan with a note stuck to it:

"Here's a casserole for your first night. Betty."

Sally pulled it out and said to Larkin, "Look at what Betty left for us, Honey. She is so sweet."

Larkin walked over to her and took a look, "I wonder what kind it is?"

"I don't know, but we'll find out!"

She warmed up her oven for the first time and shoved the Pyrex dish in. While they waited for dinner, Sally took the last two beers out of the refrigerator and said, "Let's go watch TV."

The TV they bought just a month before, now was in Larkin's bedroom. The one they got with the house was larger and in the living room by the fireplace. He turned on the Magnavox TV with the remote and the sound seemed like they were in a movie. The base was unbelievable and the picture- exceptional. They sat down on the pleated leather couch and watched the first channel that came on, because it was a John Wayne movie. Larkin loved John Wayne.

In a half hour or so the food was done. Sitting at the counter, they watched the movie from there, as they had a clear view. The room was nice and open, just like Larkin's parents house. Larkin said, "This chicken casserole is pretty good. I'm thankful she left it or we would have had to try to eat the leftovers from my refrigerator, which wasn't much."

"I know. You guessed it pretty close."

"I'll have to go to the store tomorrow after the movers come. Will you make a list for me?"

"That's a good plan, because I'll want to unpack my stuff tomorrow night. We can still eat the rest of this casserole tomorrow, too. Okay?"

"Sure. You know I like leftovers."

They finished up and moseyed back over to the couch to continue watching John Wayne. After a while and before the movie was over, he got sleepy from the beer and started to doze off. She saw it and said, "Let's go to bed, Honey."

Startled, he said, "Uh. Okay. He got up almost wondering where he was until he fully woke up enough to walk upstairs. Sally helped him for a second toward the landing and said, "You sure you can make it?"

"Yes, Dear, thanks."
"I'm going to tidy up the kitchen and I'll be right up."
"Okay."

Walking slowly into his room, he took all the stuff out of his pockets. He placed The Eraser on the night stand. He put all of his clothes in the hamper in the closet and put on his PJ's. Then he took The Eraser and went to the master bedroom. In the closet was a safe built into the wall behind the shoe rack. All you had to do is pull the handle on the rack and it moved aside, much like a picture frame would. 'Ingenious,' he thought. Bob had given him the combination when he picked up the keys and this was the first time he tried to open it. He was impressed that he got it open on the first attempt. He placed The Eraser and the bank bag with the rest of the cash into the safe and closed it. Sally came in and started to change. She glanced to her right, smiled when saw him in her closet and asked, "Spying on me?"

"No, Dear. I was putting the money and The Eraser in the safe. You'll need to know how to open it, too."

"Okay, you can show me later. I'm going to bed."

"Me, too," he said and he went over to kiss her goodnight. She started to take off her shirt just as he got there, and using his mom's advice, he didn't pay much attention to it and just kissed her and said, "Goodnight, Dear."

She smiled and continued to change as Larkin made his way to his room and a solid night's sleep. He yelled to her when he got in bed and said, "Pray for me!"

"I will, if you will for me!"

"I will. Goodnight!"

"Goodnight, Honey!"

On Monday morning, she went through a different routine because of the new house, but all in all, how do you change how you get ready for work in the morning? You really don't and neither could she. When she was ready to go downstairs, she looked into Larkin's room to find he was already up, so she went down and saw him standing by the refrigerator, looking for something. "What ya looking for?" asked Sally.

"I thought I had some cream left from the other place."

"Oh that. I opened the carton to try to pour some and it stayed in the carton. So, I threw it out."

"Good idea. I'll drink my coffee black today. Want some?"

"Sure."

He brought them each a cup over to the counter and they sat down. He said, "I've been thinking that I may have someone put a garage door opener on the garage door. It would be so much easier."

"That sounds real good, Larkin. Say, Honey?"

"Yeah?"

"What do you want for Christmas?"

"Hum. A garage door opener! But really, I have everything I need and more. I have you don't I?"

Ignoring his statement about her she said, "Yes, but I'm serious. What would you like?"

"I'd like this cast off! But, seeing as that isn't going to happen yet, I would like to go on a clothes shopping spree when I get it off."

"That's another month away. What do you want *now*?"

"I don't know. I'm sorry, Dear, but I can't think of a thing."

"Okay, but you're at my mercy."

"Aren't I always?"

"Well, I gotta get going. I'm sure looking forward to Thursday at five! Bye, Honey." She pecked him on the cheek and started to the garage. He said smiling, "Bye!"

After she left, Larkin called the wedding planner and asked how things were coming along. She said very well and was pleased to say they had the dress made and was ready for him to see. That was to be the gift Sally would open on Christmas morning. The planner also said that all the air travel was secure; the honeymoon booked, the caterer and flowers ordered, the rooms for the parents reserved, but that the details for the cake still needed to be hashed out. She'd like him to help with that and his tux, so things were on schedule. But, she needed a picture for his passport and a signature. He set up an appointment with her for the next day.

Driving along in her little Datsun on the way to work, Sally thought about her life now with Larkin. Before Larkin, she would have thought this kind of life to be boring; staying home in imposed solitude and not going out. She was content with her situation. Not because of the money, nor their relationship, but because of the peace and love she shared with this farm boy from New York. Amidst the turmoil of the Eraser, she wondered how that could be real. She knew it was because of God's hand in their lives and Larkin's love for her. She thanked the Lord and parked her truck. Behind her, the man in the blue suit parked, too.

About an hour later the movers came with the rest of Sally's things. He had them bring all of the food in and place it in the pantry. The clothes boxes went straight to her room and the rest to the garage stacked against a wall so they could sort through it and put away as they pleased. She had a lot of things. After they finished and left, he decided to tackle the food and started to put it in the pantry.

She had most of the foodstuffs and some canned goods, too. What Larkin had, she didn't and there wasn't much duplication except for coffee of which, together, they had plenty, so he put a pot on. The people had left their Bunn coffee maker and he was glad to use it because it made great coffee, and Paul Harvey endorsed it. He loved Paul Harvey, too.

He sat down when he finished the work in the pantry and had a cup of Joe, radio playing and listening to the news. He had plugged the new AM/FM into an outlet in the pantry and he was about to go turn it up when he looked out the window to see someone watching him from a house across the street. He was, of course, paranoid, but he figured they were curious as to who the new neighbors were. Larkin waved and the guy waved back. He'd have to make sure Sally had the shades closed or clothes on at night!

When Sally got home, Larkin had dinner already warmed back up again, so they sat and talked about their day as they ate. Larkin said that he really wanted to get back to working on the research, because he still had not figured out anything about Pike and the Key. It still had him somewhat, no, *really-* baffled. They also decided not to decorate the house for Christmas this year, as they had too much to do with moving in and really no time to concentrate on doing it properly. Besides, they wouldn't even be there, because they'd be at the Hotel and the Shipley's. They finished eating and Larkin volunteered to clean up while she went to unpack her clothes. He listened to his new radio while he put the dishes in the dishwasher and cleaned up the pots and pans. Even though it had cost him eleven million, he still liked to listen to it! He shook his head and chuckled when he remembered what Sally had said the other day about it. Finishing up, he went upstairs to see how she was doing.

Sally had the clock radio playing in the master bedroom and she was really getting into her work. Almost three-fourths of her clothes were already put away. He sat on the bed and watched her sort and move things back and forth until she got them the way she wanted them. He thought, 'Man, girls put way too much into this.' After about an hour, she was done with the clothes boxes and she had placed all her things in the drawers. The bad news was that she had used both dressers and Larkin wondered what he would do with his stuff when he eventually moved into the master bedroom with her. He didn't say anything about it because that really might work. He'd think on it. She moved to the closet and the wardrobe boxes next. That took less time, but still filled all the space. She had it all sorted and categorized. She really had it together. She said, "Okay, Honey. You can move all the empty boxes to the garage now."

"Okay, Dear." He hopped to it and took about three loads down and placed them on the back wall in front of the two vehicles.

When he arrived back upstairs, he found that she had stepped in the shower. He came to the door and peered into the steam filled room saying loudly, "I meant to tell you, Dear, but the man across the way was looking into our windows today. I think we ought to make sure we close the shades at night."

She answered by opening the shower door and asking him, "Why, Honey? Don't you want him to see *this?*" She pointed, laughed, and closed the door. In resignation, he just shook his head and waited for her on the bed. In a couple of minutes, she came out in her robe with a towel wrapped around her head like a swami. Coming over to him, she gave him a kiss and then asked as she dried her hair with the towel, "What do you have planned for tomorrow?"

He couldn't tell her about the appointment with the wedding planner, so he just asked, "Why? I do have to go to the store. I never made it there today."

"Well, I thought you might want to come and have lunch with me. That's all." She frowned with disappointment.

"Oh. That's sounds real good. Any place special?"

"No. Let's play that by ear." She now smiled, now understanding what he meant.

"Okay. I heard there's a new Greek place down there that has a thing called a "Gyro?" Ever heard of that?"

"Yes. They are good. I had one in Nashville last summer with my sister. I think the place here is just called The Greek Café."

"You know where it is?"

"I think so. I'll ask some of the people at work about it. Okay?"

"Neat. I'm getting in the shower. It's my turn."

He went to his bedroom, got his PJ's and then went into the master bedroom shower. Plastic bag and cast too! He loved the shower, because it was big enough to actually stand in and had two shower heads, one on each wall. It was really meant for two people and he knew it. So did Sally. He hoped she waited until after the wedding to try it out! He turned both of them on and just stood there in the middle, letting the warm water heat up his skin. It felt good with the outside temperature hovering at about 10 degrees! As he stood there, hot water running off of him, all of a sudden a smiley face appeared in the misted window of the clear shower door. He laughed and said, "Sally, cut that out!"

"Oh, Honey, you're no fun!"

He replied, "Well at least not yet, anyway."

She giggled and said, "I hope so."

She left and he got out. He took a look at himself in the mirror that went from floor to ceiling by the whirlpool tub. He hadn't noticed, but he was filling out a bit. The slim waste was still slim, but it seemed to be a little bit buffed up and more defined. He wasn't a skinny boy anymore; he'd become a man. Sally startled him when she came up and stood by him asking, "What ya looking at?"

Way past blushing, he turned and shook his head at her saying a little sternly, "Sally, what are you doing?"

"Looking at you." She came and put her hand on his stomach.

Forcefully, he removed it and replied, "Not yet. Now- *go on.*"

"I told you that you were no fun." She lowered her head and frowned.

Standing there with only a towel, he turned her around and gave her a little push toward the door. Slowly she left, and seeing the opportunity, he took another towel and snapped her on the rear through her robe. It landed with a resounding- "crack".

"OW!" she cried.

He laughed and she slammed the door as she left the room. He thought, 'I know other people our age struggle with this all the time, but they just go for it. It sure is hard and it *is* a struggle. It is so easy to sin that's for sure. I just hope I can hold out for the next few days. Lord help me! Besides, if it weren't for the Freemasons and the Eraser, we wouldn't *have* to be living this way!' He thought about that as he dried off and combed his hair. Compared to other kids, he knew his life was pretty boring. He wondered why Sally would even consider the life of seclusion that the Eraser forced upon them. He somehow had to make life more exciting for them. He'd think on that.

He got dressed in his PJ's and went out to see if she was angry with him, but she didn't seem to be, because he figured she knew she deserved it. She was watching Larkin's TV in his bedroom and waiting for him. "I sure wish we had some more beer, Honey."

"Want to go get some?"

"Naw. It's too cold after a shower and I don't want to catch a cold."

"Hey- wait a minute!" said Larkin with a twinkle in his eye, "I thought I saw a closet downstairs with some wine boxes in it. Wanna go look?"

"Sure. Let's go!" She had forgotten all about what had just occurred in the bathroom, much to Larkin's delight.

She grabbed his hand and they went down the stairs at a faster rate than he should have. The stairs to the basement were old and rickety, so they went a little slower down them because, Larkin just had to! There was a laundry room, the furnace, and a water heater down there in a partial basement, but it didn't smell like most old musty basements. It seemed dry. He led her to the closet and opened the door throwing on the light switch. Sure enough, there were three wine boxes, full of wine- a full thirty six bottles of all different kinds. "Wow!" exclaimed Sally.

Larkin pulled a bottle out and took a look at the label saying, "This is some really old stuff. This label says 1949, Sally. They probably thought it was too old to drink, so they just left it here." (Little did he know that these boxes were left behind on purpose, because of where the previous owners relocated to, much to their chagrin.)

She picked up a bottle and wiped off the dust, saying, "It just depends. You know what they say, "We will drink no wine before it's time". I say, "Nothing ventured, nothing gained". Grab a box and let's go drink some wine!"

Larkin grabbed the top case and they went upstairs to find a cork screw. Sally said she thought she had seen one in the kitchen. She looked in a couple of drawers and when she found one she held it up wide-eyed and said, "Eureka!"

They opened the bottle that Larkin had looked at first and he took a whiff. He said, "Smells fine. What do you think?"

He handed it to her and she did the same saying, "Actually, it smells pretty *good*. I'll get the glasses!"

She sounded excited to him, so he sat by the counter in anticipation of it as she placed two wine glasses before them. Larkin gently picked up the bottle and poured a little in; like he'd seen people do. Sally picked it up and smelled it again. She shrugged her shoulders and said, "Here goes!" She took a sip, smiled and said, "Its *real* good, Larkin. Pour us both a glass." He did and as he took his first sip of wine *ever*, he picked up the bottle once again to study it.

He read the label, "This is Chateau Petrus 1949. It is from the Bordeaux region of France."

Sally asked, "I wonder how much it costs?"

"I don't know much about wine, do you?"

"All I know is that some wine can get pretty expensive."

"Well, maybe I can make a list of what's down there and find out about it sometime. In the mean while, let's drink a toast. To- free wine!"

Sally held up her glass and said, "To free wine!" They clinked their glasses and took a drink. It was as good as she said it was and this was his first full glass of wine in his life.

By the time they finished the bottle, they were feeling no pain. In fact, Larkin was about to fall asleep. Sally said to him, "Let's go up and go to bed, Honey. I think we are done for the night."

He replied, "I think you're right, Dear. Let's go to bed."

He started up the stairs and almost fell back on her. She caught him and pushed him up the stairs one step at a time. He would have never made it without her. He went into his room and tried to pull back the covers, but was having one heck of a time doing it. She sat him on the edge of the bed and did it for him. Helping him off the bed, she pushed him towards the pillow leaving his legs dangling off. She chuckled, put her arms under them and heaved up. At last, she was ready to pull the covers over him. "Whew, he can't take his alcohol either! He's so innocent," she said to herself. Kissing him on the forehead, she smiled as she looked at him lying there, left him and went to bed.

Tuesday, she left for work on time with no problems, Larkin, on the other hand, couldn't get up. He wasn't doing too well and wasn't happy he had the appointment with the wedding planner. What he was really unhappy about was the fact that as a novice, he had drunk more wine than he should have. He got up and got into the shower to help him wake up. He felt a little nauseous, but that started to go away. He just stood there until he had to get out and get dressed. He was running out of time. He struggled, but he put the shopping list in his pocket and made it out the door and drove to her office.

He parked very slowly in front and walked in even more slowly. The lady saw him come in and guessed why he was suffering. She asked, "Have a little too much to drink last night, Larkin?"
"Yeah. We found a bottle of a French wine called, ah, Chateau Petrus last night and drank the whole thing."
"What year?"
"I think it was 1949. Why?"
"You drank a two thousand dollar bottle of wine last night?"
"Really? It was worth *that* much? Yeah, we found three cases of wine in my basement. We don't know what any of it is or what it's worth."
"Found it in your basement, huh? Bring me a list and I'll tell you what you have before you drink something you shouldn't. But, let's talk about what you came here for."

She pulled out her list and they went over it with a fine-toothed comb. He liked what she had done with the cake so far and they worked out the details. She asked for his sizes, so she could get the tux, but he referred her to Stephen, because he just didn't know himself. Finally, she had the dress brought out. He was stunned. It was just beautiful, in and of itself. He could only imagine what it would look like with Sally in it! He said, "It is just beautiful. You've outdone yourself."
"Thank you, Larkin. Do you think she'll like it?"

"Oh yes!"

"Do you have any other questions?"

"Just one; is Mrs. Shipley up to speed and has she made any beneficial suggestions?"

"Yes, but only pertaining to her home. She and her family are very excited about it all."

"I hope everyone is. Now remember, the dress needs to be wrapped so I can give it to her Christmas Eve."

"Larkin, this is just a suggestion, but would you wait until Christmas Day when everyone is there?"

"I don't know. I don't want to throw it all at her at once, but it sure would make a great surprise. We'd have to get there earlier than noon, which she is planning on now from the previous invitation."

"I could have Mrs. Shipley include you all in the gift opening and arrive at ten instead."

"That would work and still give her enough time to be ready. I could say her gift from me was sent there, so she would have something to open. Sound good?"

"Let's try it. I'll have Mrs. Shipley call."

"Now remember, we will be at the Hay-Adams from the twenty-second until we leave for the honeymoon. Okay?"

"Got it. Thanks for coming in, Larkin."

"Glad to. What time is it?"

"Almost noon."

"Thanks, I gotta go."

He walked as fast as he could and hopped in the car to go meet Sally. She was waiting for him at the door when he arrived. "What kept ya?" she asked.

"Oh, it was tough getting up. I think I'll limit myself to one glass until I get used to this wine thing."

She laughed at him and said, "You're a wimp. The Greek place is just down the mall. It'll only take us five minutes to walk there. Up to it?"

"It may actually feel good to get the fresh air."

She giggled at that.

They started off and Larkin kept up pretty well. He asked, "I know we didn't put anything on the grocery list for dinner tonight. Have anything in mind?"

"Do you like shrimp?"

"I do. What are you thinking?"

"How about I make some shrimp scampi?"

"I'll try anything you make, Dear."

"Good, 'cause you never know what I'm going to make sometimes. Here we are."

THE KEEPER

She pointed to the door of "The Greek Café". They went in, looked around and took the first seat available. It looked like they had a salad bar. Larkin liked salad bars. A waitress came to take their order as they perused the menu. They both ordered the Gyro, the salad bar, and Cokes. In a minute, the waitress brought their salad plates and glasses saying, "If you want more than one salad plate, just let me know. I'll bring you another." She winked at Larkin.

"Thanks," said Larkin. Getting up, they went over to the salad bar. He said pointing to the dressings, "They have that ranch dressing we had the other night over at Luigi's. I like that."

"They are all different, depending on who makes it. All you can do is *try* them."

He piled a huge salad on his plate and started back to their seat. Hers fit her plate just a little neater and when she saw his she exclaimed, "You glutton!"

He smiled at what she said and as he sat down he said a prayer saying, "Lord I thank you for this larger portion of salad than Sally's and for her, the best fiancée a guy could have. Amen."

When he finished, she unfolded her napkin and said smiling, "Suck up."

The food arrived, and the waitress, dressed all in white with an apron stained with various condiments, sat it down in front of them as Larkin was still eating his salad. Sally was ready for the main course and she dug into the sandwich as she said to the waitress "Thanks!" He followed suit and he commented that he really liked the taste of the meat. He would order it again someday, he said.

They finished and she needed to get back to work, so they paid and started the walk back. He told her, "I'm going to the store- *now*, so I don't buy too many extra things. I binge buy when I'm hungry."

"Sounds like a good idea, Honey," she said as they arrived at the front door. He kissed her goodbye and she went in. The guard, Jim, waved through the window at him and Larkin smiled and waved back. He would miss working there.

He went back to his car admiring it once again as he looked at it on the street. He drove all the way down Jefferson to 3rd and watched a bus almost hit a pedestrian and slam on the brakes to avoid him. Then he drove up to D and took a left, just so he could drive past the Albert Pike statue snuggled in the park. He made the left just before the light turned red and slowly drove past it. It was no different than the one in the Temple, except, this one had bird droppings all over it. 'That fits,' he thought. He drove past, still in the dark about the Key. Where was it?

83

When he got to the store he was feeling much better than when he got up that morning. He took a shopping cart, "the one" with a bad wheel, and took the list out of his pocket. As he didn't know the store, he just went through every isle picking up the items on the list and looking for bargains on the way, cart making a funny ca-thump, ca-thump as he pushed it along. He did add some ice cream to the cart and some candy bars. He went to the meat isle and got the shrimp, added some steaks and hamburger, too, but, by the time he got to the back of the store the cart was full and he knew the list wasn't needed anymore. He'd picked up way too much, but they didn't have much at the house anyway. When he paid, the bag boy said it was the largest order he had all day. He helped Larkin out to the car with it and Larkin gave him a tip. "Groovy. Thanks, Mister," he said, "we only get tips this time of year."

Larkin smiled at his comment and replied, "You're welcome and Merry Christmas."

Larkin drove home and got out to open the garage door. He remembered then that he'd forgotten to call about the opener. He parked and carried the bags to the landing. Because there were so many, he wondered if he could or should install a dumbwaiter to the pantry from the garage. The house had the garage tucked under it to save space and it made for a lot of walking up stairs. He'd have to think on that.

After about six trips, he finally had carried it all up to the kitchen and put away. He was bushed. The cast wore him out sometimes, but he reasoned, just think how much muscle mass he was building under there! He sat down and remembered Sally wanted some beer, but he couldn't buy that, so he called to tell her that if she wanted some, she should stop and buy it on the way home. He dialed, but Sally didn't answer, Mr. Shipley did, "Shipley here."

"Hello, Mr. Shipley, this is Larkin."

"Larkin, I'm so glad you called when you did, as Sally is out doing an errand for me. I just want to say that we are so excited about your plan for Christmas Day."

"I haven't spoken to you since then, Mr. Shipley, and I want to thank you also for your sharing of your family's day, home, and resources to do this for us. I'm sincerely grateful."

"Oh, I'm glad you asked. It is a pleasure to do it."

"Will Sally be long, Sir?"

"No, I expect her soon. Is there a message I can give her?"

"Well, this is awkward. But, as I can't purchase beer yet, tell her that if she wants some tonight, she must stop on the way home and get it."

His boss laughed and said, "I'll tell her, Larkin."

"Thank you, Sir. Goodbye."

Larkin turned on the TV and went to sleep.

Sally got home and came up the stairs to the kitchen. She heard the TV on, but didn't hear or see Larkin. She put her beer in the fridge and went into the living room. Larkin was lying down asleep on the couch. She came over, sat next to him and kissed his face. He woke up and said, "Hi, Sally. Did Mr. Shipley tell you I called?"

"Yes, he did, and I stopped and got a couple of six packs. I'm not going to run out so fast this time."

"Good. Want some help with dinner?"

"No, but you can come over and sit and talk to me."

"Okay."

She walked over to the fridge and took out a beer for herself and asked, "Want one?"

He balked, considering his last experience with alcohol, but said chuckling, "Sure, why not?"

She handed it to him and sat hers down, so she could get the food out. As she began to prepare it, they talked about the Greek Café and the rest of her day. She said, "I'll still be glad when I'm done with work."

"So will I, Dear."

She had him get a few things out of the pantry for her and it began to turn into a shared cooking experience, just like up at the Family Palmer's kitchen. Sally said, "This is starting to feel like home, Larkin."

"It is. It is home- for now."

The next couple of days went by very quickly. By the time she got off work on her last day, she was excited and ready for the Christmas holiday. She saw it as a new beginning- an end of one era and the start of a new one. She would now have the best boss in the world and she knew she could work with him! When she got home, Larkin was in the home office looking over the documents again and trying to come up with a connecting thread between people, places, and events. Maybe it would lead to something. Maybe it would lead to the Key. And then again, maybe not...

Back home in Brookfield, Larkin's parents went along with life without their son and missed him greatly. The void was accentuated with the absence of Tom. The farm was running smoothly because of Percy and Arville, however, and the excitement of going to D.C. on Christmas filled them with joy. They hoped that it would all go off without incident and the "they" would not be tempted to do something.

Chapter Four

The Wedding

After work her last day, Sally came in the door and yelled, "I'm home!" She ran up the stairs and came over to Larkin sitting at his desk so fast that when she sat in his lap his office chair rolled back across the room all the way to the window.

Larkin said, "Whoa girl, are you excited or what?"

"Yes. I'm soooo happy! I'm done, I'm done, I'm done!" she said kicking her feet up and down, one shoe flying up to the ceiling. Her eyes got wide and she asked excitedly, "Want a beer?"

"Let's go have a beer!"

They both stood up and she kissed him passionately. Then she took his hand and led him quickly down the stairs, running to the kitchen. She pulled two beers out of the refrigerator and asked him as they stood there, "Did you get packed for the week at The Hay-Adams?"

"No, not yet. I need to go to the store tonight and get another pair of pants. Want to go with me?"

"Where?"

"I don't know. Penny's?"

"Let's wait. You can go get pants while we are at the hotel."

"I guess we could, couldn't we?"

"Yup. Let's just pack and get ready tonight, okay?"

He didn't answer as if in agreement with her question. Instead he asked, "What's for dinner?"

"I don't know. How about hamburgers?"

"Yeah. We can try out the Jenn-Air."

She made the patties while he got out the condiments and fired up the Jenn-Air. It worked well, but he thought it was loud. The fan that sucked the fumes out was powerful, but sounded like a mini-jet plane. They placed the burgers on it; juices sizzling as they fell off onto the heat and it cooked them to perfection. In a way Larkin was disappointed, because he just couldn't smell them cooking the same way as outdoors on a grill. They pulled some chips out of the pantry and sat down to eat. He said the grace. "Lord, we thank you that you provide all our needs and so many of the extras. We pray you are with us as we change and do new things. Be with us as we stay away from our home and keep all evil from us. Amen."

Sally said a loud, "AMEN!" They dug in.

Afterwards that night, Sally had another beer and Larkin sat watching her and the TV as she packed for two hours. To him, it seemed that that is all she had been doing lately. (In reality, it was.) He had finished in fifteen minutes. When she finished, she came over to him and said, "I'm so tired, Honey. I think I'm going to bed. I'm going to go brush my teeth." Turning, she took off her shirt and went into the bathroom. He went to his room and changed into his PJ'S. He lay down and in a few minutes she came in and said to him, "Don't forget to wake me up early."

"What time?"

"What time do we see the judge? I forgot what you said."

"Eleven-thirty."

"No hurry then. About eight, I guess."

"Okay. Goodnight."

She bent over and kissed him, and being satisfied with that, she walked toward her room. Larkin set the clock and turned off the light. He said one more prayer the whole thing would go off without a hitch.

When the alarm went off, Sally was already up. Larkin got up and went in to use the bathroom, except that Sally was in there. She was standing by the mirror doing her face in her bra and panties. He was too tired to deal with it. She said, "Good morning, Honey! I'm so looking forward to staying at The Hay-Adams." He went over and gave her a kiss.

He asked, "Did you make any coffee yet?"

"Yup. Its ready."

"I'm going downstairs."

He went down and poured a cup and went straight into the downstairs bathroom and sat down. He just didn't need company for that.

He went back upstairs afterwards and got dressed. His cast was getting ragged and he wondered what he could do to make it look better. He thought about it for a minute and got an idea. He called out, "Sally. Do we have any white shoe polish?"

"Why?"

"I want to polish my cast."

"Huh?"

"Do we?"

"Yeah. It's in the hall closet."

"Thanks."

He went downstairs again, found it in the last place he looked, and sat at the kitchen table to put it on, only he couldn't reach the whole thing. He had to call Sally to help. "Sally, will you help me?"
"Be right down, Honey."

She carried her suitcase down with her and sat it next to the pantry and door to the garage. "What do you need, Larkin?"
When she saw him, she knew, and went over to help. Taking the applicator from him, she got to all the hard to reach places. It looked pretty good. Larkin inspected it and said, "Thanks, Dear. Take it along so I can touch it up later?"
"Okay. You should go get your suitcase and the suit bag."
"Going right now," he replied obediently, springing into action.

When he got back downstairs, he headed to the door and the garage with this first load. He'd come back up to get hers the next trip. She came down with him after they locked the doors and set the alarm system. Everything fit in the trunk nicely and they jumped in the car full of excitement. He said, "Hey. Wait a minute. What time is it?"
She laughed and looked at her watch knowing they had left too early, "It nine-thirty!"
"Want to go back up or go have breakfast?"
"Perkins would be good."
"Perkins it is." He put in the key and started the car.

They drove toward UMD and found the Perkins. They ate wasting no time, somewhat annoying the waitress, and when they finished, left to go to see the judge. Sally was nervous. She had never been in a courtroom, much less having a judge ask her questions in his chambers. They arrived at the complex, parked, and went in, telling the clerk they were there. She told them to have a seat by all of the other people waiting and she'd call them when it was their turn. That's what he always hated about government- it always took too long and there was always a wait. Sally excused herself to go to the bathroom, so Larkin knew he'd be going in to see the judge alone for a minute. It was just the way that things always work out. He was right, because the clerk came to get them as soon as Sally went in the restroom door. Larkin had to ask the clerk to send her into the Judge's chambers when she came out.

When Larkin went into the Judge's chambers, he introduced himself to the balding man with a mustache and asked him, "Your Honor, did Pastor Olsen explain to you that my fiancé' doesn't know we will be married on Christmas Day as yet and that it is to be a surprise?"

"Have a seat, Larkin. Yes, he did. Don't worry." Just then, Sally came in and Larkin introduced her to the Judge. He asked them all the questions a clerk would when applying normally. Showing his sense of humor he asked, "You're not related in any way are you?"

They all laughed and Larkin answered, "No, your Honor."

"Well then, your application is approved. You can get married anytime in the next three years." He signed it, smiling at them.

The two got up and he handed the application to Larkin. Larkin thanked him and the judge said, "Pay the clerk on the way out and good luck, Kids."

"Thank you, your Honor," replied Sally.

Larkin happily paid the clerk and they left to go to the Hay-Adams.

Larkin pulled up to the door in his Lincoln and Chester was standing there ready to great them, his breath visible outside in the cold from under his brown muffler. Opening the door for Sally first, Chester said, "Welcome to the Hay-Adams, Madam." He was surprised when he looked over and saw Larkin and said, "May I have the valet park your vehicle, Mr. Palmer?"

Sally was impressed and looked at Larkin who responded, "Yes, Chester, please do."

Larkin parked and pushed the trunk button for Chester to remove the suitcases. Mike came out to assist him. He waved at Larkin as he and Sally went in, arm in arm. Sally was in awe at the way the place was decorated for the holidays. She almost tripped, looking up at the garland and bows that hung all around them, and gawking at the tree at the top of the stairs that was simply- stupendous.

They looked refined and dignified in their Sunday clothes, and when Henry looked up and saw the pair coming toward him he was pleased, and he beamed when they got to the front desk saying, "Good morning, Mr. Palmer, it is so nice to see you again."

"Thank you, Henry, likewise. Henry, this is my fiancée, Miss Sally Britt, of Tennessee."

"A pleasure to make your acquaintance, Miss Britt." He again directed his words to Larkin and said, "You will be in room 319 on the inside, Sir. I'm sorry there is not a room with a view for you."

"No problem. It is quite good; actually."

Larkin signed the register and Henry gave him the key. Mike was already by the elevator waiting for them. After they got on, Mike pushed the button and the elevator went up. He asked Larkin, "How long ya gonna be here, Larkin?"

"I think a week, Mike."

"Nice," he said, gum cracking as he spoke. When the elevator stopped, they stepped out and Mike pushed the luggage cart to the door of the room. He let them in and they removed their coats and gloves. Mike put the baggage in the bedroom and stopped to say goodbye, and get a tip he knew would be coming from Larkin. He handed him a hundred as Sally walked into the bedroom. Mike whispered and asked, "You inherit a bunch of money or something?"

"As a matter of fact, Mike, I did!"

Suddenly, Mike got serious and said softly, "Oh. Sorry, Larkin. But, thanks."

Larkin laughed and said, "No problem, Mike. Merry Christmas."

"Same to you." Mike tipped his hat and left happily.

Larkin went to the bedroom to find Sally putting her clothes away and hanging up the things in the suit bag. She wanted to look her best there. She wanted to "Put on the Ritz". Larkin asked, "What do you think?"

"I love the place. Before you ask, this bed by the bathroom is mine."

"I knew you'd pick that one." He came up to her and kissed her as she put the last of her things in the top drawer. She melted in his arms. He stopped, because he had another plan. He switched gears.

"Have you thought about where you'd like to eat lunch, Dear?"

"How's the restaurant?" After the kiss, she composed herself enough to reply.

"It's very good actually, but I think we should dine there tonight."

"We should "dine" there?" Sally asked, smiling.

Larkin gave her a funny look and said sharply, "Yes. We should. Their lobster is the best."

The phone rang. Surprised, Sally picked up not having any idea who it might be and for that matter, neither did Larkin, and she said, "Hello?"

"Hello, Sally, this is Mrs. Shipley."

"Why hello, Mrs. Shipley, how are you?" Larkin shook his head when he heard who it was and he went to put his things away, too.

He overheard her side of the conversation and he knew what it was all about, because- he had planned it! When Sally hung up, she told him that they were invited to open gifts with them a little earlier than planned. Larkin said that was no problem. She said, "Good", because, she had already accepted.

Larkin said, "Good." He smiled.

Sally went into the bathroom and Larkin turned on the TV. He wanted to know what the weather predictions were for the weekend. Not that he planned to go out much, but he did want to shop a bit and go to church, for which he'd drive them himself. The weather man said clear and cold, much of the same, except that there would be a possibility of snow flurries on Christmas Day. He didn't know whether to believe him or not.

Sitting down, he picked up the newspaper on the table. It had been a while since he'd read the paper. He didn't like the drivel nor the commentary presented by most reporters, because it was not reporting and just their opinions. That- was supposed to be left for the editorial and opinion pages! He thought, 'I have half a mind never to read the paper again.' He pulled out the ads- lots of ads, mostly for Christmas shopping. He didn't want Sally to see them, but knowing her, she somehow already had. He didn't expect to find one for blue jeans, but surprisingly he did; at Kmart. He took it out of the pile and set it aside.

As he read, there was an article which told about Christmas light displays and he wondered if Sally would like to go on a tour of the city. He called down to the desk and inquired about it, but Henry referred him to Chester. Chester said that one of his friends took people around the town in his limo for a hundred dollars for a three- hour loop around the city. For a private tour it was five hundred. Larkin asked him to see if he could book it for a private tour that night. Larkin hung up before Sally came out of the bathroom, so he went to see what she was doing.

He walked in and she was standing at the sink adjusting her makeup. He could tell she had used the restroom, but he didn't say anything and she said, "Let's go out and get you some blue jeans like you wanted. Kmart has a good sale."

"How did you...?" Larkin trailed off not completing his question as she walked away from him toward her coat. When it came to shopping, Sally knew it all.

When they got to the door, Larkin asked Chester to hail a cab for them. As they waited, Chester said to him out of the side of his mouth,

"Couldn't get it for tonight; tomorrow. Okay?"

Larkin nodded "yes" and Chester made the "Okay" sign. They got in the cab and as they did, Larkin told the driver, "Take us to Kmart, Driver."

Overhearing Larkin's request, Chester closed the door for them and just smiled.

They had not changed their clothes, so they seemed out of place at Kmart, even to themselves, but that kind of attention really amused Sally, so much so, that she tried to play it up. That embarrassed Larkin as she made him come out with the blue jeans on under his suit coat, which he had to admit, looked kind of good together, in a strange "country" sort of way. There were so many shoppers and she was enjoying it. He on the other hand...

Larkin was never so glad in all his life to get out of the men's department! They walked through the rest of the store and she commented on cute things for Christmas. As they walked past the women's department she kept on going and he asked, "Don't you want to look here?"

She looked at him like he was crazy and then he figured it out, *she* didn't want to look like *she* was "slumming it", but it was alright for him to do it! 'Women!' he thought, 'Always a double standard.' Though for him, Sally could do him no wrong. He bought the two pairs of jeans and they went back out to the cab which had waited the hour for them. The cabbie was impatient, but he could tell he would have no problems in getting his fare and even a nice tip. When they got in he turned, his puffy afro rubbing on the car's ceiling, and he asked hesitantly, "Where to?"

Without asking Sally, Larkin said, "Reece's. I'm hungry."

When they got there, he dismissed the cabbie and gave him the fare, and a fifty for a tip. The cabbie was delighted and said, "Merry Christmas. Thanks, Mister."

Larkin just nodded and waved, and the cabbie drove off. They went in and the waitress took them to a different place this time and Larkin was actually glad of that. He figured they wouldn't run into Ellie anyway, as she was probably in the Riviera already. They sat down and threw their coats in the booth with them and they ordered some coffee. The waitress left them menus and said, "Be right back."

The booth was against the window, which made it a little cooler there, but it also made for viewing people rush about in the cold, and gave them an appreciation of being out of it. Sally said to him, "What do you have planned for us this evening, besides dinner, I mean?"

"Nothing, really, and I thought we could just sit by the fire in the dining area and drink some wine. IF, I can bribe someone, that is. Think they'd mind if you bought it and shared with me?"

Sally laughed and said, "Larkin! Bribe someone? I heard they are considering bringing back the eighteen year old drinking age, but by the time they make up their minds, you'll already be twenty-one, Honey."

He shook his head and laughed as the waitress sat their coffee in front of them. She took their orders and they sat and talked. When they had finished eating lunch, he asked the waitress to call a cab for them, at which she said with a smile, "I will, Sweetie, but it'll cost ya extra." She winked and left. Sally waited a second and as the woman walked away, she broke out laughing! Larkin was embarrassed by it and he just blushed as usual. When the cab arrived and they left, he had made sure he left their waitress a nice tip.

Going back to the hotel, they went to their room to rest before dinner. Mike noticed the Kmart bag in Larkin's hand and asked him on the ride up, "Go slumming, Larkin?"

"No, I think *you* call it shopping, Mike."

Mike laughed, pointed and said, "Touché', Larkin."

The elevator opened and Larkin said to him as they exited, "Have a good one, Mike."

They went to their room and settled in. Sally wanted to take a nap, so she got undressed put on her robe and lay on the bed. He went over to her and gave her a kiss, placing his hand just a little too close to her breast. At least a little too close for his comfort, but that too, was part of his plan. He could tell that this was working, so he stopped and said, "Sweet dreams. I'll wake you early enough to get ready for dinner."

Somewhat flustered she replied, "Okay, Honey."

Larkin walked over to where he put down his Kmart bag and getting out his new pants, tried to find a way to duplicate the cut on the pair he already had, and after a couple of minutes of frustration, he got them out of the drawer to compare. He couldn't believe how ratty they were looking! Sally watched him from the bed, falling in and out of sleep as he tried to accomplish the task. He took out his pocket knife, which he had placed in the pair of jeans on purpose just for this operation and started to cut away. Where was Stephen when you needed him?

When Larkin finished with the alterations, he thought how it was a shame that he had to do that to a couple of pairs of brand new jeans. Maybe he really *was* more suited for shopping at Kmart? He took them and put them in the drawer and in so doing, noticed the closet door was slightly ajar. He knew he had closed it when they unpacked, so he looked inside. His tux was hanging there! He looked at the leg and saw that it, too, had been modified to fit the cast. He hung it to the back, so that he wouldn't have to answer any premature questions and even if he did, he'd just tell Sally the Shipley's sent it over, as the Christmas affair was to be black tie. He knew she was already prepared, because her Christmas Day dress was hanging there.

He walked over and looked at her sleeping so peacefully, and wanted to join her on the bed, but he was going to have to stay in his suit all day and this evening, so he didn't want to get undressed and then have to put it back on. As a result, he walked out of the bedroom, closed the door and sat in the chair in front of the TV. He turned it on low with the remote and fell asleep in the chair.

He woke to the ABC news with Harry Reasoner. Pulling out his watch he looked at the time, hoping he hadn't slept too long. He had made a reservation for 7 P.M., but it was only six. Going to wake Sally, he turned the light in the bathroom on so as to wake her slowly. He went to kiss her and she woke, and taking his hand, he placed it where he had it before. She would have had him keep going, but he broke her kiss and said, "I told you I'd wake you in time to dress. I want the best looking girl in the place on my arm tonight."

She smiled at him and said so very properly, "And you shall, Mr. Palmer. You shall."

She jumped up, ran into the bathroom and turned on the shower. She took off her robe in front of the door and never looked to see if he was looking, but he knew she knew he was. He wondered where she got all of her energy. He went over, closed the door for her and turned on the light in the bedroom. Then he went back to the living room to wait and closed the bedroom door. He watched an episode of "All in the Family" while he waited. He liked the character of Archie and thought the way they portrayed Edith was demeaning, but he supposed that was what they wanted him to think. He particularly disliked the character of Michael, who, although intelligent, he thought was an idiot for his rebellious and truly uninformed ways.

Sally came out about five minutes before they should go down to the restaurant. When she opened the door, he saw the most beautiful woman he had ever seen. Dressed in a black evening gown, her sleek hair covering the low cut neckline, she was, indeed, what she said she would be- the best! For a brief moment, he stood looking at her and then finally, came over to her and took her arm as she waited by the door. No words were said as they left. None needed to be.

Gracefully, they walked down the hall and got on the elevator and then, she finally spoke. "Did you say the lobster was good here, Honey?"

"Oh yes! It is great! I had it the last time here and Mr. Shipley even paid for it."

"Really? You had dinner here with the Shipleys?"

"Oh yeah. That was before you really knew me. But yeah, I know that's what I'm going to have."

"Well, maybe that's what I'll do, too."

They got out of the elevator and went toward the dining room arm in arm. The fireplace next to the entrance was blazing and the couch in front of it was occupied by two little old ladies that Larkin nodded to as they walked past. He could tell they were speaking of them as one of the ladies pointed ay Sally and placed her hand in front of her mouth leaning to her companion and whispering something to her. They went to be seated and were met by Sam who smiled upon seeing the beautiful Sally on Larkin's arm. He welcomed them saying, "I saw you'd be dining with us again, Mr. Palmer. It is good to see you. Do you have a table preference?"

"Nice to see you, too, Sam. Could we have Gotti's table again?"

"Yes, Sir. Follow me." Sally looked at Larkin funny after that request, but she figured she could ask him about it.

Sam led them to the back and pulled the closest chair out for Sally. She sat and as Larkin sat down Sam said to them, "I must inform you that your meal has all been arranged and paid by the Shipley's this evening. They hope you both enjoy it."

Astonished Larkin replied, "I'm sure we will Sam, but could we ask what our entre' will be?"

"They know your love of lobster, Sir."

They smiled and Larkin said, "Thank you, Sam."

As Sam walked away, Sally said, "That is so sweet of them. They are the nicest people and I sure will miss working with Mr. Shipley. He's taught me so much."

"I know and I already do. It has been strange not working in B-102!"

They both laughed at that and Sam brought out a bottle of champagne. It was the best of the house. He opened it and had Larkin taste it. Larkin nodded his approval and Sam left them. Sally picked up her glass and said as a toast, "Here's to free wine!"

Larkin raised his in affirmation and said, "To free wine!"

Sally said softly, "Little did we know your wish would be granted and you didn't even have to bribe someone." She giggled and asked softly, "So, tell me about "Gotti's" table?"

"Oh, yeah. I guess that he likes this table when he comes to town, because he can sit here in the corner and see everything that goes on and no one can come in from behind. I thought about that the last time and observed he might be trapped back here that way though. I guess he could always shoot his way out!"

"I guess," she replied giggling and taking a sip of her champagne.

Sam brought their soup; it was bisque. They took the time to pray and to them, they felt like everyone was watching their display of faith. They didn't care either way, because the people either thought it refreshing or offensive. All they knew was that for them to skip it, would be unnatural.

The soup, salad, and rolls were good, but Larkin, after two glasses of champagne, was ready for the lobster. In between courses they had talked leisurely, but it was time to get down to business.
He had an immense appetite that evening. He finished his sixteen-ounce lobster and when Sally couldn't finish hers, he ate it as well. He sat back after that and Sam said as he took their plates, "We have baked Alaska for dessert, Sir."

Sally waived it off, but Larkin said, "Bring one, Sam, we'll share."

Sally's eyes got wide and she said, "I wondered how the "bubbly" would affect you. Lots of people get drunk real fast on it, but you just get hungry!"

"Can we take the rest with us?"

"Oh, I think he may let us," she whispered smiling.

Sally moved over next to Larkin when Sam brought the dessert. She took a couple of bites, and she was just too full to continue, but Larkin polished it off easily. They sat there for a few minutes. He put a tip for Sam on the table. Then Larkin stood, picked up the two wine glasses and pulled the rest of the bubbly out of the ice bucket as he passed by. The couch by the fire was vacant now, so he led Sally there and motioned for her to sit. He gave her the wine glass and he poured her another. Doing the same for himself, he took a seat next to her. They each took a sip and sat their glasses down on the table in front of them. Taking his arm and putting it around her, she nuzzled her head into him and they sat silently watching the flames dance from log to log. After a bit, the night doorman came and placed another log on the fire. They were glad no one else had come by to try to sit there, or at least they had not seen that to be the case, but if it had, they would have most likely left the lovebirds alone to while away the night.

Sally began to get sleepy, the affects of the champagne most likely, and he said, "Let's go up to bed, Dear." She didn't respond, but merely yawned as she got up and took his arm to walk to the elevator. When they got to the room, she kissed him inside the doorway before he closed it and the neighbors saw them in each other's arms. The older couple paused to observe them, and smiled as they moved on toward the elevator. Ah; young love.

Sally went to the bedroom and began to change. Larkin checked his wallet to see how much money he still had with him, as the day had lent for many opportunities to spend. He was still okay, but he'd brought both his checkbooks with him, which brought to mind something he wanted to talk to Sally about.

She was in the bathroom in her robe brushing her teeth. He walked in and said, "I forgot to tell you what I thought I'd do with my old checking account, Dear."

She finished brushing, bent over the sink and spit, then asked, "What's that, Honey?"

"I think I'm going to just make it our household account and add your name to it. You can pay the bills and use it for groceries and the like. Then after a while I'll withdraw some of the interest in the others and put some in it. We should be fine that way."

"That's a good idea. Now come to bed."

She lay down on her bed and watched Larkin get undressed. He hung up his suit and walked into the bathroom in his underwear to take a leak and brush his teeth. She followed his every move as he went and when he came back he switched off the lights leaving it pitch black in the room. He didn't bother with PJ's and got into his own bed. She took off her robe and got into her bed naked, which Larkin couldn't see and didn't know. He asked, "Pray with me, Dear?"

"Go ahead, Honey."

"Lord we thank you for this day and the beauty of it all. We appreciate fully your care in our lives, the burdens you give and the opportunity to serve and do your will in it. Now Lord we ask you to keep all evil from us and protect us from all sin, for we know we are sinners in need. Thank you for your mercy. Amen"

"Goodnight, Dear."

"Goodnight, Honey."

The next morning Larkin got up before she woke and she lay there sleeping, covers partially fallen to the side. Her body lay exposed and he was surprised to see her sleeping naked. He went over to her bed, covered her and proceeded to the bathroom. He took a shower and when he came out he walked to the closet wrapped in a towel. She woke and came over to him without her robe. He saw her and pulled her to him kissing her as he had the other day, from deep within him. She tensed and wanted more, but he pulled her away and said to her, "Aren't you cold?" She didn't answer, but just looked at him with wanton eyes. From her skin he knew she was cold- goose bumps all over. He led her to her robe and placed it on her. Deep inside he knew she wanted to be led somewhere else, but he continued to wet her appetite and plan for later.

Somewhat disappointed, she walked into the bathroom and slowly closed the door trying to understand what just had happened. When she got in there and took off her robe, she thought to herself, 'What is he doing? Why is he tempting me like this if he's not going to deliver?' She opened the shower door, got in and stood there for a long time thinking, and praying that God would somehow help them. Then it hit her- they could get married! She hurried to finish her shower and went back out to talk to Larkin, but he wasn't there. Shoot! Where was he? Stuck on the door was a note saying, "Went down to get us some coffee. Be right back."

While he was gone, she got into some casual clothes for that Saturday. She remembered she should call Mrs. Heidelmann about church, so she picked up the phone and called her. Sally set up the time for Sunday morning, but asked what time the Christmas Eve and Christmas Day services were. Sally said, "We'll be at church in the morning as normal, but I think we'll go to the midnight candlelight service. I doubt we'll come on Christmas Day due to our commitments, Mrs. Heidelmann."

"Oh that's fine Sally. I'm getting too old to go to the candlelight service, but I'll tell you, it is just beautiful."

Just then Larkin walked in with their coffee. He sat it down as she finished her conversation with Mrs. Heidelmann.

He asked, "Who were you talking to?"

"It was Mrs. Heidelmann. I just set up times for us to go to church with her. Say Honey, I've got something I want to talk to you about and consider."

Larkin picked up his coffee and took a sip. Sally did the same and she continued with what she was saying.

"I was thinking. We have a license. We have no reason not to do it, so why don't we just get married? We don't have to wait. It doesn't have to be a fancy wedding in the church or in June or anything like that."

"You mean just go back to the Judge?"

"Yes."

Larkin now knew he'd been driving her as crazy as she had him, but he stuck with the plan, because it was just too close now. "You don't want to have your family or my mom and dad there?"

"Not if it means waiting one more day. No. I just can't wait anymore."

He paused as if to think about it. "Okay, Sally. We'll do it next week after Christmas before we go back to the house. We wouldn't be able to arrange anything before then anyway."

She was ecstatic! She jumped up into his arms and gave him a big kiss saying, "Oh thank you, Honey!"

'Boy,' he thought, 'is she ever going to be surprised.'

He let her down and gave her a kiss. She wanted more, but he said, "Dear, we've made it this far, we can make it a few more days. Be patient, it will be worth it."

She looked into his eyes trustingly and said, "I know. But it's so hard."

"It is hard. So we need to direct our focus somewhere else. I was going to surprise you but, guess what I have planned for tonight?"

She got excited again and asked, "What?"

"I booked a private limo for us to tour the city to look at all the Christmas lights."

She began to cry again. "Oh Larkin, you are so romantic."

"I know, Dear. I know.

They went and had breakfast in the restaurant, but not wanting to make it a long drawn out affair, they just ordered toast and coffee. They needed some fresh air, so they decided to take a walk past the White House. They bundled up, said "Hello" to Chester and walked out onto 16th and over to Lafayette Square. The weather was brisk that day, and they walked quickly, just to keep warm. She took his arm and he held her close. It wasn't a gentile stroll through the park. There was no one else at all around them, and they figured most people were occupied shopping for last minute Christmas gifts.

As they walked Sally asked, "I've noticed you don't have a present along with you for me, Honey. Did you forget to get me a Christmas present?"

Larkin played it coy and said to her, "If I remember right, this stay at the Hay-Adams *was* my gift to you. Remember?"

"Oh yeah," she said disappointedly.

But just to brighten her day he added, "But, I sent your present over to the Shipley's so you could open it there."

She stopped and started to cry again and said, "Oh, Honey, you're so romantic."

He laughed and said, "You're starting to sound like a broken record, Dear. I must really be romantic."

She stopped again and kissed him saying afterwards, "Much more so than I ever imagined."

He smiled and they walked on.

They passed the White House walking through the loop. Someone was standing on the Truman Balcony and they could see him distinctly, because the noonday sun shone directly upon him. He was bent over leaning on the rail looking out past them and as they went by, they waived at him. He returned their wave in kind and they wondered if it was Carter, or just some secret service agent trying to be funny. As they walked along, a flock of birds flew overhead, their wings slapping in unison and sounding as if the cold winter air would turn their wings to ice. They swerved and swished around the trees, moving apart and coming back together again, flying as if they had purpose, but going nowhere and landing not.

They were starting to get tired and their lungs sore as they walked back up Madison to H St. When they finally got back to the hotel, Chester opened the door for them and they hustled in. Larkin looked at Sally's nose and ears and they were as red as her hair. It was a longer, colder walk than they had bargained for and they certainly had gotten their dose of fresh air! They went up to the room and took off their coats. Larkin picked up the phone and dialed room service. "This is Larkin Palmer in 319. Could you bring up a couple of hot cocoas for us? Thank you."

Sally had gone to the bathroom and she came back shivering all the way. She put her arms around him and said, I need something to warm up with."
"I just ordered some hot cocoas for us."
"That's not what I had in mind, but it will do for now." She smiled, looked up at him and kissed him. He said, "Gotta go."
She knew what he meant and let go of him.

Larkin walked toward the bathroom as someone knocked on the door. Sally went to answer it and let in the room service person. She expected a man, but it was a woman of what Sally assumed was South American decent, kind of like Pilar was. She left the tray and Sally handed her a tip. Nothing was said except a "Thank you," by Sally. Neither Sally nor Larkin thought anything of her. But, they should have.

She poured them each a cup. Larkin came out, saw the steaming hot drinks and picked up his cup. Sally came over to him and asked, "What do you want to do until the tour tonight, Honey?"
Before taking a sip, he blew on the chocolate concoction and said, "Let's take a nap."
"I could go for that."

He took her cup from her hand and placed the both of them on the cart. Taking her by the hand, he led her to the love seat by the TV and turned it on. They sat as usual in front of the tube and watched until they fell asleep.

The phone rang and Larkin got up groggily to answer it. "Larkin, this is Chester. Your ride is here."

"Oh my," he said, "we'll be right down Chester." He hung up the phone and said to Sally, "Wake up, Sally, we overslept!"

She roused and said, "What? OH!"

She jumped up and they put on their coats and gloves walking quickly to the elevator. He said, as they walked "What are we doing? You know, we really don't have to rush, we have it for three hours- *alone*." They got in the elevator and when they came out they walked arm in arm, just a little more relaxed than when they left their room. Chester greeted them at the door and opened the limo for Sally. She got in and then Larkin and he mouthed a "thank you" to Chester who tipped his hat to him.

The ride around town was well planned by the tour guide. He was an older man, named Gerry, and he said he'd been doing this for thirty-five years now, starting in 1943 to make some extra money driving in his personal car. He said, "Those were the good old days before all the cabbie and limo regulations. They try to control everything nowadays." He explained each and every exhibit they went past, how many years the people had had it up and how many lights they contained. He was a very knowledgeable and interesting fellow, and they had a great time. He even had some finger food and a bottle of wine for them to share and Sally opened it. It was a German wine called Liebfraumilch, which Sally said she had seen while in Germany. They drank a glass each, but that was enough as they wanted to be able to get up and go to worship without trouble in the morning. It was a night of peace, lights, and love for the two and they vowed to do it every year. Gerry finally let them out about a half hour later than they expected and thanked him for all of it. Larkin gave him the fee and the same amount for a tip saying, "Blessings on your Christmas. See you next year." When Gerry saw the tip he said, "I'll call you *first*, Larkin. Merry Christmas!"

Chester opened the door for them and Larkin handed him a twenty saying, "Thanks for arranging that for us. Do it again next year would you?"

"Will do, Larkin."

They went up to their room and got ready for bed. Larkin put his PJ's on and went out and turned on the TV. Channel four had an episode of "Hee Haw" on which Larkin thought was a hoot. He really liked the person of "Grandpa" who he thought would fit in just about anywhere.

Sally came out from the bedroom in her robe and said, "What ya watching?"

"Hee Haw".

She sat next to him for a minute and when it went off he said, "I think it would be better to sleep in bed than on this love seat again don't you?"

"Yup. Let's go."

They turned off the tube and walked slowly into the bedroom, getting into their own beds. Sally seemed to be content with his plan to marry next week and it had helped cool the embers, so to speak. He was grateful to God for that, but Larkin wondered why God placed such a drive in the human spirit. Was God afraid the world would never be populated if He had not given us a sex drive? He'd think on that. They prayed and went to sleep.

In the morning the wakeup call came on time, which Larkin requested due to the evening before. He didn't want to be late for church. He kissed her good morning as she lay there and he went to the bathroom first. As he finished she came in and sat down as he turned out of the way. He began to shave and watched her in the mirror as she got ready. Her movements contained no waste and it seemed she had the process down to an art form.

They were ready a little before schedule and decided they had time to eat first. Larkin called Chester to have the car brought around. They went downstairs after Sally straightened Larkin's tie. She said, "I wish I'd have bought you a tie for Christmas. Where did you get this at Woolworth's or something?" He didn't say a word but thought, 'Or something!'

They placed their orders and Larkin sneezed. Sally said, "I hope you didn't catch a cold from all that fresh air we got yesterday."

"Frische luft ist gesund, nichtwahr?" he replied.

Sally took a sip of her coffee and said, "It's supposed to be, but I think it only applies in Germany today."

They ate quickly and headed to the door where the car was waiting and all warmed up! They climbed in and headed to Mount Olivet Lutheran.

Larkin was looking forward to asking Pastor Olsen about new member classes and about doctrine. Sally was anxious about it as well. They parked, went in and walked into the narthex which was decorated for Christmas. Mrs. Heidelmann was there waiting for them as always and she wished them a Merry Christmas to which they replied in kind. They went into the sanctuary and were in awe at the way the chancel area was arrayed, with trees that seemed to reach up to the sky, decorated in hundreds of white lights which proclaimed the birth of the Light of Heaven. Sitting in their usual place, Pastor Olsen came out to welcome the congregation to worship. It was a special order of service that day with no communion and had special music featuring the bell choir and the mass choir. The service focused on Jesus the light of the World and Pastor Olsen's message was inspiring in that he urged all to proclaim Christ crucified sent as a child to bring light to the message of hope. Even the man in the blue suit was touched by the message.

All in all, the service lifted them up and gave them peace knowing Christ came for them, even though they knew they were still sinners. The whole of it brought tears to Sally's eyes and a smile to Larkin's face. The recessional music boomed out by the pipe organ was joyful and the Christmas spirit was in them all. As the congregation walked out they spoke together in happy voices, smiling and shaking hands with everyone wishing them a Merry Christmas. As they got to Pastor Olsen, Larkin shook his hand and told him for both of them that they wanted to join the next new member class and they had lots of questions.

He asked if they'd be joining them for Christmas services, which Larkin thought was a good smoke screen, and Larkin told him they'd be there at candlelight service that night because they had a commitment the next day. Sally overheard this all and Larkin was convinced she was still in the dark about his plans.

They said goodbye to Mrs. Heidelmann and wished her a Merry Christmas. They told her they would come by in the next day or two to bring by a special gift for her. She said to call first and she'd be happy to see them because she missed Sally, and Sally cried as she gave the woman a hug goodbye. Larkin watched Sally as she talked to the aging woman and was proud of his soon to be wife. She was a lovely woman of good heart and soul, always prepared to do good for others, caring, and sweet. He felt so blessed. They got in the car and Larkin said, "It's time to do some shopping, and then we have some stops to make."

Sally said, "I'm along for the ride, Honey. Lead on!"

Larkin drove them over to the local Rescue Mission and they went into the hall. He saw many men sitting inside out of the cold weather. Walking toward the office, an older man in a suit came up to Larkin and said, "You look like you need to see someone young man. Can I help you with something?" His name tag read, "Pastor Wells".

Larkin replied, "What is your greatest need at the mission here this month, Pastor?"

"I guess it would be food and heat bills; like always. Why?"

"How much would cover it?"

"About ten thousand, I guess."

Wells motioned for them to follow him and when they went in his office, he offered them a seat. Larkin said, "Although I have my own cross to carry in this life, Pastor, the Lord has always been by my side blessing me. This year he has blessed me in so many new and special ways," he took Sally's hand and continued, "but He has especially blessed me financially." He took out his check book and wrote a check for the amount and handed it to Pastor Wells, who like Sally, began to cry.

"I've been praying that God would provide a miracle this year. Things have been way down due to the Carter recession. You," he looked at the name on the check, "Larkin, are our miracle this year. Thank you so much."

Larkin nodded at him, stood up and started out. As they went toward the door Larkin stopped to talk to a couple of the men, wishing them a Merry Christmas and telling them the Savior had come for them, not just 2000 years ago, but today. Pastor Wells shook his hand and they left. Sally took his hand as they walked and she said to him, "I love you, Honey."

"I love you, too, Dear."

When they got in the car she asked, "Where to next?"

"A store. Where's the closest department store?"

"Penny's. Go straight and left at the first light."

She led him to Penny's and they had to park way at the end of the lot. She asked, "What do you have in mind, Larkin?"

As they walked in he said, "Well, this first." He dropped a hundred into the pot at the Salvation Army ringer and Larkin said to him, "Merry Christmas!"

"Thank you, Sir, and God bless you!"

To which Larkin replied, "He has my friend and He does."

They walked in and Larkin said, "We need that present for Mrs. Heidelmann, one for Harry, and one for the Shipley's. And don't forget the kids! Go for it girl!"

She saluted him and said, "Yes, Sir! I'm on it. Just follow and watch the master." She paused and asked, "How much?"

"No limit."

"Well, that makes it easy."

Larkin knew she might have an idea what each could use and he, of course, did not. He may as well abdicate the role of "shopper" to her in this case and get the job done. He followed along and watched as she grabbed this and that. They took it all to have it wrapped and all he had to do is write the check. He got by for less than a thousand dollars, thinking he should have possibly set a limit after all. They put it all in bags and headed out. It was an eventful day and a show of the love of God, not only to the world, but to each other.

They went back to the hotel and left all the gifts in the trunk until they were to go to the Shipley's. They were supposed to go and pick up Harry on the way the next day, but they wondered what he was doing that night. Larkin asked Sally, "I wonder what Harry is doing tonight? Do you think he'd want to go to church with us at midnight?"

"Oh. I don't know Larkin. That's kind of late. You know how he falls asleep so early."

"Yeah. I guess so. He might not be able to get up early enough to go with us to the Shipley's." So they dropped the thought and decided to go alone. It didn't matter, because Harry wasn't alone.

They changed clothes and went down to the restaurant for dinner. All Larkin had ever eaten there was seafood, so tonight he wanted to have a steak. After they were seated, he asked Sam what the best cut of beef was there. Sam said, "Try the filet, Larkin. It's the best."

It was the first time he'd called him Larkin and he took notice and replied, "Thank you, Sam. Would you bring me a good white wine? You choose."

Sam was pleased that Larkin trusted him enough to do this so he said delightedly, "I shall, Larkin. But you know white should not go with red meat." He winked at Sally and left them.

Sally had chosen the prime rib and sat her menu down. Sam brought the wine, took their orders and left them alone. Larkin tried it and said he liked it a lot. Sally said she liked the wine they had in the limo better. They were starting to now have opinions on wine! Larkin said, "Since when are we wine experts?" He cupped his hand by his mouth and said softly toward her, "I'm just glad they are serving me." They laughed about it and he said, "Well, maybe someday I'll be a "legal" wine expert. All it takes is practice, I guess."

Sally laughed again and said, "We'll just have to practice then. I'm looking forward to tonight and tomorrow at the Shipley's. This has been a very nice weekend."

"I'm glad we decided to do this. It *has* been very nice."

Sam brought their salads and they began to eat. They talked and ate slowly, knowing they had plenty of time before church. Besides, they had nothing else to do but be with each other and that was the reason they were there. Larkin thanked Sam for the suggestions for their meal as they stood to leave. He had paid him already, but had not given him the tip, for which Sam was waiting. Larkin knew it and was just playing with him, so he put his hand in his pocket and took out a hundred and handed it to him. Sam's eyes lit up and he said to Larkin, "You are most generous, Sir. Thank you and Merry Christmas."

"Same to you, Sam."

Sam bowed slightly and went toward the kitchen.

It was only nine o'clock and as they strolled past the fireplace it was occupied by an older couple holding hands much like they had there the night before. Sally asked him, "Is that what we look like, Honey?"

He noticed how they looked at each other, like they were made for each other. He replied, "I'd like to think so. Only we're younger. Wait a minute. Is that Rudy Vallee?"

"Naw. Couldn't be. Could it?"

It was.

She smiled at him and put her head next to his arm as they continued to their room. Again she looked at the decorations, pointed out this and that to Larkin and saying she'd like to do that at their house. She started to cry again, stopping as they walked into the foyer under the chandelier and Larkin asked her what was wrong. She said, "Larkin, I'm so happy. God has truly blessed me and I'm so grateful to Him for sending me you."

He was so proud and happy with her, and he took her in his arms and held her tight. Neither of them would have given up that moment for anything. Finally, after what seemed like an eternity, he said to her, "I can't think of why He would take away and give to me as He has this year. But this I do know, I love you with all my heart and soul, and for this, I am grateful." He bent over to kiss her as tears of joy streamed down her face. She smiled as he kissed her softly and they turned to go upstairs and change for church.

Larkin turned on the TV when they went into the room and the weather man was saying how cold it would be that night. It was going to be cold for sure, but there would be some snow on Christmas Day. Sally went to the closet and took out her dress and looked through the closet to prepare for the morning when she saw the tux. She wondered why and how, and called out to Larkin, "Larkin, what's this tux doing in the closet?"

He thought, 'Oh oh.' He went into the bedroom to explain.

"Oh, the Shipley's sent that over the other day and I forgot to tell you. It seems tomorrow will be a black tie affair."

"Fancy Christmas, huh?"

"It seems. But what does it matter? Look. They even had it tailored to fit my cast. Isn't that something?"

"Wow. I should still be fine with the dress I have. It's actually the nicest one I own."

Larkin knew the dress and he said, "You'll be beautiful." He pulled her to him and gave her a kiss.

She pulled away and said, "Let me get dressed now so we won't be late. We better get there at least fifteen minutes early. They say this is the best attended candlelight service in D.C., because of the children's choir. It's supposed to be fantastic."

"Well then, no dilly dallying. Let's get moving."

He was glad she believed his story, which was really stretching the truth, but to some degree was still the truth. He thought God and Sally would forgive him in the morning- maybe even now.

He called down to have the car brought around and told the night doorman they'd be down in five minutes. They finished getting ready and went down to the car. Even though Larkin didn't know the night guy, who appeared to be about twenty, he went over to him and asked him, "Say, what's your name?"

"Sid," he answered.

"Sid, are you Jewish?"

"Yeah, why?"

"Would you be offended if I told you Merry Christmas?"

"No Sir, I hear it all the time."

"But do you know what it means?"

"Not really. The rabbis just say he was a good guy."

"I tell you what Sid, I don't know much about Judaism and you don't know much about Christ, the Messiah, who was a Jew. How about if we sit down one day and tell each other about each other?"

"That would be cool. Where do you live?"

"On Ridge."

"Hey, that's only four blocks from me."

"Give me your number and I'll call you next week."

He wrote it down and gave it to Larkin. He put it in his pocket and said, "Here's a tip for you, Sid." He handed him a twenty and said, "Happy Hanukkah and Merry Christmas."

"Thanks, Sir."

"It's Larkin, Sid."

Sally watched this whole thing happen. She got in the car with him and as they started off she said, "That was amazing how you witnessed to him, Larkin."

"It's what Pastor Olsen told us to do today, Sally."

"Yeah. You're right."

She thought about that the rest of the way to church. She remembered how the Bible said we should be doers of the word and not merely listeners. The events of that day were Larkin's way of showing her how he was a doer. She was learning to respect him as the leader and as her- man.

They arrived early, but had trouble finding a place to park. Sally was afraid they wouldn't get a seat, so she made him almost run to the church. His cast wasn't cooperating well with that tonight for some reason. He laughed as he thought to himself, 'It probably needs another paint job.' The usher gave them each a candle in a holder along with the bulletin. They found a seat about half way up on the same side as usual. The place was as packed as Sally knew it would be. The organ started to play pre-service music. The sanctuary was filled with electricity tonight, but as the service began, the lights were lowered.

The children led the service off by singing, "Liesel Reiselt Der Schnee." Larkin knew it wasn't really a hymn usually sung in churches, but he figured Pastor Olsen knew most of his parishioners wouldn't know the difference. These youngsters did such a wonderful job in the a cappella song, that the people wanted to cheer, but it was not the practice to applaud in this church, much less at this type of service, and it was to be a holy thing, done to worship the Lord.

The order of service was printed for them to follow and the children did much of the singing. They had their own bell choir as well and it sounded as if the bells of heaven peeled out their voices in the praise of the newborn King! The final hymn was Silent Night. It was *always* that hymn. The children sang the first two verses in German and the congregation joined in at the last in English. As they began to sing, the usher took a flame from the candle in front and passed it through the congregation, and by the time they had sung the last verse, the place was ablaze with light! It was a sight to behold. And then, when had they finished; complete silence. They filed out that way, lost in the serenity of God for that one moment.

Once outside, the cold brought them back to reality, and they hustled out to the car and hopped into the frosty, frozen Lincoln. The leather seat cracked from the cold and Sally said, "It's freezing on my butt. Turn on the heat."
He replied, "You don't get instant heat!" He started it up and they drove to the Hay-Adams on the deserted wintery D.C. streets. They could hear the tires in every turn as the cold hard rubber crunched on the pavement. They pulled in and Sid came out to take the car from them.

He said goodnight to them as they ran into the hotel. Larkin waved back, glad to get inside.

They were tired, but Larkin didn't think he'd sleep that night before Christmas... They went up to the room and he tucked Sally in. She too, was beat, and she wanted to get to sleep so she could get up in the morning. He did too. They kissed, thanked God together, and lay down. Sally slept. Larkin laid there too excited to sleep.

In the morning, Sally woke up first and came over to Larkin's bed. She crawled up beside him and kissed him. He woke and she said, "Merry Christmas, Honey!"
"Merry Christmas, Sally."
"Time to get up, Sleepy Head."

She patted him on the head and she went into the bathroom to get ready. She went first, because she just plain took longer. Larkin had to pee, so he went in after she got into the shower. She heard him come in and she said, "Don't flush; it may take the water."
He yelled back, "Okay, I won't."
He peeked as he went by, she was beautiful. But, he had to wait. It was so steamy in there he had to get out. In more ways than one! Whew! Why did she use so much hot water?

It was his turn in a few minutes and she came out, preparing to lay out her clothes. She wanted to be all prepared. They still had a couple hours to be there, but she was nervous. She didn't know how nervous Larkin was in the next room. He couldn't think. He was tired. He was panicked all his plans wouldn't come off. Trying to calm down, Larkin said a prayer and left it all to the Lord to handle. He'd done everything that *he* could.

When he had shaved and come out, Larkin called down to Chester to have him pull the car around. Sally was still putting on her makeup. She was almost done, but had run out of something. It was no problem she said, but Larkin could tell she was a little miffed at herself. They both began to dress and she asked him to zip her up. When Larkin got the tux on, he asked her to tie his tie, because he had never done one like it before. They both walked over to the mirror and looked at themselves, then at each other. They smiled. It was time to go pick up Harry!

Chester had the car ready and waiting for them, and Larkin felt bad Chester had to work on Christmas Day. Larkin gave him a hundred bucks and told him, "Merry Christmas."
"Thanks, Larkin. Nice tux."

The two lovebirds drove over towards Harry's house. The sun shone brightly and the steam from the vents on the roofs of the houses billowed up off of them. As the night before, there was no one out on the roads but them. They pulled up to the front and Harry saw them from his window. Harry wouldn't miss this for the world! Larkin left Sally in the car with the engine running and he went up to help Harry with some gifts he had. He took them from him and put them in the trunk with theirs. By that time, Harry had made it down the stairs and over to the car. Larkin opened the back door for him and he said, "Thanks, Larkin. Hello, Sally. Merry Christmas!"

Sally turned in her seat and said, "Merry Christmas, Harry!"

Larkin got in and they headed to the bosses house. At this point, it seemed more like a work Christmas party to them and probably more so to Sally, who had no idea of her fate that Christmas Day in Washington, D.C.!

When they pulled up to the door there were four or five cars there already. Sally said, "I wonder who all the cars belong to? I didn't think anyone but us was coming for this." Larkin smiled. They got out and went to the trunk to get all of the presents. Putting them all in their arms, they went to the door. Sally rang the bell and instead of their maid answering, Mrs. Shipley herself came to greet them. She said, "Hello everyone; Merry Christmas." She came to Sally to hug her and Sally went and placed her cheek to hers. The maid came and took her packages and Sally began to take off her coat revealing the beautiful dress she wore. Larkin and Harry had come in and put their gifts on the floor of the foyer. They gave their coats to the maid as well and Mrs. Shipley said to them, "Please follow me to the ballroom. We've set up in there."

Sally gawked as she followed her in, amazed at the extravagant decorations in the Shipley home. As they walked into the ballroom, there sat Sally's mother and dad, as well as Larkin's parents. Sally's mouth flew open in surprise and she said, "Mom and Dad! Oh, Larkin." She assumed he had brought them there for Christmas and it was a surprise for her. She was, in part, correct.

They all called out, "Merry Christmas!"

She went over to Larkin, gave him a kiss as she began to cry and said, "Thanks, Honey."

They all began to talk and no one was to say a thing about it, the wedding that is, until she opened her gift. They all sat down by the tree taking places by her parents, and sitting by the fireplace, which was burning cedar logs. Everyone had arrived, so Mr. Shipley had the girls distribute the presents to each person. Of course, the little Shipley girls opened their gifts first and then went off to play in another room with their nanny. The adults began to open their gifts and when it came around to Sally, she picked up the largest package, which was from Larkin, of course. She read the tag and said, "Thank you, Honey", in advance of opening it. As she pulled the tissue back and saw the dress she knew what it was. She sobbed with her hand in front of her mouth. Then Pastor Olsen came in the room, he having just finished the Christmas Day service. She waived for Larkin to come to her and she asked, "Is this for," she gulped as she cried and tried to contain herself, "today?" Larkin shook his head "yes."

She put the dress box down, rose to her feet, walked slowly over to him and put her arms around him. Smiling she said, "There will never be another as romantic as you." She kissed him and they all clapped and cheered.

Kidding, Larkin put up his hand and said, "Please hold the applause until she changes and we get married." They laughed.

She picked up the box and the wedding planner appeared at the back of the room. Larkin motioned for Sally to go with her. She showed her to the changing room and told Sally the plan. It was then Sally realized how much had gone into this scheme of his and what he had done. She began to cry again. The wedding planner said, "He told me you cry a lot." She handed her some tissue and kept helping her with the dress.

In the mean while, the group all went to another room where a setting was placed for the wedding. The seats were all set out, the isle lined with poinsettias, with white bows on the chairs, and an organist played music as they waited for Sally. Larkin was elated and happy it had gone the way he had planned so far. 'Why wouldn't it?' he thought, 'I gave it to the Lord.' He went up to Pastor Olsen and he said to him, "I told you so."

"You didn't need to Larkin, I knew. I could see in her eyes how much she loves you."

The wedding planner came and told him she was almost ready and gave him the bill. It was twenty-five thousand dollars, but Larkin was pleased and wrote the check. He also wrote another to Mount Olivet Lutheran Church. He handed them both to her and asked, "Would you give this one to Pastor Olsen after we leave?"

"Sure", she said smiling.

"Merry Christmas and thanks."

They got the signal that she was ready and the men walked up to the front. Harry was to act as the Best Man. Mrs. Shipley was the Matron of Honor. The music started and the three Shipley girls dropped petals of roses along the isle to the front, which was short, because there were but three sets of four seats. Her dad gave her away and Harry handed him the ring he took off of Sally's finger before she went to change. He also gave him a ring the wedding planner had purchased for Larkin. Mrs. Shipley took a seat and Pastor Olsen began.

He followed the Order of Holy Matrimony of the Lutheran church. He did all of the things Larkin expected, all of them, "I do's" and "I wills". In time, Olsen came to the ring and this part hit them both the most. Pastor Olsen chose a version that many pastors don't when they ask them to "repeat this after me". He started with Sally who repeated his words, "Larkin, with this ring I marry you, my worldly goods I give to you, and with my body, I honor you." She began to cry as she finished, "In the name of the Father, and the Son, and the Holy Spirit. Amen." She placed the ring on his finger. He had Larkin repeat the same thing to Sally. When he finished he placed his Grandma Mary's ring back on her finger.

Pastor Olsen asked them to kneel on the cushion in front of them. He said, "Now that Sally and Larkin have committed themselves to each other in holy matrimony, have given themselves to each other by their solemn pledges, and have declared the same before God and these witnesses, I pronounce them to be husband and wife, in the name of the Father and of the Son and of the Holy Spirit. Amen. What God has joined let no man put asunder. Amen."

They stood and the pastor said, "Ladies and gentlemen. I introduce, Mr. and Mrs. Larkin Palmer. Larkin, you may kiss the bride!" Of course, he did what Pastor Olsen told him to do!

Everyone clapped and cheered, the family, Mrs. Heidelmann, Harry, some of Sally's friends from work, and even the Shipley's staff had come into the hall and they, too, joined in the congratulations. The music played and they walked toward the door. The photographer, a man the Shipleys knew, took pictures faster than a loose Japanese tourist!

The wedding planner had them come to the side of the hall where they cut the one tier cake and let the people get pictures of them as Sally shoved her piece into Larkin's mouth so hard he almost choked on it! She giggled, and he just let it go, not wanting to get even on this one and he just placed a piece in her mouth very gently and tenderly. The photographer got all the pictures they had asked for and then they were ready to leave. The guests were to remain, as Larkin's planner had arranged a meal there for them, compliments of Julia Childs.

They shook everyone's hand, Sally cried and hugged both sets of parents and the girls gave everyone some little bags of bird seed to throw after they got outside to leave. Sally took Larkin's' hand to go out and the folks followed along throwing the bird seed until they got to the limo the planner rented for them. Getting into the car, Sally waved at their parents and smiled from ear to ear. Larkin did the same. The driver pulled out and headed toward the hotel. Sally cried the whole way back and held Larkin in her arms. She was so happy! As there was no train of cars behind them, the driver didn't honk the horn. Besides, there was no one on the streets of D.C. on Christmas Day; except that one other car.

The limo drove into the driveway of the Hay-Adams. Chester opened the door for them in shock as Larkin had told no one there of his plan. He said to them, "Congratulations, Mr. and Mrs. Palmer."
Sally gave him a peck on the cheek and said, "Thanks, Chester." Chester didn't wipe it off and he smiled.

Taking Larkin by the hand, Sally and her new husband walked triumphantly to the elevator. Guests came up to them and congratulated them while also wishing them a Merry Christmas. The ride up to the third floor was an eternity and Larkin could sense that ever present reality in their lives begin to flame up in his wife; not to mention himself.

When they arrived at their floor, as she already had him by the hand, she led him down the hall at a crisp, but respectful walk. Larkin opened the door and picked her up to cross the threshold. The dress got in the way and she laughed at how he had to maneuver her into the room; first to the side and then a back and forth swing. Finally, he succeeded and dropped her to her feet. She landed in front of him and he closed the door with a kick of his foot. Taking off her veil, he dropped it behind him on the floor. The rest of her clothes went straight to the same destination. She helped him with his tie and then the rest. Taking his hand, his wife led him to his bed. There, happiness was found in each other's arms. As usual, Larkin slowed Sally down. This inexperienced farm boy made it, this once in a lifetime experience, soft, slow, and tender. It was something they would remember the rest of their lives, because it was worth the wait. They lay in each other's arms the rest of the afternoon, sometimes asleep, sometimes- not. Sally didn't ask about how he had pulled off the wedding that day yet, but threw her being into what she had waited for. Finally, when they were finished, they fell to sleep.

The next morning, Larkin received a million questions from his new wife as he stood in the bathroom. First, she wanted to know if all the parents went home, because she wanted to see them.

Secondly, she had to know about the surprises and all the details. Last of all, she wondered about the honeymoon.

He wondered why that was the last thing she asked about. "Oh-the *Honeymoon*! We leave on Friday; for Hawaii," said Larkin, smiling.

"Hawaii!" she screamed in delight.

"But, I wanted to finish out our week here first and make it as special as we thought it would be. We have to rush nowhere. We have the rest of our lives to be with each other."

She walked up to him standing by the sink and put her arms around him. She was content. She told him it didn't matter there weren't hundreds of guests, or all of the things associated with a big church wedding. The only important guest was the Lord and He was truly there. She was content.

They dialed up room service and spent the rest of the day in the room doing what newlyweds do. There was no one for Sally to see, because the parents had gone home.

Wednesday morning the sun was shining brightly and the weather was finally supposed to break. The arctic air had subsided and the jet stream allowed some warm Florida air to come toward the Northeast. It was supposed to be forty-five degrees that day, but Larkin didn't know whether to believe the weather guy again. It never did snow on Christmas Day! Sally wondered about all of their gifts and where the car was. Larkin told her that the wedding planner was to put everything in the Lincoln and take it to their house. But first, she wanted to give some verbal "thank you's".

Sally called Mrs. Shipley first and spoke with her for almost a half an hour. She thanked her profusely and asked that she convey the same to Mr. Shipley. Mrs. Shipley said, "Please thank your husband for the generous gifts for my daughters, they will truly appreciate going to Harvard."

Her eyes grew wide, because Sally didn't know Larkin had done that and she'd speak with him about it later. Then she called her parents and talked to them for longer than that. And last of all, she called Shirley and Lawtin, so she could speak with them. Larkin got on the extension and talked as well. They no longer spoke as much like children, but more as peers, but with caution until the newness of it all wore off. They laughed and cried as they spoke of Larkin's tactics and all the surprises he came up with to pull it off. Sally said she had been completely in the dark and never even guessed it, but she knew God wanted it to be when she wanted to get married this week as well. Shirley said, "When Larkin

told me he was going to surprise you into marrying him, I just shook my head, but then I thought, "How romantic?""
"This entire affair has been that way. He does so many little things that surprise me. You can tell he loves me."

Sally started to cry again and she set the phone down to go get a tissue. When she left Larkin changed the subject and said, "Hey Mom, how are "things" up there?"
She knew what he meant and replied, "It all seems to be fine Honey, why?"
"Oh, I had a little altercation here before the funeral, but it has worked out to our benefit like it always does, until they find another excuse. They said I have until I graduate to stay here, so we'll see." Unfortunately, Larkin's false sense of security in this had led them to be unaware of the man in the blue suit from time to time.

Sally got back on the line and said, "Where were we? Oh yeah..." She went on talking to Shirley and Larkin sat the phone on the hook and turned the TV on low. He overheard her from time to time, especially the part where she tried to whisper and she said, "Yes, Mom. He's better than I ever thought..." and she giggled. Then she said, "Yes, Mom, it was worth the wait." He just shook his head and smiled.

She finally hung up and came out to see him. She hadn't dressed yet, because she had just started to get ready for the day, but it didn't matter anymore and Larkin grabbed her by the waist and held her. He kissed her and asked, "Want some coffee?"
"Actually," she answered, "I want some breakfast. I'm starving. Let's go downstairs."
"Okay. But you have to get dressed first. "

He swatted her on the butt and she went to the bedroom to get dressed. He was all ready, so he sat down and watched the tube until she came back. She had put on the most comfortable clothes she had and still look respectable to go to the dining room. He had put on one of his new pairs of jeans and a "preppy" sweater. They were ready to go.

They went down to the lobby and walked to the restaurant. They went hand in hand and the people they passed smiled as they noticed how happy they looked together. Some of them knew they were newlyweds, but others didn't. There was just an aura around them and it was good.

Sam welcomed them to the dining room and congratulated them on their marriage. He had heard the news from Chester. They ate Eggs Benedict, first time for Larkin, and he actually liked them. Sally said,

"Let's go over to the house, open our presents and bring the car back over here."

Larkin wiped some goo off his chin with the napkin and said, "Sure, Dear, that's a good idea."

They stopped at the door and told Chester they would need a cab and then went up to get their coats. The maid had already been to their room and she had even hung up everything they had just abandoned to the floor. Especially Sally's wedding dress, which Larkin had moved and stood up next to the corner like a mannequin with no arms. Grabbing their winter garb they started to the door and Sally remarked, "Oh that reminds me, I better start getting us packed for our honeymoon while we're home. Can't wear this stuff there!"

"You should have been a scout; you're always prepared."

"Military brat; that's what it is."

The cab drove a little slower and a little out of the way and Larkin got a bit perturbed. It wasn't so much the money, but the idea. He figured he just wouldn't tip him to convey a message. When they got out he handed him the fare, but the man asked, "Hey, Bud, no tip?"

"Not this time," Larkin said, "but if you treat me fair next time there will be."

The cabbie understood and said, "Oh." He drove off as the two kids walked up the stairs to their home.

Everything was as the planner had said. Sally told Larkin she needed to call and thank her too, for doing such a wonderful job. Larkin replied, "You know I paid her pretty well for it?"

"Yes, I figured, but she must really care to do something like that on Christmas for us."

"I guess so." Larkin shook his head in agreement. He had not even thought of that.

They opened their gifts, which weren't very many and they found things that meant something to the givers, because they knew they didn't need a toaster or a blender. They were touched by them all and Sally sat each one aside with the card so she could write thank you cards to them. Sally cried at the opening of each gift, knowing their intensions, and that the giver loved them.

When they got to the last of them, the present they had bought for Mrs. Heidelmann was there, too. They had promised they would come by to see her, so Sally said, "Let's go to see her and then drop by and take Harry to dinner tonight."

"I think that would be great, Sally."

"But first," she shouted, "let's pack for Hawaii!!!!"

"Dear, you start to pack and I'll let Harry know the plan, okay?"
"Okay." She was happy with that, loving to pack and to plan.

Larkin called Harry at work and said, "Hi, Harry! What's new?"
"Larkin! How are you two, Son?"
"We are fine. I thought I'd call and invite you to dinner with us tonight."
"I'd like that, Larkin. Are you sure you two want to share your alone time with me? You know what I mean?"
Larkin laughed and said, "We have plenty of that kind of time, Harry. We wouldn't be calling if we didn't want to be with you, would we?"
"Where are we going?"
"We hadn't talked about it. Where would you like to go?"
"You remember that place you and I went for steaks, Bobby Van's?"
"Oh, yeah. We did go there. That sounds great."
"I got to go, Larkin. But, I want to say thanks for the Christmas gift. It's a real nice shirt."
"Thank Sally, she's a good shopper. See you later. Bye, Harry."
That reminded Larkin and he called to Sally, "Hey, Sally! Where's my Christmas present?"
She called back, "Your? Oh my goodness! I forgot to give it to you!" She ran into the master bedroom from his room, stopped right in front of Larkin and said, "Oh, I'm so sorry, Honey! With all the excitement and everything I forgot all about it. It's in the hotel room under your bed."
"Under *my* bed? Hey, that's pretty smart!"
"But I can make it up to you," she said with an evil grin. She put her arms around him and slowly pushed him toward the bed kissing and caressing him. They made love there in their own bed for the first time.

They slept for a bit and when Larkin woke he said, "Hey, Sally. Call Mrs. Heidelmann and tell her we're coming. I'm going to take a shower." He went and got in the shower with the stupid bag on his cast and he heard Sally speaking with her old landlord on the phone. He could tell it was a happy conversation with laughing and loud phrases on Sally's end. He got out and got dressed again and as he walked into the room Sally closed the call.
She said, "She was gabby today. She wants us to come as soon as we can, because she has plans at four."

They drove over to her old apartment, which had been rented out again to a student, and gave Mrs. Heidelmann her gift, and then excused themselves to go spend the evening with Harry. Sally said it was nice to see and be with them both and Larkin said he thought they should make it a practice to spend an evening with each of them a month. Of course they'd see Mrs. H (which they now had come to call her) at church, but it would still be a nice thing to do.

When they arrived back at the hotel, the first thing Larkin did was go to his bed, throw back the covers, stick his head under it and look for his Christmas gift. He found it and pulled it out. It was small, and he plopped right down on the carpeted floor, his back against the bed, and began to open it as Sally came into the room to watch him. The box was four inches by four inches square and he shook it to see if it made any noise- nothing. Sally said, "I hope you like it and it's not much because you said you already had everything and didn't need anything."
"I know. What is it?"
"Open it, Silly."
He opened it with reckless abandon, paper coming off of it faster than a tornado. He stopped abruptly and then slowly opened the top of the box looking inside. It was a real nice- tie! Larkin just laughed. So did Sally…

The next couple of days went by quickly. They checked out of the room early at The Hay-Adams on Friday and wished everyone a Happy New Year. Sally wanted to get home quickly to unpack and pack the things she had set aside, because their flight to Hawaii stopped in California for the night and it boarded at noon tomorrow. When they got home, she packed them both with the things she had set aside already and she said to Larkin, "I think we're going to have to buy you some things when we get there Larkin."
"Like what?"
"Shorts, for one thing. And maybe a swimming suit?"
"How am I going to swim with this on my foot?" He pointed to the cast with a funny, quizzical look on his face.
She chuckled and said, "It's not that you have to swim, but that you have one on when you sit on the beach!"
"Oh. Beach etiquette?"
"I have to tell you everything."
"That's' why you're here, Dear."

Sally went through her mental checklist and closed the suitcases up for the last time. Larkin had gone to the safe for some more money and put one of the checkbooks in there with the remainder of the cash. He wondered if he should take The Eraser with them, but he didn't because he didn't feel threatened and all *seemed* to be calm. He felt God was protecting them and in control. He came out of their closet and asked, "Do you think two thousand in cash is enough?"
"Did you bring a checkbook?"
"Yeah."
"Then it's enough."

Larkin laughed at that one.

She pulled his suitcase off the bed and said to him, "Get mine will you, Honey? It's heavier."

He laughed again and asked sarcastically, "You really need me don't you?"

She smiled and stopped next to him and puckered up her lips and replied, "Sure do. Lay one on me." She closed her eyes and waited face forward and body prone.

Larkin obliged her and he said, "Now you're using me for kisses. When will it stop?"

He laughed, grabbed her bag off the bed and they headed to the car to leave. He set the house alarm and looked around, not that looking around made much of a difference, but he wanted to do a mental checklist, too. He said, "Well, I guess that's it. We're ready. Let's go to Hawaii!"

Chapter Five

The Honeymoon

The flight to California went like a breeze. Larkin had never flown that far before. Sally told him to just wait, because the trip to Hawaii was longer! He liked to have the window seat so he could look down through the clouds and see the tops of the houses, the rivers and lakes, and especially the patchwork of the fields. He daydreamed the whole way, wondering what the people were doing down there, what the farmers were growing, and if this was God's perspective of all of us, too? Only God knew all the answers to the questions. And God took care of all creation, even though each part, place, and person was different.

Sally woke him from his daydream and asked, "What ya thinking about?"
"God."
"What about God?"
"Oh. How he takes care of all of that," he said pointing out the window, "without even trying. And how all the people do what they do without ever noticing what God is doing."
"I never thought of that, Honey."
"See?"

The stewardess came and brought them a drink and some peanuts. However, Larkin was hungry. He asked if they'd have lunch and he found out they'd be coming through with a sandwich in about an hour. He took the snack and told her "Thanks." Thinking he could wait if he had that, he drank the Coke pretty fast. Sally was fine and she just sat there reading the magazine from the seat pocket in front of her.

Somewhat satisfied, he took a little nap and he dreamt about The Homestead and the trees. His uncles were not present in his dream, just himself walking through the orchard and taking care of it. It was much like he was in the Garden of Eden, mist all around, but with cool air in the evening. Again, Sally woke him from this dream with her hand, softly squeezing his arm and saying, "The sandwich is here." He sat up and pulled the tray table down in front of him. They each took one and commented that it was pretty good- for airline food. He thought about his dream and hoped that one day soon he'd return to the Homestead.

When they deplaned in Los Angeles, it was 70 degrees. It was a shock and they had to take off the coats and sweaters. They took a cab to the hotel the wedding planner had reserved for them for the night and settled in to get some sleep before the long trip in the morning. Larkin was excited when they got there and checked in, because of the palm trees and the flowers, even in the *wintertime*. He put the suitcases in the room and he left Sally saying, "I'm going to go out and see the pool."

She smiled and hurried to finish what she wanted to put away so she could join him saying, "Okay! Be right behind you."

It was so beautiful in Los Angeles! When he got to the pool, there were people swimming and sitting in the late afternoon sun. It had been a warm winter and the water was still somewhat warm enough to swim. A song called "California Sun" was playing on some loudspeakers by the pool. Not that he could go in, but he still stuck his hand in the water and took a feel of it. Felt cold to him! After he got back up, a woman in a bikini walked past him and gave him the eye. He smiled, but didn't say anything, and just then, Sally came up and said, "I saw that, Larkin Palmer."

He blushed and told her, "I may be all yours, Dear, but I ain't dead."

She laughed and took his arm and they walked around the grounds finally going into the bar. Larkin wondered what would happen there and he was right to do so, because the bartender asked if he was old enough to be there. Sally answered and said to him, "He's not, but I am. I guess I'd like a couple of beers for myself to go?"

He shook his head and with resignation said, "Okay. Let me see your ID."

Sally got it out of her purse and showed it to him. He asked what kind she wanted and he went to get them. Sally paid, because Larkin could not. Putting them in a bag, the bartender went back to cleaning glasses and the two left and walked up to the room.

They sat in front of the TV drinking the cold Buds and talked about how different it was there in California. Sally said, "I've never been to Hawaii, but if you think *this is different*, just wait until you see it there."

"You want to go over to McDonalds and get a burger? I saw one across the street."

"That would be nice for a change. I actually *like* fast food."

"I like almost anything, even though I haven't necessarily had it!"

She laughed, took the last sip of her beer and the two walked over to eat at the Golden Arches.

They each ordered a Big Mac, fries, and Coke, and then sat down at a table someone had not yet cleaned up. It had ketchup on one of the chairs and Larkin wiped it up. Sally watched him do this and was impressed that he had a servant's heart. It was part of why she loved him so. After praying, before he took a bite, Larkin all of a sudden held up his burger and began to sing out loud, "Two all beef patties, special sauce, lettuce, cheese, pickles, onions, on a sesame seed bun." Sally was laughing and putting her arm over her head in embarrassment as he stood up to finish for the people who were listening to him. They clapped and cheered, and he took a bow.

Sally asked, "Larkin, are you trying to embarrass me?"

He sat back down, laughed, and said, "That's for Kmart," and he started to eat.

She laughed, rolled her eyes, and said, "I guess we're even."

They finished up, threw the trash away and walked down to the beach. The sun was setting and the gulls flew over them as they went toward the pier on the sidewalk. Larkin was very interested in the plants along the way, especially those growing in the sand, like the sea grass. Much to his dismay, Sally didn't want to get sand in her shoes, so they had to stay on the path. The wind had begun to pick up and her hair blew back behind her as they stood on the planks of the pier and watched the sun sink slowly into the water. The ozone level was high and the sky was filled with red hues and blue streaks. It was simply breathtaking. When the light was almost gone, they decided to head back to the room and go to bed.

Larkin called the cab company and reserved one to come get them and take them to the airport in the morning. Sally got ready for bed and Larkin just took off his clothes and climbed in. It was a new feeling this, "freedom", they had in marriage. Larkin thought about that for a minute and got the Gideon Bible out of the nightstand. 'What had Paul said?' he thought. He looked in Galatians. "Here," he said out loud. Sally came out of the bathroom in a teddy and asked, "What?"

She came over, sat on the bed by him and looked into the Bible to where he pointed and read, "Galatians 5:13, "You, my brothers, were called to be free. But do not use your freedom to indulge in the sinful nature; rather serve one another in love."" Larkin looked at her and closed the Bible.

Sally looked at him and said, "That's us, isn't it?"

"Yup. I'd say I'm happy we've done it the way we did. It was worth it."

"Then love me, Honey."

She kissed him and he loved her. It was their honeymoon!

Rising early, they got going in the morning, wanting to have time to eat before the cab came for them. The hotel had a greasy spoon attached to it so they went there and got something quick. The coffee there was great! Larkin dipped his toast into his egg and watched a little girl take a spoon of oatmeal and launch the sloppy contents at her brother seated across from her. Her mother didn't like that much and the girl got a swat for doing it while mom tried to clean it up. Larkin smiled and pointed without saying anything as he saw it, and Sally turned from her grapefruit just in time to see the boy wipe the mess from his face. She giggled. The waitress brought their check and they got up to pay the cashier. Larkin left a tip and paid, and then the two went to the room to wait for the cab.

They sat waiting and Sally said, "Just think, Honey, in just six hours or so, we'll be in Hawaii."

"Just six hours, huh?"

"Well, at least we got about half of the trip done yesterday."

"Yeah. At least it wasn't all in one day. Do they have direct flights from D.C.?"

"I'm sure they do, but I wouldn't want to do it."

"Me either."

The Yellow cab drove up and honked. Larkin pointed and said, "There he is. Let's go!"

"I'm excited, Honey!"

"Me, too, Sally. Me, too."

The flight to Hawaii was different than the trip to L.A. For one thing, the plane was much larger and it was fuller. Also, they had an "in flight movie" and if you wanted to watch, you just put on a set of headphones they gave you and plugged them in. This was all new to Larkin and Sally was having fun watching his reaction. He was so innocent and naive in some ways, but not at all in others. For the rest of the flight she just watched him, and a couple of times he caught her doing it and wondered what she was doing, but not saying anything to her about it. They had been watching the movie, but Larkin fell asleep, because that's what media did to him, and she turned in the seat facing him and watched him, thanking God for him and wondering why He had brought them together. She fell asleep watching her new husband and the two woke about an hour before they were to land because some little kid was having trouble with his ears and started to scream. The mother did as much as she could, rocking and consoling him as he held the sides of his head, but there was really nothing she could do. Larkin woke first, looking at Sally who had been watching him before she dozed.

He brushed her hair away from her face, and leaned over to her and kissed her. He didn't care what the guy next to her thought about it, because he'd given them a funny look when he'd been demonstrative before and in fact, the guy had been snoring and almost fell face first into the back of the seat in front of him. Sally smiled at Larkin as she woke and asked, "Where are we?"

"Over the ocean," wise cracked Larkin.

"But how far from Hawaii?"

"I'd say about an hour. They already said to sit and belt up."

"Good, but I have to pee and I can't wait another hour!"

She got up and headed to the restroom. They didn't give her any trouble and said the previous restriction was due to some turbulence. When she got back, Larkin went to do the same. He had never used a rest room on a plane before, so it was something new for him. He thought, 'I wonder if Sally would like to see this "first" for me too?' He laughed as he went in. When he got back, the flight crew asked all the passengers to be seated and prepare for landing. They belted in and watched the plane land through the window. Larkin said, "I have to admit watching all that water go by, just wasn't as interesting as going over land."

Sally smiled and changed the subject by asking, "Did the planner reserve or book anything for us to do on the trip or are we on our own?"

"Oh, the only thing she booked was a tour of Pearl Harbor. Otherwise, we can do what we want."

"That's good, because all I want to do is relax and sit on the beach."

They didn't have any carry-on baggage, so they went to pick up their bags when they came off the plane at the claim area. Larkin went over and tried to grab one as it went by, but was unable because he couldn't keep up with it in his cast. He felt like a dweeb. The next time it came by there were more bags gone adjacent to it, so he had longer to grab and this time he got that one. Sally saw the other and grabbed it. They went to get a cab, but as they walked to the door a driver with a suit and cap on stood holding a sign with "Palmer" on it. Larkin saw it and asked, "Are you waiting for Larkin Palmer?"

"Yes, follow me please."

The driver took them to a limo parked outside and placed their bags in the trunk while they got in. Larkin said to Sally, "She didn't tell me this was going to be a first class trip! But, I guess I should have expected it."

The driver took them to Waikiki Beach and their hotel: The Moana Surfrider.

When they arrived, he let them out at the door and a large woman in a Mumu, who seemed to be a local, came up to them and said, "Aloha! Hello, Mr. and Mrs. Palmer, my name is Julie. I'm going to be your liaison during your stay here in Honolulu. Anything you need, want to do or see, come to me and I'll make it happen."

Sally said, "Thank you, Julie."

Julie placed a lei over Sally's neck and said, "Please come with me to sign in."

She led them to the front desk where they received their key. The desk clerk said, "Your suite is on the top floor of the tower facing the beach. I hope you enjoy your stay."

Larkin was amazed and said, "Thank you. I'm sure we will."

The bell hop picked up their bags and Julie led them to the elevator. As they waited Julie said, "I'll leave you now. Here's my card. Call if you need anything."

"Thank you," Sally said.

They went up to their room and although small compared to the Hay-Adams, it was very nice. Larkin was impressed by the architecture of the building with its columns and beautiful windows. He gave the boy a tip and he closed the door behind himself. Sally was at the window looking out at the beach and pointed down to the left saying, "Look Larkin! It's Diamond Head!"

"Yeah. Look at that view! It's neat. Hey, are those Banyan trees I see down there?"

Sally laughed and said, "Trees are your life, Larkin."

"No not really, Dear, I just like them. All kinds. But, not as much as you!"

He picked her up and carried her over to the bed. Kissing her softly, he lay her down and made love to her. Afterwards he thought to himself, 'Boy, honeymoons are great!'

Larkin went into the bathroom while Sally put away their clothes. After seeing what the people were wearing, he knew he needed to buy some clothes. But, he didn't want to look like a tourist. He wanted to look like a local. Sally came in to go to the toilet and he told her what he was thinking. She suggested, "Call Julie, she'll tell you what to do."

"Good idea."

He picked up her card from where Sally had sat it down and called the number. "Julie, this is Larkin Palmer. Say, I need to buy some clothes, but I don't want to look like a tourist. I want to look like a local - with flair. Have any recommendations?"

"That's easy. Wear sandals, shorts, jeans, Aloha shirts, tees, and a skirt for your wife. Don't wear swimsuits anywhere but the beach. If you go to church or do business, wear business casual. Got it?"

"Got it."

"Go off the beach a ways and you'll get better prices, too. Anything else?"

"Nope. Thanks for the help."

"You're welcome. Oh, and Mr. Palmer?"

"Yes?"

"Don't go in the water with that cast." She laughed a loud boisterous laugh and hung up.

Smiling, he said out loud, "Always a comic in the place".

Larkin told Sally what Julie told him. Sally said, "Well, you have a tee and your jeans for now, so we'll go shopping in the morning. In the mean while, let's put on a swim suit, go sit by the pool and have a drink."

"Ah, I don't have a suit remember?"

"Well, I'll put on a suit, you make cut offs out of one of your pairs of jeans and then we'll go sit by the pool!"

"Great! Where's a scissors?"

"Call Julie."

Larkin called Julie again and she sent up a pair of scissors. She told him to be careful with it or he might get hurt. Larkin thought she was funny. While he cut off his pants, the old ones, Sally changed. She came out of the bathroom and Larkin's eyes flew wide open. He said, "Where did you get that?"

She turned around as if to model it and said, "You like, Mister? I got it through a mail order place. It's nice, isn't it?"

"It's got to be the smallest bikini I have ever seen, but you're right it's nice, in a small kind of way."

She put on a wide brimmed hat and grabbed her sun screen and said, "You coming?"Larkin put on his cut offs and out the door they went.

The pool was beautiful, but at this moment, Sally was obviously the point of focus! The guy's heads turned to watch her as she passed, long red hair trailing behind her. She was a knockout! And she was enjoying the attention. Larkin walked along side her to protect his territory and he could see the looks of disappointment. A woman in a two piece was staring at Larkin and Sally caught it, but Larkin didn't react on the way by. They went to the bar first and ordered a MaiTai. The bartender, named Guy No Wei, came up to him and Larkin just knew he was going to ask him for his ID, but instead he said, "I assume you are married to this lovely woman and if you are, have her place this flower behind her left ear. It is a signal to the men that she is taken." He placed a flower on the bar. Larkin picked it up and went over to Sally as they waited for their drinks and he pushed her hair aside gently to put the flower behind her left ear.

Sally said, "That's sweet, Larkin."

"Not as sweet as you may think, Dear. It's custom. It means you're mine."

She smiled and gave him a kiss saying, "*That* means you're *mine*," just as the bartender brought the drinks. "Your room number, Sir?"

"Penthouse suite. And thanks for the info, Guy." Larkin gave him a ten for the tip.

Guy replied, "Anytime. Thanks."

They found two places to lounge by the pool and sat down. Sally asked, "Hey Larkin, want to see these guys go nuts?"

"How?"

"Put this sun screen on my back would you?"

He was surprised by this. He had no idea she was like that. She had never exhibited it before. But he went along with it- this time.

Sally lay down on the lounge chair with her back up. She pulled her hair aside and handed him the sun screen. Larkin opened the bottle and squeezed some into his hands. She had him rub it in all over her back and legs until she was satisfied he had hit all the spots. As he rubbed he watched the other guys and she was right, it was like they wished they could take his place. He was glad she had the flower and that she was his wife. They sat there until the sun went down, just about two hours. Which was a mistake, because when they got up to the room, fair skinned, freckled Sally was starting to show a little red, even if she had sunscreen on, she still burned. Larkin wasn't so bad, having only burned a little on his neck. If he believed in Karma, he would have thought this was her reward. He smiled at that.

She took off the bikini and walked into the bathroom to look in the mirror. Larkin followed her to see, too, and he said, "You look like the girl in the Coppertone ad!"

"And it's starting to hurt too," she boo-hoed.

He came over to her to hug her and she said sharply, "No! Don't touch me! It hurts."

She started to cry, not because it hurt, but because she couldn't be held on her honeymoon! Larkin thought a minute and said, "I'll call Julie!" She followed him out to the phone. Larkin called Julie and asked her what people did for sunburn. She told him and Sally heard, "Ah ha, Yup. Okay. Really? Got it. Thanks."

Sally was still standing there naked and he took her by the hand and led her back into the bathroom. He turned on the tub and said, "She said to take a cool bath to relieve the burning. I need to go and get some aloe lotion to rub on you to help heal it. In the mean while, she says don't lie in the sun for so long. And it just depends on how bad it looks in the morning."

"Thank you, Honey." She gave him a kiss and started to get into the tub, which was indeed- cool. He could tell.

He said, "I'll be back as soon as I can." He went out locking the door behind him and got on the elevator to go to the gift shop. But, the gift shop didn't sell aloe lotion. He asked the lady where he could get it and she replied, "Kmart."

"Of course," he replied.

He went to the front desk to find Julie and he said to the clerk, "Is Julie here?"

"No, but how can I help you?"

"I'd like to find some aloe-based lotion for my wife, but the store here doesn't sell it. They say Kmart does. I'd like to see if I could send someone on your staff to go get it for me. Is that possible?"

"I believe that can be arranged, Sir. Just a minute."

She called someone and in about a minute a man came to the desk that looked like one of the guys that does the fire dance in Hawaiian shows. In fact, it was, and his name was Akoni. He stuck out his hand and introduced himself with his Hawaiian accent. "Hi. My name is Akoni. I can help you."

Larkin said, "Thanks. I hate to put you through just going to the store for me, but if you don't, my honeymoon is going to be cut real short; if you know what I mean."

Akoni smiled and said, "I do, Man. What do you need?"

"Something for her sunburn; like aloe lotion."

"Oh yeah, that stuff works gooood and it cools the skin."

"So I've heard. Here's a hundred bucks. Will you bring it up to us?"

Akoni smiled and looking at the hundred said, "For a hundred bucks, I'll take it to the moon. Be right back."

Larkin looked at him and said, "Thanks, Akoni, but to be safe, get two?"

Akoni winked and left.

Larkin went back up to the room and Sally was still in the tub. She actually looked worse. It almost appeared she was getting a welt or two on her skin. He didn't want to seem negative about it, so he told her that Akoni was going to get the lotion for her right away. He said, "I promise I'll rub it on gently."

She started to cry and said appreciatively, "I love you, Honey."

She stayed in the tub until Akoni came back with the lotion and when she got out, she looked like an octogenarian. Larkin took some towels and laid them on the bed and she lay face forward as Larkin poured generous amounts of the lotion on her. At first it was cold to the touch and it felt good, but after a bit, it began to wear off and he had to apply it again. Larkin said out loud for his benefit, not hers, "It's going to be a long night."

"What, Honey?"

"Oh, nothing, Dear."

She put up her hair and didn't put anything on that night, and just lay on top the covers so nothing would have to touch her skin. She was miserable. From time to time Larkin would put some more lotion on her, but it didn't last long and she thought it was hopeless. In fact it was, until the skin started to heal itself. That would take a couple of days- best case scenario. It was a restless night for them both and not for the reason Larkin or Sally would have liked. Larkin said a prayer that the Lord would heal her quickly; for both their sakes.

The next morning, on Sunday, Larkin had to do something more for her, so he went to the store downstairs again and bought some over the counter pain relievers. He wished he had something stronger for her that would put her out and give her some rest. He went to Julie again, who was standing by the desk. "Hi Julie," he said.

"Hi, Mr. Palmer. How's your wife?"

"Not too good. The lotion helps, but she can't get any rest. She needs something to help her get some rest."

"I see. I'll call the company doctor and see what I can do."

"Thanks, Julie."

She made a call and in a couple of minutes the doctor called her back and told her that he'd call in a prescription to the drug store down the street. Larkin was grateful as usual. He told Julie, "You should have never volunteered to be our liaison."

"Who said I did?"

She *was* funny! He laughed and walked away.

Larkin went to their room and told Sally the story and she just cried. She was overtired, miserable, and disappointed. They had missed church in Hawaii, too! He gave her a couple of the pain relievers and hoped they'd bring the others soon. In a while, Akoni came to the door with a pharmacy bag. He handed it to Larkin and said, "They put it on the room."

Larkin still handed him a tip and said, "Thanks, Akoni."

He took it to her and she swallowed one of the pills with a big glass of water. She lay down on the bed like the night before, au natural, and he drew the curtains completely to block the light for her. It didn't take long and she was out. He was glad and in some ways, more relieved than she. He lay down and took a nap. It helped a lot. She, on the other hand, was going to be out for a long time and so he went down to the pool to get a drink. As he walked to the pool he smelled the ocean and could almost taste the salt in the air sent by the breeze coming straight off the bay. He watched the people for a while, but got bored with that, wishing he were doing some of the things they were enjoying , so instead, he went over by the Banyan trees to look at them and their history there. For him, it was interesting to say the least. While he stood there peering into the tree, he became aware of someone standing next to him. It was the woman from by the pool. She said, "You like trees?"

"As a matter of fact, yes, I'm an arborist."

"A what?"

"A caretaker of trees. I specialize in northern hardwoods."

"Hardwoods?" she smiled, "My name is Barb. Yours?"

He blushed, finally looking at her face and saw a flower under her right ear. She was single.

"I'm Larkin Palmer. Nice to meet you, Barb."

"Where are you from, Larkin?"

"Well right now, my wife and I are here on our honeymoon and we live in D.C.. How about you?"

"Oh," she said disappointed, "I live in Seattle."

"Are you here with a group or something, Barb?"

"Yes, I belong to a scuba club. We come here to dive every year."

"That's one thing I've never done."

"You should do it while you are here, Larkin, it's amazing."

"I'll think about it, Barb."

Just then her group went by and motioned for her to join them. She said goodbye and left Larkin to himself. He was grateful to the group.

He decided to go up to the room and see if Sally was awake. When he got there she was still out, but was rousing. He had not had anything to eat all day except snack food at the bar and a drink, so he was hungry. If she was able, he hoped to get her to put some clothes on and go down for dinner. That is, *if* she was able. If not, he'd call room service. All he knew is that he wanted his wife to be comfortable and he prayed for her.

She woke and he was sitting by her side. She put her arms around him and he didn't put his around her. He knew better. She asked, "How long have I been out?"

"All day, about seven hours. Do you feel better?"

"Maybe a little. At least I got some rest."

"Would you like something to eat? Can you get dressed to go down to dinner? Or do you want me to call room service?"

"I don't want to just sit here. Will you help me put a light top on and some shorts?"

"We can try, Dear."

She got out of bed and went to the bathroom first, and when she came back she asked him to put some more aloe on the sunburn before she put on her clothes. Larkin picked up the bottle and put some on very lightly. She handed him the top and she held her arms up so he could just drop it from above. He did a good job and it came to rest in the right places. She could not wear a bra. Then he had her sit on the edge of the bed and he pulled her shorts on her legs part way up. He said, "Get up, Dear." She got up and he pulled the shorts to her waist. She was totally commando- top and bottom. He asked, "How does it feel?"

"Not as bad as I thought it would."

"Good. Let's go. I'm starving."

She took his hand and they started down to the lobby. She still looked a mess, her hair undone, no makeup, and now a burn that shone like the noonday sun. The elevator door opened and the bell rang for the first floor. They got out and went toward the restaurant. Sally squinted as she had not been out of the room or the halls all day and it was bright in the lobby. Larkin was glad they didn't have a dress code like the Hay-Adams! They got a table and the waitress brought menus. Sally asked, "What should we eat, Honey?"

He could tell she was in a totally dependent mode right now. Otherwise, she'd just tell him what she wanted. "They say to eat fish while on an island. Have the steak when you get home."

"That makes sense. Can I get the grouper?"

"That's what I was thinking of."

Larkin ordered for them both and skipped the alcohol that night. They drank water with lemon and she shivered in her chair due to the air conditioning and her being so underdressed. Her top showed just how cold she was, too. The food came and they ate more quickly than they wanted to, because they really wanted to take time to enjoy it and themselves. It made for a less than enjoyable meal. They finished and asked for the check, so they could go back to the room. Before they could get up to go, Barb came by with the dive club and waived at Larkin. Sally wondered what that was all about and she looked perturbed. Larkin paid and he whispered to her, "I'll explain in a minute."

They walked toward the elevator and Sally asked, "Is that the girl from the pool that gave you a look the other day?"

"Yes, but wait and let me explain."

"Sure. I get sick and you just go off having fun with another woman on our honeymoon while I lay in pain in our room!" She stomped her foot and headed to the elevator at a high rate of speed.

Larkin called after her, "Sally! Wait!"

She didn't. In exasperation he said, "Women."

He waited a couple minutes to go up to the room, hoping she would calm down and let him explain. Not that he had anything to explain, because he was just a victim of circumstance. He opened the door and she was sitting on the chair next to the desk, because it was wood and had no material to stick to her skin. He went over to her and asked, "Are you going to calm down and let me tell you what happened?"

"Go ahead." She tried to cross her arms in front of her, but she couldn't, because it hurt.

Larkin smiled and said, "I was down there looking at the Banyan trees and she came up to me and introduced herself. I told her we were here on our honeymoon and she said she was here with her scuba club. She left and that's it."

"Really?"

"Really."

She stood up and put her arms around his neck and gave him a kiss and said, "Oh, I'm so sorry, Honey. I didn't think I was the jealous type until now. I guess I love you more than I thought."

"Gee, thanks, Dear."

"Oh. I didn't mean it that way. It's these pills, Larkin. I can't think." She started to cry again.

Larkin asked, "How does it feel? Want to take another cold bath?"

She nodded, "yes", with a pouty look on her face.

"Okay. Come on."

He led her into the bathroom again and turned on the water. As the whirlpool tub filled, he helped her get the clothes back off, but he had to almost peel the top off of her real slowly so as not to take skin off with it, because her back had started to shed in large patches. She was a mess and he felt for her. He pulled her shorts off, took a look at how bad it was, which on the bottom wasn't as bad with less peeling, and she got in slowly trying to get used to the water a little at a time again. Larkin said, "That bikini bottom decal you have on your butt is kinda cute."

"Don't be funny! It hurts too much to be funny." She asked, "Will you get me another pill, Honey?"

He asked, "How many can you have a day?"

"I don't know."

Larkin picked up the bottle and read it. "It says two a day. I guess you're okay then."

He gave her another with a glass of water.

She said, "Will you get in the tub with me?"

He asked, "If I do, can you deliver?"

She looked at him and said mischievously, "We aren't missionary's you know."

He smiled and said, "Let's make this a quick bath then, because if that pill kicks in, you'll fall asleep on me!" They laughed as Larkin took off his clothes and got in real slowly. It didn't help much when she splashed him though. It *was* cold!

They got out in about a half an hour, Larkin's cast sticking up out of the tub to keep it dry, and just for long enough so that the bath might do some good, which Sally felt it did. Larkin helped her dry by patting her skin with the towel so as not to peel the skin off too quickly. He dried himself and not getting dressed, went to bed. She followed. From that moment on she was in charge. The night didn't turn out as bad as Larkin thought it was going to. Instead, he was quite pleased.

They slept in that next day in Honolulu and the pill Sally took didn't wear off as quickly as the day before. It was Monday and it was *supposed* to be another day of sitting by the pool. Larkin didn't think much of that without Sally, so he let her sleep and he went to the free brochure stand and found a few places they could go that they both might be interested in. They already knew they'd be going to Pearl Harbor on Wednesday, so they would have to think of things for them to do the rest of the week and try to stay out of the sun. Although he hoped she might be able go to back outside into the full sun by Friday, he wondered about that, and had his doubts.

When he went to the room, Sally was up and about, trying to get cleaned up. He was surprised to see that. The Movie "Blazing Saddles" was on TV loud, so she could hear it from the bathroom. She felt better, and she vowed never to do something that stupid again. She was standing there naked, putting on her makeup and fixing her hair. Larkin asked, "If you fix your hair first, won't we mess it up trying to put your top on?"

"Not if you help. You'll see."

She finished up and said, "Okay, same shorts as yesterday."

Larkin picked them up and helped her step into them. Still commando style. "See that pink halter top there?" She pointed to the chair. "Let's try that today."

Larkin retrieved it and shortened it up to place it over her head. She directed him, "Now, just stretch it over my head and hair until you get to my neck and back. Then just let it fall out. Hopefully, it won't stick."

She held up her arms and he did it exactly like she said and it worked perfectly. Except when he let the last part down, he playfully pinched her someplace sensitive. It didn't hurt her, but she just wasn't expecting it and she yelled, "Larkin quit that!" He ran and she chased him around the room until she caught him by the door where she pinned him to the wall. She kissed him and said, "Honey, I love you." This was getting to be the playful, old Sally again!

Larkin showed her the brochures and they picked a couple of places they might like to see. Sally said, "How about we go to a couple of places today, rest tomorrow, then the tour, a couple more on Thursday and then try to relax by the pool or on the beach for a bit on Friday? If- I am able." He laughed. She put her arms around him and asked again, "Okay?"

"Sounds like you're getting back to your usual self. Sure. What's today?"

"I figured we could do one for me and one for you each day. First, we'll go to Foster Botanical Gardens for you and then shopping downtown for me."

"You're genius. Let's go eat."As they walked out of the room past the TV, Mongo struck the horse in the head and it fell down knocked out. Larkin pointed and said, "I love that part." He switched off the TV.

After eating a late breakfast Larkin asked her, "Do you want me to reserve the limo and we do this in style?"

"If I were well, we'd walk the whole day, but considering the circumstances, why don't we have them drop us off and come back and pick us up?"suggested Sally.

"Smart." They went over to the desk and told Julie and she set it up. They told her they'd be back down with Sally's purse in a minute.

On the way to the elevator Larkin said looking at his feet, "I never realized that wearing sandals would be this comfortable. I could get used to dressing this way all the time."

"Sandals? You mean- sandal? So could I." She laughed.

Larkin laughed, smiled and asked, "You mean, like that?"

She blushed and said, "You know what I mean. And yes, this is actually pretty freeing and comfortable."

He smiled again, glad to see she could blush and asked, "How are you doing? Feel okay still?"

"Oh, you're sweet. Yeah, I'm okay."

They retrieved her purse and hat, and off they went to the Botanical Gardens. Larkin was excited.

They made quite a stir when the limo dropped them off at the Gardens. The people looked at them like, "Are they famous?" Little did these people know just how famous Larkin Palmer was in the annuals of Masonic History, even if there was no written record of it by them and only verbal history passed on from Grand Master to Grand Master. He was glad he didn't have to deal with that there, too!

They went through the entrance and paid, picking up a map of the site. Larkin was visibly excited and Sally smiled at him, because she thought it was cute. She took his arm and snuggled to him and asked, "Where to first, Honey?"

"I thought I'd like to walk in a loop from right to left. We can save the orchids for last. My interest is all the old trees Hillebrand planted in the 1800's and the Act 105 trees." She just looked at him like he was speaking Martian, so he said, "I'll explain as we go, okay?"

"That's better."

"Let's go this way," he said pointing to the right. Sally loved the fact that so many butterflies were attracted to the plants there, flittering and flying all around them. Larkin thought it funny she spent more time looking at them than the plants. The middle terrace had gingers, aroids, and palms that Larkin said he just loved. They went back to the herbs section next and Larkin pointed and said, "Look! Its a rare Encephalartos inopinus!"

Sally said, "Really?"

Knowing she had no idea he laughed and said, "It's from Africa and is related to succulents, like the aloe plant that we rubbed on your back."

"Well, I like it then."

They bypassed the prehistoric glen and didn't spend much time there, because much of it was still fledgling, having opened just a few years before. So they went to walk through the palms in the back corner of the property. The canopy was stupendous, not only in the palms, but everywhere in the gardens, which in a way made Larkin sad, because the gardens were the only oasis of history in Honolulu as now there was just concrete, glass, and blacktop all around. He was sure Hillebrand would not recognize the island if he were alive. At least the Fosters, who last owned the garden property, saw to it that this postage stamp of preservation should be attempted. Larkin pointed to the Act 105 "Exceptional Trees" in the palm section as they went, explaining what they were. He said, "We have lots of what I'd call "exceptional" trees at The Homestead."

"I'm sure you do, Honey," Sally answered.

When they made their way down the path to the upper terrace, he pointed at a tree about fifty feet tall with bright red pods hanging down like grape clusters from the branches. Sally pointed and asked, "Those are pretty, Larkin, what are those?"

"That's what they call "Colville's Glory". They're from Madagascar. They are pretty aren't they?"

They stayed a long while in the upper terrace because Larkin had to go and actually touch many of the trees for himself. He was a "hands on" kind of guy!

They finished up at the orchids like Larkin had planned and he was amazed Sally was not getting impatient, because the whole excursion there at the gardens had already taken four hours. But he knew this part of it would interest her the most, and it did. He told her how Dr. Lyon, a Minnesotan, had taken his own orchid collection of over 27 years and with it, made this an outstanding exhibit. The late Dr. was truly a dedicated man. They left the orchids, because Larkin was afraid Sally would pick one. He didn't want to get put in jail today! But, he thanked her for letting them go to the Gardens. She replied, "I had a good time, Honey. I have to say, I didn't know you knew this much about it, especially tropical stuff like this."
"Before I met you, I used to read a lot."

When they walked back to the gate, they didn't call the limo because they saw a restaurant across the street called "Zippy's" and they were hungry. Larkin said, "Let's go eat what the locals eat."

They walked through the doors and instantly knew they were in the right place. Sitting down, they looked at the menu and the waitress came and greeted them saying, "Aloha, I'm Lo Lani. What can I get you?"
Larkin replied saying, "Hi! I think we already know what we'd like." They told her Furikake Grilled Salmon for him and Miso Butterfish for her.
"Drinks?"
"Cokes."
"Thanks. It'll be out soon."

She walked away to put in their order and they looked out the window at the gardens. Larkin saw a man standing leaning against the fence at the entrance. He didn't pay any attention to it figuring he was just waiting for someone to pick him up. They talked until the food came and they prayed like always which got some real funny looks from the other patrons. They ate and thought the food was fantastic!

As Larkin finished his meal, he looked out again and the man was still there. He wore sunglasses, shorts, and a blue Hawaiian shirt, but somehow he looked familiar to him. Then it hit him! The man in the blue suit! He didn't show any panic, and in a way he felt important and impressed that they had sent this guy to tail him on his honeymoon, even though he had warned them to back off, consequently, he was upset.

After paying Lo Lani, they went out the door and walked back toward the Garden entrance to use the pay phone and call the limo. The antagonist went into the gift shop before them. Larkin walked in with Sally and he went to the phone while Sally shopped. Larkin kept an eye on the guy while he talked. He arranged their pick up and walked past him on the way to Sally. He stopped and turned standing back to back to him while the man looked at a trinket. Larkin picked up a souvenir and said to him, "I know this was a nice way to get a free vacation, but I think you should go home and leave me alone." The intruder dropped his trinket with a clang as if surprised he had been spotted. He turned, walked away without saying anything and hustled briskly to his car, driving away. Larkin smiled as he watched him leave and called to Sally, "Hey Sally! Look. This carving is made of Banyan tree!"

The limo arrived and they paid for her things and went out and got in. Not knowing where to go, they asked the driver, "Say, could you take us to the best shopping area away from where we "mainlanders" shop?"
The driver chuckled and said, "Sure. We're on our way."

They pulled up in front of "Hawaiian Wear Unlimited". Sally said, "Oh, I've heard of this place. Have you ever heard of "Hilo Hattie" Larkin?"
"Can't say that I have, Dear."
"Well, follow me and I'll give you a course on shopping, "Hawaiian style"."

They went in and spent at least two hours spending money on clothes and a few gifts to take back for family and friends. Sally was now in her element and having a lot of fun. The guy "in the blue Hawaiian shirt" was gone, so Larkin relaxed. He saw a shirt he'd like to have with palms and a sunset on it, with shades of red, yellow, and brown. She "let" him have it, but suggested two others that she bought for him. He wondered where he'd wear three Aloha shirts back on the mainland. As long as she was having fun, he was too. Besides, he still had four more days on the island! She held up a Mumu to herself and Larkin said, "That looks great!"

The driver waited and after paying, they walked out and got in the limo, but Sally wasn't done. She asked the driver, "Can you take us to a cheap souvenir shop?"

Before he could answer Larkin asked, "Is there such a thing?"

The driver said, "Well, no, but there are better. I'll take you to Ala Moana, but you'll have to bargain shop."
"Oh, I can handle that," said Sally rubbing her hands together.
Larkin asked her, "How are you feeling?"
"I feel the burn from time to time, especially now that I've been perspiring, but I'm okay."
"Good. Then on to Ala Moana!"
The driver hit the gas and off they went.

When he dropped them off, the driver told them to call when they wanted to be picked up and he'd come to get them. Larkin thanked him and he drove away as they gazed upon the large open air market place. It was huge! Sally stood thinking about the enormity of it all and where she would begin to utilize her skills in the art of shopping. It was like a dream of heaven to her! To him, maybe the other place? She just started up the right side of the market, leading her novice husband to observe her. He wasn't going to tell her he didn't care. He just wanted her to have fun.

By the time they finished going up the right side, Larkin's cast had taken its toll and he was getting tired. Even the sandal was beginning to rub him the wrong way. Sally was beginning to feel it too, as her sunburn turned a little redder again. She had bought enough to say she didn't need anymore and in fact, Larkin wondered where they'd pack it all! She was ready to pack it in, which disappointed her, but made him, well, glad. Larkin put a dime in the pay phone and called the limo. He laughed when he told him to come back so quickly, but so they didn't have to walk back to where they began the excursion; Larkin told him exactly where they were.

They only had to wait for a brief time and the driver picked them up and took them back to the Moana Surfrider. Larkin gave the driver a hundred tip, for which he was appreciative. He said to Larkin, "Call anytime and asked for Clyde. I'll drive *you* anywhere."

When they got back to the room, well, Sally set her shopping bags down and collapsed in the desk chair. She said, "I have to get back in the tub, I have sweat all day and the salt is starting to burn. Help me get these clothes off."

With that command, Larkin went over, stripped her slowly, having learned a lesson from this experience in gentleness, and watched her get in the tub as it filled with cool water. He put a baggie on his cast and jumped in the shower. He got out and she watched him walk around the room naked and for which he played up for her. In fact, he started to become a bit excited and she noticed. She didn't say anything, but got out of the tub after washing off a bit and said, "Come with me, Honey."

Taking him by the hand, she led him to the bed and proceeded to repeat the event of the night before, as she was still too sensitive on her back for anything other than that. Larkin didn't mind at all and finally after a while they fell asleep with Sally lying on top of him. Larkin now knew who put the "Honey" in the term "Honeymoon"; it was women. Oh my- how glad he was they had waited for things such as these!

They woke about two hours later to hunger pangs and they started to put on some of the things they bought from Hilo Hattie. He really liked his shirt which had a red anthirium on it. Sally did, too, and laughing she said, "That's you a couple of hours ago! Rub some more aloe on me would you?"

Larkin blushed, to which he wondered, "Why?" and he went up to her, gave her a kiss and rubbed on the lotion.

When she was about ready to go she asked, "Will you drop my mumu over me?" Her hair was straight down her back and she was still naked, which began to excite him again, but getting that idea out of his mind, he just picked the mumu up and she held her arms high. He let it unfurl down around her and then helped her pull her hair out and place it down the back of the dress. She looked beautiful! She said, "I'm ready! And you know what?"

"What, Dear?"

"I'm really getting to like going "commando"."

He smiled and laughed saying, "Let's go have some Polynesian!"

The hotel had a special evening of entertainment and pig roast that night. The Hula girls were impressive swinging their hips from side to side, wearing coconut shells for bras, and they asked some of the men to come up and participate in the dance, to which Larkin declined. As the newlyweds sat and watched the show, they drank Mai Tais out of coconuts with little umbrellas on them. After a while, Akoni came out with two other men carrying fire staffs and joined the dancers on stage. As the two ate the roasted pig and poi, (which Larkin thought to be "icky", so he stuck to pineapple) the men danced with precision and timing. Akoni came right over in front of Sally and threw the stick up in the air, catching it just inches from the top of her head! The audience applauded, the men took their bows and started off stage, but Akoni stopped in front of them, bowed to Sally and she told him, "Thanks for the aloe, Akoni."

He saluted her and ran off. They had a wonderful time and even got to keep the coconut glasses!

When they got back to the room, Larkin turned on the clock radio and found a station that played soft romantic contemporary tunes. Sally noticed and didn't flinch knowing what he had in mind. She went to the bathroom and coming out she saw he was out of his clothes and in bed. She said, "That isn't going to do, Honey!"

He looked at her disappointedly and said, "Are you tired?"

"No stupid! You have to get his Mumu off of me! Or do you want me to do a hula like the girls in the show tonight?" She started to swing her hips back and forth slowly to the music.

He laughed getting out of bed and came over to her, obviously ready for her to come to join him. She caressed him and he waited for her to raise her arms to remove the Mumu. She did and he looked at her back. The peeling was in advanced stages, and despite its flaky appearance, was starting to look much better. He was glad to see it, for it made her less on edge and a lot happier. Taking that into consideration, he picked her up and lay her down on her back. She didn't react except to welcome him into her arms. Just then, Barry White came on singing, "Can't get enough of your love Babe." Sally asked, "How'd you do that?"

In all seriousness and not trying to be trite he replied, "I'm just *so* romantic you know." Kissing her, he did all he could to prove it to be so and yet, he was cautious and tender.

On Tuesday morning they didn't bother to get up at all. They just lay in bed and he'd rub more aloe on her, they'd make love, and then they'd fall back to sleep again. By evening they were getting hungry though and Sally said, "Let's see if we can find a good place for dinner besides our own hotel."

She went to get ready and Larkin called the desk to see where they recommended. Julie said to him, "I'm supposed to tell you go to go our restaurant, Mr. Palmer, but if you don't tell them I told you, I'll tell you."

"Okay. I promise."

"Go to Dukes. It's great."

"Want something to go?"

Julie laughed and said, "You're funny, too! You want the limo?"

"In an hour. Bye, Julie."

"Have fun, Mr. Palmer."

He helped Sally put on the nicest of the Mumus after she got cleaned up and then he took a shower, too. He naturally noticed there was a great deal more humidity there and the result was he had to take more showers than he was used to. After getting dressed he thought he looked good, but she was- a knockout! Even with the sunburn, which she was able to somewhat hide, she was, in his opinion, the most beautiful woman in Hawaii.

The limo driver knew where to go, because Julie had made a reservation for them and told him where. Duke's was just down the way on the beach and when the driver pulled up, he let them out to the sound of the nightly entertainment. The place was cool! It had all of the ambiance that anyone could ever hope for, even on a Hawaiian postcard! It also had quite a bar and it seemed like the place was hopping! But yet, it had just enough light to be romantic, too. Julie had told them the right place to come to. They were seated and they decided to have shrimp cocktails and a drink before they ate. The waitress gave Larkin a look about his age when he ordered, but she saw their rings and let it go. They talked, watched and listened while they sipped on the drinks and ate their shrimp, becoming totally absorbed in one another. Sally's drink had gone down quickly and Larkin asked, "That must be good, what did you have?"

"It's called a "Dig Me Daiquiri". Want one?"

"I like my Mai Tai. But you can have all you want. Remember though, we have to get up early for the tour tomorrow."

Sally ordered another drink and they placed their food orders, lobster for Larkin and seafood Luau for Sally and the waitress said, "I'll bring your salad bar plates back in a second."

Larkin's eyes lit up and he said, "I must be in heaven. They have a salad bar, too!"

The food was fantastic and they enjoyed the whole night at Dukes. Not wanting to leave after they ate, they went into the bar for about two hours and watched the people dance. Most of the folks were very obviously feeling no pain and it made their time go by quickly. They were really having fun listening to the music, sipping their drinks, and watching. But Larkin knew they should go or they would be hurting in the morning, so he took his wife by the hand and went to call for the limo. Thinking about that for a moment he said instead, "Want to walk back? It's, like, right next door. See?" He pointed down the beach and they could see the tower where their suite was only about four hundred yards away. Sally smiled and looked at him with her loving eyes as if to say "yes", and she took his hand to brace herself as she leaned to take off her shoes as they went out the door.

The air was cooler and the ocean breeze blew gently as they made their way back to the hotel on the beach. They were not the only ones down there and other lovers would giggle and laugh as they passed them by. They walked upon a couple lying in the sand making love. Stopping for a moment, they turned to walk another way. Sally giggled and took Larkin by the side with her arm. Before they went up to the steps he took her by the waist and pulled her to him and said, "I love you, Sally Palmer." She kissed him deeply, sighed when she stopped to look at him while he shook the sand from his feet and they went up to their bed, lost in the fourth night of their honeymoon.

The clock went off early at six a.m. on Wednesday, because they had to be in front of the hotel at eight to get on the tour bus with the group to see Pearl Harbor. She told him which shirt to wear this time and he helped her put on a different Mumu after rubbing more aloe lotion on her back. Today she put her hair up and tucked it under her hat. He had bought a pair of Polaroid sunglasses because they would help him see under water at the Arizona memorial, to which he was looking forward to seeing. Putting them on, he teased her saying, "Hey these work well, I can see through your Mumu."

As she still was not wearing anything under it, she was alarmed and asked half way convinced, "You cannot?"

"No, just kidding, but I sure wish I could!"

She came over to him, slapped him lightly, and gave him a kiss saying, "Come on Honey, let's get some breakfast."

They went downstairs and had fruit, a muffin, and coffee. There were a lot of people out already and they assumed that most of them would be going on the tour with them, and they were right. The bus was already parked out front and some of the people started to file up there to get a seat they were comfortable with. Larkin knew he would need an aisle seat because of the cast, so they gave the others the opportunity to get aboard first. They got in last and much to their delight the front two seats were empty. This was perfect for them, and Sally sat on one side with Larkin on the other, cast hanging out into the aisle.

The driver was excellent and gave them some background information about what they were going to see on the tour on the way over. "Good morning ladies and gentleman. My name is Alec and I'll be your tour driver today. Today we will be visiting the history of the attack on Pearl Harbor on December 7th, 1941, by the Japanese. Our destination is the USS Arizona. I want to make sure that you get as much out of your tour as possible. Sooooo, if you have any questions at all, feel free to ask me anything you want. Well, *almost anything!*" The people laughed at his joke. "Seriously folks, you can interrupt me if you want to ask a question, but after I answer it for you, it will be your responsibility to remind me where I left off!" They laughed again. "Please sit back and relax while we travel over to the site and I'll talk to the guy with the cast sitting by me."They chuckled again and he hung up his microphone on a hook above him.

He asked Larkin, "So what's your name and how'd you do that to your foot?"

"I'm Larkin Palmer, and the beautiful woman behind you is my wife, Sally. I fell from the snow going down the steps to my apartment."

"Wouldn't happen here would it?"

"Nope. Here it would be geckos."

"Ha. Good one, Larkin; geckos."

Alec took them to the Visitor's center and said, "Okay, this is our stop. Now people, listen up!" They got quiet and he resumed. "The tour is self guided, so I'm not coming with you! When you go into the visitor's center you'll see a movie and you can go through the museum, too. There are other things to see and do, so knock yourselves out. The tickets are free and it's first come first serve. Sometimes 5000 people a day go through it. So don't wait. Get them! The trips out to the Arizona are timed and depart on a regular schedule. I will be parking here now until 1 p.m. That should give even the most patriotic American and most interested history buff plenty of time to get back here before I leave you. Oh, there's no food on site, so if you get hungry, get back soon! Any questions?" No one had any. "You disappoint me people! I thought you'd have at least one. See you before 1 p.m.! Repeat that with me- 1 p.m., 1 p.m., 1 p.m.!"

The Palmers got off first because Larkin was in the way! Larkin waved goodbye to Alec and Sally took her husband's arm to start into the visitor's center. A special movie was just about to begin, so they got tickets and went into the theatre. The movie was about twenty minutes long and it talked about the vessel itself and the attack on Pearl Harbor on the "day of infamy", but focused on the battleships' fate and the loss of 1,177 of her crew members. By the time Sally came out, she had cried twice. They went to go through the museum, but because it was a slow day, they called their ticket group and they had to go to get on the boat to the memorial. They could come back and look at the museum afterwards.

Most, if not all of the people in the tour bus, came out on the boat with them to the memorial. The pair got off and walked up the ramp, Larkin putting his sunglasses back on to look into the water at the sunken battleship. His feelings got the best of him as he realized he was looking into the final resting place of so many soldiers. He began to cry and when Sally saw *his* reaction, she cried as well. In fact, as the group walked along the deck and peered down, they, too, became somber. When they got to the Remembrance Wall, Larkin could do nothing but pray for the families of the many men that gave their lives for their country. They looked at the model and compared what they saw to it. Finally, it was time to go back to shore. The ride back was mostly in silence; not many of the people were jolly, but it had made them at the beginning of the year 1979, reflect upon their freedoms and how they come. Freedom is not free. For this Palmer man, he was determined to always be prepared to fight evil. Someday, he knew not when, destiny would lead him to have to complete his Grandpa's plan; the fight against another New World Order.

When they got back to shore, they finally went through the museum as did most of the others. As 1 p.m. came around, the group was all in the tour bus *ready* to go. Alec had seen this reaction to the memorial many times before, therefore, he was not the funny guy he was on the way out. He merely announced they'd be back to the Hotel in fifteen minutes. When they got back, he thanked them for coming with him to the Memorial and said, "Goodbye and aloha" to them all. He did say, "Next time you take a tour, tell them you had a guy named "Wise Alec" for your driver!" They all chuckled somewhat again, many shaking their heads.

As Larkin got up, he handed him a tip and asked, "I suppose you really don't get many tips do you?"

"Not really." Alec held up the folded bill and said, "Thanks, Larkin." The bus emptied quickly.

After that they went up to the room. They didn't say much. Instead of talking, Larkin turned the TV on and just sat there for a while because Sally was in the bathroom. When she came out she sat next to him and they just held each other. Finally, trying to bring them "up", he asked, "What are we going to do tomorrow?"

"We are going to Diamond Head and the Dole Plantation to eat some pineapple."

"That sounds great. What about tonight?" She answered his question with a question,

"I was thinking disco?"

"Disco huh? Where?"

"A new place called "DA Waiting Room". Are you game?"

"I'll try anything once. What do I wear?"

"Jeans and a tee are fine."

"How about you?"

"A skirt and a shirt! But let's eat something before we change. Okay? I'm hungry."

"Me, too."

He called down for room service and had them bring up a burger for each of them as they had been eating a lot of fish. They wolfed them down and then decided to take a short nap before they changed as well. The "short " nap turned out to be three hours and they decided to skip the disco and just go down to the pool bar to drink, listen to music, and maybe even dance.

The attire planning didn't change though and they changed out of the clothes they had worn that day. They were in better moods than that afternoon and went down to the bar with smiles on their faces; determined to have a good time. Guy was there and he asked what they wanted to drink. Larkin said, "Mai Tais; of course!"

"You got it!"

They waited with their backs to the bar scoping out the crowd and listening to the music. It wasn't strictly Hawaiian music tonight, but dance music, and people were dancing in an area by the pool under lights held up by a couple of Banyan trees. The sky was clear, the moon was out and the stars were actually visible in the night sky. It was a romantic setting for sure and one that after the first drink began to have an effect on the newlyweds. They sat at a table next to the dance floor and when a slow dance came on, they got up to give it a whirl. They could not remember having danced before, so this was their first dance, their wedding dance, and they were the only ones on the dance floor. The song began to play and they hadn't ever heard it before and Andy Williams began to sing, "The Hawaiian Wedding Song". By the time they had finished Sally was crying and much to their surprise the people by the bar clapped and yelled out "Congratulations!" They had been set up and Guy was the culprit. They walked back over to the bar and Larkin said to Guy, "Thanks Guy. That was nice."

"You're welcome, Larkin and Sally. Here's a drink on me. Congratulations."

"Thanks, Guy," said Sally.

The two walked back over to their table with women grabbing Sally to congratulate her and guys telling Larkin "Way to go!" When they sat down the music began to play again only this time they sat and drank their Mai Tai and watched the other people. This didn't last long though and the mood to dance struck the red haired woman and she took Larkin's hand, leading him to the floor. She put her hand on his shoulder and held him close as Eric Clapton sang "Wonderful Tonight". For the rest of the night they danced the slow ones, with the final dance being "Fever" by Peggy Lee. They finally started to their room when Guy closed the place down and wanted to go home himself. He figured it was his own fault for getting them started. They said goodnight to him, and they went up to bed. It was a wonderful night.

Larkin got up before Sally that Thursday morning and went down to get them coffee. He had two cups in his hands and was on his way back up when Julie approached him and said, "I heard you closed the place down last night, Larkin. Get lucky?"

Larkin blushed, but got even with her by saying in a serious tone, "Do you always speak to your guests this way?" She didn't know how to

answer and began to panic when he asked her, "I did. Did you?"He
walked away whistling and she cracked up laughing so loudly they could
hear her at the front door.

Sally was brushing her hair when he came back with the coffee
and he sat it down by her chair. He took a sip of his and it was still too
hot. Sally pushed her hair to the side and Larkin took a look at the
sunburn. "I think it's looking good, Dear."
"It feels a lot better. I hope to get some sun tomorrow. I didn't
bring my suit to wear it just once!"
"That's not a suit, it's a postage stamp."
"You like it."
He went over to her, kissed her and said, "Yes. *Everybody*
does."
"Oh. Will you put some more aloe on me before I get dressed?"
"Of course!"

He picked up the now open second bottle of aloe lotion and he
repeated the same procedure they had done so many times before, but
this time it became more sensual than therapeutic and before long the
two honeymooners were "honeymooning". He marveled on how God
had designed such a symbol of their love to be this much fun. When
they finally called down to tell Julie to get the limo ready, it was getting
late and she asked him, "What is taking you so long up there "lover boy?"
He played along and said, "Let's just put it this way Julie, it was a
labor of love I didn't mind doing."
Sally overheard him and she paused with putting on the last bit
of mascara to shake her head and make a funny face.
Julie started to laugh again and said, "I'll have the limo ready
when you get here."

They had the limo drive past the Dole Plantation first and they
tried pineapple straight from the fields. It was just so fresh and if they
could have, they would have stayed there all day long. As Larkin took a
bite he said, "Did you know there's about 30,000 pineapples to an acre
out there? I wish we could put that many apple trees in an acre." Sally
laughed and watched one of the field hands unloading pineapples for the
stand.
She asked, "They hand pick all those don't they?"
"Yes. Its hard work and kids still help out during school
vacations."

Sally was in awe at how fast the people there cut up a pineapple.
The man who cut theirs twisted off the top in a snap, cut it into four
pieces, trimmed off the outside, and cut it into cubes in less than a
minute. It was amazing to watch! They spent a little while longer looking

around, but Larkin wanted to go to Diamond Head. However, they bought some juice to take back to the room and wished that they could take a case of pineapples home with them. Larkin just didn't think that would work that well.

The driver took them back the way they had come and then down along the coast for the view. They watched the surfers and wondered what it would be like to follow that lifestyle. Sally watched the birds along the way and told Larkin she'd like to get some bread and feed them in the morning. Larkin told her the resort didn't like people doing it for obvious reasons. When the limo went past Kapiolani Park the road changed to Diamond Head and they were right below the landmark. The driver said at the stop sign there, "You can either walk from the lot below up to the top or I can drive you up there. Which would you like?"

Sally replied, "Drive us up and we'll walk down. You can meet us down here."

"Good plan, Mrs. Palmer," he replied.

He turned and went up to the top, dropping them off. He knew he'd never get a tip if he didn't; no matter how nice Larkin was. He could tell she was an independent woman.

As they looked around they were surprised to see what had been placed in the crater by the military. The lighthouse was especially interesting to Larkin and he thought it was a cool view of it from their position, but wanted to go see it when they went to the road below again. As all of the military structures were built turn of the century, they were beginning to become a bit run down and some decommissioned, but Larkin bet they could be reactivated and function once again. As they walked to the edge, Larkin saw the bunkers built out of stones by the military and commented on how different they were from the rock wall on The Homestead and yet, he said, served a function very similar. Finally, they decided to start the decent to the bottom and went into the cave. They didn't have a flashlight, but the people in front of them did and to a very large degree, they relied on theirs to get down the 225ft tunnel. After that, there was a concrete walkway down which curved back and forth all over the place. Larkin figured they put it in to keep the trail from eroding, besides, in some spots the trail would have fallen away and made the climb impossible. By the time they got to the bottom, they had done a lot of walking that day. Larkin was tired and his cast was starting to look shabby again. He'd have to borrow some shoe polish.

The driver was where he was supposed to be and Larkin asked him to take them to the lighthouse. The driver said, "You realize the lighthouse is not open to the public. The Commander of the 14th Coast Guard unit lives there."

"Oh," said Larkin disappointedly.

"But, I'll drive you by."

Larkin replied with resignation, "That's fine. Thanks."

They drove by rather slowly backing up traffic a bit. Craning his neck up to look at the tower, Larkin said," I'd sure like to be able to see and touch that lens. They don't make them anymore."
"What's so special about it, Honey?" asked Sally.
"It's a Fresnel lens. They bend the light from one point and direct it outward in a beam. They are very interesting and rare. They are truly a work of art."

As there was about a ten foot apron, the driver pulled onto the side of the road to let the traffic pass by. A man was standing by the mail box, so Larkin rolled down the window and asked him, "Sir. Do you know the people who live here?"
"Yes. That would be me."

Larkin looked back to see if he would get hit getting out of the limo and quickly jumped out leaving Sally and the driver in awe. Larkin took out his wallet and quickly got out his Smithsonian ID. "I'm assuming you are then the commander and probably Admiral?"
He didn't answer.
Larkin went on and said, "I apologize for taking up your time Admiral, Sir, but I'm Larkin Palmer and I work in the history department at the Smithsonian in Washington, D.C.." He stuck out his ID to show him and continued. "I've always been fascinated by the Fresnel lens and I've never been privileged to see one. I was wondering, Sir? As long as I'm in Honolulu?"
The admiral smiled at him and said, "You've got balls, Palmer. I like that. Follow me. Oh, is she with you?" He pointed back at Sally, whose head was sticking out the window of the limo.
"Yes, Sir, she's my new wife."
"Newlyweds? Tell her to come, too."
Larkin waved her to come and she got out running across the busy road to them as the admiral waited to give them a private tour.

They talked as they walked, the admiral asking them a little more about themselves and their jobs. The commander told them he had been in D.C. for some time as well, but didn't like being confined there like a ship in a glass bottle. He took out his key and opened the door and as they looked around, he told them about the lighthouse and how it just takes care of itself nowadays, just needing maintenance to keep afloat. He pointed at the stairs and asked, "Want to see the lens now?"
The two just nodded their heads and he led the way up the metal curved stairs, each step creating an echo in the round structure.

He explained how the place was occupied by the 19th Lighthouse District until 1939 and how it was taken over by the Coast Guard after WWII. There even used to be a radio station there. He explained the lens in more detail and that now the light just blinks instead of being a steady beam. He said pointing out to sea, "They can see it for 18 miles out there."

Larkin went up next to the lens and peered inside looking and trying to observe all the refractions. He looked at the admiral for permission to touch it. The admiral just nodded to him and Larkin stuck his hand on it. It was like a giant, cool, clear icicle, ready to melt when the hot light came on beneath it. He withdrew and took a look out toward the ocean asking, "Do we know how many lives have been saved by it Admiral?"

"God only knows, Son."

The admiral started back down the stairs and the two mainlanders followed him down. After they went outside, Larkin shook the admirals' hand and thanked him for his hospitality and service to his country. Sally thanked him as well, said good-bye and they let themselves out through the gate that locked behind them. The admiral waved goodbye yelling to them, "Congratulations and have a nice honeymoon in Hawaii! Aloha!"

They got back in the limo and the driver just shook his head and said, "I don't know how you did that Larkin, but you sure got some big cohones."

He replied, "That's what they say." He said it again under his breath so only Sally could hear, "That's what they say."

The driver left them out at the door of the Surfrider, and Larkin gave him a tip, telling him they'd need him in the morning as well. He tipped his hat and thanked him, closing the door and going to move the limo to the barns.

It had been a long day and they were tired. If they did want to eat later, they decided to call room service. For now, Larkin wanted to go and take a shower and then hit the sack. Sally on the other hand-didn't…

Larkin took the plastic bag off the dresser he'd used before and wrapped it over the cast. He was getting tired of that exercise, and hoped that when he got back to D.C. to see the doctor, he'd get the pesky thing cut off! He got in the shower and in a minute Sally joined him there. She wasn't there for the shower. After the shower, Larkin really did need to take a nap and Sally joined him there, too. They never did get up that night for dinner.

The last day of their trip was finally upon them. They wished it wasn't the case. Even though it had started off to be an awful honeymoon, only because of the sunburn, it had turned out to be an amazing one! They dressed casually as before and went out to go downtown to the Royal Palace and roam the area. They didn't want to stay too long, so they had the driver drop them off and told him to come back at noon so Sally could get more "exposure" to the sun. At least those were Larkin's words. Sally slapped him as soon as they got out of the limo. Larkin just laughed.

They went to Lolani Palace and took the tour. The guide started on the veranda and told them how King Kalakaua and his Queen lived in the Palace. He pointed across the street and said, "The king's statue is across the street at Judicial Plaza. If we didn't send people over there to see it, they wouldn't ever get visitors, unless they were crooks!" The group laughed and he said, "For them, the key is in the statue!" The group laughed again.

Larkin's face lit up and he got excited. He pulled Sally away from the group by her arm almost yanking it out of the socket he was so excited. Annoyed with him Sally asked, "What are you doing Larkin?"
"I KNOW WHERE THE KEY IS!" His "gift" had *finally* kicked in.

Just then the tour guide led the people past them and smiling from ear to ear Larkin said loudly as they walked away, "THANK YOU SIR. YOU ARE THE BEST TOUR GUIDE WE'VE EVER HAD! THANK YOU, THANK YOU, THANK YOU!" Seeing as they had just started the tour, the guide got a perplexed look on his face when the two ran away and he just shook his head as he went on with the group.

With that exclamation of gratitude, Larkin ran out onto the veranda with Sally in tow, down the steps and into the front yard of the palace toward the plaza and the statue across the street. He didn't stop until they got there and they breathed hard from the run. When he finally caught his breath enough he said, "Look at that statue. What do you see Sally?"
Pausing to take a breath herself she said, "Just a bronze statue. Why?"
"Well," he said taking another breath, "just imagine this statue isn't King Kalakaua, but is the one in D.C. of Albert Pike. Okay?"
"Okay! But- what?"
"Okay. Whenever anyone walks by, they just look at a statue and think nothing of it. It's just a repository for bird poop. Right?"
"So what's the point, Larkin?" Sally was getting impatient.
"Well, if you remember, it's just like the one at the Temple. He's standing there with his right arm outstretched and a book under his arm

on the left. People walk by it every day and don't think anything about it. Well, Pikes clue said, "The key is in the book". Right?" She was now listening intently and nodded in the affirmative. "Well the guy across the street just solved it! He said, "The key is in the statue!" Sally, the Key is in the book, in the statue, in the park!"

Sally's eyes lit up! She got real excited and said, "You may have it, Larkin! But how do we get into a statue?"

"That's for us to figure out when we get home. A little while ago I didn't want this to be our last day here, but now I'm glad it is. I want to get home." He planted a big kiss on her lips took her by the hand and went to call the limo.

When they got back to the room, Larkin was a pack of nerves about to tense up into a ball. He packed all his things and was making sure he was ready to go home the next morning. Usually that was Sally's job and she did it at the proper time, which she thought would be that evening, so this was particularly annoying to her. She said to him, "Larkin. Relax, Honey. You can't do anything from here. Let's enjoy the last little bit of time we have here."

He calmed down a bit and said, "I suppose you're right. But this sure is huge."

"It is. Come help me change."

"Do you need me to help you still?"

She looked at him and didn't answer for a second. "No, Silly. But don't you want to?"

He said, "Oh. Yeah!" He followed her into the bathroom to help her put on the teenie weenie bikini.

After more than a bit of time, they went down to the pool to take a swim. Of course, "they" was Sally and he watched her swim around the pool for about a half an hour while he drank his Mai Tai and tapped his cast on the ground in time with the music. He'd become kind of fond of the drink and wondered if they had them in D.C.. He hoped so! Sally got out of the pool and came for a towel. She didn't want to get another burn, so she just wrapped the towel around her, put her hat on, and plunked her butt on the lounge chair. She said, "That was refreshing. Want to walk on the beach for a bit?"

"Yeah. We haven't really done that much, but let's wait until the sun starts to go down. Okay?"

"Yes," she said, gulping after having taken a swig of her drink, "I don't want to take the towel off and get another sunburn."

They sat there a little longer drinking Mai Tais until the sun was about to set. Finally, Sally took off her towel and gave it to Larkin. She left her hat on her head and they got up to walk along the beach until the sun had sunk into the ocean. The lovebirds walked barefoot on the sand as it began to cool from the heat of the sun and watched other couples come out to see the sun take its final dive for the day. Walking hand in hand, they said nothing, listening to the waves sound against the shore and pier, while birds flew to find their perches for the night. When the sun had finally extinguished itself beneath the waves, Larkin lay down the towel and they made love on the sands of Waikiki.

As they checked out the next day, Julie came up to Larkin at the desk and said, "I'm glad to have been able to serve you two while you were here. It's been fun and I hope you had the best time of your life while here in Honolulu."

"You and the staff have done a great job, Julie. We want to thank you, too."

Being a wise guy, she suddenly took out a piece of paper from behind her back and handed it to him saying, "Here's your bill for the extras! Aloha!" She giggled and walked toward new people coming in the door.

Larkin had been approved for check writing, so he wrote a check for the extras and the limo driver picked up their bags. It was time to go home! But first, he left Julie a tip. On the hundred dollar bill he wrote this caption coming from the mouth of Ben Franklin; "I got lucky in Waikiki!"

Chapter Six

The Dead Letter

By the time Sally and Larkin got off the plane in D.C., she knew the honeymoon was over! Not so much that Larkin would neglect her and their relationship, but she knew Larkin would delve back into this work with a vengeance. Even before the flight from Honolulu to L.A. was over, he had devised a way to retrieve the Key. He only needed the right time to accomplish it.

The first thing they did when they walked in the door to their home was call the parents! Sally called her mom, but her dad wasn't home. They talked for almost an hour and Sally promised she'd send some of the pictures she took with her Brownie. It was the same for Larkin, as Lawtin wasn't home either, because he had gone to town to pick up a few things for Shirley. They talked to Shirley for almost as long, but Larkin told her about some of the things they'd seen and especially the Lighthouse adventure.

They hung up and sat down by the kitchen counter. Larkin said, "Say, Dear, I was thinking that things are going to be a little different now that we are married and we ought to come up with a plan as to how we are going to do things."

Sally sat down with a glass of water took a sip and with some reservation asked, "Like what, Honey?"

"First thing I'm going to do is move into the master bedroom. The other bedroom is just a place to store some of my clothes and we might want to move some into a couple of your drawers, so it is no longer my room. The master is "our" room now."

"That goes without saying," she replied.

"Secondly, I'll be going to school on Mondays, Tuesdays, and Thursdays now, so while I'm at school you can take care of the household things and help with my stuff on the days I'm off. I'll have to study in the afternoons and evenings of the days I have school, too. But, I think in order not to burn ourselves out, we should try to keep the weekends free from as much as possible and take off as many evenings as we can. I know one thing for sure and that is I want to get out and maybe go for a walk each evening with you; if we can. What do you think?"

"You chauvinist!" She rolled her eyes, laughed and continued, "Oh, that's a lot. But I have to admit, it all sounds like a good idea. After I get the place down pat, I know I can do more for you, too, especially in research. I'm just grateful that I don't have to work at the 9 to 5 job environment anymore. I liked Mr. Shipley as my boss, but I know I'm going to like Mr. Palmer more!"

He was concerned now about what he had said and asked her, "Did I sound like an egoist?"

She kissed him and said, "No. I understand where you are coming from."

He said, "I hope you never stop taking those benefits from your boss."

She looked at him puzzled and he explained, "The kisses." She smiled and kissed him again. He said, "Let's go unpack."

Kidding him, she replied in a lowered voice, "Yes, Boss."

They unpacked and Sally moved some of her stuff where Larkin's used to be to make it easy. They both felt grungy, so they got cleaned up before trying to make dinner. Sally put on her robe and didn't get dressed, but Larkin put on some jeans and a tee before going down to the kitchen to scrounge for food. The wedding planner had left a couple bottles of champagne for them and when Larkin saw them, he tried to come up with something to go with them for dinner. He was tired and wanted something simple, mostly because he didn't want to burden Sally with fixing a big meal. She was tired too! Sally looked in the pantry and Larkin looked in the freezer. He said, "We have some breaded shrimp we could fry or a frozen pizza."

Sally held up a couple of cans and said, "It's either beef stew or chili."

Together they said, "Shrimp."

Larkin said, "Wait a minute! We just got back from a vacation where all we had was seafood. We were supposed to eat beef when we got back."

Sally laughed and replied, "Oh well. I guess we're in a rut."

He chuckled.

Sally started the shrimp while Larkin put a can of green beans on the stove and baked potatoes in the microwave. Then he took the champagne out to the back door and opened it. They were glad he did, because it spewed all over and he caught the foam with his mouth to avoid spilling so much. Sally said, "That's your first glass!"

He laughed and said back, "No! That was *your* first glass."

They laughed and he got out a couple of glasses to have a drink before dinner. Larkin held the bottle up and looked at it asking, "I wonder how much I spent on this?"

"She, (meaning the wedding planner) probably knows."

That reminded Larkin, "I forgot to tell you! You remember the bottle of wine we drank from the case we found in the basement?"

"Yeah?"

"Well, she says we drank a two thousand dollar bottle of wine that night!"

"What? Is the rest of it worth that much?"

"She said to bring her a list and she'd find out."

"I'll make it and take it to her. Wow. Isn't that something?"

He brought the bottle over to fill her glass again and said, "Our lives are really something, Sally. We are so blessed, we Palmers, even if we are cursed."

Ignoring that statement she asked, "Are you trying to get me drunk?"

"No need."

"Pretty cocky aren't we?" she asked in the third person.

"Yes," he replied arrogantly and took her in his arms, bending her over to kiss her.

When he let her back up she said, "Whew! Enough of that stuff for you!"

They ate and laughed and went to bed early so Larkin could test the bed in the master bedroom. They both liked the new arrangement.

They got up on Sunday and headed to church. Mrs. Heidelmann was glad to see them and she patted the seat next to her as Sally made her way down the pew to their seats. Sally knew she'd have a million questions for her, so she'd suggested to Larkin they invite her to eat lunch with them afterwards. The service was long and Larkin was hungry when they finally shook hands with Pastor Olsen. He said, "I'm so glad to see you're back. Looks like you two got some sun in Hawaii."

Larkin just burst out laughing and said to him looking at Sally who was smiling, "You don't know the half of it, Pastor. I'll tell you sometime."

Sally piped in, "No you won't, Larkin!"

Pastor Olsen asked him to call to set up registering for new member classes and they walked out to the narthex to speak with Mrs. Heidelmann. She accepted their invitation for lunch and she asked them to follow her to the house so she could drop off her car.

They had a great lunch and told her about the whole thing; the Hay-Adams, the details of the wedding surprise, and the honeymoon. Afterwards, Mrs. Heidelmann took Sally aside when Larkin went to the restroom and being rather snoopy asked, "I heard you two kids made a commitment to keep pure until you got married and that must have been tough when you were living together, but how did you do it? If he was my boyfriend, I wouldn't have been able to resist!"

Sally laughed and said, "I tried Mrs. Heidelmann, but he wouldn't let me. I used every trick in the book, too. He's a good man and he wanted it that way. I respect him for it and I know he loves me."

"I'm glad for you, Sally. God is good to those who love Him."

Sally took her hand and said, "Yes, I know. Thank you."

They watched Larkin return and they both just giggled as he walked toward them. He noticed and he asked them with a smile, "What are you two laughing about?"

Sally answered him saying, "Just girl stuff, Honey." Mrs. Heidelmann just smiled.

Larkin paid the bill and they left to take her home. On the way they proposed that they do this once a month and Mrs. H said she'd like that.

After they dropped her off, Larkin was curious about something and he asked Sally, "Sally, would you mind if I drove by Pike's statue?"

"Now?"

"I'm kind of curious to see how many people go by there on a Sunday afternoon."

"Okay."

Larkin drove past and because there was a parking spot in front of it, he parked. They got out and stood looking at the statue. Larkin had wondered, since Hawaii, if the man in the blue suit had been snooping around, but he had not been and definitely was not on a Sunday. They had never seen a tail on Sunday and that was good. He walked up to the effigy and Sally followed. It was a mess, with bird droppings all over it. Sally asked him, "How are you going to get up there, Larkin? He's tall."

"Here's the plan. I load a ladder in the truck with cleaning supplies and some tools in case we need them. We come over here on a Sunday when no one is around or possibly tailing us. We pretend to be cleaning the statue and look for entry into the book somehow. When we find what we are looking for, we finish up and leave."

"What if someone asks us what we are doing? Like the cops?"

"We just say I got community service from a judge and this is the only day I can do it. What do you think of the plan?"

"I think it'll work. Actually, it's brilliant."

"I know. We just have to find a time," his voice got higher as an idea came to him, "like, when it's raining!"

They got back into the Lincoln and started home. As they had to pass Harry's house on the way, Sally asked, "As long as we are close, want to stop and see Harry?"

"I think that'd be nice."

Larkin parked out front and the two hopped out and walked up to the door. Harry didn't come right away and Larkin was tempted to use his key and go in, but he thought that wouldn't be good because they might alarm him. Finally, he came to the door putting on his glasses and pushing his hair back as if he had been taking a nap. Harry opened the door and waved them in saying, "You're back! How nice of you two to come by and see me. Come in and tell me about your trip."

Harry had tons of questions about the trip and Hawaii. When Larkin told him about the lighthouse tour he said, "You got to see a Fresnel lens?"

"I *even touched* it."

"Wow! You touched a Fresnel lens."

Not to be outdone by a lens, Sally said the first thing that came to her mind, "We got to walk the beach and even go to the USS Arizona."

Harry replied, "Is that so? I bet the Arizona was interesting, but kind of a hard thing to look at, huh, Sally?"

"Yeah, most of the people went away pretty down."

"Well, that's why it's called a memorial, I guess. Say, would you guys like a beer or anything?"

Sally said, "Sure. Want one, Honey?"

"Yeah, I'll take one, Harry."

Harry got out three beers and they sat and talked for about another half an hour. Sally thanked him for the wedding gift and said it would work well for them. Seeing it was getting late, Sally said, "I guess we should go, Larkin. You have to get ready for the first day of classes in the morning."

Larkin stood up to leave and thanked Harry for the beer. Harry gave him a manly hug and said, "I sure miss having you two around."

Sally said, "Oh, Harry, we thought we'd like to have dinner with you once a month or so. Would you like that?"

"Sure would. Just let me know when."

"Okay, we'll give you a call."

They went out the front door and got in the car to go home after a long day away. Larkin asked her when they got in the Lincoln, "What did Harry give us for a wedding gift?"

Laughing she said, "I don't remember!"

When they got home it was about six o'clock and Larkin went into the office to plan his first day back to school. Sally thought it prudent to go do thank you's for the wedding gifts!

They started to get hungry about two hours later and the newlyweds decided to put the frozen pizza in the oven and watch TV. Too tired to do any more that day, they just wanted to sit there. The buzzer on the oven timer went off and Sally got up from the couch to pull the pepperoni pizza out before it burned. It turned out perfect, however, and Larkin took a couple beers out of the refrigerator and brought them over to the counter. The movie, "Gus", about a soccer playing mule was on channel six. Larkin asked, "Did you see this in the theater?"

"No. It's kinda funny and has some good actors in it. I like movies that a family can go to."

Larkin smiled and continued to watch the antics of Tim Conway until they were done with the pizza. There were two pieces left, so she put them in the refrigerator. He cleaned up the pizza pan and she threw away the trash and wiped up. After he finished that chore, he turned off the tube just as the credits began to play. It was an end of another day and he thought about how even these little things with Sally, like winding down on a Sunday night, was something he'd always remember as part of the good times of their life. Little did he know...?

The next day they put their plans in action, or maybe it was said to be *his* plan, but it seemed to work well. Sally got all of her tasks done and Larkin was way ahead on his school work already. He received his grades from the previous semester and he was still a 4.0 GPA student. Sally asked him, "Did you call Pastor Olsen today about the class?"

"No. I forgot. Let's try now. It's only three." She smiled, but said nothing about it.

Larkin dialed and instead of his secretary picking up, Pastor Olsen answered himself. "Mount Olivet Lutheran Church, this is Pastor Olsen."

"Hi, Pastor. This is Larkin Palmer. Where's your secretary?"

"Oh, hello, Larkin! She goes home at three. What can I help you with?"

"I thought I'd call you to enroll Sally and me in the new member class."

"Good! It begins this Saturday morning at nine o'clock. It runs until ten-thirty each week, finishing at Pentecost. If you complete it, we will welcome you in as members and then you may receive communion."

"Sounds good, Pastor. We'll be there."

"Oh Larkin, want to tell me the story about the sunburn?"

"In person sometime, Pastor."

"It must be a good one then," Olsen chuckled.
"It was funny to me, but not so much for my wife."
"I'll see you Saturday. Bye, Larkin."
"Bye, Pastor."

Larkin was in luck, because Sally had gone to the bathroom half way through his conversation with Pastor Olsen and she didn't hear the last part about the sunburn. She came back into the room and she asked, "Did you call the doctor about getting your cast off?" This time she chuckled audibly and so did he.
"No! I forgot that, too!"
"Want me to?"
"No, I'll try right now."

Larkin dialed the doctor and talked to his secretary. She set up an appointment for Friday afternoon to have it removed and boy, was Larkin happy! Hanging up the phone, Larkin jumped up, grabbed Sally's hands and danced around the room in joy swinging her around like a mad man. He was going to be set free on Friday!

Friday didn't come as quickly as Larkin wanted it to, but come it did. All morning long he'd look at his work, set it down, pace around the room and then repeat the process. He was driving Sally crazy with it as she read from a resource book and finally she just said, "Quit it, will you Honey? I can't concentrate."
"Oh. Sorry, Dear. I'm just excited."
"Come here, I have something to show you. It's about someone in the Palmer Journal and is very interesting."

Sally handed him the book and he began to read. He stopped and said, "This is a report on the Anti-Masonic movement of the time and how the anti-Masons blamed the Masons for the death of Morgan. Interesting. My Great Grandpa Lawton just filled in the missing parts of the puzzle in the Journal for us. They obviously added another dead body to the mix. All of these people are Masons. Just shows you that all of the stories in the Journal are true, Sally, because my family was there." He sat the book down and took her by the waist to say, "I'm hungry."
She thought he was being amorous and she asked, "What do you have in mind?"
"Grilled cheese."
He let go of her and started to the kitchen. She laughed and followed along saying, "That wasn't very funny, Honey."
"I thought it was," he said, sprinting the rest of the way out of her reach.

They ate their sandwiches and afterwards, he went to get ready for his appointment. Putting all of the paperwork away again, she wondered if he had put a copy of all of it in the safe. She went to ask him as he dressed. "Say Honey, did you put copies of all these documents in the safe, just in case?"

"Yes. In fact, these are the copies of the original copies. I don't think they'll try to get into the house with the alarm system on though."

"Okay, just wondered."

Looking at himself in the mirror he said, "I'm all ready to go lose some weight."

The cast came off without a problem and the doctor said the x-ray showed a good mend. On the way home Larkin said, "Boy does it ever feel good to get that cast off. Look at how white my foot is! I actually overcompensate and exert too much force when I lift my leg now. I suppose that'll take time to get used to again. But you know what I think?"

"No. What do you think?"

"Let's celebrate! Pizzaaaa!!!!"

Sally looked at him in a maniacal manner and they both screamed, "Pizzaaaaaa!"

Stopping at Luigi's, they commented that they hoped they had as good of floor show as last time. They ordered and this time they got Italian sausage with the pepperoni, just for something different. They watched the pizza fly into the air and the cook just caught them like it was nothing- a small feat. It was the same guy that got into the fight with the customer the previous time they were there and his name, they came to find out, was Mario. They had been talking to the waitress who noticed Sally's ring and asked if they had gotten married since the last time she saw them and they said "yes."The waitress's was named Vi, and she congratulated them. Watching Mario was almost as good a show as the argument of last time. The pizza flying through the air was mesmerizing. Vi finally brought theirs and after praying, they washed it down with a whole pitcher of Coke.

Bringing their ticket to them, Vi also brought them a bowl of spumoni and said, "This is a wedding present from us." She pointed at the crew and Mario, who waved and smiled from behind the glass windows of the kitchen. They thanked her and waved back at Mario knowing this was the place they'd always come to for pizza. On the way out, Larkin skipped, hopped, and twirled to the car, almost like a giddy schoolgirl in happiness over the loss of the cast. It was a good celebration!

The weekend began slowly for the newlyweds, as they slept in and didn't get up until almost lunch time. The phone rang to wake them and it was Pastor Olsen. "Larkin, this is Pastor Olsen. I called to find out if everything was alright?"

Then it dawned on him that they had missed the first class. "No. Oh Pastor, I'm so sorry. We made a mistake and forgot to come to class! Please forgive us, it won't happen again!"

Olsen laughed and said, "It's okay, Larkin. You can read the material and make it up, but try not to let it happen again. You're forgiven."

"Oh thank you, Pastor. I got my cast off yesterday afternoon and the excitement of it all made me forget to set the alarm. Can we get the materials from you after church tomorrow?"

"I'll have them ready. See you tomorrow." Hanging up the phone, Olsen said to himself, "Ah, to be a newlywed again!"

Sally said, "We forgot to go to class. How could we miss that?"

"I was just so excited. We'll go next week and do makeup. I feel like such a dummy and I don't want to let Pastor down." He also now knew that Olsen held his people accountable and he liked that.

The phone rang again and this time it was Mr. Shipley. "Hello, Larkin, this is Mr. Shipley. I'm glad to hear you are back."

"Thank you, Sir. And thanks again for all that you did for us at Christmas."

"It was our pleasure and Mrs. Shipley is so fond of you both, as I am. Larkin, I've called to tell you I have made a decision about the Seward file. I wanted to wait until you were back and I had given it enough time to do consider it. I hope you concur with me that this is a very sensitive thing. That being the case- I have decided to wait to make an announcement until your research is complete and your paper, and findings, ready for submittal. I want it wrapped up tightly so they don't consider us a bunch of Anti's or conspiracy theorists. It has to be watertight. Do you agree?"

"I want to say, Sir, that I am disappointed, but understand your reasoning. It will take me a while to do what you ask, but it will be worth the wait, I believe."

"Good. As I said before, I will continue to pay your wage personally until it is complete. Expect a check to be mailed each month. In the mean while, you will still be considered staff with full benefits and authority."

"Thank you, Sir."

"By the way, how was the Honeymoon?"

"Very fine, Sir. We had a great time."

"Good! If you need anything or would like to make a progress report, call me anytime."

"Thank you, Sir."

"And Larkin, you know you didn't need to pay for my children's college education."

"I know, Sir. I hope it shows what the Shipley family means to us."

He could hear Dan get choked up and he said, "Thank you, Son. Goodbye."

"Goodbye, Dan."

Larkin hung up the phone. At first he was a bit miffed by Shipleys' decision, but Sally calmed him down trying to appeal to his intellectual and forgiving natures. She was successful, but then he became disappointed and down.

She said trying to cheer him up, "Now all you have to do is put your nose to the grindstone and get it done."

"I will, with your help, Dear."

"But we can't let anyone sidetrack us with any more distractions. Once we get the Key, we need to focus on the file and nothing but the file."

"All we have to do is wait for rain on a Sunday afternoon."

On Valentine's Day, Larkin surprised Sally, blindfolding her and taking her to the Hay-Adams for dinner. He had to pull strings to get the reservation, but they got their usual table. Sam was their waiter and it was like old times. They saw Chester just as he was leaving to go home after his shift and Mike as he took some bags to the elevator. They decided to make the Valentine Dinner a yearly thing for them. Sally was glad Larkin was remaining so romantic and attentive to her even now that he had so many things going on.

Easter came and went, but it was still cold outside and they had not had a seasonal rain yet. In fact, it was only twenty-five degrees on Easter, the wind was blowing and it was threatening snow. The two never missed another of Pastor Olsen's' classes and they got to ask all of the questions they had on the minds. It gave them new understandings and the light bulb of their own faith went on in their heads more than once as they learned from the Word of God. It was the week before Pentecost and they were excited that they would be taken in as Adult Confirmands the next week at church. Sally had been pressed into service with the Women's Missionary League and Larkin was happy she had a little more to do because she was so efficient. She often just read or tried to look for things to do for him to fill her daily routine.

Larkin didn't want her to get bored. Consequently, he took her out on the weekends to concerts of all types and the Symphony, which she enjoyed immensely. The community had noticed them, especially the group the people from the Smithsonian ran with, and they had also been invited to some of their homes for societal gatherings. Along with that, comes charity work, but Sally didn't want to be involved with that quite yet and stuck to the group at church. Larkin, of course, was the financial purse that was tapped and he didn't mind giving to causes he had a proclivity for. All in all, they were becoming a well-known pair of young D.C. socialites untied to the political machine. Larkin liked it that way, because he owed no one any favors. But their nemesis didn't like this much and it seemed as if Larkin was rubbing their noses in the situation. And they were right.

When the Saturday before Pentecost arrived, Larkin was ready to put his plan to retrieve the Key into action. What he didn't count on was the fact that the weather had become suddenly warm and a big rain storm was coming in from the Florida Keys. He thought, 'Isn't that apropos?' Therefore, he loaded everything up into Sally's truck and got ready to go to see Pike after church on that Sunday. Sally came to the garage and saw him loading up and said, "Hey, are we going to clean bird poop tomorrow?"

"Yup! Take a look. I have the ladder, screw driver, rain gear, rags, gloves, soap, to make it look authentic, a hammer and a large putty knife."

"Putty knife?"

"In case the poop is real thick."

"Icky!" she said in disgust.

"Well, the book is in a good resting place. I wouldn't be surprised if there isn't even a nest or two resting there."

"You're in charge," she proclaimed.

"All you'll have to do is hold the ladder and watch out for the crap I scrape off!" He laughed at that one.

"Don't you dare hit me with bird crap, Larkin Palmer!" She slapped him on the arm and smiled. She changed the subject and asked, "Say, Honey. Did you forget to have someone put a garage door opener in?"

"Yes, I did. I never got around to it. Can you get somebody?"

"I'll take care of it. Let's go up and eat lunch."

He bent over, gave her a kiss and said, "I think I'll have cereal."

"Cereal?" she asked.

He ran up the stairs ahead of her, still happy he had his cast off and thanking God for his good health.

That afternoon Larkin took the film from the trip to Hawaii to the store and picked up the pictures he'd dropped off before Christmas. Sally wanted to get some copies made for the folks and get them sent out soon. Larkin wanted to see the pictures of the die they took at The Homestead. After paying, he went out to the car and got in. Opening the envelope of double prints, he sorted through them to the two pictures of the die she took in the basement. He sat them on the seat and found only three. Looking again he could still find only three- one of them was missing! Unfortunately, the one copy that was missing was one of the better ones. Were "they" at it again? IF they were, they knew the treasure was, at least at that time, uncovered and in the Palmer families' possession. That- was a huge problem...

Pentecost Sunday morning they were so anxious that they were ready early. The two decided to go ahead and eat a big breakfast so that they didn't have to take time to stop for lunch when they came to get the truck and change. After cleaning up the dishes Sally took off her apron, and hanging it up she asked Larkin, "You know dear, when I first read the Journal with you back home, I wondered what happened to the other 99 erasers that had been cursed. What do you think happened to them?"

"I've wondered that myself," he replied. "I figured there were many possibilities, like they were never sold and were just placed somewhere by Nairne, because he did write that he'd retained as many as he could or maybe those that were sold were used like any other eraser and the people didn't know about the curse. Or that there may still be some out there that are being passed on just like ours. I think that if that were the case we'd know, because the Masons would have used it on us, but to answer your question, I just don't know, Dear."

"We'll have to think on that."

"Ready to go to church?"

"Ready!"

The confirmation service was very meaningful to them. Fourteen youth were confirmed that day and seven adults like themselves and they all sat in the front so they could participate in the service. The whole congregation was smiles and the new communicants received the Lord's Supper for the first time that day. It meant a great deal to them to be included in something they now truly understood. Of course, Sally cried when she received the Lord's Supper, but Larkin smiled and was happy, now that he knew he had received forgiveness in it. To them, -this- was what life was all about! Why anyone would not want to be one of Christ's was beyond them.

Afterwards, the participants stood beside Pastor Olsen to receive congratulations from the congregation on the way out the door. Everyone welcomed Larkin and Sally into the fellowship with open arms. Of course, Mrs. H was ecstatic. She bragged on them as if they were her own, which in a sense was true, because she had no children, nor family. It occurred to Sally how much she was like Harry. Then she thought, 'Why don't we introduce them?' She'd have to talk to Larkin about that idea.

They said goodbye to her and headed out the door. Larkin was suddenly in a rush, because the storm had moved in and it was raining. Since getting his cast off, he had bought a new suit from Stephen for Easter and he didn't want to get it wet. They ran to the car, got in, and brushed their rain soaked hair away from their faces. It was going to be a long day. Larkin hoped the rain would subside some before he had to do his "community service".

They pulled the Lincoln into the garage and got out. Sally said, "I'll definitely call to get the door opener tomorrow, Honey."

"Thanks. My suit looks like a "swimming" suit right now." He wondered why neither of them could remember to call the door guy! Was it Divine intervention?

Changing quickly, they came right back down to the garage. He handed Sally her rain gear and said, "If we have this on from the beginning, we may not look too much out of place."They put the gear on and got in the truck. It was the first time that Larkin was able to drive the truck because they hadn't used it when they were together since he got his cast removed, so he said, "You drive Sally, I'll get the door."Sally got behind the wheel and started to back out of the garage while Larkin waited for her. He got in after shutting it and said, "Let's go clean crap off of Pike!"

"Ick!"

Sally parked right in front of the statue as Larkin had before. There was no one around and traffic was minimal because of the weather. Larkin pulled the ladder over to the front side of the image and leaned it on the right armpit. It was sturdy there and had a good vantage point. Sally brought the bucket of other stuff over to him and he had her hold the ladder as he looked up at the book. The rain had subsided a bit, for which Larkin was thankful, and after putting on his gloves he climbed to the top of the ladder and said, "Yuck!"

"What?" Sally asked.

"There are three nests here all sealed into the top of the book with poop. It's a mess! Toss me the putty knife."

Sally got the putty knife and threw it up to him with the precision of the baseball pitcher she used to be. He threw the nests to the ground in a way so as to miss Sally and took the putty knife to task scraping two inches of bird droppings off the book. "Hey," he said, "there's a clasp type arrangement here that goes over the book, just as if it were a real one. No one would ever think it may be functional. Toss me up the screw driver, would you, Sally?"She actually threw it to him and he caught it first try. Sticking it in between the book and the clasp he pried on it. It was too sturdy. "I'm going to have to have the hammer too, Dear, but don't hit me with it!"Sally laughed and threw it up end over end. He caught it handle first and said, "Nice throw."Taking the hammer and screw driver, he hit the clasp a couple of times. It broke loose! He checked to see if it would open and it gave way! Throwing the tools down to Sally he opened it the rest of the way. Inside the book was, of course, a – metal box! This was no surprise to Larkin and he said to Sally, "Wow; déjà vu!"

He didn't want to open it now, in the rain and out there, so he threw it down to Sally. He closed the book clasp back up and started down the ladder. Larkin looked around to see if there was anyone there, but no one had been around to approach them, so they quickly picked up all of the equipment, got in the truck, and started home. As Sally drove, Larkin shook, but he finally calmed down enough to open the box. The clasp on it was stuck, so he had to break it with a plier. Wrapped in a cloth bag was a small brown book and on its cover was its title- "The Key to Curses."

"This is it!" shouted Larkin.

"You don't have to shout, Honey. I know it is." She smiled.

"We need to put this in the safe right away."

"What my question is," asked Sally "is how it got there?"

"Better yet is, are there any others like it?"

"I suspect not. Or they wouldn't be looking for it, too!"

They got home and Larkin placed the book in safe next to The Eraser. Before he did, he found that there were 225 pages of curses and their antidotes, or "releases" as Pike called them. The one pertaining to The Eraser was evident which Pike named, "The release of a curse on an object of destruction." At least Larkin *thought* it was evident to be the one. 'Ironic,' he thought, 'they both, the Key and the Eraser, take away.' There were so many antidotes he'd have to see which one fit. One thing he was sure of was, that the Mason's knew which one fit and that they should never see the Key.

Larkin sat on the bed after taking off his rain gear, exhausted from the ordeal they had just gone through and pondering the situation. He sighed a sigh of relief. Sally came in, sat next to him and stroked his still wet hair saying, "Want to take a shower?"

"Yeah, I have to get out of these wet clothes, too. The rain gear works, but not that well."

"You're not getting the picture, Honey." Sally stood up, took his hand and led him to the shower.

They lay in bed for the rest of the afternoon, sleeping after the shower and what Sally had in mind. The phone rang about six o'clock and it was Shirley. Sally answered the phone, but Larkin picked up also and said, "Hi Mom. I've got some great news. We found Pike's Key. We aren't in as much danger now."

"Where was it, Honey?"

"In a statue of Pike in the park. In a metal box. Pretty ingenious."

"I'm glad you found it. How are things otherwise?"

Larkin thought he heard something on the phone, but was unsure and kept on with the conversation. Unfortunately, Dean now knew more than Larkin wanted.

The two told her about church that day, their classes, what Mr. Shipley had said and all the other things they thought a mom might want to know after not hearing from them for a while. They figured out what she *really* wanted to know about when she asked, "Pregnant yet?"

"Mom!" said Larkin.

"Why can't I ask if I'm going to have a grandchild? What's the harm in that?"

"You're so embarrassing, Mom."

Sally said, "No, not yet Mom, but we're working on it. We'll let you know when it happens."

They talked for a bit more and Shirley told Larkin she'd tell his dad about the Key and all the other news. They hung up and the kids just looked at each other and said, "Pregnant yet?"

"Mom has her way with words," said Larkin.
"Yup. Short, sweet and to the point. That's why I like her so much."
"I'm hungry. What's for dinner?"
"Spaghetti."
"Okay. Let's go."

Larkin got up and pulled Sally bare from the bed. She protested, "Larkin, I don't have a stitch on. Let me put on my robe."
He did a double take on that one and asked, "Are you cold?"
"No. I don't want the guy across the street to see me."
"Since when are you so modest?"
"Well, I don't know. All I know is that *this* is for you."
After pointing at herself, she put on her robe and started downstairs. Larkin thought to himself, 'I guess we're making some progress. I thought I was living with a nudist.'

They ate dinner and drank a bottle of wine Sally had bought a couple of days before. He asked if she had ever given the wedding planner the list of the names of wine in the basement and she said, "Yes, but she hasn't gotten back to me on it."
"I guess I'll wait until she does before I call a carpenter for the wine cellar."
"Why would that make a difference?"
"I guess if I knew I had some expensive wine I'd think it was worth it to build it."
She laughed and said, "You're a scream."

The next couple of months flew by. Larkin's work had become tedious and was dragging on. His classes at UMD were almost done for the semester and he and Sally had really settled into a routine. Sally had become involved with the bell choir and from time to time she'd bring home her two bells and get them out and practice with a cassette tape. He went to hear them practice a couple of times and he was proud to say she was doing well.

Sally and her parents had been in touch and they wanted to know if they could come to Tennessee for a visit in the summer, but she put them off until they found out what was happening at The Homestead with Tom's replacement. Larkin wondered if his dad would want him to come home during the summer to help train the new hand. His name was, Peter Hollins. He and his family, consisting of his wife Eve and two teenage boys, James and Luke, had moved into the house. So far, Lawtin was happy at what he saw in his practical knowledge, his education and application thereof, and especially his work ethic. He even thought the boys possessed some of their dad's traits as well. Larkin thought he'd call Lawtin after UMD was out and ask him about it. The time was now. Larkin picked up the phone and called. Shirley answered and Larkin said, "Hi, Mom, it's me."

"Oh! Hi, Honey, how are you?"

"Just fine, Mom. Is Dad home?"

"Yes. I'll go get him." He could hear her yell, "Its Larkin. Come to the phone, Lawtin." She came back to Larkin and asked, "You're not calling to tell us you're pregnant are you?"

Larkin sighed and said, "No, Mom."

Lawtin got on the extension and said, "Shirley, will you quit asking him about that? What's up, Son?"

"I'm about finished with my classes and I wondered how things were going up there with the new man and all. Do you think I need to come and give him some tips or anything?"

"Actually, Son, I think Percy and I have made a good pick in this man. He's doing just fine out there. He runs the place as well as Percy does here. I'm pleased with him."

"I'm glad to hear that, Dad."

"Now, you can always come up to visit if you want though. It's been kind of lonely without you kids around."

"We might just do that, Dad. I'm kind of burned out from it all. Sally's folks want us to visit too, so maybe we'll go to see them and then come see you. I'll talk to Sally about it when she gets home from the store and call you in a couple of days. Okay?"

"That sounds good to us, Son. Say hello to her for us."

Shirley chimed in, "Love you, Honey."

"You, too, Mom. Bye." Larkin hung up and wondered if "they" would give him any trouble back home if they decided to visit.

Sally came home from the store and Larkin helped her put the groceries away, each and every item in its perfect place. She handed him a couple bottles of wine and asked him to take them down to the new wine cellar. He said, "I'm sure glad we told the wedding planner about the wine, the one bottle she sold for us paid for the cellar. Now I think I might have her sell another one so I can buy more wine!"

Sally laughed at him and said, "Come on back up and help me make dinner, I saved one bottle for us to drink."

"Okay. Be right back."

Larkin went down to the basement on the new stairs he also had the carpenters build, because the old ones were rickety, and turned on the light. A cat jumped out from behind the door, scaring the crap out of him, and he dropped one of the bottles to the floor, breaking it. He said out loud, "How'd that cat get in here?" He looked around the basement to find that one of the windows was open a bit. It was somehow *left open*? It had contact points for the alarm on it, so no one had broken in. Ah, the carpenters! They must have left it open sticking lumber through it as they worked. So why hadn't they noticed it before? "I guess no cats came in before!" he said to himself. The cat had climbed up a shelf next to the window and gone out, so he just locked it back up. But it made him think about their security and that they needed to be more careful.

He cleaned up the mess and went back upstairs to help his wife. She asked, "What took so long? What was all the noise about down there?"

Larkin told her what had happened and she said she felt like there was something different the last couple of times she was down there, but didn't see the window open. Larkin said, "Let's be more careful when we have people over to do things for us. Oh, when's the garage door guy coming?"

"Tuesday."

"I'll be here. And maybe we ought to use the alarm system every day?"

She nodded in the affirmative, saying, "Yes. We'd have known about that sooner."

They talked about the proposed trips to their parents during dinner and they agreed that since they had not ever been to Tennessee together, they would stay two weeks there and then one week in New York. Not only to be fair, but so as to not provoke "them" to do anything while they were in New York. Larkin gave the task of getting it all set up to Sally, because she, in reality, was better at it than he. Besides, he still had one test left to study for. Sally was excited about her task! Larkin wasn't excited about his.

The test went fine, and he felt he had aced it as always, and Larkin was done for the summer. Dr. Perkins had a meeting with Larkin before he left and he assured Larkin his grades from independent study at the Smithsonian were top notch after his conversation with Mr. Shipley. He said he was also quite pleased about Larkin's grades on campus and that the professors suggested he be allowed to tutor and quite possibly apply for a position on staff after graduation. Larkin said, "I'm honored, Sir, but my heart is on the farm and more than likely I shall return there to put into practice what I've learned."

"Just keep it in the back of your mind, Larkin. Would you?"

"Yes, Sir." Getting up to leave Larkin said, "I'll see you in the fall, Dr. Perkins."

Shaking his hand Dr. Perkins said, "Have a nice summer, Larkin."

Larkin walked out of the building with a sigh of relief and a sense of freedom, at least for the summer anyway. He did face one problem in his future plans however, and that was the Masons didn't want him in Brookfield, or D.C.! When he got home to Sally, she was on the phone with the airlines confirming their reservations. It was set up to fly into Nashville for two weeks and then to Albany like they did before. They'd stay until the first of July and then fly home. And, she was all packed already!

What Larkin didn't know is that the Commander had received the missing picture of the die from the man in the blue suit. Larkin had not seen him follow and drop off the film. When he knew the pictures would come back in three days, he was there to go through them before Larkin did, as the pickup was self serve. He put the die picture in his pocket before anyone noticed and now, the Commander knew. Yes, McPherson knew the family had dug up the treasure. He knew the Palmers had found the Die *and* the Key. Now, all that needed be done is determine the correct time to retrieve what was theirs...

On the Tuesday before they left the installer from the garage door company came to the door. Larkin went to the door and he said, "I'm from Capital Door Service. I'm Marty."

Larkin looked at the guy and said, "You're Marty McKee! You were at UMD with me."

"Yeah! Hi, Larkin. I didn't know I was coming to your house. Nice place!"

"Thanks, Marty. C'mon in. Hey, how come you're working for this door company?"

"I took your advice, Larkin. I told my folks I wanted to be a cop. So, I dropped out and got this job part time while I train to be a cop. Hopefully my grades will be good enough to get in. Thanks, Larkin!"

"I'm glad it worked out for you, Marty. I'll take you to the garage."

He watched Marty install it all and the door opener worked great. He even set it up on the homes' alarm system. When he finished, Marty thanked him and said, "I appreciate the work and all you've done for me, Larkin."

Letting him out the front door, Larkin said, "Bye, Marty. Nice to see you again."

The trip to Tennessee was better than Larkin thought it would be. The early summer weather wasn't too warm yet and the people who lived in Columbia were very down to earth like the people back home. There was a difference however, and that was all the "ya'lls and fixin to's".

It took a while for the Yankee to get used to the Southern drawl, but he did and paid "no mind" to it.

Larkin and Sally were uncomfortable with the sleeping arrangements at her parents' home, because her old room was right next to theirs and you could hear almost everything between them—everything. Larkin decided that they should refrain from "anything" while there and Sally agreed but said, "Just wait till I get you to your room back home, Honey."
Larkin blushed and replied, "I will. I mean, I can't wait. Really." She slapped him on the arm and gave him a kiss.

While there, they went to see many of the local points of interest, especially the Civil War sights. Larkin found the Confederate graveyard at Carnton Plantation in Franklin to be very interesting. Although he had read a great deal of Civil War history, he didn't know much about the bloodiest battle of the war. The fact that so many were killed in the Battle of Franklin in such a short time astonished Larkin, but he was disappointed to see that the battlefield had not been preserved like Gettysburg or other sites. The forefathers of Franklin either had no vision for preservation, or were so dismayed of the carnage, the loss of their sons and companions, that they allowed the site to be lost forever. There were always reasons for actions, and these had been lost to history.

They also visited the Parthenon in Nashville, which he found out was an exact reproduction of the Parthenon in Greece. He was surprised by the detail and the history behind its completion. He was disappointed however, by its condition and how the concrete was decaying. Even though the structure was less than a hundred years old it needed restoration. 'Nothing lasts forever,' he thought, 'I hope they restore it.'

Sally's family took them to some local events while they were there and made them promise to come back for "Mule Day" sometime. Her parents, who were Church of Christ, even allowed them to go to the local Lutheran church called Trinity. Even though these Lutherans used the same hymnal and the same order of service as they did back home, it was still done differently and it was interesting to see the cultural implications of diversity in worship-at least for Larkin. Sally didn't notice the difference.

One night, her folks took them to the Grand Old Opry. Larkin had heard of it before, but had never been into country music, especially the old times stuff his Grandpa Elias and uncles would listen to on the radio at night. That night, they sat in the balcony, up enough rows they couldn't look over the edge and get vertigo as they observed the people in their seats below. The lineup was different every night Sally said, and tonight they were to see a couple of her mom's favorites; Little Jimmy Dickens and Jean Shepard. The Opry, as it was called, had moved out to a place called Opryland in 1974. The old Opry was downtown and needed restoration and expansion for the huge audiences that now attended.

They wanted to go out and explore the theme park the next day by themselves and leave her folks at home, but Sally said to Larkin softly as her folks sat next to them, "I don't think we'll lose them Honey, they like the park."

Larkin just shook his head and resigned himself to the fact that it might be the case they'd be with them. Besides, it was a *family place,* and he knew what family was all about! He'd be happy- either way. Larkin laughed and tapped his foot when Dickens, who was called "Tater" by those who knew him, sang the song "Take an old cold tater and wait". Larkin thoroughly enjoyed the Opry that night. He thought, 'I guess I just might be more country than I thought.'

The next day, much to their delight, Sally's dad received an invite to go fishing on Old Hickory Lake with a buddy he'd not seen for a long time. He asked Sally if she'd be upset with him if he went and being a good daughter, with her own hidden agenda, she feigned sadness and told him, "I'll miss you Daddy, but we'll find something to do." He thanked her and gave her a peck on the cheek as he grabbed his fishing hat, sunglasses, and a lure on the table, heading out the door to his pickup. Her mom had a sewing project to get done, so Sally said to her, "Mom, I think Larkin and I are going up to Opryland today. Okay?"

"Oh that's nice. You two go and have fun!"

Larkin and Sally looked at each other and smiled. Sally asked her mom, "Can we borrow the car, Mom?"

"Oh sure. You know where the keys are."

"Thanks!"

The two were excited about having a day alone in Tennessee, so they got changed and headed out the door as fast as they could. Sally drove her mom's old Dodge Dart and when they arrived at the entry to the theme park there was no one in line to buy tickets. They paid for a day pass and parking and drove all the way to the front. It was still early, the doors having opened just a half hour before. The weather had changed the day before and the forecast was more like Sally remembered- hot! Dressed in shorts and tees, they both were ready for a warm summer day, but mostly for FUN!

Sally had been there just one time before on a trip back to visit in 1974. The park was new then and she saw from the park map at the entrance that they had added some new rides and lots of shows. That was the thing she liked the most, all of the shows you could see with entertainers from all over the country trying to make it in the music business doing skits, music, and dancing for the entertainment of the theme parks' visitors. It was, in her words, "Great!" The rides were what Larkin liked the best, and after it got hot and humid that day, they went to the "Big" Log ride. As it came down a large ramp it would splash water up onto a bridge that you'd walk on to the entrance of the ride. If you really wanted to get wet, that was the place to stand. Larkin did this repeatedly, and he held Sally so tight the first time she couldn't avoid the water, which of course, soaked her entirely. At the end of the day they were completely spent and on the way home to Columbia, all they could do is yawn and say what a good time they had.

The people in Tennessee were very friendly and Larkin was impressed at how easy it was to get to know them. However, after the two weeks were up, they were ready to leave, especially Sally, which to a degree, surprised Larkin. After he thought about it though, he came to realize she had been in D.C. for five years and she had become accustomed to living on her own. He could sense a tension there which he could not describe, because there wasn't anything like it back in New York at his parents. They thanked her parents for having them and she had them packed and ready to go even earlier than usual. The next day they got on the plane to fly to Albany.

As they deplaned, the remembrance of the last time they came to New York flooded back. The funeral and the sad events were something they'd never forget, but they were here for a different reason this time and they had come to have fun! Even though he didn't say anything, nor did they discuss it, Larkin hoped it would be different than at her parents and he was sure she did, too. While driving down the road towards Brookfield, Sally asked him questions that had been on her mind since the last time, just different pieces of the puzzle of Larkin's' life she still had not seen or heard. Like; "Where was Ginny killed?"; "Can we go to her grave?", and "How come your parents never had any other children?", and on, and on. Larkin did the best he could to answer them all. However, he was sure she'd have more and he didn't mind, because he knew she just wanted to know more about the man she loved.

The road seemed to take forever going to Button Hill. It always seems to be that way- long roads going to a place and short roads going back home. Sally couldn't wait to get there and kept asking Larkin how far it still was. He must have told her five times, "It's not far." Obviously, Sally thought of going to his parents much differently than going to her own. He couldn't understand it, but thought he'd think on it. One thing he did know was that she acted like a five year old in the car!

Shirley was waiting for them knowing they had surely landed and were on their way home. She was a pacer, and Sam just watched her going back and forth across the kitchen floor. The two women finally had their excitement fulfilled when Larkin pulled into the driveway. Sam barked when he heard the car and went to the door, hopping up and down in anticipation of Larkin's arrival. Larkin whistled, knowing Sam was back at home now. Shirley opened the door for Sam and he flew out to see them. Sally's dog, Sam, had gotten run over by a truck and she didn't find out about it until they had arrived in Tennessee, which disturbed her greatly, so for her to see this Sam, was soothing to her and she bent down and gave him a kiss. Larkin made a funny face at that and said, "Don't kiss me for a while." Sally smiled back at him. Shirley came out and gave Larkin a hug and then Sally. As they walked in Shirley patted Sally on the stomach and asked in her ear, "Pregnant?"

Sally just nodded her head "No" and the two didn't let on to Larkin what they were talking about.

Larkin carried in their bags and Lawtin met them at the door. He opened it for Larkin and he took Larkin's hand and shook it hard as his son sat the bags down on the kitchen floor. "Glad to see you, Son," said Lawtin.

"You too, Dad. I didn't think we'd ever get here." Meaning, he was worn out from all the questions.

Sally understood, however, and said to her in-laws, "I was driving him crazy with questions along the way."

Lawtin raised his head and opened his eyes a little wider showing he understood that position his son was in; trapped in a car with the "Inquisitor". He'd been there before himself many times. "It's never too early to be in that position, Son. Welcome to the club."

Shirley said to the kids looking at her husband with a scowl, "Come sit down and have a drink. You can tell us all about your trip to Tennessee." Shirley gave them a glass of lemonade and sat down at the table with them.

"Go ahead, Dear, tell Mom about what we did in Tennessee." Larkin took a drink of the tall cool glass of lemonade as condensation dripped off the sides of the glass to the table. Sally began her story and went over all the places and things they did, including going to church. Shirley could somehow tell they weren't real excited about their visit, but she didn't ask if anything was wrong either. She figured Larkin would say something if there were a problem- which he didn't.

When she finished her story of their trip, Sally went to the refrigerator and looked inside.

Shirley asked her, "What are you looking for, Sally? Hungry?"

"No, Shirley," she replied, "I was wondering what was for supper?"

"Fried Chicken."

Sally smiled and said, "Good. Thanks, Mom."

"I gotta pee, Larkin," said Sally, and she ran to the powder room. Larkin went to get their bags and go upstairs with them, and his mom said, "I didn't make up the spare bedroom this time, Larkin."

"Mom! Quit that!"

Lawtin smiled and said to him, "Does Sally drive you crazy that way too, Son?"

"You don't know the half of it, Dad."

"I can imagine," he replied.

Sally came back and asked Shirley if she could help with supper and she just answered, "You know your job."

Sally started to set the table as Larkin went to the room with the bags and Lawtin turned on the nightly news. Larkin came back to talk with his dad and the girls chatted as Shirley did her magic with the chicken and fixings. Soon they were praying, eating, talking, and laughing like they had done before. Larkin observed this and said to himself, 'Now, *this*, is a family.'

After supper the girls cleaned up and the guys continued to talk about the farm and the recent purchase of more cows. Lawtin told him Percy said the production was up and costs remained almost the same, so consequently, profit was up, which was always good. Larkin asked if they could go over to meet Peter in the morning and Lawtin said he didn't know why not. Besides, he wanted Larkin to look at the trees to see what he thought about their condition. "Are you concerned there's a problem, Dad?" Larkin asked.

"No, but as long as you are here…"

Larkin smiled, happy his dad thought that much of his opinion and knowledge.

The girls finished up and Larkin was tired so he said, "I think I'm going to hit the hay. Good night."

Sally said to Shirley, "I'm going up, too. What time is breakfast?"

"Sleep in tomorrow. How about eight?"

"Okay. If we're not up- call us. Goodnight, Mom and Dad."

Sally followed Larkin up and he went to the bathroom. She came in as he was finishing and she got out her toothbrush and put toothpaste on it, standing at the sink pushing up her lips to look at her gums like he used to do with the mules. Larkin came over to her observing this behavior, but shrugged it off and said, "My mom sure wants us to have kids doesn't she? Man, what's with her?"

"Oh, she's just excited, that's all. The prospect of that is very important to her. I don't blame her at all."

She put the toothbrush into her mouth and began to brush. Larkin just went into his room and began to change. It was the first time as newlyweds they would be together in a bed in his room at home. It was weird. Sally came in, took off her clothes, and got in bed- sans nightgown. Larkin asked, "Up to your old tricks, Sally?"

She smiled and said, "No tricks this time are needed. Come to bed. Remember what we haven't done while back in *my* old room?"

He shut the door to his room, took off his clothes and came to bed. It wasn't as weird as he thought.

In the morning his mom called up to them and said, "Soups' on!" He looked over at his clock and was amazed they had slept that long. Sally stretched and he grabbed her and brought her to him. He wrapped himself around her, not playfully but in *that* way, and would not let her go until he said softly, "Love Me," and kissed her tenderly. She accepted it and submitted eagerly. It didn't take long anyway and he said immediately afterwards, "We had better get down there or she'll come up after us." Fear gripped Sally's eyes not wanting to be caught in that position and she jumped up, pulled on her jeans and a shirt, and went downstairs before Larkin, who went to the bathroom.

As Sally walked into the kitchen Shirley smiled and asked knowingly, "What kept you?"

Sally just smiled back at her and said, "Let's just say it's never too early to make hay."

Shirley grinned, but didn't comment.

Lawtin came in from going out to get the paper and the screen door slammed behind him waking Sam from a mornings' nap. He turned on the radio on the way to his seat and sat down unfolding the paper, looking at the front page. Without even looking up he said to the two women, "Looks like the county is trying to spend our money again."

He went on with no elaborations and the women just shrugged and kept on with their conversation as Larkin walked into the room saying cheerfully, "Good morning!" His mom turned and looked up from the pancakes she was stirring and asked him already knowing full well why, "What got you in such a good mood this morning?"

He grabbed Sally around the waist and hugged her and replied, "Let's just say I mind my mother."

She and Sally laughed at that one and he just shrugged not knowing what they had talked about before. He poured himself some coffee and sat next to his dad while the girls finished preparing breakfast.

His dad said setting down the paper, "I called Peter and he's expecting us in about an hour."
"Okay. It'll be nice to see the place. I miss it." He turned and asked Sally, "Sally, do you want to come along to The Homestead?"
"Actually, your mom and I have plans already."
"Really? Okay. We will only be gone for a little while, anyway."
"Us, too."

After breakfast, the men went over to look at The Homestead and have Larkin meet Peter, while the girls went into town to look for some things on Shirley's grocery list. It wasn't much of a list, but she couldn't find those things the other day while in Schenectady. Sally got the feeling someone was watching her, so she turned slowly to see a man looking at her and Shirley from the end of the aisle. She knew what it was about and "who" it was, but paid no mind and would tell her husband when she got back to the farm.

Larkin was as impressed with Peter and what he'd been doing with The Homestead as Lawtin was, and that was good. Peter seemed to have a true love for his work and the new responsibility he had taken on and it was evident in the care he'd taken to do his job. Larkin looked at the grove of trees his dad wanted him to, and saw no problems, but was glad his dad and Peter were cautious about it. The men left to go back to the farm with peace about the whole situation at Larkin's place- The Homestead.

As they drove back in the truck, Larkin finally started to come to realize that the place, The Homestead, was his. Without him living there it was just a mental note or intellectual knowledge. But by being there and walking in *his* orchard, it made it more real to him. He was glad his dad had found someone he could trust to work it and take care of it the way it should be until he could return.

They drove up to the farm just at the same time the women did. Sally got out joining Larkin as he went to the barn to see Percy, placing her arm around his waist and hugging his side. Shirley smiled at the two kids and took the sack of groceries into the house, followed by Lawtin who had to go to the bathroom. Sally told Larkin about the man in the store and he just said that now "they" knew they were there, but didn't think they'd bother them if it was just a vacation. Besides, he had brought The Eraser with him and it was in his pocket.

Percy welcomed them as they came in the door to the barn. He was glad to see them again and he asked Larkin if he wanted to help. "Not today, Percy."

But Sally said, "I want to!"

"What?" asked a surprised Larkin, "you've never milked a cow before- have you?"

"No, but there's always a first time. Show me."

Larkin looked around, found a bucket and took Sally over to Betsy, the gentlest of the entire herd. She was waiting for Percy to attach the milking machine, but Larkin took a stool and sat it down next to her. He showed Sally how to squeeze the teat and express the milk. Then he had Sally sit and try it. She actually did quite well and Larkin was impressed. Betsy didn't mind the difference, even if it had been a while since she'd been milked by hand. When she was through, which Larkin determined for her, Sally picked up the bucket of milk and Larkin moved Betsy out of the stall and out to the pen.

Sally was proud of herself as well and she took the milk into the house with them for the family to use. When Shirley saw her bring it in she asked, "What have we here, Sally?"

"I milked Betsy this time. I figured we could use it. Okay?"

"Very good, Sally! There are a couple of pitchers in the cabinet there, but wait a second and I'll show you how to strain it."

Sally took out the pitchers and placed them in the sink. Shirley showed her how to strain the milk through a cloth and poured the milk into the pitchers. Taking a glass, Sally filled it from the pitcher and took a drink. She said, "This is sooo good. I wish I could do this all the time."

Lawtin said to her, "You can. Anytime you want."

Sally came over to him and gave him a hug and said, "I know. We will be here someday, Dad. Just pray."

Larkin smiled as he watched all this and he took the empty bucket saying, "I'll take this back out to Percy. Be right back."

Sally replied, "Okay, Honey." She put the milk in the refrigerator as he went out the door. She rubbed her hands a bit after he left, realizing that they were sore from her first time of experiencing the chore of milking. She determined not to tell her husband about that.

Larkin had heard what Sally *had* said and took it to heart. He knew she wanted what he did and that was to return to Brookfield to live. He knew he had some plans to make in order that it might come to pass, but he also knew he had to complete what was in progress in their lives now. He knew the Seward information was just too important to drop and he wanted to complete his education. Even though they had enough money to live without ever having to struggle, Larkin wanted to satisfy his own sense of accomplishment. He went into the barn and stood there watching the life he used to be so involved with. Truly, he missed it. Sitting the bucket down by the others, he waved at Percy and Arville as he walked back out the door to go up to the house. He knew he had to come up with a plan so they could come home. He'd think on that.

The rest of the days they were there went by so quickly they were sad to know on Saturday they only had one more day before the flight back to D.C.. They had just hung around the farm and didn't do much else except go to church and tell Pastor Johnson they had become Lutherans. He wasn't upset with them at all and was glad they had been involved in their becoming better Disciples of Christ. Since this was the first time the people at church had seen them since the wedding, they all congratulated them, including Mr. Berry. That Sunday night they began to pack for the flight and Sally cried the whole time. Shirley wasn't much help in that regard, for when they did the dishes they both would talk a while and then cry. Larkin was both happy and sad for Sally- happy she had become so close to his mother and sad because she really didn't want to leave. Neither did he.

The next morning went much like the last time they were there and it was difficult to go out the door to head to Albany. But they had to and they said their goodbyes once again. Shirley put her head in Sally's window and said to her before they drove off, "Make sure you me call if you know."

"You know I will, Mom," Sally said and Shirley patted her face and waved goodbye. They pulled down the road and after waving at Mrs. Weaver next door on the way by, headed to Albany. Larkin didn't have to ask what that was all about with his mother and he didn't say anything, but just smiled a half-hearted grin.

They arrived in D.C. just in time for dinner and they just stopped to eat at a McDonalds on the way. Sally didn't want to stay, so she made him go through the drive through. They didn't order any drinks because Sally said, "Just get some burgers and fries, Larkin. We have drinks at home."

"Okay, Dear."

He did so, and they got home before the food got cold. When Larkin drove into the garage he said, "Man it's nice to finally have the garage door opener. I'm glad we got it done before we left." They left their suitcases in the trunk and went up to eat. He could come back for them later.

Sitting down at the counter Sally said to her husband, "Will you get a couple of beers out of the refrigerator, Honey?" He sat the food on the counter and took out two beers. Opening the bag, Sally found that the people had made a mistake and given them the wrong order. It had a fish sandwich, two burgers, and three fries. Sally said, "From now on we need to check our order before we leave the drive through. It's getting worse all the time."

Larkin sat next to her and gave her the beer and said, "I don't think it will ever get better. Let's pray."

Larkin thanked the Lord for the safe trip and their food. He also asked for a way to be able to go home for good. Sally smiled when he finished that prayer and said to him, "We both know that's what's on our hearts. We just have to find a way and make a plan. God's timing is what's important."

"You got it. Do you want the fish?"

Sally's words were true, because often man's plans are not God's plans...

They ate and Larkin went down to get their stuff while she went to take a shower. The bags were heavy, especially hers. Shirley had sent some syrup and jam back with Sally, so he sure hoped they weren't broken in her suitcase. He didn't smell anything, but he knew they had gorillas as baggage handlers these days. He finally got the bags up there and Sally was almost done when he went into their room. She called from the shower and said, "Will you bring me my robe, Honey? I forgot it."

"Sure will!" he yelled back at her.

He pulled it off the hook on the back of the door and went to give it to her. Placing it on the top of the shower door he said, "There you go, Sally."

"Thanks, Honey."

He was glad she was getting used to actually wearing her robe.

They put away their things that night and found all the glass jars to be intact. Sally said, "I'm going to eat this all up and you don't get any."

"Better not. Or you won't *get any.* If, you know what I mean."

Sally's mouth flew open and she said, "Ah! You couldn't stand it if you didn't get any of *this,* Larkin Palmer!"

"The jam?"

She pouted and said, "No. You know what I mean."

She sat down on the bed like she was pouting, but of course, she was faking it. Larkin came over to her and she grabbed him and lay him down on the bed, tickling him on his stomach, which was the only place he was ticklish. Afterwards, they went to sleep, glad to be home.

They got settled into their lives once again and things got back to normal. Larkin had lots of time for his research and Sally helped a great deal. The two of them went everywhere together and were seen walking about in the city every night. They let no grass grow under their feet and were having the time of their lives together now that they were man and wife. Everything seemed to be going absolutely perfect, except for what Shirley had wanted, and Sally was still not pregnant by the end of the summer and classes for Larkin were to begin. Sally wasn't disappointed and neither was Larkin, but the pressure from Shirley began to bother her a bit. Sally understood and tried to let it pass every time they spoke to his parents. They knew they would be parents when God said the time was right. They just did what they wanted and what God told them to do; Love one another.

By the end of the summer, Larkin was about a third of the way completed with his project. It was a lot of work and sometimes it multiplied as he found more information. However, he gave Mr. Shipley a report before school began and he was satisfied with all that Larkin was doing. The good part was that Mr. Shipley and Dr. Perkins had arranged for his summer work to be included as college credit for independent study for "The American Civil War", which was a senior level class. Larkin was pleased with that news.

He had not seen the man in the blue suit, nor had "they" tampered with his home while the Honeymooners were away that summer. He was glad "they" left him alone after their surveillance stunt in Hawaii. The Eraser was back in the safe and Larkin started locking his project up each night as well, because it was just so- damning. He knew that if the Masons knew he had what he had in his safe, they'd kill them for it- plain and simple. What he thought they didn't know is that he also had- the Key. Studying it would be their next priority. He thought Sally may need to be the one to begin that task. He would find out that he was wrong about that, too.

The summer turned to fall and their walks became less frequent, much to his dismay, and colder, much to hers. The trees were turning and Larkin would pick up the leaves and explain to Sally how they did so.

She already knew all of that, but she didn't mind him yammering on about it. He was glad they didn't have a yard to rake, but missed all the colors at The Homestead and the apple picking time. Larkin made returning to his NY home, now that he had found his true love, his top priority. He had come up with a plan to implement this once he graduated, not before. Sally was just as eager to go to New York as he, so she agreed with the plan and thought it to be the only way. The plan was a little dangerous because of their destination, but they would be safe where they were now in D.C. (Actually, they were safe nowhere, because Marty had come to work on the garage door...)

UMD was a little fuller with many more new students the fall of his junior year. He could tell, quite simply, because there were fewer places to park. On days he didn't want to drive, he still took the bus. Larkin only had two classes this fall semester and they were both on Wednesday. This gave him a lot more time during the week, but they were more intense and time consuming because they were both upper level classes. Sally continued with the bell choir at church and Pastor Olsen had a big Christmas program planned this year. It would require a great deal of practice and that she stay in D.C. for Christmas. That news disappointed Shirley, who wanted them to come home to Brookfield for the holiday. Larkin pondered them going for Thanksgiving, but had not made up his mind. He'd have to see how his classes were going.

They put the Seward project to the side for a bit when he began classes, so he could concentrate on them, and Sally started the project of reading the Key and deciphering it. No matter what, they always quit working at 5 PM and spent the evening together, except for bell choir practice night, of course! On that night they still ate together and Larkin studied and did papers, if required. It worked out well.

One day, Sally was working on the Key. She had been comparing some of the curses and hieroglyphics in it to other reference books and she began to cry. Larkin came up to her and asked, "What's wrong, Dear?"

"This is so evil, Larkin. This book is terrible and the man who wrote it must have been possessed by the devil himself. It is extremely difficult for me to clear my head and thoughts from this garbage after I have been reading it for a while. I don't know if I can do it anymore, Larkin."

"I didn't know it had that effect on you, Dear. I'm glad you have a strong faith or you may not have been able to do what you have already. I understand if you want to stop, but one thing is for certain, you totally understand from this research what we Palmers have had to deal with, don't you?"

"Yes, I do! I didn't realize how evil it was. I think I may have found the curse and the retraction we want anyway. Read here." She pointed to page 37 and read the curse for "Cursing objects for killing." And under it was the retraction, "Removing curses from objects that kill."

"I believe you are right. This is all we need. And they can't do a thing because it says right here in order to remove the curse on the object it must be in your possession! So, don't work on this anymore. Got it?"

"Thank you so much. It's just so terrible." She stood and gave him a hug and he wiped the tears from her eyes and kissed her.

Larkin started to set the Key down and he realized something, "Say, Sally, isn't it odd the document was number 37 in the Seward file and this is on page 37?"

"That is odd; a possible coincidence?"

"Maybe, but what if it was put that way on purpose by someone that *knew*?"

"Who? What would it prove? That Seward and Pike were out to get each other?" She went on with another question, "You mean like Albert Pike killed Sec. Seward after all, through Gen. Barton the chemist and Dr. Verdici?"

"Maybe. And Seward knew and placed the document in the file as number thirty seven. But how would he have seen The Key?"

"Don't know and don't know if we can link anything there, Honey."

"You're right. Let's call it a day and go down to have a beer."

"That sounds great," she said with a sigh.

From that moment on Larkin held back on the things that would upset Sally about the Masons. For her to encounter the pure evil side of it was too much for her to handle and more than such a sweet person should have to. As he had told her, he was glad she had the faith she did so as to keep the devil away from her mind in the exercise. As time went on, he just asked her to provide some of the footwork for the research, for which she was better suited anyway. All in all, Sally had come to truly see what the family had to keep at bay and struggle against, for themselves and their country. From then on, Sally placed as a priority to pray that God would protect them every night. Larkin did the same.

UMD had let out for Thanksgiving recess and they had still not bought tickets to fly to Albany. Larkin had put it off until the last minute, but now felt comfortable enough to go. However, could he still get tickets for them to fly this late in the game? He had Sally contact the travel agent that Mr. Shipley used in order to call in a favor. The woman that she knew said she'd do her best and call back later. While they waited, Sally decided to go ahead and pack, because she trusted God would get them the flights. They'd only be able to be there for a week and then Larkin had to be back for classes. Getting the tickets would be a blessing. She prayed. When the phone finally rang, her prayer was answered in the affirmative. They would leave in the morning!

Larkin was so happy that he took them out to dinner at Harry's favorite place, Bobby Van's, but without Harry. They had been keeping their promise to go out with him and also Mrs. H. They never did get the two together because she was much older than Harry and they thought he'd be offended anyway with that kind of match making. Larkin really didn't like Sally's idea, and after she thought about it some more, she scrapped it. They went alone because they wanted to be alone. By the time they got back to the house they decided to go to bed because the flight was early. Thankfully, Sally had them all packed because she had believed…

The flight was full and when they got off the plane the last available rental car in Albany was waiting for them. They were excited as usual, but were also sad because they knew they wouldn't be able come back for Christmas. It took forever to get to the farm, not because the roads were bad, (in fact they were pretty good this year), but because, once again, the roads seemed so long. When they finally pulled into the drive, Sally jumped out and ran to the door before Shirley and Lawtin even realized they were there. Sam didn't even have time to come and greet Larkin! Sally threw her arms around Shirley and gave her a big hug and said, "Oh, Mom, it's so nice to see you!"

"It's nice to see you, too, Sally. Any news?"

Sally shook her head no. "Don't worry, Mom, it'll happen when the Lord wants it to."

Shirley shook her head "yes" and went to the door to greet Larkin.

Larkin came in with the suitcases and his mom grabbed him and gave him a hug. He kissed her forehead and said, "Hi, Mom!"

Lawtin came from the bathroom and said, "Glad to see you made it before supper. I didn't want you to miss the fried chicken."

Sally's eyes lit up and she said, "Thanks, Mom. You always serve that the first night for me."

"Don't mention it. I like to make it anyway."

They all sat down at the table and talked for a while and Larkin said, "At least we have a few days to be over fried chicken before we eat turkey!"

They all laughed and Lawtin said, "That reminds me, we've had some wild turkeys come through and I haven't seen that in years. No- *decades*. Want to try to bag one?"

"Really? I didn't know they'd come back and I thought they were only in Southwest New York."

"The state did some transplanting and other management, so we'll see how it goes, but if I can get one, I'm going to try. Let's go on Monday when everyone is back at work."

Sally said, "I'm going upstairs to put our clothes away, Honey."

Larkin replied to both of them, "Okay."

Shirley took one bag and Sally the other, talking their way up the stairs like always. After they left Larkin continued, "How did the apple picking go? Were the numbers up this year?"

"Peter says we got two bushels per tree more. Not much, but he says the quality was much better and they sold more at The Homestead than ever before. So, they received more money per bushel."

"Everything else okay over there?"

"Yes, I think so. Why?"

"Oh, I don't know. You just can't predict what "they" will do."

"I know. The farm is doing much better and with the new cows we are up to record productions and profit. Based on that, Percy will be getting a good bonus at the end of the year."

"He'll be thrilled to hear it, I'm sure. Dad, be right back."

He ran up the stairs like he had so many times before and went to the bathroom. His mom and wife were still in their room putting things in the dressers and talking away. They'd laugh and cackle from time to time and Larkin was so glad he'd found someone like Sally. He went in afterwards and put his arms around Sally's neck and hugged her from behind. She smiled and looked back at him and he asked, "You two about done in here? I'm getting hungry."

"Yes, Son, we are. I'm going right down there. Coming, Sally?"

"Yes, Mom."

The two turned and marched right out of the bedroom and down the stairs singing, "Hi Ho, Hi Ho, it's off to work we go." Sally puckered her lips and tried to whistle the rest like in the movie, but she couldn't and just started to laugh.

They all talked as Shirley made supper and Sally did what she could to help. Larkin looked outside and thought he saw snowflakes. Getting up from the table, he went to the window and pulled the shade back and sure enough- it had begun to snow! "I didn't know it was supposed to snow, Dad. It looks like we got here just in time."

"They said we had a chance, but I never believe a thing they say. It should help us hunt if it sticks around until Monday."

Shirley said, "Larkin, let's eat this bird first and we'll think about the other later. Come sit down." Setting the food on the table, she sat down and they all held hands while Lawtin prayed. It was nice to be back.

After dinner, the guys went in by the fire and the women brought some coffee to sip on as they watched the oak burn and talked. On the way from the kitchen, Sally stopped and looked out. She remembered the time she and Larkin went out behind Harry's and played in the snow. She loved it. Just maybe, she could talk him into it again. She didn't say anything about it until Shirley and Lawtin went to bed and left them by the fire. "Want to go out in the snow, Honey?"

"It does look good for making snowmen and snow angels."

"Well then- follow me!"

Sally grabbed her coat and headed out the door with Larkin in pursuit, throwing his coat and gloves on as he went. They stopped under the yard light and she began to roll a ball of snow bigger and bigger until she couldn't move it any longer. Larkin was doing the same and he stopped rolling it a little smaller than hers so he could place it on top of her base. He lifted it up and it fit well. Sally started another ball and Larkin patted together the other two with snow to give it stability. She stopped right next to him and the ball was the perfect size. Larkin lifted it up and placed it on "Frosty". They repeated this one last time for his head and she was too far away from the rest, so Larkin had to pick it up and carry it all the way over to the "man". He stopped once to rest because the snow was very wet, heavy snow. Finally, he put his head on and cemented him all together. It was a great looking snowman. Sally went to the driveway and picked up some rocks for buttons and eyes. He looked like a million bucks! Getting tired, Sally lay down in the snow and made one snow angel before they went in. She did a good job, was totally wet, and more than cold- freezing! Larkin said, "C'mon, let's go in." He took her by the hand and they walked in quietly, the snow falling peacefully to the ground, covering the earth as a blanket, ready for slumber. They went upstairs and took a shower to warm up and went to bed clinging to each other, safe and secure under the covers. After the long day they were exhausted, and fell soundly asleep.

Shirley woke them with a call to breakfast that Saturday, and they put their PJ's on before going down to eat. Lawtin was in his usual place reading the paper and Sally went to set the table. Life for them while they were there had almost become a routine, one with many lapses of time, but a routine, nonetheless. On the way downstairs and into the kitchen, Larkin almost stopped to pick up the phone to call his uncle, but then remembered. He was saddened by it and took a minute to compose himself before going in by the rest of them. Shirley made pancakes and sausage that morning and she brought out some of her syrup. As he walked into the room Larkin said excitedly, "Well, well, I'm finally going to get some syrup."

"What do you mean Larkin? I sent some home with you last summer." said Shirley.

As he unfolded his napkin and put it on his lap he said, "If I remember correctly, my dear wife ate it all AND the jam."

Sally put her hand in front of her mouth and laughed saying, "And he even threatened me for doing it."

Lawtin asked Sally in disbelief, "He threatened you?"

"Yes. To withhold his manly obligation from me if I did."

They all burst out laughing and Lawtin said, "From what I've heard from down here, he won't live up to that threat."

The two kids blushed and Lawtin said, "Let's pray before we eat. Dear Lord, for all your many blessings and especially for this new day, we thank you. Thank you for bringing us together again and we pray you will make it permanent soon. Amen."

"Amen", they all said.

They ate and looked out at the snow through the window. It was still coming down and Larkin feared another storm like in D.C. the year before. There was already about six inches on the ground, but by the time they were through with the meal, the sky had cleared and the sun was beaming down on a beautiful winterscape. The pines held the heavy snow like shimmering white wedding gowns and the snowman they had made stood out like he needed a mate. Sally looked out and said, "He looks lonely. Let's go make him a wife!"

Larkin had really already had his fill of playing in the snow, but he figured that Sally, being from Tennessee, had not, so, being the husband he was, he went along with her plan. In just a little while, they had made a wife for Frosty. Finally, when she was satisfied with their creation, Larkin said, "Let's go for a walk." She didn't say anything, but took his hand and they went toward the road, walking in the eight inches of snow. It had begun to warm up a bit and the snow was melting and falling from the trees, crashing down at times around them along the way. The sun shone off the canopy of whiteness and made it blinding at times and Larkin wished he'd had his sun glasses. They talked a bit as they walked and Larkin asked, "You know, I've come to realize that I don't really know a lot of things about you."

"Like what, Honey?"

"Like for instance, have you ever done drugs?"

She looked at him like she was insulted and replied, "No. You wouldn't think you'd have to ask that question."

"No, that's true, but lots of kids experimented and still do in the dorms. It's the times."

"I know, but I never thought it was something I'd do, so I didn't. You?"

"I was brought up in seclusion out here. I never had the opportunity and when I was old enough, I knew better."

"I've noticed that none of your family swears much," Sally commented.

Larkin laughed and said, "Nope. No need. Sometimes, I'll say and occasional "dang". Grandpa Elias would let out the "s" word once in a while though."

They walked for a bit more and when they came to the corner, Larkin said pointing to the fence post in front of him, "I used to wait right there for Ginny when we'd ride our bikes over to uncles'. We'd meet here so she didn't have to ride all the way to my house."

Sally smiled at her husband and took him by the arm and said, "You were a nice guy even back then. Do you miss her?"

He looked at Sally like it was a trick question. She said, "Don't worry, because it's not a trick question."

He said hesitatingly, "Yes, Dear, but not in that way. I miss her as a person and a dear friend."

She nodded her head thoughtfully and they turned around to walk back up Waterman Road.

That night after supper, Shirley asked Larkin where they were going to go to church the next morning. He hadn't thought about it, but he made a decision for him and his wife. "We'll always worship with you when we come home, Mom. There's no sense driving that far to a Lutheran church, unless, we come home to stay." Shirley smiled and Sally didn't say anything. No problems. They all went to bed early.

The next day as they arrived at church, Larkin paused and looked up the street at his old school, and that part of his life seemed liked eons ago to him, but it was not and he knew he had grown so much since then. When the Palmers went in, he could tell the people at church were happy to see them again. It seemed the congregation had gotten used to the fact that they were a couple and the ghost of Ginny had finally been put away from their minds. Church was fuller, almost to capacity, as many of the children and their families had come home for the holiday. Pastor Johnson was happy about that of course, and his sermon was a little more upbeat and not so filled with fire and brimstone this Sunday. They stayed and shook hands with a few of Larkin's friends from school afterwards. Some had come home from college, and some had gotten jobs in Albany or Schenectady. They wanted to know if he was coming home for Christmas, but he told them they'd be in D.C. this year. When Shirley overheard him say this, he could tell she was not pleased. He knew she'd come to accept it.

They went home and got out of their "Sunday-go-to-meeting" clothes and ate a little lunch. Being a bit sleepy, Larkin decided to go upstairs and take a nap, so he lay down on top of the bed. Sally had stayed downstairs with Shirley, but after a while came up to join him. They slept until dinner time and Shirley called them down with, "Soup's on!" He woke with her in his arms, unaware she had even come in. Smiling, he kissed her and she hugged him tightly. He got up and went to the bathroom and she followed him in and stood there waiting her turn. He had been somewhat cured of his case of "shy bladder syndrome" since he'd been married to her, not because he had gotten used to it, but out of necessity, as she was always around. He finished and he went to wash while she took her turn. It seemed she always wanted someone there while *she* went, especially if she had to linger. But it was not advantageous to stay then! He went downstairs before her, and when she came down he asked, "Did you wash your hands?"

She slapped him on the arm and said, "Yes. I always wash my hands."

"What are we having, Mom?" asked Larkin.

"Pot roast, potatoes, and carrots, with gravy and rolls."

"You spoil us when we are here," remarked Sally.

Lawtin shook his head and said, "She doesn't cook like this for me all the time anymore. I want you to visit more often." He finished saying, "But not for just that reason kids. Let's pray, "Lord thank you for this food, the loving hands that prepared it, and for our family. Amen.""

"Amen," they all said.

The rest of the week went so quickly because they were enjoying themselves and each other. They did all the things they would do if they lived together like this every day. They worked, they played, they lived life; life like normal everyday people; living like normal everyday Christians, challenged by sin, the world, and evil. Each one of them struggling to live in two realms, the world and the church, and trying to balance them out as Disciples of Christ. As perfect as it was for them, they knew they were both sinners and saints. And as they had this short time together, they wanted to make the most of it because as Christians, not just family, they loved one another.

Larkin did go over to the Homestead to visit the cemetery by himself one afternoon as Sally rested, but as the snow had drifted over most of the graves he merely pulled up Chase Road, he only took a picture with Sally's Brownie camera, turned around in the driveway and headed back to Waterman Road.

The guys never did get a turkey; except at the market! They had gone in to buy one from the butcher as a last resort. To them it was admitting defeat in the quest for a "traditional" meal; whatever that was. Actually, all Thanksgiving meals are traditional, whatever tradition is followed. The Palmer Thanksgiving meal was short one person this year, and Sally took Tom's seat at the formal dining room table. Lawtin thought it was the only way to go and Sally was honored. They took each others' hands and Lawtin asked Larkin to say the grace. He began, "Dear Lord. You give and take away, and through it all we praise you for your providence in our lives. We thank you Lord for this family and for the opportunity to serve you in all we do each day. We thank you now for this food and all of your blessings. Amen."

They all joined in, "Amen."

Shirley had outdone herself! The turkey was great and they were assured of enough leftovers for sandwiches, pot-pies, and turkey ala king. Not to mention the turkey divan! The rest was perfect, especially the pumpkin pie, which Sally deemed out of this world! They laughed, talked, and planned for the future. The future they hoped for when Larkin graduated from UMD. At least that was the plan…

On Friday, Larkin wanted to go out and spend part of the day in the dairy control room and observe the equipment that was put in to upgrade the facility during the past summer. Getting up early, he left Sally asleep and went down to the barn in his bibs, just like old times. Percy was getting the first group hooked up to the milking machines and Arville was blowing his nose as he walked in and waved. Larkin just went into the control room and took a seat in front of the board. They had set up a TV in the room and they could look out and see what was going on with the cows and watch TV all at the same time. This was nice! It worked well and Percy was proud of what he had done under Lawtin's direction. Percy considered it "his" control room. Larkin understood why.

Not staying too long so as to wear out his welcome, Larkin left Percy and Arville and went in the house, getting there just in time for breakfast. The others had already prayed without him, so he bowed his head and prayed. Sally brought him some bacon and eggs saying, "You can leave my tip under your plate."

"My tip to you is get out of this business. It doesn't pay."

"That's so funny I forgot to laugh."

"Where did I hear that? Oh, it was on Saturday Night Live the other night. I think it was. Wasn't it Sally?"

"Yeah, that was it."

Lawtin asked, "You guys watch that show? I'm asleep by then."

They laughed and Shirley said, "He usually falls asleep so he doesn't have to talk to me while I sew." Lawtin got a funny look and Sally just smiled and looked at Larkin saying, "You won't fall asleep on me will you, Larkin?"

"Do you sew?"

"Not really. But the ladies want me to learn to quilt."

"Well, you can't do that by the fire, so I won't have to worry. No, I won't fall asleep on you. You usually fall asleep on me." Sally got up and was blushing, and picking up her plate she put it in the sink to rinse. Changing the subject she asked, "Anybody else want seconds?"

"Nope," said Shirley and Lawtin both smiling at Larkin's last statement.

"Do you have any more bacon and toast?" asked Larkin.

Sally picked up the last piece of toast and the plate with two strips of bacon, and gave it to him, kissing him on the cheek. Larkin said, "Thanks, Dear."

"For the food or the kiss?"

"Both," he said shoving a piece of bacon in his mouth and smiling.

She sat back down and they talked, drinking the rest of the coffee in the pot. It was to be another lazy day, but what else were holidays for? The problem was that they had to get ready to leave again and they were putting it off as always.

A little while later, Larkin was caught by his dad, standing and looking out of the window, daydreaming about his childhood. "Does it change much, Son?"

"What do you mean, Dad?"

"Out there. When you live here, you don't see it change. But, do you see it?"

"If I see it with my eyes, I see the change," he said, "but if I see it with my heart- it never changes."

Lawtin put his arm around his son's shoulder and nodded, truly understanding what he meant.

Knowing she had to pack, Sally grudgingly went upstairs to begin the task. She wanted to stay again and never leave. As she packed she cried, and Shirley came up to help by talking to her about their lives back in D.C. As always, she pried and wanted to know why they weren't pregnant yet. And as always, Sally reiterated the fact that God was in control and they did what they could according to the plan. Sally said almost chastising her, "Mom, have faith! Sooner or later it'll happen. In the mean while, we will have fun as we are supposed to. Blessings come when God wants them to."

"Oh, I know. Forgive me. You know I'm just so excited. I want to be able to hold a grandchild."

Sally put her arms around her and gave her a hug saying, "I want that for you, too."

The next day they got in the rental car before breakfast and drove to Albany for their flight. This time their parting was so much more painful and difficult. Larkin didn't want to have to leave his parents like that again, so he determined to not go back until he was done with college. No one but God knows the future though and His plans are not ours.

Christmas came quickly and Sally went all out in decorating the house. She established their traditions and Larkin abdicated that task to her gratefully. Besides, it was her strong suit and it was great. When they had kids it would be even better. The "Bells of Christmas" was such a special event at Mount Olivet Lutheran that the place was packed for all the Christmas services. It was fantastic and there was even an article in the paper covering it. Sally had such a good time in her role in the bell choir that she volunteered to help the director throughout the coming year. They went on their yearly limo ride to look at the lights and they were glad they had. The Christmas away from home in New York was different for them, especially Larkin, but he wanted them to have "their" Christmas established and there was no time like the present. At least there were no snow storms that year!

However, as they always seem to do, the seasons came and went, school went on, and before they knew it another year had passed. Larkin's folks waited for the call to tell them they'd be there again for the holidays, but it never came. In fact, Sally had not been calling Shirley much because if she did it was always a disappointment for her to hear the news that they were still not having a baby. Larkin was about finished with his Seward report and was afraid that the Secretary would renege on his promise to release it when he finally was done. God forbid the Masons would learn it was in this form, because it was irrefutable. However, if they did know, their lives would be in even more danger!

But, regardless of the ever-present danger in their lives, Larkin had it together! Life was good and the young married couple was very happy. His grades had placed him Summa cum Laude and he was looking forward to graduation in the spring. He also had their retreat from D.C. well planned. He didn't think it necessary to sell the house, because it was a good investment, but they could keep it and visit from time to time. He wondered about his foes and if they had any idea that he'd found the Key. In fact, he'd thought that one day this week he'd go over to the Temple to throw them off and look at some more documents just for the fun of it. What a perverse sense of humor!

It was May and the whole of D.C. was in bloom. Larkin especially loved the cherry trees. The sun shone through the windows waking the two as they lay together, Sally's arm stretched across Larkin's chest. He got up and she roused, and she watched him go to window to look out at the trees and then to the bathroom and return, as she did most mornings, smiling as he put on his clothes. He asked her as she stretched her arms back over her head, "Do you want to go to the Temple with me today?"

"I forgot you wanted to go back there. No. I think I'll pass on it. It's too evil and I can sense it. But you be careful."

"He promised they'd leave me alone until graduation. I'm still safe for a week. Besides, the list my Grandpa Elias started is now complete and I have over 350 names of the top Masons in the world. If I don't come home you know where it and The Eraser are. You can use it as a bargaining chip, to win the day or if it need be, for revenge." After he said this, he knew how much he hated the rubber square in the safe.

"I know and I truly understand. But right now I have to pee." She got up, threw on her robe, went to the bathroom and wasn't feeling well, but dismissed it, because a flu bug was going around church. Going downstairs Larkin made some toast and coffee for them and when they finished he just got up, said goodbye, kissed her, and went out the door.

He drove with purpose and actually wondered what he would look at when he got there so as to not disturb "them" more. After he parked, he went right in and there was his old "friend", Dean, standing at the welcome desk. He addressed Larkin right away, "Why, Mr. Palmer, what a surprise. What can we do for you today?"

"As I only have one week left in D.C., I thought I'd look around one last time for clues to the Key."

Dean smiled and said, "Oh yes, I will be so happy, I mean, to assist you if you need anything. Feel free to go into any of the public areas. Good luck!" Dean laughed as if he thought Larkin was an idiot.

'Boy,' Larkin thought, 'are *you* ever an idiot, Dean.'

He went into the open library and looked at a few books on Pike, and placed two out on the table when he left to make it look like he was still "on the trail", so to speak. He left, waving goodbye to Dean as he went out the door and the sense of evil left him as he returned to the Lincoln and drove away.

Dean went in the office and told the Commander that Larkin had been in to which he said, "Did you send him the warning letter I told you to?"

"Yes, about two weeks ago."

"You wouldn't think he'd have the balls to come in after reading that. I've always known that kid to have guts, that's for sure."

"You're "dead right", Boss!"

"Are our associates ready?"

"Yes, Commander!"

"Then give them the "green light". If we can't get him with the Key we'll get him this way."

They laughed and laughed.

When he returned home, Sally was in the pantry with the ironing board down, going over Larkin's' graduation gown with the iron. It had been delivered the day before all wrinkly and crinkly, and Sally knew that just wouldn't do. She looked up and smiled at him when he threw his keys into the bowl on the counter where he always put them and he asked her, "Hey, what are you doing?"

"Oh, just ironing your gown. How'd it go at the Temple? Everything okay?"

He came up to her, they kissed and he said, "Yeah, it was fine. I know they want me gone for sure. I think Dean has even been dreaming about it. I wonder how they'll react when I submit my paper and the Secretary releases my findings?"

"We had better be packed and out of here," replied Sally.

"You got that right. What's for lunch? I'm starving."

"Anything you want. I'm not too hungry. Make yourself a sandwich or something while I finish this up, okay?"

Larkin thought that was odd, because she was always hungry, but he just shrugged his shoulders and made a sandwich for himself. He turned on the TV and the phone rang. Larkin picked it up and it was Harry.

"Hi, Harry, how are you?" He put the phone on his shoulder and began to eat.

"Just fine, Larkin. I keep meaning to tell you when I see you, but I keep forgetting.

There are some pieces of mail that have come for you in the past couple months and I put them downstairs with the pile of things you forgot to take when you moved out. Are you ever going to get that stuff? Before you move back to New York, maybe?"

Laughing Larkin replied, "I guess I had better. Yeah, we'll be over before we go. I want to see you and say goodbye. Like, maybe, the day after graduation on our way out of town?"

"That would be great, Larkin. I'll be at the graduation you know."

"My parents are coming too, and I'm excited to be done. Don't worry, Harry, we'll still have the house and come back from time to time."

"You had better! I'll see you there Friday night then! Bye."

"Bye, Harry."

On Thursday, Larkin's' parents came to town and when they got there, they were impressed at the house. They hadn't been to see them all of the time he had lived in Washington, except for the wedding. They never went many places for sure, but they needed to come to see their son graduate. They drove the whole way in the truck, because Lawtin didn't like to fly and the kids needed it to move.

Larkin needed to go to the Smithsonian to submit his Seward project for his final grade. He was excited about it, but thought it might be best it be released the Monday after they left, instead of while they were still in town. He'd request that from Mr. Shipley when he submitted it. He asked his Dad if he wanted to tag along, at which Lawtin accepted. Leaving the girls behind to catch up, the two men got in Larkin's Lincoln and drove to the mall and found his usual parking place, so his dad didn't have to walk too far. Larkin showed Jim the guard his ID, (not that he had to, but it had been a while since he'd come in) introduced his dad to him and they went up the stairs to Mr. Shipley's office. His new secretary, Sandra, had worked out well. She said, "Hello, Larkin, how are you? And who's this with you?"

"Sandra, this is my Dad, Lawtin Palmer."

"In town for the graduation? You must be proud of this guy! We are. Mr. Shipley is expecting you. Go ahead on in."

"Thanks, Sandra."

Lawtin and Larkin just looked at each other and went in to Mr. Shipley's office after knocking. He stood up from his desk and said, "Hello, Larkin, how are you? And Lawtin, how nice to see you again!"

"Yes, Mr. Shipley, it is nice to see you as well," Larkin replied. They shook hands and all sat down.

Larkin handed the file containing his project to Mr. Shipley. It was now about six inches thick and Larkin said to him, "It has become quite lengthy, but it is most complete. I found substantiating resources and tried, with varying degrees of success, to corroborate every claim that Seward and Barton made. I hope it is what you need to go ahead and show the world our claims are true; that the Masons, of the North and South, did conspire to kill Lincoln, Seward, and Johnson. I also ask that you wait until I have left D.C. before you release the information."

Shipley looked at the document, sat it down, and thanked Larkin for his work saying he'd wait until he'd been able to read the project before he released it. He was sure that what Larkin had done would be sufficient to proceed. He wanted him to know he would be welcome back on staff at any time if he should wish to continue at the Smithsonian. Larkin thanked him and said, "I'll miss all of this and you, Mr. Shipley."
"I'll miss you too, Larkin. Goodbye, Son."
Getting up from his chair, he smiled at his former boss and Lawtin followed him out.

Larkin and Lawtin went down the stairs toward the car, but first went by to introduce Lawtin to Harry. Harry saw them coming and got up to greet them. "Hello, Larkin. Hi, Lawtin how are you?" Larkin had forgotten they had already met at the wedding. Because- he had left for the honeymoon!

They said their hellos and Larkin told Harry that he had just given Mr. Shipley his project. "I sure wish I knew what was going to happen after that comes out, Larkin. You'll either be the most famous man in the country and a hero, or a laughing stock and a hated man."
"I know, but either way, I won't be here."
"True," said Harry, "Well, I better get back to work. Nice to see you again, cousin Lawtin."
"You too, Harry. See you tomorrow night."
Harry said to Larkin reminding him, "Don't forget to come and get your mail and things."
"I won't, Harry," replied Larkin.

While the guys were gone, the girls were packing up so they could load some of their things into the pickups when the men got back. They wanted to leave the house complete, so that if they came to visit or work, they could just move back in. However they had to have all their clothes and miscellaneous things packed to take with them. They had almost everything ready when the men returned. Sally asked, "How did it go?"
"Just fine, Dear. I expect he'll release it next week after he has read it."
"Good. We have all this stuff for you to carry down to the trucks whenever you're ready."

"We're ready," father and son said in unison. Looking at each other and laughing, they loaded their arms and took the first boxes down to the garage to fill Sally's pickup first. When it was full, they put a tarp over the top of her truck just in case it rained. It was packed tight and looked good. They put his dad's truck in the garage and parked Larkin's car on the street so they could load that truck as well, and keep it safe before they left Saturday. The plan was for his parents to leave from there, and Sally and Larkin would leave, go to Harry's, and then start out for New York. The hour was almost upon them.

The next morning on Larkin's graduation day, Sally called the kids down for breakfast, "Soups' on!" It seemed odd, because they were at their own home and not in Brookfield.
Larkin said to Sally, "Sounds the same no matter where she is."

Sally was just finishing drying from a shower and she came over to Larkin and said, "I'll be down as soon as I dress." She kissed him, he squeezed her tush and she went to the closet to get the clothes she had kept for the day. She wasn't feeling well again that day, just a bit of the flu she thought, but she wasn't going to say anything and spoil Larkin's graduation day.

Larkin went down to the kitchen and said to his mom, "Trying to use up some of the stuff we have before the move?"
"That's right. So this is going to be a big meal. We have three kinds of meat and pancakes with eggs on the side. Want some coffee?"
"Wow! I'll get it, Mom. Thanks." Larkin poured himself some coffee and he asked his dad, who was sitting there reading the paper, if he wanted another cup, too.
Lawtin said handing him his cup, "Yes, please." As Larkin poured the coffee, Sally came down the stairs to the kitchen.
"Smells like we have a lot of food here this morning," she said.
"I think we'll have leftovers from breakfast," commented Larkin.
"We'll have breakfast for lunch, too," said Lawtin, smiling.
"What time do you have to be at the auditorium, Honey?" asked Shirley.
"I'm supposed to be there at two. I think you could get there at three-thirty and still be fine."

Everybody got to where they were supposed to be for the graduation and on time. Larkin stepped across the stage and his four lone fans in the room stood up and applauded as he accepted his diploma. The Vice President gave the address that day, only because Dr. Perkins was his friend and they didn't know who else to ask. However, Larkin knew Mondale was a Mason puppet, too. It was ironic that Larkin had done so well in the nation's capital where it was run by so many

Masons, especially at UMD. God had been good to protect him there. As the crowd was dismissed, Larkin ran to his wife and said, "Was that cool or what?"

"You looked great, Honey. Give me a kiss."

Shirley said, "Me too, Honey." After kissing his wife he leaned over to his right and kissed his mother. Harry and his dad stuck out their hands and congratulated Larkin as well. He was now an educated farmer.

The troop made it over to Larkin's house afterwards and they invited Harry along to eat dinner there too, to which he gladly accepted. Larkin had bought steaks for everyone and they fixed them on the Jenn-air, which Shirley was mystified by. Larkin thought it was great that his dad and Harry were getting to know one another. Harry was almost as close to him as were his uncles and he was so glad that God had led them to know one another. Lawtin and Shirley would not drink wine with their meal, but they didn't mind if the rest of them did and Larkin got out one of the many new bottles he had bought from the sale of the second bottle of the rare wines they had found in the basement. The wedding planner got twenty thousand dollars for that one. He had over 1500 bottles in the cellar now and the remainder of the rare ones on a special shelf.

When Harry got sleepy, Larkin offered to drive him home, rather than getting another cab. The two got in the car and Harry put down the window in the cool spring air. It was refreshing after drinking the wine and Harry felt better when Larkin pulled into the curb and stopped to let him out. Harry had to move in a rocking horse fashion a couple times to get up. Larkin laughed at him and said, "See you early in the morning, Harry."

"How early?"

"I think we will be here by seven or so."

"That's fine. Thanks for dinner. Goodnight, Larkin. Congratulations!"

"Night, Harry."

Harry shut the door and walked up the steps to his house waving at Larkin as he went in. Larkin drove off feeling a bit sad knowing he would only see him one more time for who knew how long.

Sally was waiting for him when he parked out front and she set the alarm when he came in. She had been nervous the whole night knowing the time had almost run out for their warning from the Commander. Larkin had locked the car up and the trucks had been in the garage the whole time, so she felt like everything was secure. Larkin could see the worry on her face and said to her, "Dear, the Lord is with us and no matter what happens, we will be fine."

"I know. Just give me a hug." She cried, as always, and they walked up to their bedroom. She went in to change and Larkin said goodnight to his parents who were across the hall from them. They were all tired and it was going to be a long drive back to Brookfield tomorrow.

He went in to change and she was in bed already. She watched him take off his clothes and as he started to put on his PJ's she shook her head no at him and motioned for him to just come to bed as he was. She was scared and he knew it, not wanting to have him like usual, but to need him, to feel secure and not feel vulnerable, but protected and loved. They made love so tenderly and went to sleep.

The next morning came early and they ate leftovers heated in the microwave. The rest of the food they threw out, knowing it would go bad anyway. Then, when everyone had gone to the bathroom one last time and saying goodbye, Larkin's folks left for Brookfield. Larkin and Sally each got in a vehicle and headed to Harry's.

They both parked out front and Larkin picked up a suitcase he had some space in saying to Sally, "Go to the front door and ask Harry to come to the back and let me in, okay?"
Sally had been feeling bad again this morning and felt nauseous, and while holding it back she said, "Okay, Honey." She went up to the front door and rang the bell while Larkin went around to the back. Harry answered and said, "Good Morning, Sally."
She responded, "I don't feel so good Harry. I have to use your bathroom. Go let Larkin in the back will you?" she asked as she ran to the bathroom. Harry went to the back and opened the door for Larkin and he started down the stairs to show him the things waiting for him. Larkin came in the back door and saw Harry going down the stairs and as Harry got to the bottom stair he said, "What's that smell and why is it so dark in here?"

Just then Larkin got to the second stair, the same stair he had fallen on so long ago, when he realized what the smell was—gas! He yelled, "Harry, don't turn on the light. Its' gas!" The explosion's force knocked Larkin all the way back up the stairs and out the door into the back yard. The house was instantly engulfed in flames, especially the back steps and kitchen. Larkin had been protected by his suitcase because he was holding it in front of him. His pants were singed and smoldering on the bottoms and his hair was hot to the touch. He sat where he had landed for a brief moment, trying to shake off the explosions force, finally crying out, "Sally! Harry!" He knew there was no way into the back. Running to the front door, he couldn't get in that way either, as fire poured out the door and windows. He assumed they were both dead, so acting quickly, almost instinctively, he walked away leaving his car, thinking that if the Masons thought he were dead, too, he may have a chance. He cried, was angry, devastated, and upset, and as he turned the corner on foot two blocks away, the fire department came rushing past him toward Harry's house. Sally and Harry were dead. He needed to get away from there!

The "dead" letter that the Commander had sent was never opened and destroyed by the fire in Harry's basement. "They" had struck again and had won the battle, but not the war...

Chapter Seven

The Trip

Larkin walked around town in a daze for most of the morning until he came to the bus depot. Fortunately, he had taken the rest of the cash and checkbooks from the safe and put them in his pocket along with The Eraser, the list, and his passport. He bought a ticket on the next bus going west and it was headed for Houston.

Back at Harry's, the fire department had to call another truck to help with the blazing fire. They had extinguished the fire in the front quickly and realizing there was still someone alive inside, went into the structure to pull them out. It was Sally! The blast had thrown her from the front of the toilet as she vomited into it, through the curtain and into the tub, landing on wet towels from Harry's morning shower. She was spared because as the fire drew close to her, she covered herself with the towels and turned on the water in the tub. The fireman told her by the truck that if she hadn't thought quickly like that, she probably would have died. She had a bump on her head and had inhaled a lot of smoke, but otherwise she was fine. Many of the neighbors had come over to see what had happened and all a distraught Sally could do is ask about Larkin and Harry, but the firemen couldn't find either of them and couldn't answer her questions. She cried because she thought, 'Larkin's dead'. The fire and rescue people talked with her for a long time to determine if she was fit to leave. When Sally asked the fire chief if he'd have Larkin's car taken to the house and gave him the key, they thought she was coherent enough to drive. When they told her it was alright for her to go, she got in her truck and headed toward New York leaving it all behind. There was no longer any hope. Larkin was dead; Harry, too.

Larkin stared out the window as the bus went on mile after mile. He couldn't imagine why they would want to kill Harry, too, except that he had left them and he was a traitor. Remaining in a trance, he thought of his wife, her death and what it meant. He wanted to get out the list right now and kill them all! But no, God would show him the way to wage his next battle and to take vengeance at the proper time. Would he, a mere man, play God? After crying for a while he fell asleep. He woke to some guy trying to pick his pocket and in a rage he said, "Touch me again and I'll kill you." The guy held up his hands and moved back from him. He could tell Larkin was serious. Shoving his valuables and the Eraser deep into his pocket, he went back to sleep until the bus pulled into Houston.

The pickpocket exited quickly and Larkin got off the bus, and walked down the street to the nearest diner. It was an old 50's style diner, with white Formica tables; "s" curved metal chairs, and a counter the length of the building. Sitting down on the metal stool at the counter, he ordered a hamburger and Coke. There was an older Amish or Mennonite man and his wife sitting in one of the five booths down a little ways from him on the back wall. They finished up about the same time and Larkin smiled at them, being used to seeing the Amish, and as he paid in front of them said, "Hello, Brother."

"Good day to you," replied the man. Larkin nodded as he went past them to the door and he walked to the street not knowing where he wanted to go. The couple came out and saw Larkin standing on the sidewalk bewildered and more noticeably, disheveled. They got into their truck, drove up next to him and the man said through the window, "Need to go somewhere, Son?"

Somewhat exasperated Larkin replied, "I don't know where to go, Sir."

"I'm going to San Mario if you want to go that way."

"Thank you."

Larkin threw his bag into the back of the truck and climbed in next to the man's wife who had moved over. The man asked him as he began to pull onto the road, "What's your name, Son?"

"Larkin Palmer, Sir."

"I'm Martin Yoder and this is my wife, Sarah. Palmer, hum, I knew some Palmers back up in the New York area. You kin to them?"

"Probably so, what are their names?"

"Harry and Tom, of Brookfield, I think it was."

Larkin got choked up and began to cry, but holding in the tears said, "They were my uncles, Mr. Yoder."

Seeing his reaction Mr. Yoder said softly, "I'm sorry to hear of their passing, Larkin. It has been a long time since I've been in your neck of the woods."

"Uncle Tom passed two years ago and Harry has been with the Lord for almost eight years now and this morning..." Larkin stopped mid-sentence and began to cry. The two just let him cry and didn't interrupt, and Larkin turned and put his head against the frame of the truck in silence.

Mr. Yoder drove for a couple of hours and had to stop for gas. Larkin got out to use the restroom and when he came back, he joined Martin and insisted on paying for the fuel before they left the station. He was grateful and thanked Larkin for the blessing. Opening the door to the truck, Mrs. Yoder got in first and Larkin took the place next to her again. Larkin felt a little better and they drove on again with Mr. Yoder humming "Amazing Grace". God had done Larkin an amazing favor by sending him the Yoders and once again, he was along for the ride.

When Sally arrived at the farm, she ran into the house, flung herself onto the floor in a corner of the kitchen and broke down only able to say rocking back and forth, "Larkin's dead, Larkin's dead." She finally came out of it only after Shirley soothed her in her arms for an hour or so, but she was equally as distraught as Sally from the news. Lawtin just sat there at the table in shock and unable to ask any questions as to how or what had happened. They just took Sally's word for it that their son was dead.

The Yoder's destination was the home of some friends in San Mario. They too, were Mennonite and offered to take Larkin in for the night as well. He felt safe with them and gladly accepted their offer. The smell of food cooking was in the kitchen and the visitors were welcomed to sit down and talk at the table as the women finished the meal. This environment made Larkin think of home and gave him a sense of peace, even though his insides were being torn apart. The women finally had the meal on the table and they all held hands to say the blessing, which the man of the house accomplished. He asked especially that the Lord would be with Larkin, not knowing what the matter was. It was out of love for Larkin he asked this, not even knowing his circumstances. In that act of love and kindness to a stranger, Larkin saw the Word in action and he felt peace.

They ate and sat around the table afterwards talking about their plans for their trip and their final destination, which Larkin found out, was Costa Rica. 'Costa Rica!' thought Larkin. It was the place that Sally wanted to go for their honeymoon! And it also was the place she said you go to because no one else went there. The men talked about the dairy they were planning to start in a new town and how they sure wished they knew someone that had knowledge of the dairy business to help them out. Larkin had not said anything until this time as it was none of his business, but when they got to this point in the conversation he had to step in, "Brothers, I believe God sent you to me today, but I also believe He has sent me to you. I am your man."

He told them of the farm and his success and knowledge; of the innovations he had brought and implemented, and of his new degree in agriculture from UMD. The men were astonished and praised God for His sense of humor, timing, and His goodness. Larkin told them to pray about that he might go with them and he'd do the same that night. He was given a cot to sleep on in the laundry room and because of the demands of the day, he fell fast asleep.

The next morning the men were reading the Word and praying at the table, while the women listened and prepared the food. He went to the bathroom and came out to sit with them and listen, and pray. But he knew in his heart what God had in store for him and why He'd brought them together. Even if Sally had survived, which he truly believed not to be the case, he knew he should leave, if for no other reason than that at some future time, her life might be spared again. After breakfast, Larkin, once again, told them he'd like to go to Costa Rica with them. They concurred that they saw the hand of God in it and accepted him into their plans. They asked him about his faith, his church, and his past relationship to the Lord. With it all they were satisfied, especially when he told them he was named after a Quaker man the family once knew. At this news they laughed, and with it he became a member of the group. He offered his resources to them and they accepted, and he was glad he had brought some of his money along and his checkbooks, but he'd not use that resource for a long time so as to not show "them" he was alive. When the convoy of three trucks and a stock trailer with six cows headed South, Larkin was riding along.

The newspaper headlines in D.C. read, "Home destroyed by blast. Two missing; feared dead." Dean brought the front page into the Commanders' office and laid it on his desk. Picking it up, he read it and smiled saying, "Well, we don't have to worry about him anymore."
"What about his wife? Do we go after her?" asked Dean.
"I think we'll leave her alone. She'll suffer the rest of her life. That's even worse than death sometimes." He laughed, wadded up the newspaper and tossed it in the trash.

Mr. Shipley read the news as well, but quite different from the Commanders' reaction, he was distraught to see what had happened to both men whom he had employed and become quite close to. He could hardly work that day and threw the paper across the room in a rage. He now had a decision to make, "Was he to risk the wrath of whoever killed Larkin and Harry and release the Seward report? Or would he bury it along with his friends?" He sat back and pondered the question for a few more minutes and finally made the hard decision and wrote across the file, "Sandra, file report with Seward file." To protect his family, he decided to bury it.

The trip went slowly through Mexico as they had to stop often for the livestock to rest. This was really no problem, because they were on no time table. They got there when they got there and no sooner. Larkin was actually enjoying seeing these new places and peoples, but was still suffering greatly, especially at the end of the day when he'd pray. He was not angry with God, but angry with men. He struggled with it and had The Eraser in his hands more than once. He prayed for patience and that he might be able to forgive, but he really didn't want to forgive. That night he truly missed his wife and thought about her gentle ways, her kindness, and thoughtfulness. He recalled her spunkiness, playfulness, and her sexiness. And yet he remembered her for her devotion to him and the love they shared. With all of it behind him, he decided to let her go, forget the pain and give her to the Lord. He fell asleep knowing God was with him and in control.

Arriving in Costa Rica, he found out the country was smaller than he thought. The town was to the East of the capital and it was called Rita. It was no more than a hole in the wall and the people friendly, but very poor. The surrounding areas were farms, but were very primitive in their operations. He was looking forward to the challenge of their mission, but now saw so many other things he could help with. Now he understood the term "mission". That is what the Mennonites were all about here in Costa Rica. Although they came to begin a dairy operation, they came also to proclaim the Gospel. And that was to be done by example and in the way they led their lives. Hopefully, nothing would get in the way of that mission and their focus obscured by the world and the ways of it.

At first, it was all grunt work. Building the dairy all from scratch, not only took resources, but muscle. He came home dead dog tired many times, but was rewarded by the accomplishments he saw each day. This was especially true when they had an Old Fashioned barn raising and put it up in a week with the help of almost all of the Mennonite men in the country and some help from others. He grew to appreciate what his parents and forefathers in Brookfield had done for him there, after having done this now himself. They ran out of money from time to time and Larkin did what he could to help, but could not use his accounts in the USA due to fear of "them" finding out he was alive. He put as much of the cash he had left into it and when he got to a certain level stopped, saving what he must, so that one day he may return to the USA. Consequently, he lived like the people he had joined, efficiently, economically, thriftily, but always trusting in the Lord to provide. He was given a primitive shack to live in, with leaks in the roof and no furniture, out behind the main house close to the barn, so that he had some privacy. It wasn't much, but for the time being, it was now home.

Their community there in Rita was two families and himself; the Yoders, Martin and Sarah, and the Johns family, Emil and Frieda, and their sons, David and Jacob. They went to worship about twenty miles away at a congregation served by Brother Johann Epp, called "Iglesias Menonita Casa de Dios". There were about ten other families there who were members and some had been there for about fifteen years already. They had made very little progress in conversions from the local population, which was discouraging to them, but they had hoped that someday that would change. The first time Larkin came there, they welcomed him with fervor and were impressed by him, so much so, that two of the brothers with daughters eyed him as a potential son-in-law. But, when they found out of his recent loss, they withheld their ideas and didn't approach him.

Larkin began to dress in the Mennonite style and had grown a smallish beard and mustache. He kept it neatly trimmed and actually looked quite dapper, which didn't help a thing when the daughters would see him each week at church. However, remaining single was number two on his priority list, while number one was staying alive. Both were cause for holding to the status quo.

His education and knowledge made him quite famous there when he put them into action and applied them amongst his new brethren. His fame bothered him as he had hoped to remain under the radar here as well, because he remembered what had happened in D.C. The community began using his ideas and production went up. Getting equipment was the hardest hurdle to jump, but ingenuity made up for it when necessary. He continued to try to meet current needs, but came up with plans for the future and had long range goals that surprised even Martin. In it all, he showed his faith in God as his strength and provider.

One day, Brother Martin lost his only pen. It wasn't much, but he wasn't happy because he'd have to buy another the next time they went into town. Larkin overheard him talk to Sarah about it and he said to him, "Go look in the barn by Betsy's stall." He did later in the day and sure enough, Martin found his pen in front of the stall! From then on people would come to him, (many were from the local Catholic population and somewhat superstitious) much like his Grandma Mary, to help them find lost objects.

The years flew by and life in Costa Rica didn't change much. The only thing he saw that did change was the jungle in the hillsides as it grew larger and taller. He found the trees and plants to be very interesting and the Mangos were his favorite. However, the birds would come to raid them and he'd always have to shoo them away. There were so many mangos on the trees there was really no need to not let them have whatever they wanted from them anyway. He did a lot of walking, not because he had to, because they always had the trucks, but because he wanted to. He had nowhere to go quickly. No need to set timetables.

He walked all over the countryside when he was not working, enjoying God's creation, studying it, especially the trees, and making friends with the locals along the way. And of course, he'd think on life, which at times, was not beneficial to his mental well being.

He didn't pay much attention to what was happening in the world and when the American newspaper would come by mail to the house each week, he wouldn't read it. He didn't know Spanish when he arrived there, but now going on his nineteenth year in Rita; he had become quite proficient at it. He helped the locals often and had become well known, not only for his giving of himself, but his smile and love for them all. He had improved his living quarters quite a bit since he arrived, but it wasn't what you'd call a house back home, but he didn't mind and it met all of his needs. He had put a toilet in a lean-to on the side of it with a barrel on the roof for solar heated water, just like back at The Homestead and when the Yoders or Johns' needed another, they'd come out and borrow his bathroom and shower once in a while. He didn't mind that, because they shared everything. The Brethren didn't ask about his money back home, and he did feel guilty about not using it from time to time, but he had no choice. Someday he hoped to change that. He'd grown out his facial hair and now had a full beard. He kept it as neat as always and he looked very handsome. He was the only confirmed bachelor in the group his age, because the rest of their men all were married at early ages- the girls even earlier. All those who wanted him to be a son-in-law had given up on the idea a long time before.

Back in Brookfield, Sally was working the barn, listening to the radio as she finished milking Mrs. Hoxie. The Bee Gees were singing, "The Way I love You." Listening to the words, she could not continue and picking up the pail of milk, shut it off and headed towards the house, brushing a tear from her face with her work glove.

At that very same moment, Larkin was moving his bed in order to catch a mouse that had scamper under it. He pushed aside his suitcase resting there and in so doing, accidentally turned on the radio he had taken out of his drawer at home so long ago. Hearing the music playing, he thought, 'What in the world?' He pulled the case out from under the bed and opening the front pocket, he removed his old transistor radio from therein while it played, "How deep is your love?" by the Bee Gees. He listened for a moment and shut it off. Larkin had missed the entire Disco era, but placed his radio on the top of his dresser.

The farm had done well while he was there. The Mennonite community had grown and now was almost single handedly responsible for most of the milk production in the country, as well as cheese. The community of brethren had also done well financially and for this Larkin was thankful. He was grateful that God had given him purpose there and most of all- peace. Larkin had never given up hope that Sally might be alive, no matter how slim the chance could be. That damned Eraser!

Although he'd lived with them a longtime, he did not totally share his ideas about his faith in Christ and hid from them that he truly had remained a Lutheran at heart and continued to hold those things dear that he and Sally had been taught by the good Pastor Olsen so long ago. Hopefully, he would one day be able to practice it fully once again. They turned a blind eye to this because they knew he was a righteous man and he had done as St. Paul, becoming "all things to all men".

Living there was also a time of introspection for him. He struggled with the memories all the way back to his days of finding out about The Eraser, reading the Journal, and all the notes and letters that made up the entire story of the curse, and finally the bullying and harassment by the Masons and their sons. His forgiving side said, "That was a long time ago." The human side came out in rages at times, especially when he thought of Jim Coon and what he had done to him and how it finally killed Ginny. Last but not least, Sally and Harry being killed in D.C. by McPherson, which always brought him to tears and resignation to the fact that she had been killed by "them". He prayed that he would not come to use The Eraser at times, but by prayer and asking God for patience, and by keeping busy with good deeds amongst the people, he was able to go on. But that didn't mean he still didn't struggle, he was indeed human and he was afraid at times, feeling lost and alone. He asked God for help, forgiveness and peace. In reality he was hiding in Costa Rica, from "them" and especially at times, himself, and from God. He was sometimes totally unable to resolve in his mind the dilemma he was in. In fact, he could not, without his faith and hope in God's promises.

What he also failed to understand was how so many members of the great secret society, no matter which branch, could be deceived by those who knew the whole truth. Even he knew what it was all about and he wasn't even a Mason! So many men just thought they were joining a club or fraternity. But why didn't the lower ranks want to know? Or did they? Where they merely pawns in the great plan of the Illuminati? He did know this, however, that many of them would not believe him even if he told them! He felt sorry for them and hoped that someday they would come to know the truth about Freemasonry before it was too late, just like Nathan B. Forrest had.

The time came close to his birthday and on the 12th of June in the year 2000, he was to be forty. The brothers didn't celebrate birthdays. But he did by making a decision; he was going to go back to the USA. Larkin didn't tell Martin or Emil. Then one day, he was sitting and eating breakfast with them as Martin was reading the paper. Martin held it up and on the back it said, "Masons plan International Convention in D.C. to discuss New World Order." Larkin was visibly eager to read it fully and Martin was surprised as he sat it down and Larkin picked it up. Larkin never read the paper. The convention was to be in September at the Walter E. Washington Convention Center. He thought, 'That must have been built since I left.' What really piqued his interest is that they expected 150,000 Masons from all over the world to be in attendance. Because of their agenda, he knew he needed to be there, too. He sat the paper down and said to Martin, "Brother, I'll be leaving you soon and I wanted to tell you so that you are prepared to find someone to do my work."

"I had a feeling that you were becoming restless. I will miss you, Brother, and I pray you'll come back some day." Martin shook his hand and Sarah came over to him and hugged him.

Martin asked, "When will you leave?"

"As soon as possible. I have a long trip ahead of me."

After about a week's time, Martin had found a young brother from a family about six miles South, that was willing to come and help in Larkin's stead. So, Larkin felt comfortable enough to pack his things into the suitcase he had brought when he came. It was dusty, but no worse for wear, because he hadn't gone anywhere in all that time. As he put his meager belongings into it, he found something in the back pocket. He pulled the square package out and looked at it. It was the Trojan that his mother had used for the "Mom" test with Sally some twenty- two years before. He smiled, shook his head and laughed saying out loud, "I guess that I never needed it." He threw it in the trash. Anything more than one suitcase was too much to take, so he gave everything away as his neighbors and friends needed, even his old radio! He took out The Eraser from the back of his dresser and his checkbooks which were gathering dust. Larkin put them in his pocket and then was all packed. He'd leave in the morning. As he lay in his bed that last night in Costa Rica, Larkin thought of a book he'd read so long ago back in his home town library. The historian Thomas Carlyle had said in it, "Our main business is not to see what lies dimly at a distance, but to do what lies clearly at hand." He knew his time was now.

They fed him well that morning, saying a prayer for safe travel, too, and gave him a sack of food to take with him for the trip. Martin had arranged a ride for Larkin into Santo Domingo. There he could get a bus. He said his goodbyes and he walked down to the next road where he was to get his ride. Along the way, he stopped and picked two mangos and put them in his sack, too. The brother picked him up in his old

Datsun pickup, which just happened to be blue. He smiled when he saw it and thought of Sally once more. Throwing his suitcase in the back they headed for the big city. Larkin, appreciative as always, thanked him for the ride and got out at the bus station. The buses there were quite different, and he piled on next to a woman with a bird cage in her hands. She didn't want the seat by the window, so he pushed past her and he sat there much to his delight. After about two hours on the road the bus stopped and let out many of its passengers. He still had an hour to go to his next bus. This one stopped at the border and then went back to Santo Domingo. He fell asleep that last hour because the lady had gotten off and he sat in the seat alone. Finally, when the bus stopped, he woke and got out onto the dusty road.

He had kept his passport up to date just in case he had to make a trip and this was much to his dismay, because he knew he risked detection by doing so. However, no one ever caught it, he thought, because he had just reapplied from his original passport of twenty years ago. He still had to go through four countries, but those border stops usually went easily, especially now that he spoke Spanish. He had no troubles, as he thought would be the case, because no one bothered the Mennonites. They usually had no money, and if they did, it wasn't much. Besides, he looked as poor as the rest of them and smiled and said hello all of the time to everyone. He got a bus in Mexico City that would take him all the way to the border of Texas. He was actually getting excited to be going home. He was only thinking of one thing now- The Eraser.

The border guard looked at his passport and went through his bag for contraband. He didn't know why, because he still looked like he had when he left Costa Rica; a simple and plain man- period. Larkin walked through the facility when he finished and went straight to the bus station. He got on the first bus to Houston and when he got off after sleeping the whole way, he walked to the bank across the street. It happened to be a branch of his bank in D.C. and he went to the counter still carrying his old suitcase and talked to the cashier there. "Hello. I'd like to know if I can still use this account. It's been inactive for years and I'd like to see what the balance is today." The woman didn't give him much of a look when he said this and just took the checkbook from him and entered the account number. She looked at the balance and said, "Just one moment, Sir."

She went over to the branch manager, told him what she had seen and pointed at Larkin as he stood waiting. He came back with her and said, "Do you have any ID, Sir?"

Larkin smiled, pulled out his passport and handed it to the man. He looked at it not once, but twice, comparing it to Larkin's face, mostly because of the beard. He was finally satisfied and said, "Although your account has been inactive for this entire time, Sir, it has continued to accrue interest."

"And what's the balance now?" inquired Larkin.

The man gulped and said, "The balance is forty-five million dollars, Sir."

"I see. I'd like to withdraw ten thousand dollars if you would help me with that."

"Yes, Sir!" said the manager and he went to the safe to get it. He came back counting the new bills out for Larkin and put them in a bank bag for him with his receipt.

Larkin undid his suitcase and after taking some of it for his pocket, put the bag into it and said, "Thanks. Oh, can I use your phone to call a cab?"

Pointing toward the door he said, "Sure. Just sit at that desk over there."

Larkin called a cab and took it to the airport. Opening the door, he gave the cabbie a tip and got out. Things had changed a bit since he had flown the last time. It looked to him like people didn't enjoy flying anymore. They rushed about almost faster than the planes themselves and no one had a smile. He went to the counter, bought a ticket and the cashier asked, "What credit card would you like to use, Sir?"

"I don't have a credit card. I'll pay cash." She looked at him funny and he thought that to be odd that cash didn't seem to be the way to pay anymore. After paying, he had about an hour to wait and decided to keep going to the gate.

He walked toward the concourse and had to go through security to go to his plane. They put his bag on the scanner and the man stopped it and wanted to open it. Larkin went through and waited for them to finish and they took his bank bag out of his suitcase and questioned him about it asking for his passport. They asked him where he got it and why he was carrying so much money. He asked, "Why?"

The guard answered by saying, "Criminals who work for the drug cartels often launder money across the border for them. It's illegal. Is that what you are doing, Sir?"

"No. I just withdrew it from my account before I traveled. The receipt is in the bag. Look in there."

Sure enough, the receipt was there and they asked, "Could we see the checkbook account you took it from then, Sir?"

Larkin pulled it sharply out of his pocket and handed it to him. The bank teller had updated his information and the current balance was now shown. After looking at it the man's eyes got wide in disbelief and he said to the guard assisting him, "Let's allow Mr. Palmer to pass. It's okay." They gave him back his things and money saying to him, "I'm sorry, Mr. Palmer, we need to be careful nowadays."

He said to him, "Things have changed since I've been gone. And all of this because of- cash!"

The guard didn't smile.

There was a restaurant there on the concourse and he decided he was hungry, so he went and ordered a hamburger with fries. He was surprised it cost almost five dollars and wondered what had happened. He thought, 'No wonder I have so much money in my account- inflation!' He sat and gave thanks, eating it fast so he could go to his plane, which he heard over the loudspeakers was now boarding. As he walked to the plane, he took a look around him to see how things had changed. He was appalled at all the tattoos, the blue and red hair the kids were wearing and the bare midriffs with navel earrings. He thought, 'What's that all about?' The good thing he saw was that there were no more bell bottoms and big hair. He also was amazed that everyone seemed to be using computers for almost everything!

He had the window seat in row 21, sitting next to a woman with a set of headphones on who was listening to music on some smallish device. He didn't care what part of the plane he was in as long as he got the window seat. Nodding to her as he sat down he said, "Hello." He sat quietly and looked out the window, remembering the last time he had been on a plane with Sally. It didn't take long for him to begin to daydream and he thought about what it would be like with her again, in love and happy. Larkin woke from it in a swelling rage, and was determined to go through with the plan his Grandpa Elias had envisioned so long ago. It was, in some ways beyond his control, a God ordained plan, with him as some pawn moved to complete the task. He felt helpless, hopeless, and held hostage by so many forces. Still, he knew he must go on with the plan. The New World Order would not come about on his watch as Keeper!

It was almost six o'clock when he deplaned at Dulles and he took his bag from the carousel and headed toward the door. A black man asked if he wanted help and Larkin just shook his head and continued on towards the cab stand. He hailed a cab and got in. The cabbie looked at him as if to ask for directions and Larkin said, "Four-o-six Ridge."

"You got it."

He was surprised to see that so many changes had taken place in Washington. Many places had been torn down and new multiplex condos put in their places. The stores had almost all changed names or been remodeled into something else and it looked as if there were less houses and more commercial buildings. Nothing remains the same. The cab pulled up to his house, at least he thought it was his house, and let him out. Was he home?

CHAPTER 8

The Eradication

Larkin really didn't know what to do at this point. He still had his keys, so he took them out of his pocket and then noticed in the window that there was a sticker saying the house was protected by Brinks Security. Was the alarm changed? Had his parents sold the place? To be sure he didn't enter someone else's home; he looked in the windows first. He saw his furniture and everything he left there twenty years ago. He walked around back to the garage and peered into the dirty window panes. There sat his Lincoln. It was still his house! Larkin walked back to the front door, put the key in the lock and turned it saying, "Here goes!" It opened and as soon as he went in the alarm sounded. Running to the keyboard he entered his birthday 61260, and Valla, it went off! It was, indeed, still his house! He sat his suitcase down and closed the front door. Taking a walk around the rooms downstairs, it was if he had stepped into a time capsule. Nothing had changed, except it was mighty dusty. It was as if no one but the alarm people had been there since he left. He ran upstairs with his bag, a little slower than he remembered doing so many years ago, and looked around up there as well. It was no different- just vacant. He picked up the princess phone next to the bed, listened for a dial tone, and to his amazement, it was still hooked up. And it seemed all the other utilities were on as well. There were just no people. He plopped down on the bed and began to cry once more, remembering his dear wife and the life he once knew.

After a good cry, he composed himself and went to the bathroom. He looked in the closet and found some linen they had left, so he went to take a shower and get cleaned up. First, he looked in the dresser for some clothes, but only found a pair of old blue jeans he'd cut in Hawaii. He took off his clothes and thought he'd just continue to wear them as a cover. No one ever noticed the Mennonites, except in D.C., he might not wear his hat. After showering, he felt better and he went to the kitchen to see if there was any food there at all. There were canned goods, but they were all out of date and some popped up and exploded from being bad. He knew he couldn't eat anything there and the refrigerator was empty, but was cold! He'd have to go to the grocery store and out for supper that night.

Going back upstairs, Larkin put all his clothes away knowing that this would have to be his operations center for the next month as he planned for the September event. He went into the closet, opened the safe and took a look inside, and all that was there was his copy of the Seward report and dust. He picked up the papers and wondered whatever happened to it. Did the Secretary release the information? He also wondered, "What happened to the Key?" He shook his head in wonderment. He sat the papers back in there and placed The Eraser and the list in the safe with most of the ten thousand he had withdrawn that morning. He kept some cash for groceries and dinner, and thought about where he could go and not be recognized as he ate. As the walk would not be too far and the atmosphere dark, he decided on Chinese; at least if the restaurant was still there!

Before he left, he went down to the garage, opened the door to the Lincoln. Therein, he found keys in the ignition. He recognized them as Sally's. 'Hum,' he thought, 'how did they get Sally's keys to bring my car home?' He'd ponder that. He found the car to be in perfect condition and it still only had 12,007 miles on it! It had a bad battery, tires, and of course, the gas in it would need to be drained, but he bet it would still run! He'd take care of all that later. He closed it up, went upstairs and set the alarm on the house, venturing out the front door to go to dinner. He still liked to walk, and he was curious to see how the neighborhood had changed along the way. People looked at him strange, mostly, he thought, because he looked like a Mennonite farmer! He thought he may have to do something about that after all and would do some investigation about style and dress so he'd fit in better without being recognized. Right now, he did not blend in!

When he started down the street, he looked past the first few signs to see if the restaurant was still there. It was! He was happy to see it and when he went in he was greeted by the same waiter, much older now, but just as pleasant. Larkin wondered if he would recognize him, especially because of his beard and dress. At first he didn't seem to, but when he took him to the same table as always before, he knew. In fact as he sat down, he whispered to Larkin, "Very nice to see you again, Sir."

"Thank you. Same to you," Larkin replied in kind. He ordered and looked around the room to see what had changed there. Not much! In fact, it was still the same old pictures, paint, and decorations that were there twenty years ago. They seemed to be timeless and there was really no need to change them. His food came and he listened to the other people in their booths and at their tables talk about their days and laugh. He saw a young couple, who seemed to be in love, lean to each other and kiss from time to time, speaking softly so no one would hear them, and smiling all the while. He thought of Sally and their first meeting there and hung his head wishing she were there with him once more. When he finished, he picked up the bill and left the fortune cookie on the plate. As he paid he thanked the waiter, gave him a tip, and started out the door, but the man stopped him by saying, "I hope to see you again, Sir."

Larkin turned, smiled at him and said, "Maybe so my friend."

As he walked down the street, he knew he would not be able to go shopping that night, because he was just too tired. He walked home and put it off until the next day. He had to plan his next few weeks and he already had ideas, but he had a lot of learning to do, because of being gone for so long. It was, indeed, like he had died and come back to life!

He went in and decided to watch some TV and find out a few things. The country was in an election year, and a man named Bush was running for President against a man from Tennessee named Gore. He wondered if either of them were Masons, but figured they both either were or were beholding to them. He was delighted that the TV in his bedroom worked, mostly because the man at Wards was right, the Hitachi was the best, but he didn't like what he saw on it. It was different programming than before, lots of violence, inappropriate situations, and sex on TV now. The ads were interesting to him and he wanted to find out more about computers and how they might help him. It seemed that a thing called the" internet" had come into being and there was lots of information there to be found on almost any subject. He'd call someone about computers in the morning, too. Even though he didn't know about them, he did know he had a lot of things to learn in the next few weeks!

He started to go to bed and fluffed the comforter on it to get all of the dust off. Dust went up into the air in a plume and coughing as he inhaled it, he decided to just fold it over double and clean it later. He didn't want the neighbors to know he'd come back, so he'd drawn all the curtains and only used the lights when he needed to. He didn't know if that would work, but he was going to try to lie low as much as possible. He got in bed and read his Bible looking for guidance in what he was planning and wondering if God could forgive him for it. What he was thinking of doing was surely premeditated, and if men could prove it, they would lock him up for the rest of his life or even worse, give him the death penalty. As a Palmer, he knew that this action, no matter how big or small, would one day come to him as it had all of his ancestors before him. There was no peace for Palmer men, only the curse of The Eraser.

Larkin prayed and wanted to go to sleep, but it was difficult to do so in the bed he had shared with Sally. He smelled the sheets to see if her scent lingered there after all of these years, but it did not. He got up and turned the bedroom light on and looked for anything that was hers, but she had packed very well before she left. The dressers, closet, and nightstands were empty. Even their wedding picture that had been on the dresser facing them was gone because she treasured it so and it had gone to Brookfield. He sat and cried again, unable to contain himself because he still loved her so much. He was tempted to just pick up the phone and call his parents, if they be alive, but knew he should not until he was finished with what he'd come to do. In fact, he thought he may not even call, but just go home. It was the time.

The next couple of weeks were busy, learning, planning, and preparing. Not to mention, cleaning, fixing, and buying. He had someone come and fix the Lincoln there at his house because he knew it couldn't be driven the way it was. He even had to put new tires on it because of the dry rot. When the man was done he said, "Boy, you've got a great old car here, Mister."

He decided to purchase his own computer to help his planning. The man who sold it to him said he was the first Mennonite man he had sold one to and he laughed at him when Larkin asked, "Who's Bill Gates?" Taking it home, he read the directions out of necessity and setting it up at his desk, he plugged it in and used the telephone cable for his internet connection. This was called "dial-up" service he found out and was slow. But it didn't matter, because it was free and he didn't want to set up any other types of services from the house. Wondering about the rest of the services, he called the utility companies to see where they were sending the bills for them, and finding out they were going to his parents house he was thankful for them once again.

Larkin searched the web for the names of those Masons of the 32nd degree and above coming to the convention while comparing the list to the one he had prepared so long ago. Some of the men had already died, so he scratched them off his list. He was glad to find out that both Mr. Rojas and R.E. Jensen had died as well. He didn't want to have to erase their names. Those of that rank that he did find, he put a check mark next to, and those he could not confirm, he left alone. Larkin purposely removed any names of high profile Masons and Illuminati, especially the former president. Some names he added to protect his family back home, and he wondered if that was just revenge. He felt it not to be and in fact, had come to the conclusion that none of this, in reality, was vengeance at all, but the logical conclusion to a condition created by the menace themselves. He recalled the Journal and the Leviticus verse stamped on the back, 'Indeed,' he thought, 'an eye for an eye.' There were also other names to be added, new minions of the ranks of men like Pike, who succumbed to the evil they were enticed to follow. He now had a complete list, but how exactly would he implement the plan?

On the morning of September 11th, 2000, Larkin went out for a walk. He had not been able to go past Harry's old place on U Street as yet, but today he felt he must face it and decided to walk rather than drive the Lincoln. He made his way down the streets in a reserved mood, not knowing how he'd react when he saw where his two best friends were killed. He supposed that it would all depend on what he found there. Who owned it now? Would it be rebuilt? What would he find?

The street was one of brownstones built in a row with no space in between them. He was afraid to proceed down the street when he arrived at the corner, but he went on asking God to be with him and give him peace as he got closer. Arriving at the spot where Harry's house had once stood, 1776 U Street NW, the Mennonite man smiled and then began to cry. There wasn't a new home there, but merely a vacant lot next to a liquor store, with trees and a neatly kept lawn with wild flowers growing in the back where Harry's garden used to be. Some of the trees were still those that were there before and they'd become the majestic examples of the area they now were. He wondered who would pay to have this kept up, but his question was answered as he walked into the yard and stood by a bench placed for passersby. On it was a small plaque which read, "Dedicated to Harry Hall and Larkin Palmer who died on this spot May, 16th, 1981." He knew it was his family. Sitting down on it in the cool spot under the trees, he watched the world go by him and remembered his wife. 'Wait!' he thought, 'where's Sally's name?' He turned around and read the plaque once more. It only mentioned him and Harry, and not Sally! Was she alive? He stood up excited as he had never been before. What should he do? Should he praise God right now? Should he jump for joy? No, he needed to find out and then finish the plan. Especially if she *were* alive!

He ran toward the house and kept on going at full blast until he could run no more. He stopped, caught his breath, and started up again. When he got to the house, he ran up the steps and went in, almost forgetting to turn off the alarm. He went straight to his computer and got online. He thought, 'There must be a phone directory for Brookfield.' He found whitepages.com and typed in the town and the name Sally Palmer. The search came up, "4 results nearby". There was one in Fayetteville, Syracuse, Cazenovia, and Brookfield! The last one was on Chase Road! Sally was ALIVE! He wept and thanked the Lord the rest of the night. He wanted to call her right that minute, but, he could not. Larkin would not compromise her security ever again and he was so happy.

He searched the internet the next day for evidence of the release of the Seward Project and found nothing. He tried many different ways and came to the conclusion that Mr. Shipley had never released it. But, he questioned, why? Had he betrayed him? Was he really one of *them*? He found out that he had retired years ago and still lived in D.C. 'He must be almost 85 by now,' he thought, 'maybe I'll go and see him.'

Little did Larkin know, but that very same day, the Masons of rank had come to D.C. early for a preconvention meeting. It just so happened, that Commander McPherson was in charge of the convention festivities as host Lodge. He said to his brothers assembled in the convention board room, "Fellows. We are at a time in our history where all men will be united under the veil of Freemasonry. For you see Brothers, the New World Order is finally to come to fruition. We dreamed of this so long ago when our forefathers came to this great land. Now that we are in place to take control here and across the world, we finally may now put it into place. The New World Order has arrived!" The applause was great with shouts of bravo and McPherson just smiled as he began again, "Twenty years ago, we achieved a great victory in removing a menace that had plagued us since 1792- The Palmer Family.

Since it was removed, we have gone forward with our plans almost unchecked. We have infiltrated all the lands and governments. Even now, unbeknownst to the feeble minded Islamic dissident groups, we have allowed them to flourish and they do our bidding without them even knowing. They are such fools. By the end of this convention, we will have come together to place it all into practice and you will take to your lodges your marching orders. So be it!" The men rose to their feet and applauded for McPherson uproariously.

When McPherson sat down, Dean brought a representative from New York to his table. Dean introduced him, "Sir, this is Billy Coon from the Lodge in De Ruyter. He has a very interesting question to pose to you."

The Commander said to him, "Sit down, Coon."

Billy pulled up a chair and said, "Thank you for seeing me Commander. Do you remember the treasure that the Palmer family stole from us and Morgan?"

"I've received a picture of the die. Yes, and I've waited a long time for this."

"We know they have it on the property somewhere. We just don't know where. Now that Palmer has been dead for the past twenty years and there is no trace of The Eraser, I believe it to be safe to pursue the matter. It must be worth hundreds of millions in this market and we could use it to help bring about our plans."

"Very good, Coon. I think it is worth pursuing. Will it take physical force?"

"It may take some convincing of the family, but it shouldn't be a problem."

McPherson laughed and said, "Do what you must."

"Done," he said as he got up and went back to his own seat. The New York Palmers were now in danger!

The next week Larkin refined the rest of his plans and did his research on the convention center. He found out about the hall where the meetings would take place and the schedule for each day. He found out about security and the computer system. He knew all he could about them and more, he surmised, than they would have wanted him to. *If,* they knew he was alive. He determined not to go to the convention center until it was absolutely necessary and only for the purpose of setting up the plan.

Everything being in place, he was happier than he had been in years. He now knew what it was like to cry like Sally did, because he cried tears of joy almost every day as he waited to implement the plan.

He relaxed the last few days, walking on the mall and going to the sights like the tourists did. He even went by The Castle and walked around his old place of work, finding that he recognized no one and that they had changed the place considerably.

It had been such a long time since he'd enjoyed life and in finding that love was alive, he felt like he did as a kid once again. He could not wait to see her. Yet, he did not want to envision what it would be like, so as not to be disappointed. What had she done all these years? He could only assume she'd gone back to live by his parents and now lived on The Homestead. He was glad she'd not married and still had his name, but was she involved? So many questions he had and only a couple more days to go before they could be answered.

He had gotten used to being in the house again, had cleaned it up somewhat, got rid of all the bad food, and even went down to the wine cellar to check it out. He had not had a drop of wine all of this time, and he wondered how his collection of wines had stood the test of time. Opening the door, he realized that they were all now vintage wines. May some were now vintage vinegar? He picked up a bottle and took it upstairs with him. Going to a drawer in the kitchen he found their corkscrew and he looked at it for a moment, remembering the day they had moved in and Sally had said, "Eureka" when she held it the first time.

Larkin removed the cork from the bottle of 1979 Glen Ellen white zinfandel and took a sniff. Smelled good! Larkin poured himself a glass and raised it saying, "To Sally, may we be drinking here again soon!" That night, despite his circumstances, he felt no pain.

Sitting down on the sofa, he clicked the remote to find there were so many new channels on his TV. He came to the History Channel and stopped. It was a show on Ronald Reagan and his political rise from being Governor of California to President of the United States. He watched for a while drinking his wine and falling in and out of sleep, as was his custom in the evenings. (Even without the wine.)He awoke to a clip from a speech in 1964 shown in black and white. Reagan said, "You and I have a rendezvous with destiny. We will preserve for our children this, the last best hope of man on earth, or we will sentence them to take the first step into a thousand years of darkness." He clicked off the TV with the remote after that and said, "Thanks, Ronnie." He got up and went to bed. He was struggling with finally going through the action of using the Eraser and the wine only softened the blow that was to come the next morning for Larkin; the day of The Eradication!

He got up slowly that next morning, thinking about the task he had to complete. If it had not been for the wine, he would have not been able to sleep. He asked God for forgiveness, not for the wine, but in advance for what he and his Grandfather had planned and what now, in a few short minutes , was about to come to pass. Putting it off, he went to the bathroom, got dressed, ate breakfast and watched the news. The reporter talked about how the convention of Masons was in its last couple of days and how they were touting all of the wonderful things they did in the community. Larkin laughed at that as he sat his coffee mug on the counter. He said out loud, "I can't put this off any longer." He went to the safe to retrieve the Eraser.

He sat at his desk, Eraser box in hand, and once more questioned himself and wondered if he could do what he was about to do. Taking the list from the drawer, he sat it next to the weapon he would use to rein in the evils of Freemasonry once again. Even if they were only brought to their knees for a short time, the momentum of the New World Order would be diminished. With that, Larkin was satisfied. He bowed his head and trembled as he said a short silent prayer. Picking up the box when he finished, he opened it to see the letter from Lawtin Palmer Esquire that he had read so long, long ago. He opened it slowly and read it once more:

Dear Sons,
In the course of a lifetime are many mistakes,
To remove the mark, this is all it takes.
With malice it never take away,
For with consequences you must pay.
Use it sparingly. Strive for perfection.
If you do, you shall receive God's election.
Destroy it not for you all shall be,
the object of its hostility.

Lawtin Palmer Esq. -1770 A.D.

He wept bitterly.

Then, after a deep sigh, he took the Eraser in hand and began at the top of the list. He had erased about half the page when the smell, the foul stench of death became more than apparent to him. He stopped. Placing the Eraser next to his nostril, he took a sniff expecting to be overwhelmed with it. But no! It smelled of rubber! The stench was from its use only, evil emitted in the action of its curse. He continued until the list was gone. The Eraser was now almost half used, hopefully, by him, for the last time. Larkin placed the Eraser and empty page back in the safe, closed it with a sound "thud", and he went out for a walk...

The last day of their convention, Larkin had gone to the convention center early. Dressed in an Italian suit, and having trimmed his beard and hair, he looked quite refined and distinguished as he made his way into the empty hall. He had made a digital image of himself taking the list and rubbing The Eraser across it. He knew there would be other pictures shown that night, so he found the Power Point presentation on their computer which was already set up on sight, hoping he'd remember how to use the program. He had to move fast, as he was afraid he'd be found out, so he added the image as the last on their presentation. He didn't care if he was recognized or if anyone even figured it out.

Larkin knew he had them, even if they did recognize him. Who would ever believe that he killed them with a rubber eraser!? The cops would laugh at them! He just wanted them to know what had caused the rash of deaths that were soon to begin. If- they were wise enough to understand at all.

With that mission accomplished, he left the center and was never even seen. On the way out of the building he felt free, safe, and secure, and somehow justified that God's will was being done and that the country, and more importantly, his family, were removed from the grip of their power- at least for a time. This was a war like no other, a holy war, and invisible war to all but the players involved, and the Family Palmer had just won another battle, and yet, he felt awful.

He had driven the Lincoln and as he went towards home he turned another way and headed to Mr. Shipley's. He just had to know what happened. He drove in his driveway and parked in front of the portico. Even though the Lincoln was old, it still looked remarkable out in front of Mr. Shipleys' mansion. The butler came to the door when he rang the bell. Looking at the distinguished man standing at the door the butler was impressed and taken aback.

Larkin said to him, "Mr. Larkin Palmer to see Mr. Shipley."
"Are you expected, Sir?"
"No," he laughed, "Not at all. But he will see me, I'm sure," he said with resolve, "please, announce me."

The butler turned, went away and came back momentarily, somewhat flustered, and said, "Follow me, Sir."
Leading him to the garden entrance they went out to the patio and stepped onto the flagstone walkway. The butler motioned and said, "He is on the veranda, Sir."
Larkin nodded and said, "Thank you," and proceeded out to greet him. As Larkin approached him, Shipley turned and looked at Larkin in fear, not knowing what to expect as he greeted his ghost from the past. Larkin walked up to him and said, "Hello, Mr. Shipley."
Larkin didn't extend his hand to greet him and Mr. Shipley walked over to him, white as a ghost himself. "I suppose I owe you an explanation, Larkin. Walk with me."

They began to walk the gardens, with water splashing from the fountain by the pool, which leant to have a calming effect upon their discussion. Larkin was not angry with him, but only desired to know what had happened and he told him so. Shipley explained that he had become scared after his and Harry's death and wanted only to protect his family. His girls were too important to him and he dared not risk their lives in order to release the report and bring "their" wrath upon them. He said he felt guilty about it, but figured he could always release it if circumstances allowed. He begged his forgiveness. Larkin went up to the man who at this time looked as if he were to cry and held out his hand to him. However, Mr. Shipley pulled him to him and hugged him, finally released from the guilt and happy his friend was alive.

Mrs. Shipley watched all of this from the window and when the two came together, she smiled and walked out onto the veranda greeting Larkin herself, amazed that he was alive and looked so good. She asked, "Would you join us for lunch, Larkin?"
"I'd like that very much, Mrs. Shipley."

They went to sit on the patio and were served lunch there under the awning on the expansive wrought iron table, shaded by the trees placed strategically in the garden area. They caught up on twenty years of the past as they ate and when the discussion finally came to Sally, Mrs. Shipley asked him, "Does she know you are alive, Larkin?"
"I'm afraid not. I just found out *she* was alive. I leave for home in the morning."
"We wish you well, Larkin. Please come back with her sometime. You are always welcome in our home."

"And you at ours. We will be in D.C. from time to time I'm sure." He got up to leave.

"What time is your flight, Larkin?"

"I think I'm going to take the bus, Mrs. Shipley."

She looked at him oddly and said, "Don't you have the resources, Larkin? Would you like a loan?"

He laughed and said, "Oh no, Mrs. Shipley, forgive me, but I have plenty of money. My accounts sat idle for twenty years and grew to a very substantial amount. No, that's not it. I actually enjoy being out amongst the people."

"I see. Then be careful and Godspeed. Thank you so much for coming to see us."

"Thank you, Mrs. Shipley. Good bye."

Mr. Shipley stood and went with him to show him to the door. He seemed relieved and also at peace knowing that Larkin was his friend and more importantly- alive. They shook hands once again and said goodbye. Before he went out the door, Larkin turned and said to him as if his peer and no longer his mentor or boss, "You know I have a copy, don't you?"

"I assumed. Use it wisely my Son." As Larkin drove away, he could do nothing but smile.

The Temple Commander sat at his table and watched the final presentation by the representative from Australia. He spoke of the coming "New World Order" to be established and as the final words were said in haste in order they might adjourn the fiasco of a convention, another picture came to the screen.

No one knew what it was about or who it was. It was just a man at a desk, seeming to be correcting papers with an eraser in his hand. McPherson looked at it and it didn't register at first. Then he looked more closely at the face and slowly it began to come to him. It was Palmer! With The Eraser! He pointed at it, stood up and began to say, "PPPalmmer." Gasping, he collapsed and fell dead into the table before him. Dean, who sat next to McPherson, just slumped forward in his chair shortly after realizing the very- same- thing.

Larkin drove into the garage and pushed the button on the garage door opener. It began to close and he said, "I sure wish I could have used that button more before I got killed." He laughed and started to go upstairs to pack. After turning on the TV in his room to listen to the news, he hung up his new suit and decided to leave it there, because he thought he wouldn't wear it in Brookfield anyway.

As he packed, he listened to reports coming from the convention center of mysterious deaths thought to be caused by food poisoning or Legionnaires' disease. The deaths had amounted to about three hundred and panic was setting in as the Masons stared to leave in droves before the final ceremonies. What the authorities could not explain is why only Masons of the 32nd degree and greater, except one, had come down with the illness and died.

That night Larkin went to bed early, praying the next day would go well and thanking God for his mercy. He hoped the Masons would never touch him or his family again and that they would now get the message that the Palmers would not be pushed around! He felt confident that he would now be able to move about freely, until such time that this generation all died and the next generation would start this all up again. He prayed not. He knew differently however, because they always returned to try to control and reclaim that which they thought to be theirs- the right to men's liberty. That was why he did what he did, and because he knew he may never pass on The Eraser. He was just too old to have a son.

Chapter Nine

The Homecoming

When Larkin got up in the morning, he was nervous and shook thinking about seeing Sally once again. He had made sure he locked up everything and prepared the house again for an extended absence. The neighbors had actually come to think he lived there and no one questioned him as he came and went. He even waved at the guy across the street one day, who seemed to be the only neighbor that knew him or had known him before. He called a cab to take him to the bus, because he didn't want to carry his suitcase that far. He had dressed in his Mennonite clothes in order to slip under the radar when he got back to Brookfield, because he didn't want to be recognized until he knew for sure things were under control there as well. Before the cab arrived, he removed some money from the safe for the trip and put The Eraser in his pocket. He left everything else there. The cab pulled in up front and honked the horn. Larkin closed up the safe, hurried downstairs, set the alarm and got in the cab saying, "To the bus station, please."

Larkin got on the bus and had the rest of the day to ride what would have taken four hours to drive. At first, he thought about the plans of the Freemasons. What really were their intentions with this new form of "The New World Order"? When they said they would take over every country, just what did they mean? Would they actually control the economy, the banks, commerce, each man, woman, and child? He cringed at the thought of losing his constitutional freedoms. Would that ever happen? Did he forestall their plans, or merely postpone the inevitable?

He sat alone and there was no one near him and he had plenty of time to be nervous about it all. He wondered how his parents were, if Percy still worked for them and if Peter and his family were still on The Homestead with Sally. He'd have plenty of time for all of his questions to be answered. He wasn't planning on going anywhere ever again. When he got off the bus in Brookfield, it was almost four o'clock. He figured the sun would be going down in a couple of hours, so he'd better get to hoofing it. He looked around to see if anyone was paying attention to him and in fact the focus was on the local mortuary, as business seemed to have picked up in the last couple of days. It seemed that some of the local Masons had gone to the convention in D.C. and had died while there due to some mysterious disease. Four local men had perished; The Grand Master, who was a lawyer, a man who was a doctor, and including the Coons, father and son.

Larkin walked quickly toward home, recalling all the times he'd walked or ridden that route on the way to and from school. He took a breather under the tree at the Coon place where Mrs. Hoxie had found him beaten up and where Jim had once threatened him and Ginny. He kept on and remembered so much along the way, his life passing like a reel of motion picture film, frame after frame with each step towards home. The memories came to him, of the boxes and treasures, the riddles and clues, and finally, The Eraser and what it had done to him. When he got to the corner of Academy and Baldwin Roads, he stopped. There on the corner was a sign and he smiled as he read it, "Palmer Orchards- Since 1792."An arrow on it pointed to the left. He wanted to go both ways, right to the farm on Waterman Road and left to The Homestead on Chase. He would see his parents later and knew there was really no choice to make and he headed toward The Homestead: To his Homestead and his wife- to Sally and the rest of his life.

As Larkin walked, he began to sweat in the afternoon heat, as it had been a warm fall. Stopping, he took off the hat he wore drying it and his scalp with a bandanna, and he put it back on taking up his walk again. As he approached Chase Road, Larkin turned and had the afternoon shade of the trees on his left as he walked closer and closer to his destination. He began to shake, not from fear, but from the expectation that he would see her once again. However, if there was one thing he had learned the past twenty years it was patience, and he could wait until he got to the end of Chase Road.

As he finally turned onto the gravel road called Chase, Larkin noticed that the trees looked good and were full of fruit, and he knew someone had been doing a great job caring for the place. As he approached, he saw that there was something very different. To the left on the south acreage, near the home that his Grandma Mary had grown up in was a new house that looked strangely familiar. With a covered porch and two stories, it fit well in this country setting. It sat back from the road where he had planned to build after he and Ginny were married, but had forgotten all about so long ago. Then it dawned on him; Sally had built his house! She had taken the plan he'd drawn and built it for herself. What a woman!

229

He picked up the pace as he drew near, becoming more excited with every step. He glanced at the cemetery as he went by, but as he drew closer, he saw the new customer outlet store and parking area behind Uncle Harry and Tom's house and there in the trees was a young man, about twenty he thought, working on a ladder. He saw Larkin walking toward the house and climbed down to greet him. Their paths crossed at the gate to the yard of the new house and the young man said to Larkin, "Hello, Sir. I saw you coming down the road and wondered if I could help you? We don't get many people walking out here that way."

"Yes, you can," Larkin replied, "is this the home of Sally Palmer?"

"Yes, Sir, it is."

"Is she home?"

"Yes, but is there something I can do for you, Sir?"

The young man was becoming protective and impatient with Larkin and so Larkin slowed it down and asked him, "What's your name, Son?"

"Larkin, but my mom and grandparents just call me Junior. What's yours, Sir?"

Larkin's heart fell to the bottom of his soul. This, was his *son*? Sally was pregnant? He almost fell to the ground collapsing at this news and Junior scrambled to help him. His son didn't know him. How could he know him? He looked like any of the Amish in the area, why would he even expect that his long forgotten, dead father would be there in his arms now? Junior helped him up to the porch and had him take a seat on the bench. Going to the door Junior opened it and called out, "Mom? Would you come here and help?"

From inside, Larkin heard the radio playing a song he had never heard before. It was a group called, "Mercy Me" and they were singing, "Almost Home". For a brief moment he thought, 'How apropos'.

Suddenly, Larkin realized Junior had called for Sally. Larkin stood up and faced the door and as she came out she stopped dead in her tracks. Realizing who she was looking at, she began to cry, placing her hand slowly in front of her mouth. Junior didn't know what was going on and he asked, "Mom? Are you alright?"

He watched his mother as she slowly approached her husband, this stranger on their front porch, as she put her arms around him in tears saying as she buried her face in his chest, "Oh, Honey."
Slowly, he placed his hands on her head and pushing it back, kissed her on the forehead saying, "Oh dear, Sally."

Junior looked at the man being hugged by his mother and then he recognized him from their wedding picture that sat on her dresser- this was his father! That couldn't be! He approached them and said, "Dad?"
Larkin smiled from behind his tears, extended his free arm to welcome him into the hug and replied, "Son!"
Junior asked, "Dad, what have you been doing for twenty years?"
Without a lost beat his father answered, "Son, do we have a story for you." Sally looked at him and smiled from behind her tears, and as they began to walk into the house Larkin said to him, "Junior, this is the tale of the curse of The Eraser!"

-------------------------------- To Be Continued ---------------------------------

ABOUT THE AUTHOR

C. A. Fiebiger, is a native of Roseville, Minnesota, attended Eastern Montana College in Billings, Montana, now MSU- Billings, receiving his BA in History, with a minor in Philosophy in 1987. He released his first book, The Baker and Malachi, in the summer of 2013.

He currently resides in the Nashville, Tennessee area with his wife Shirreen and daughter Tara. He has two older children, Gary and Candace, and four grandchildren.

Watch for the release of the third book of the series, "The Keeper's Son", soon.

www.cafiebiger.com